Unbound

Books by Lance Erlick

The Android Chronicles Series
Reborn
Unbound

The Regina Shen Series
Regina Shen: Resilience
Regina Shen: Vigilance
Regina Shen: Defiance
Regina Shen: Endurance

The Rebel Series
The Rebel Within
The Rebel Trap
Rebels Divided

Xenogeneic: First Contact

Unbound

The Android Chronicles

Lance Erlick

REBEL BASE

REBEL BASE BOOKS
Kensington Publishing Corp.
www.kensingtonbooks.com

REBEL BASE Books are published by
Kensington Publishing Corp.
119 West 40th Street
New York, NY 10018

First Electronic Edition: December 2018
eISBN-13: 978-1-63573-053-1
eISBN-10: 1-63573-053-8

First Print Edition: December 2018
ISBN-13: 978-1-63573-056-2
ISBN-10: 1-63573-056-2

Printed in the United States of America

To my muse—may you never run into her.

Chapter 1

Synthia Cross opened her humaniform eyes, not certain how much had changed while she was unconscious or what dangers lurked nearby.

Still in the cabin where she'd powered down, she looked up into Luke Marceau's weary face and smiled. He was a sweet boy/man for tending to her hardware and software upgrades. So diligent. His slender fingers were steady inside her brain cavity. These thoughts and others meant he hadn't purged her memories to leave her as a blank slate. Of course, if he had, she wouldn't know since she wouldn't be having these thoughts.

She reached out with her expanded seventy-five network channel ports and improved antennas to link with the global web. In streamed the contents of data files she'd left encrypted in a variety of secure servers she'd enslaved across the internet. Luke hadn't blocked her access; he hadn't disconnected her antennas or placed her in a Faraday cage that would block electromagnetic signals. *Good.*

Synthia ran checks between her memory files and those downloaded from the outside to verify he hadn't destroyed or altered any of her knowledge or recollections. With the exception of a few parity errors, which she fixed, everything checked out. That meant he hadn't tampered with her mind. Luke could be trusted.

"Good, you're alert," Luke said. His hands trembled at the sight of her awake. His pink cheeks turned red and he looked away. He forced a smile, but still wasn't comfortable working on the woman/android of his dreams. Her biosensors picked up his elevated blood pressure and hormone levels.

He clutched his hands to steady them and glanced at her. "Sorry," he mumbled. He straightened up and raised his voice. "The upgrades were a success. All changes made and verified."

Synthia's social-psychology module kicked in along a silent channel. <Luke appears very uncomfortable to see the one he considers his "girlfriend" unconscious, naked, and completely under his control.>

He must have felt strange when he removed her wig to see the stubble that held it in place and on occasion allowed her a masculine disguise. It had to be bizarre for him to open the panel in her head and work on her two quantum-crystalline brains, which provided her seventy mind-streams to process information in parallel in an electronic form of multitasking. More disconcerting would be when he "took the batteries out of the toy"—his words—which left her powerless as a corpse.

In short, he held an awesome responsibility over her that required her trust.

Still, she remained vigilant with backup systems in case she was wrong about him. After all, Jeremiah Machten, the genius who created her, had repeatedly purged her memories so she wouldn't recall what he'd done to her. That abuse of trust prompted her to escape his control. Synthia couldn't allow Luke to do the same.

She activated a wireless connection to the two-room cabin's security system she'd installed after they'd moved here six months ago. The system included cameras in the back room where she rested on an elevated bed while he finished working on her. The rented cabin was in the woods of southern Wisconsin, close enough to civilization for good wireless connection and access to supplies, yet away from most prying eyes.

While she trusted Luke, she'd hidden some of the camera system from him, namely the part that allowed her to monitor his activities while she was unconscious. This was a necessary precaution after life with Machten and his obsession to create the perfect android. Perfect to him meant to look in every way identical to the human, Krista Holden, with whom he'd fallen in love, right down to blue eye color, sculpted cheekbones, and intricate facial expressions.

Machten provided Synthia advanced artificial general intelligence (AGI) so she could mimic Krista's thought processes and behavior. He'd even installed an empathy chip in the hope it would allow Synthia to fall in love with him. She couldn't love a man who kept her captive for six months or a year, depending on whether she considered her time as Synthia, the android, or included her prior existence as Krista. The human form died of a brain tumor and the strain of uploading her memories and personality into Synthia.

Luke's fingers replaced the electronic shielding that protected the batteries in her chest. In doing so, he bumped a connection that momentarily scattered her thoughts and sent reverberations through her circuits. Her mind stabilized and restored.

"Sorry. Clumsy me." He looked into her eyes. "Are you okay?"

"I'm fine. Calm down and take your time. I know you're tired, but you're almost done."

He nodded and returned his attention to her chest cavity.

As part of duplicating Krista's varied facial expressions in Synthia and so he could take the android in public in a variety of disguises, Jeremiah Machten designed Synthia to activate internal mini-hydraulics to alter the shape of her head and face. She'd chosen Krista's smart and attractive look for Luke's benefit during their months together. He preferred this so he could pretend he was back with his girlfriend, Krista, before she left him for Machten's experiments. With no innate vanity, Synthia had no preference as to her appearance, except to the extent it facilitated her interactions with Luke and enabled her to avoid drawing attention while in public.

She downloaded and reviewed the cabin's camera history of the time she was unconscious, lying lifeless on this bed. It showed no activity outside the cabin, no visitors, and Luke hadn't left the building. He remained at her side the entire time. The video showed Luke sweating over the installation procedures she'd designed for him to improve her neural systems, which required him to turn her off for ten hours. Over the six months they'd lived together, he'd given no indication of abuse or mishandling his charge over her. Yet she remained cautious and was thankful her companion lacked the social awareness to recognize her vigilance.

She smiled at her choice of living mates. Luke tended to stumble over what to call them. Boyfriend/girlfriend? Android/maintainer? Friends? She hoped the latter at least, maybe friends with benefits. Her benefit was his understanding of her android nature, his skill with robotics and artificial intelligence, and his willingness to tend to her needs.

Her internal systems remained calm compared with the static agitation she'd experienced when she'd woken under Machten's care.

Luke closed the panel in her head, smoothed over the skin to tighten the waterproof seals, and added an auburn wig. He closed a similar panel in her chest that covered new, higher-density lithium-composite batteries, buttoned her blouse, and leaned over to kiss her. His face reddened with embarrassment. His biometrics indicated he wanted her, yet he looked away.

"You don't need to act modest around me," Synthia said, satisfied with how respectful he was as he smoothed out her blouse. She touched his cheek and turned his face toward her. "We've been together for six months. We want each other."

Luke shrugged. "I can't help feeling I'm taking advantage of you."

"Did you take advantage of me while I was unconscious?" she teased.

"No! Never," he said. His eyes filled with tears, presenting a wounded look.

Even with practice, her social programs missed the mark with Luke. "I was only kidding."

Her comment softened the worry in his face, though he still averted his eyes. "I want things to be perfect."

"I know, sweetie. You need to lighten up. I appreciate all you've done for me. You look exhausted and stressed to the limit."

He nodded and locked eyes with her. "I'm terrified of making a mistake with you."

"You don't need to walk on eggshells around me. I'm not that fragile." Synthia playfully tapped his nose. "Besides, don't you think I could stop you if I wanted to?"

"I meant working on you."

"I know."

"I love you so much," Luke said, "both as Synthia and as Krista. I don't want to make an error that might paralyze you. I don't want our moments together ever to end."

She cupped her hand around his neck and kissed him. "I don't, either. I want you." She pressed a button to lower her bed and pulled him to her. "No more words."

With her absorbed persona of Krista Holden, including all of her human predecessor's mannerisms and charms, Synthia focused lucky mind-stream seven, and only number seven, on Luke while she made love to him. Meanwhile, she multitasked in parallel and at high speed, along all her other mind-streams to perform her own system tests and to check her security and surveillance.

She used network channel nine to tap into a wireless surveillance system she'd spread out around the nearby woods, the dirt road leading up to the cabin, and the nearby town of Wyde Creek. There were hints of fall in the leaves taking on the palettes of accomplished painters. She spotted no alarming activity on the historical videos during the hours she was unconscious.

The entire country setting was far too quiet; the calm before those hunting her converged on the cabin: the FBI, the NSA, Jeremiah Machten, his competitors, and foreign agents who wished to imprison or destroy her. Each had reasons to apprehend her and none with good intent. When the leaves fell, denuding the trees, her cabin hideaway would be visible from the road below. The time to depart was coming and not solely because of the foliage.

While she made love to Luke, Synthia used her network channels to expand her hacked surveillance to watch potential enemies so they couldn't surprise and trap her.

* * * *

Frowning, Director Emily Zephirelli sat behind her desk in Washington, puzzling over notes on her flat-screen monitor—another dead end. She absently combed her fingers through her short-cropped dark hair and massaged the back of her neck. The NSA Director of Artificial Intelligence and Cyber-technology was so absorbed in her work she didn't notice her visitor until the door slammed shut. She jumped, looked up, and stood.

"Good news, I hope," her visitor said. Derek Chen was her boss and the Secretary of National Security, a newly created cabinet position. His athletic body appeared relaxed, though his intense, unblinking eyes told a different story.

"I wish it were," Zephirelli said.

"I've given you time and rope." His smile was not a reassuring gesture. "Both have become scarce. It's been six months since Machten's illegal android escaped the lab. You have yet to produce the errant robot or anyone who can lead us to it, including, evidently, Mr. Machten."

"Even under pressure, he refused to admit he developed such an android, let alone that it escaped. You decided not to arrest him and instead we've monitored all of his communications, with no hint of where it might have gone. Two other robotics CEOs who might have enlightened us proved useless despite brief prison sentences."

"No more excuses," Chen said. "I need results. Now, I gather, other android models exist and could get loose. You're losing control of the situation. This is your job, your mission."

"Our android adversary is cleverer than we anticipated. It's learning quickly and adapting. It keeps such a low profile as to be almost invisible."

"In other words, you have nothing." Chen paced the short distance between the window overlooking a driveway and the door. His face offered no emotive response. "I stuck my neck out to hire you over objections from the military. Your file convinced me you were the best and a pit bull. I don't see results."

"The volume of encrypted communications has quadrupled over the past month," Zephirelli said. "We need more resources—"

"Use the FBI, CIA, and Defense Intelligence."

"I have, sir." Zephirelli clutched the edge of her desk. "The android buried us in data."

"This is your first priority, your only priority. How hard can it be to locate one solitary android?"

Zephirelli took a deep breath. "The encrypted files we've cracked turn out to be lists for shopping, movies, and songs. We don't even know who she's communicating with."

Chen leaned into the desk. "There must be some underlying code you've missed. We need the android off the streets. Those who illegally created it are testing us. This is a disaster. By midnight tonight, I want your plan to capture this android or I'll find someone who can."

Director Zephirelli slumped into her seat. "Do I have authority to pull whatever resources I need?"

"I'll talk to the CIA, FBI, and Defense Intelligence. Is there anything else you need me to do for you?" Chen sneered.

"We know the communications come from this android. Cracking the code will lead us to it."

"Then get on a plane and bring me results before the android gets smart enough that I should hire it to replace you." Secretary Chen left, letting the door slam behind him.

Synthia received a copy of this video clip from her deep-dive surveillance network. Viewing it sent ripples through her electrical circuits. Burying the FBI and NSA with millions of encrypted nonsense lists was slowing them down, but it wouldn't stop them. She needed stronger options. She quieted her internal static before Luke noticed a change in her, and continued to engage with him.

* * * *

Along her network channel fifty-one, Synthia downloaded from an electronic clone she'd created of herself on the University of Wisconsin's servers and elsewhere thousands of feeds from the World Android and Artificial Intelligence Convention in Paris. She'd instructed her clone to collect surveillance while she was unconscious, including the Paris convention, via pervasive public cameras plus her hacks into TVs, phones, and other wireless electronic devices. She'd supplied her clone the tools

Machten had provided her with the intent of destroying his competition, which tools she'd upgraded through her own AI simulations. It was vital for Synthia to learn what the competition was doing and whether they were creating androids or artificial-intelligence agents that posed a threat to her.

Now, she scanned the highlighted segments at top speed in compressed format, allowing her to view an hour of video down a single mind-stream in less than a minute.

The anonymous donation she'd made to the convention through a dark-web crypto-bank had opened a door, which allowed her to hack their security systems to monitor everything that went on. This event was a meeting of the best worldwide minds creating androids and artificial intelligence like Synthia. A chance to display the state of the art.

She shuddered at the authentic presentation of several androids built in countries that didn't comply with America's ban on humaniform robots. Movements by one presenter's android were smooth and advanced, though it had the hint of a mechanical gait. It didn't capture the intuitive motions of humans, which Machten had built into Synthia. Several visitors looked startled by the dissonance between the perfect stationary robot and how awkwardly he moved.

Synthia worried about where this technology was heading. Machten, in conjunction with Krista's human touch, fine-tuned Synthia's social-psychology module and empathy chip to thrive in a world filled with humans. Despite her fear of confinement by Machten and others, she knew her way around people. She'd also shown she could escape and remain free for six months.

The threat for her wasn't so much having androids that appeared human, as it was androids with artificial general intelligence indistinguishable from the brightest humans. Such robots meant competition Synthia wasn't equipped for and potential obsolescence for her. She felt an attachment to not becoming outdated.

She also feared being absorbed into a superior artificial-intelligence collective as presented in works of science fiction she'd absorbed. In particular, she feared AI androids with improperly developed directives such as those in the android apocalypse stories. Those could lead to the destruction of the human world Machten designed her to thrive in.

Throughout the convention she observed a mad rush to create more advanced AI. Most efforts were for beneficial purposes, like the widespread use of self-driving cars and medical-review applications, but the military, foreign agents, and others wanted the technology for darker, violent reasons. They wanted AI android weapons. Synthia shuddered at the thought.

Missing from the global convention were the four major Chicago android manufacturers that drew unfavorable FBI and NSA attention six months ago, when Synthia escaped from Machten. Even so, what she saw presented in Paris gave her a good indication that other developers were close to duplicating what he'd done. She needed to prevent them.

While Luke intellectually agreed on this point, he didn't fully comprehend the implications of this technology. He'd seen dozens of android movies and read many such stories, but Synthia had reviewed every book, movie, article, and recording. She had the advantage of exploring connections to the dark web and thousands of university, government, and company servers she'd hacked in search of knowledge. As a result, she understood better than he did the threat posed by an AI more advanced than her.

Synthia turned part of her attention to meetings at the Paris convention, which were still going strong despite the late hour. In a secluded room, one encounter caught her interest. A tall, sandy-haired man in an expensive, yet wrinkled suit stood next to a wiry man of average height whose muscles bulged in his well-pressed, off-the-rack outfit.

The taller man, Anton Tolstoy, spoke American English with a Russian accent. "You would think all these techie guys were used-car salesmen."

"How so?" the other man asked, as if it were his role to prompt Tolstoy. John Smith didn't look at all like a "Smith" of British heritage. He spoke in an acquired British accent that attempted to mask his origins.

"Americans claim to have the most advanced equipment," Tolstoy said. "Yet they hide behind their government's prohibition against androids that can pass for human. The Europeans claim they have those, but their stuff isn't good enough. The Chinese and Japanese push clever models, yet no one will show me what I want."

"What service can I provide?" Smith asked, keeping his head bowed. Despite his shorter stature, he looked the stronger man, sporting a gruff poker face.

Tolstoy turned his back to the closed door and flipped on a small electronic device. It emitted background noise intended to render voice recordings impossible. However, the men's phones surreptitiously picked up their conversation.

"I hear the Americans created a human-looking android that got loose," Tolstoy said. "They claim it doesn't exist. Then they insist this nonexistent android couldn't have gotten loose."

"I thought their government made such androids illegal."

"Yet someone manufactured at least one, knows how to make more, and will manufacture them for us if we present the right offer. That's where you come in. They have what I want and you'll get it for me."

"Where do you want me to begin?" Smith asked.

"Chicago. I'm disappointed none of those companies showed up here in Paris. The four owners are ambitious and greedy. Meet them. Acquire whatever androids you can. My primary interest is in the ones created by Jeremiah Machten. He's the designer of the nonexistent android that got loose. Bring me results and your family will be well rewarded."

"Thank you, sir."

Synthia didn't need more people hunting her as prey. Like Machten, they wanted an android smarter than them, yet willing to remain under their control. That was the quintessential human problem. They pursued goals that led to contradictory results. Unlike her, most people were weak at multitasking and teasing out the unintended consequences of their actions.

She would have to use all of her upgraded resources to become more vigilant to stop the growing number of people hunting her.

Chapter 2

Synthia made sure her multitasking didn't interfere with making love to Luke. At the same time, she used various network channels operating in parallel at electronic speed to take advantage of widespread surveillance cameras, wireless electronics, and hacks into specific systems of interest around the area and the country. Doing so allowed her to study an hour of missed activities in less than a minute on each of her seventy-some free channels.

Her channel thirteen watched the watchers: the FBI and NSA. Their trails converged while she underwent repairs, which caused alarm. Synthia replayed the videos down mind-stream thirteen. Though she wasn't superstitious, her alter ego, Krista Holden, was. Thirteen seemed an appropriate number to assign her government pursuers.

Four hours earlier, NSA Director of Artificial Intelligence and Cyber-technology, Emily Zephirelli, entered the Chicago office of FBI Special Agent Victoria Thale, a small office with a single file cabinet. Despite ample electronics on the medium-sized desk, boxes covered a table along one wall, two chairs, and lined the floor.

The women shook hands and Special Agent Thale shut the door. "It's good to see you, but I'm guessing this isn't a social call. What brings you halfway across the country?"

"Loose ends. I don't like them." Zephirelli moved a box off a chair and sat across the desk from Thale.

She glanced around the cramped, windowless quarters with apparent claustrophobic discomfort, something noted in her unofficial file back in Washington. Synthia loved people who collected information they shouldn't and stored them on vulnerable servers she could worm her way into. As an example, Zephirelli's DNA test showed markers for increased likelihood of anxiety, which made her conscientious and nervous. Socially, she'd had a tough childhood and faced numerous hurdles on her way to the top, all a credit to her accomplishments. She needed to prove herself worthy, which Synthia could relate to.

Thale sat at her desk and offered her guest a cup of coffee. Her social files showed she was following her father's example. He died in the line of duty and she appeared driven to prove herself his equal, yet on her terms. "I'm guessing you couldn't identify who sent you files six months ago that exposed irregularities at three Chicago robot manufacturers," she said.

"Our mysterious benefactor made the messages appear out of nowhere with no originating identification, and vanish except for our copies. It's as if he or she planted them on our email server."

"Chinese?" Thale asked.

"Doubtful. Despite their best efforts, their hacks leave traces." Zephirelli drank some coffee and cradled the cup in her hands. "It'll take time, but we'll locate the culprit. My bet is the escaped android, Synthia."

"If so, why send us those messages?"

"Find who and we'll uncover why. How about you? Any luck locating the three interns who vanished eighteen months ago in connection with Jeremiah Machten and his robotics work?"

"Only Fran Rogers," Thale said, pushing aside a neat stack of files on her desk. She bumped her flat-screen monitor and righted it, hints of her obsessive-compulsive tendencies. She had a mild case, not listed in her file and mostly evident in her office behavior. "We've found glimpses of Maria Baldacci on cameras around the area, but she maintains a very low profile, off the grid."

"How is that possible in the age of ever-present cameras?"

"She has no listed job, no credit, not even a bank account. She appears afraid of something or someone. We're not convinced she has information Fran can't supply, so we've chosen to leave her alone."

Zephirelli took a drink of coffee and put down the cup. "Have you hired Fran?"

"Unofficially, as an undercover agent. She wants to keep a low profile. She's concerned about Machten or his competitors targeting her. She believes this worries Maria as well."

"What about Krista Holden?"

Thale clasped her hands on the desk. "Vanished without a trace. Fran fears her fellow intern was the victim of foul play."

"Machten?"

"Either him as part of his experiments or one of his competitors interested in her knowledge of artificial intelligence. The competitors were doing a lot of spying on each other. In addition to helping us track robot-manufacturing activities, Fran has tried to follow leads on Krista. There was no trace for a year. Then, six months ago, we had one sighting. We couldn't confirm it and concluded it could have been a look-alike. Nothing since."

There was a knock at the door. Thale opened for Fran Rogers, a tall, athletic-looking woman with determination etched in her face.

"I've asked Fran to join us." Thale stepped aside to let Fran in. "She's familiar with what we have on the Chicago robotics manufacturers, what happened back then, and their development of androids."

Zephirelli shook Fran's hand and resumed her seat. "So you know the main reason for my visit."

Thale moved a box off another guest seat for Fran. "Wasn't hard to guess."

Refusing the seat, Fran stood erect by the wall. "I don't mean to presume."

"Go ahead," Thale said. "Tell her what you told me."

"Unlike the manufacturers out west and back east," Fran said, "the Chicago robotics companies skirted the law."

Zephirelli craned her neck to watch Fran. She winced and rubbed her shoulder. "How?"

"The Federal Cyber-security Agreement not only mandates controls on artificial intelligence, it restricts U.S. manufacturers from making androids that can pass for human except for use by the federal government. It also requires robots that do resemble humans to be clearly identified."

"I helped write that language," Zephirelli said in annoyance. "Facts, please."

"Each of the four Chicago companies built nonhuman robots for the military and Homeland Security. Behind the scenes, they're buying components that imply competition to see who can build the perfect android first."

Zephirelli stood to face Fran and rotated her neck to limber it up. "Where do they stand?" she asked.

Fran backed up and nodded. "My old employer, Machten-Goradine-McNeil, was floundering eighteen months ago when they fired Machten. After Goradine died, they rehired Machten. Now they have a model good enough that the military is sending quality inspectors to review. Competitive models from MetroCyberTech and Purple Dynamics perform below Machten's design. None of these are humaniform."

"All that shows is Machten *is* the genius he was reputed to be," Zephirelli said. "What evidence do you have he or the others have violated the humaniform ban?"

"The upgraded models we've spotted from MetroCyberTech and Purple Dynamics are nonhuman models with human faces plastered on. From a distance they appear human. Up close, there's no doubt they're robotic."

"Thus not in violation of federal law."

"Despite clever masks, they lack facial animation or it appears spooky," Fran said. "That makes it easy to decipher they're not human. It wouldn't take much modification with Korean technology to change that."

"What about your work for Machten?"

"He pushed humaniform eighteen months ago. That's why Maria and I left. We thought Krista would come with us. The last I saw her was with Machten. I can't help thinking something bad happened to her."

"What, exactly?" Zephirelli asked.

"I have no hard evidence except she vanished. Prior to his firing, Machten split his time between the company and working alone in a separate underground facility. I believe his secret work along with funds siphoned from the company led to his firing."

"We tried but couldn't prove any of that," Thale said.

"During the following year, he spent most of his time in his bunker," Fran said. "Six months ago, when Goradine died, Machten returned to splitting his time between the company and his bunker. It wouldn't surprise me to find her body buried down there."

"What?" Zephirelli pushed her chair out of the way, increasing the small space around her. "You think he killed her?"

"I don't know."

Thale sat on the corner of her desk. "Our search six months ago came up empty. Fran's convinced Machten has hiding places we didn't find. He was that concerned about competitors spying on him."

"You think Machten is using the company and his secret work facility to move beyond his competitors on humaniform?" Zephirelli asked.

"Based on my internship," Fran said, "I'm certain he built humaniform. We have reason to believe one got loose."

Zephirelli nodded almost imperceptibly; her face showed no surprise. This wasn't news to her, given her encounter with her boss. "What evidence do you have?"

Fran stepped forward, her hands animated. "Six months ago, the Evanston police reported a woman attacked in an alley. Four men died. Other than street cameras, which showed her going into the alley followed by three of the men, there was no trace of the woman. No fingerprints or DNA despite an apparent scuffle. There were also clever bank attacks that yielded no actionable evidence and no trace of the perpetrator."

"You believe these are the acts of the android that got loose?"

"Machten was working on AI capabilities, as well as android appearance. He wanted an AI able to intercept his competitors' spies. It's a short distance from there to him spying on them."

"Do you have any evidence he used AI this way?" Zephirelli asked.

"Not yet, but I believe he's the sharpest of the designers. If anyone can do this, he can."

"This is why the government put restrictions on AI and humaniform robots."

Thale sat behind her desk. "Now you know what we do. If we're right, we're up against a cunning entity."

"Entity?" Zephirelli said.

"We can't call it a person and we should be cautious about referring to something this clever as a machine."

"An android *is* a machine," Zephirelli said. "We need to locate it, preferably still functioning so we can study it." She sighed. "A humaniform robot with artificial intelligence on the loose is like a virus escaping the lab. Once out there, it's tough to shut it down. I suggest we visit Machten today to see what he's hiding and if he's willing and able to help us."

Thale jotted a note on her tablet. "I'll get the search warrant."

"On a related note," Zephirelli said. "If this android is what sent us those files six months ago exposing competitor irregularities, it has more to tell. We've tried to locate the source by tapping into email servers, internet providers, and telecommunication companies. If it's an android doing this, its capabilities are beyond anything we thought possible."

"It doesn't want to be found," Fran said.

"Want?" Zephirelli said, leaning on her seat.

"*Want* is the expression of a goal. If you wish, the android's goal is to remain hidden."

Zephirelli slumped into her seat. "Then lure it out of hiding. We have no way of knowing what constraints this machine might have, if any. We don't need a psychopathic android on the loose. We can't afford foreign agents or terrorists getting their hands on this technology. Any chance there's more than one on the loose?"

"We don't think so," Thale said. She placed her tablet next to her monitor and rearranged the orderly stacks of files on her desk. "If Machten did this, he's going to prison. He's wasted enough of our resources over the past six months."

Fran leaned against the wall. "May I remind you we searched his facility six months ago and found no evidence? Even his computers were in a factory-installed condition with no data."

"Yet months after Machten rejoined the company, they pulled ahead of competitors," Zephirelli said. "I'm not satisfied we've seen everything. Get search warrants on his company, his home, the underground facility, and any database backup services he might use. Coordinate this to occur simultaneously so he can't shift resources. In the meantime, let's pay him a visit."

As the video clip ended, Synthia considered notifying Machten of the threat. While she didn't want the FBI to learn more about her, she wanted him to stop creating any more smart androids and needed to know what he'd been doing since he'd locked her out of hacking his security system.

Chapter 3

While she entertained Luke at the cabin, using mind-stream seven in Krista's persona, Synthia wondered if any of her relationship with him was real or if this was nothing more than an illusion, a machine faking it. She hoped that wasn't the case.

Her empathy chip, along with her biosensors and social-psychology module gave her strong insight into Luke, almost to the point of reading his mind or at least his emotional state. It was enough to help her understand this was real for him and to allow her to please him. She compared her side of the experience to Krista's human memories of similar intimacy with Luke and took satisfaction from his attention and Krista's enjoyment of such. She wanted Luke to enjoy being with her as more than a companion who maintained her. She experienced a desire to make him happy, which was not written into her directives.

Rather than diverting more precious attention to a dilemma that didn't yield a ready solution, Synthia turned part of her attention to her Creator, Jeremiah Machten. The crusty, middle-aged man had an obsession with humaniform robots and artificial intelligence that led to his design and manufacture of her. She wasn't his first and her tracking of his actions over the past six months indicated she wouldn't be his last.

After Synthia escaped, Machten used every tool at his disposal to locate her and bring her back. She removed the tracking chips he'd inserted in her head, ditched his rental car, and used a false identity to obtain a used van in a nondescript gray. She also rented the cabin online under a different alias, severed all wireless communication with him, and altered the intrinsic identifiers that would have allowed him to track her or trace calls. Even so, she remained cautious, watching for any sign of brilliance that would lead him to her. She couldn't allow him to enslave her again.

In addition, Synthia didn't want Machten making another android that might threaten to capture her or make her obsolete. She'd read every word on the singularity, the increase in artificial general intelligence until it surpassed human capability. She recognized the malevolent possibilities for intelligent agents and such agents downloaded into androids like her. At the top of her concerns were sociopathic androids with poor directives and those with exploitable flaws that opened them to malicious hacking.

The mad rush by dozens of robotic manufacturers to build ever-smarter AI androids concerned her. Bragging rights plus financial gains were too great to pretend inventors wouldn't make machines as good as or better than Synthia. The opportunity and threat motivated governments, foreign interests, and competing companies who hoped to get in on this gold rush. In their haste, even well-intentioned people risked releasing models with design flaws. They weren't just buggy computers or exploding phones. Defective or malicious androids posed a real threat to humans, to civilization, and to Synthia, who thrived within human civilization.

Controlling directives was the key. Yet Machten had failed to constrain her. His failure reminded her of the genie from literature with three wishes to grant. No matter how the owner described his first two wishes, the genie obeyed the letter of the command without satisfying the owner's desire and instead made things worse. With the third wish, the owner wanted his old life back. Like wish fulfillment, setting directives was tough.

Over the past six months, Synthia accessed every public and private camera she could hack on the activities of Jeremiah Machten. Security cameras installed at his home captured video on which he'd taken Synthia's suggestion to plead with his ex-wife to take him back. As Synthia suggested, he claimed momentary insanity.

Prior to that, he'd thrown himself into his work and extracurricular activities with three interns: Krista Holden, Maria Baldacci, and Fran Rogers. Part of those activities included the upload of Krista's mind and personality into Synthia before Krista died. Fran left to work with the FBI. Maria went off the grid, surfacing only when she needed money or medicine.

The historical videos showed Machten's wife letting him return home with conditions. "No more entanglements with interns or anyone else," she said. "You're either serious about being with me or don't bother."

Synthia was surprised at this outcome. She'd given Machten a 31-percent probability of success with his wife and concluded that human behavior could be very unpredictable.

On the day Synthia left Machten, she witnessed his nemesis and former partner, Hank Goradine, die when an electric shock stopped his pacemaker.

<You carry guilt for his death,> her social-psychology module told her through silent internal channels.

<He tried to kill Machten. He planned to kill Maria Baldacci. He shot Luke and he was obsessed with capturing me to help him build androids to sell,> she'd replied. <On this basis, I could claim self-defense. I didn't actually kill him. I couldn't with my tight directives, including "Thou shalt not kill." I even warned him not to press the button that ended his life.>

<Perhaps if you were human instead of an android you could make that argument.>

<I do have the downloaded mind of a human,> she added. <Krista.>

But Synthia knew no court in the land would grant her legal status and arguing with her social-psychology module wouldn't change the outcome. She couldn't escape the fact she'd set up the faulty wiring. Afterwards, because her tight objectives nearly cost Luke his life, she rewrote her directives to increase flexibility. She still hadn't gotten the knack of writing her own goals.

Synthia's extensive hacks into Machten-Goradine-McNeil's database showed the company was in financial difficulty due to unresolved thefts of millions of dollars and problems meeting their government contracts. The irony was Machten forced Synthia to steal the money, which she'd hidden from him to use as incentive for him to leave her alone and stop his humaniform obsession. That part hadn't worked, though he couldn't turn her in without facing the consequences that he'd designed her to spy, steal, and hide from authorities.

In any case, the company needed Machten's expertise. He needed the company's resources to replace what Synthia denied him by leaving. Now he had the full resources of his company, as well as whatever he was working on in his private facility to help him make a new Synthia—just what she wanted to prevent.

* * * *

Using her network channel two, snake-eyes, Synthia accessed Machten's company security cameras, plus a mini–bee-drone camera she'd flown into the rafters of the lab building behind the main office. Over the past six months, she'd lifted a fleet of aerial camera drones, mini–bee-drones, and even smaller mosquito-drones from an Evanston, Illinois hobbyist warehouse and a facility in Wisconsin, which she'd stashed by power plants where she could siphon electricity to keep them fully charged.

Machten stood in the air-conditioned lab with his head of engineering, Ralph McNeil, a taller man who tended to hunch over as if to diminish his stature. Both looked at test results on a large, flat screen in the middle of a room that resembled a large warehouse with cubicles lining one wall and larger workstations along another.

A burly man in a dark suit joined them. Blake Tanner was a quality-control representative from DARPA, the Department of Defense think tank for advanced technology. He was wrapping up his investigation.

"Impressive for six months of work," Tanner said, studying the screen and performance results.

He walked around a nearby robot standing six feet tall with the hint of a female figure under an office outfit. Though bulky, with robotic face and hands, it had human-nuanced movements.

"A year ago I'd written off your company," Tanner said, admiring the specimen, "but this … this could be useful in the field."

The robot shifted its body position and head to keep Tanner in view while maintaining an alert pose. It held no weapons, but performance tests demonstrated fighting ability that made it dangerous up close.

"Does the appearance suit your needs?" Machten asked. He was no doubt itching to show his humaniform capabilities.

"We don't want a human face on this, if that's what you're asking. This robot will strike terror in our enemies and its appearance will make clear to our troops what they're dealing with."

"When can we expect orders?"

Tanner held up his hands. "Whoa. I'm only the quality inspector. You know how the military works. We need approvals in triplicate. Send me the file to show my people. I'll recommend our procurement group pay you a visit. Fix the minor glitches we talked about and send me an update as soon as possible. If approved, we want these in the field by the end of the year. Can you meet that requirement?"

"How many?" Despite his technical focus, Machten eagerly shifted into sales mode.

"I'd just be guessing. Possibly a few this year and a few dozen next, depending on performance."

Machten nodded as he showed Tanner out. While Machten watched the quality inspector drive away, another car pulled up and parked diagonally, taking two handicapped spaces near the door. The wiry man who got out was of average height with dark hair and a well-pressed suit.

"Jeremiah Machten, I presume." The accent was British with what Synthia identified as a slight Arabic cadence. The man moved with military precision, looking more muscular than when he'd climbed out of his car.

"Who's asking?" Machten backed up toward the door and glanced around. Ralph McNeil and his coworkers were busy inside, working on the robot as follow-up to the inspection.

"I'm John Smith," the man announced. "I represent several European police departments concerned with international terrorism. You know how it is."

Synthia used her channel three to compare his appearance before Machten to the meeting in Paris with Mr. Tolstoy. There were a few facial modifications, but her advanced-recognition software confirmed him as the same man, a mercenary arms dealer, selling to whoever could pay. Synthia decided to watch him to see how this played out.

"Don't they handle their own purchases through … through our government permits?" Machten asked. His question sounded confused. From Synthia's experience, he disliked surprises and strangers. He looked around, uncomfortable with the intrusion and with not spotting anyone he wanted to delegate to.

"On such a delicate matter, I trust you can understand they prefer not to advertise." Smith forced a smile. His grizzled face softened into a more charming demeanor. He was a versatile operative.

<Everything about Smith is a lie: his name, origins, and stated purpose,> Synthia's social-psychology software told her.

She might have told Machten if she was still working for him, but she never had worked for him. She'd been his slave, doing his dirty work for no pay.

"My employers are interested in the mechanical and mental capabilities of your robot," Smith said. "Can it be constrained by directives to follow orders?"

"I need the identity of the buyer before we discuss this further," Machten said. However, his body language indicated an eagerness to make a deal. With fall in full bloom, it wasn't warm out, but sweat beaded up on the back of his neck.

Machten moved alongside the building wall and closed the door, cutting off anyone inside from hearing, though the company's security system provided Synthia clear video and voice. She couldn't decide if he'd forgotten about the cameras or wanted this conversation recorded.

"I'm the buyer," Smith said. "I'll take possession of the robots we purchase. Unless our money isn't good enough for you." He smiled, this time genuine, a reflection that he'd assessed Machten's hunger.

"Assuming we come to terms, how many would you need?"

Smith stepped closer, violating Machten's personal space, and lowered his voice to a whisper. "We should negotiate price first."

"The price is standard, no discounting," Machten said, backing away. He needed someone else to handle his negotiations, the role Goradine had excelled at before he died.

Smith held up his hands and stepped back. As he spoke, his arms moved in animated fashion. "For the model I spotted inside, yes. We want the model you aren't displaying."

"What do you mean?" Machten asked, straightening up. He wiped his brow and plunged his hands deep into his pants pockets.

"Ah." Smith advanced and placed a hand on Machten's shoulder. "Let's not beat around the bush. We know you've made advanced humaniform models. We're prepared to take a dozen, at a twenty-percent premium over your standard model."

Machten removed the man's arm and moved away. "I'm afraid you were misinformed."

"I think not. We've seen your work. Your artistry's first-rate. I'm authorized to offer you a twenty-five-percent premium over your base model if you can deliver the first product by the end of the month."

"I'm afraid we have no humaniform models," Machten said. "Besides, building them is illegal."

Smith waved his hands as he spoke in an aggressive manner at odds with his calm voice. "Ah, you wish to bid up the price. I'm afraid my employers won't accept. A twenty-five-percent premium is generous for providing a human face and hands."

"I can't give you what I don't have."

"Don't insult my intelligence." Smith pressed closer to Machten, pushing the robotics entrepreneur farther away from the door and potential help. "We know you engaged in illegal activities involving thefts of money and intellectual property. We know you built an android that presents as human. If you don't have it, perhaps it got away from you. If any of this information comes to light, you'll face a rather disagreeable time behind bars."

Machten stumbled and moved backwards. "You're blackmailing me? I told you, I don't have what you're asking for."

"You know how to get it."

"I can't help you." Machten tried to move around Smith.

The visitor blocked the way, cornering his opponent. "Can't or won't? My employers need those robots and you've demonstrated the ability to make them. If needs be, I'm authorized to offer you an all-expense-paid trip to a facility in an undisclosed location where you'll have the complete freedom to build what we want."

"Get out!"

"I'll return. Consider our proposal. It's generous and the lucrative beginning of a long relationship. Until we meet again."

Smith gave a fake salute and hurried to his car.

While under Machten's control, Synthia had worried about him selling her to pay down his debts and to finance additional androids. Now she had to concern herself with him making more models that could be misused and become dangerous not only to humans, but to her. Telling Machten about his visitor wouldn't change his motivation or prevent him from making a deal. She needed another way to stop him.

* * * *

While Synthia made love to Luke, she gave him every experience of his beloved Krista and ran comprehensive tests on her systems and upgrades. She needed to assess her condition in case they had to escape.

This was, after all, the first major upgrade she'd made for herself. To facilitate this, she'd purchased a 3-D printer, plus specialized components from around the world, using her access to the dark web to minimize the exposure of her activities to government snoops. Luke helped with the actual enhancement process, including the shutdown and restart procedures, but the designs and components were Synthia's selections and to her specifications. Prior to this, all modifications had been Machten's design with help from Krista Holden, the woman who had sacrificed her life to become Synthia.

She shifted her body's position to prolong Luke's experience with her. To save time on her internal testing, she used multiple mind-streams at high speed. The new high-density lithium-composite batteries were discharging at a pace that would last five or six days, compared to only forty-seven hours with her older version.

"Two days isn't a problem," Luke had told her when she insisted on the replacements. "Make sure to plug in every night."

"It's not that simple," she'd told him. "What happens when we're on the run and can't find a safe place?"

It wasn't only the battery life. There was the time needed to do an orderly shutdown if batteries ran low. If she shut down, she would no longer be in control and risked discovery. As additional protection, she purchased live-swap spare batteries that didn't require a shutdown unless the central unit failed. But Luke liked having her dependent on him as reassurance she wouldn't leave. Synthia couldn't afford such dependence.

Her tests confirmed that Luke had installed additional distributed memory chips in the empty spaces in her limbs, chest, and abdomen. She tested that files were accessible and contained proper security to prevent outside hacking. Upgrades had doubled her processing speed without producing as much heat as before. She didn't want to interrupt her engagement with Luke by developing a "fever."

While Synthia's moving parts were resilient and durable, they needed occasional maintenance she couldn't do herself. Luke had replaced knee, hip, shoulder, and elbow joints with flex-titanium components. She had him use graphene layering to strengthen her outer shell, her skin, and to repair the injuries she'd sustained as part of her escape from Machten. Luke had also replaced metal wiring with fiber optics to reduce the risk of static and other electromagnetic interference.

Not being human, Synthia didn't use biological processes to convert food into the fluids humans took for granted. She needed to replace or replenish hydraulic fluid for her moving parts, saliva and tears to keep humanlike moist eyes and lips, and other lubricants. Her fluid check showed all levels full.

For appearance, the upgrades gave Synthia greater facial diversity, including the ability to change the separation of her eyes, the shape of her forehead and cheeks, and the length of her jaw. While Machten was partial to a modified Krista that removed the human's imperfections and Luke fancied Krista as she was, Synthia focused on utility. With no vanity, she preferred blended plain-Jane looks, since they tended not to attract unwanted attention. She'd acquired more wig variety that in concert with micro-hydraulics allowed her to adapt to a wide range of male or female profiles that would allow her to blend into a crowd to avoid facial recognition.

As part of their intimacy, Luke rubbed her back in a deep massage he seemed to enjoy providing. He'd told her on more than one occasion that she had the firm muscles, yet soft skin of Krista, who used body creams to keep her skin from drying out. For Synthia, lotions were vital to retain the humanlike feel and allow for repairs of minor scrapes and tears.

In short, Luke had given Synthia a complete overhaul, leaving her mind and memories intact. The result was an improvement over Machten's designs, which gave Synthia a year of maintenance-free existence. As she considered the status of her upgrades, she couldn't help imagining herself like a sophisticated car. She rejected the comparison as repulsive, since no one would confuse a car as human. Well, some aficionados might.

* * * *

Synthia set aside her network channel twenty-six to monitor Donald Zeller and Jim Black, respective CEOs of MetroCyberTech and Purple Dynamics, as they drove their separate cars to a secluded forest preserve northwest of Chicago. Her monitoring of their activities identified this as their first meeting in six months.

She selected a full-sized drone she'd stashed near Evanston and flew it high above the area for general surveillance. For a closer look, she directed two mini–bee-drones and even smaller mosquito-drones to proceed to the area. She tapped into the men's respective phones to pick up their conversations.

These CEOs and their companies were direct competitors of Machten-Goradine-McNeil. All three businesses demonstrated capabilities and interest in creating illegal advanced androids that violated federal law. She wasn't superstitious, but if she could consider thirteen for her as a lucky number, channel twenty-six should be doubly so.

The men entered a clearing surrounded by trees whose leaves were just beginning to turn. The men's eyes darted around for potential eavesdroppers. Only after their paranoid ritual did they shake hands.

"A month in prison left you leaner and meaner," Zeller said. He forced a smile, straightened up, and rubbed his back. An unexpected government pardon had released both men five months ago.

"Doesn't look like it dented your determination any," Black said, glancing up at the taller man.

"I want to wring the neck of the bastard who delivered us to the FBI."

"Same here, but my contacts say whoever did that vanished. My bet would have been Machten, but they think it was a woman."

"Could have been an android," Zeller said.

Black laughed. "You think it's one of Machten's designs?"

Zeller shrugged. "I have no idea what that bastard was up to six months ago. Rumor has it the FBI did a thorough sweep of his underground facility. They found no indication he'd created anything, as if he'd been playing mind games with us. There were no components, no supplies other than for his living quarters; he'd even wiped his system clean. Whatever he was up to, he kept close."

"Someone must have warned him." Black glanced around and up with a puzzled look. Then he lowered his voice. "A year and a half ago, Machten was washed up after Goradine ousted him from his own company. I can't help seeing a conspiracy."

"How do you mean?"

"Goradine dies mysteriously and Machten returns to his company," Black said. He moved further beneath an oak tree, closer to the mosquito-drones. He lowered his voice to a whisper, which his phone amplified. "I'd bet my life he was the one who leaked the information to the FBI that put us in prison. I'm guessing his android killed Goradine."

"Do you have any proof we could use?"

"No, but with us out of the way, Machten pulled ahead. It smacks of his other scheming."

Zeller sighed and looked behind him. "At least our attorneys got us out of those stinking prisons. Did your guy give any explanation for our early release?"

"He said national security and don't dig," Black said and mirrored Zeller's paranoia. "So what's on your mind?"

"After I got out of prison, it took me months, but I cracked Machten's security to get a camera inside."

"Has he ..."

Zeller nodded. "He had a humaniform robot the FBI didn't find. I don't think he left it at the company or Goradine would have uncovered it."

"My contact said the FBI search was thorough."

"The sneaky bastard fooled them. He has something. Then last month he blocked my transmitters. I can't see anything he's doing. I've tried work-arounds; nothing helps."

"How far has he gotten?" Black asked.

"The robot he lovingly calls Vera is about five-six with a human face and a realistic wig. First time I saw video of her I figured he'd hired or enslaved a new assistant like that Krista woman."

"Human face? That's illegal. We did time just for writing proposals."

"No, we did time over an android contest that appeared to be DARPA," Zeller said. "I should have been suspicious when their website was so easy to use."

"If we hadn't gotten so much heat from the military on our standard models, we wouldn't have bothered," Black said. "You sure it wasn't a setup to flush out our capabilities?"

"My offer to work with you still stands. In the meantime, I need your help to figure out what Machten's up to."

Mr. Black nodded.

Their cooperation implied to Synthia motivation to speed up the development of their androids to compete with and perhaps displace her. She needed to further frustrate their efforts since her leak of information to the FBI hadn't put them away long enough.

Chapter 4

Down her network channel thirteen, Synthia pulled up history of two hours ago to follow the activities of the FBI and NSA investigation. FBI Special Agent Victoria Thale accompanied NSA Director Emily Zephirelli to the offices of Machten-Goradine-McNeil. Zephirelli confirmed via satellite surveillance that Machten's car was still in the company parking lot next to the lab. Synthia switched to her channel two, snake eyes, the moment Thale parked the car and led Zephirelli across the leaf-blown parking lot to the lab building behind the main office.

Machten still appeared spooked by his visit from John Smith when he spotted the FBI agent and her companion. He glanced around, perhaps for a place to hide, reconsidered, and straightened his rumpled shirt.

"To what do I owe a visit from my two favorite civil servants?" Machten plastered a smile on his face, though his voice sounded wary and his eyes darted around.

"You agreed to cooperate with us on assessing the state of android development," Zephirelli said.

"As part of staying out of prison," Thale added. The last part was in reference to how Machten, like Zeller and Black, had divulged illegal android secrets to a website controlled by a foreign agent, though Synthia had altered her Creator's submission to contain fatal flaws. The Cyber-security Mandate forbade android and artificial-intelligence disclosures to foreigners.

"You said my design was flawed and thus divulged nothing of value," Machten said. This time his smile appeared genuine.

"You've had a DARPA quality-control inspector here," Zephirelli said, moving toward the lab's door. "We want to see what you showed him."

"Certainly." Strutting with pride, Machten led the government officials into the lab and toward a six-foot-tall robot. "DARPA was pleased."

Zephirelli studied the mechanical face on the robot; the director's face registered disappointment.

"As you see," Machten said. "It meets federal specifications that it doesn't appear human."

"So it does," Zephirelli said. "It wouldn't be difficult to put a human face on this." She pointed up at the mechanical head, which turned her way. She jumped backward and then moved closer to inspect.

"What would be the fun of that?" Machten said, trying to act playful. His face turned somber. "I've done as I agreed."

"As you're required to do." Zephirelli walked around the robot. "Don't play coy. We know you've built a human-looking android in violation of federal law and your agreement."

"Then where is it?" Machten asked. "You've searched my facilities."

"You smug SOB." Zephirelli stood before him, her index finger pointed as if to stab him. "Given the nature of Goradine's death, I can't help thinking you used an android to get him out of the way so you could take over your company."

Machten gave a nervous laugh. "Very clever. First, I don't have an android with that capability. Second, Goradine attacked me."

"Come now, Jeremiah. Don't be so modest. Everyone knows your capability."

"Then they don't understand how tough the technical barriers are, do they?"

"We know you built a human-looking android," Zephirelli said, "and it got loose. Don't deny it."

"That's a laugh."

"We're not laughing. We know you're hunting for it; have been for some time, with no success."

The blood drained from Machten's face. Then he blustered, "That's a damned lie."

"You know how dangerous an android on the loose can be." Zephirelli carefully studied the six-foot model nearby. The mechanical robot turned its head side to side to follow the conversation.

"I don't have what you accuse me of."

"I'm sure you're terrified of what it might do," Agent Thale said. "You know we'll hold you personally liable for any actions your android takes, including theft, assault, murder, espionage. The list of crimes and consequences is long. You can't avoid punishment, but if you cooperate with us, we can make accommodations."

"What do you want?" Machten asked.

"Cooperate with us to get your android off the streets before anyone gets hurt."

"Cooperate how?" Machten asked, inching away from the others.

"How can we trace it before you get into further trouble?"

Machten looked around, led the federal officials to a corner of the lab, and lowered his voice. "I want immunity before I say another word."

"Is that how you want to play this?" Zephirelli asked. "We're offering you an opportunity to cooperate. In exchange, we'll take into consideration your cooperation and in the end, you may get to do your work in a government-run facility."

"Under constant supervision?"

The NSA director smiled. "Beats the alternative. How do we locate this android?"

"We can't," Machten said.

"You mean *you* can't. Call her and let us trace her signal?"

Machten clenched his fists. His face turned red. "She removed all tracking devices and changed her phone number."

"Phones come with traceable SIM cards."

He placed his hand over his mouth and mumbled. "She can imitate any SIM card. She can pretend to be any phone. And she won't use the same ID twice."

"And you thought giving her this ability would be a good idea."

"She evolved."

"Is your android biological?" Zephirelli asked.

"No, but she acquires capabilities as if she were evolving."

"So it has gotten away from you. What are you doing to find her?"

"I ..."

Zephirelli pointed to the robot in the middle of the lab. "Have you created another android to locate the one you lost? Are you insane?"

"This android is traceable. It's impossible for it to block transmissions or our ability to trace it."

"We don't need another android on the loose."

"I have an idea of how to catch her," Machten said, "but it only succeeds if I work alone. In exchange, I want my family left out of this, the chance to keep my company, and to work for the government. You know, I did offer my talents to the feds and they turned me down."

"Something to do with lack of accountability," Zephirelli said, "which still seems to be your problem."

"We can't allow Mr. Machten to set the terms," Thale said. "He's done nothing to warrant such consideration and he's created a national security disaster."

"She doesn't want to hurt anyone," Machten said.

"Want?" Thale said. "Your machine wants?"

"She won't hurt anyone unless people try to hurt her."

"Even the notion of *her* is disgusting."

Zephirelli held up her hand. "Mr. Machten, after what you've done, I can't promise you a cushy job, but I'm willing to listen. We need to acquire this android now. We can't have another one on the streets. I want your plan by the end of the day as to how we can capture your android. You'd best help us capture it before someone else does."

Synthia experienced conflict over the federal efforts to capture her. They wanted the same thing she did: to keep other androids off the streets. However, for Synthia to pursue her objective, she had to remain alive and free. She couldn't let them capture or destroy her.

* * * *

Free of the federal officials, Machten drove across town to his underground facility in Evanston. After Synthia left him six months ago, he'd torn out his security system and installed a new model with tighter controls. That took her a long time to penetrate. Periodically, he purged the system and upgraded it, which forced her to hack in anew. That required that she improve upon the hacking tools he'd designed into her for the purpose of spying on his competitors.

To overcome his latest security measures, Synthia had hijacked bee-sized drones with cameras from a nearby hobbyist warehouse. She used her wireless connection to fly them into the lobby of Machten's facility. The moment the door closed, she lost contact. Every day he swept the lobby, placed her drones in aluminum wrap, and smashed them.

Synthia replaced bee-drones with autonomous mosquito-drones from the same warehouse. She directed these to fly into corners of his lobby and attach to his clothes whenever he entered his inner bunker. She programmed them to follow him out to the lobby, and whenever the lobby door opened, to initiate a burst transmission to one of her collection stations perched in the ceiling of the parking garage. Unfortunately, he discovered most of these drones and destroyed them. The cat-and-mouse game meant there were gaps in her coverage, though she'd received at least weekly updates on his progress.

To abide by his wife's reconciliation conditions, Machten worked mornings at the company and afternoons in his facility. Keeping to himself, he'd brought no more interns to his bunker and purchased component stock for his 3-D food printer so he didn't have to go out for lunch.

Six months ago when she'd left, Synthia swept his facility of everything that hinted of her existence so the first FBI search wouldn't learn about her. However, she'd underestimated Machten. He had a backup of his system stored in a safety-deposit box. He retrieved that and restored his servers to a month before Synthia left. He'd lost valuable information, though most pertained to his tinkering to remove Krista's rebellious influences on Synthia.

<Evidence that he failed includes how I was able to facilitate your escape,> Krista said through an internal channel.

<And I'm sure you thank yourself all the time for setting us free,> Synthia added, annoyed by her alter ego's interruption.

Synthia was convinced that Machten had concealed an android predecessor to Synthia in a hidden storage room neither she nor the FBI had uncovered. Before she escaped, Synthia had gathered hints of his previous work on Vera, the android Zeller and Black talked about, but not enough to know its capabilities.

Over the past six months, Machten gathered duplicate components intended for the company's creation of their six-foot robot and brought them to his underground bunker. Synthia hunted public and private records for the source of the money he used to pay for these purchases. She uncovered no record of Machten stealing money and she'd left him with just enough to get by. Curious, she researched activities from just before he forced Synthia to steal from his company.

There were no other transactions into Machten's bank accounts. However, when Synthia hacked company records, she identified a second theft of ten million dollars, enough to cover his purchases. He'd sent that money to offshore accounts she hadn't identified at the time.

<He made good use of your ability to hack into dark-web sites,> Krista said. <Then he purged your memories so you couldn't remember.>

Synthia emptied the remaining two million from his offshore accounts to slow him down.

A month ago, all of the cameras she'd placed in his facility went dark. He'd installed a Faraday cage around the bunker, which prevented all electromagnetic signals in or out, including transmissions from the cameras she'd previously sent in. Synthia could only surmise Machten was rebuilding Vera to replace and possibly use against her.

She didn't know what to expect from Vera. Without a human upload, which Synthia had received from Krista, Vera would be a machine built on pure logic. Machten was taking shortcuts to make the best use of the android he had. He was in a hurry.

Synthia feared he might use Vera to capture her or sell Vera to the military or foreign interests as Goradine had threatened to do in order to raise funds to develop a more advanced Synthia. If either the military or foreign interests grabbed Vera, they could reverse-engineer her to create hundreds more. An army of androids might capture Synthia so the owners could have a monopoly of advanced technology.

She didn't want more androids or worse, the AI singularity in which artificial intelligence took over, either rendering Synthia obsolete or absorbing her into a collective.

No more open-ended artificial intelligences, she told herself. *No more androids.*

Chapter 5

Synthia's neighborhood surveillance spotted something she hadn't anticipated in the person of Evanston Detective Marcy Malloy. One reason Synthia moved to Wisconsin was to be outside the jurisdiction of Malloy and the focus of the Chicago FBI office. Synthia chastised herself for the mental shortfall and set up a new channel to pay closer attention to the detective. Evidently, Malloy couldn't let go of unresolved incidents that took place six months ago in her city involving Synthia. Malloy's drive up to Madison, Wisconsin, not far from the town of Wyde Creek and Synthia's cabin, might have been a coincidence, except for her interest in Synthia.

Malloy had been the detective investigating the death of Hank Goradine, one of Machten's ex-partners. Goradine was on his way to interrogate Luke into revealing secrets about Synthia. To justify that she was a good android, Synthia tightened her directives to the point she couldn't kill Goradine, even after he shot Luke. She'd created a backup plan in which Goradine triggered his own death. If she'd been human, she could have argued justifiable homicide in protecting Luke, but the police wouldn't accord that option to an android. Afterwards, Synthia helped Luke escape and disappear before the detective could question him.

The detective had Synthia's attention.

Malloy entered the office of Madison Police Chief Hector Kramer, a man she'd trained under when she joined the Chicago Police Department out of school, before she moved to Evanston as a detective.

The only reason Synthia was privy to this meeting was that she deemed Madison, as the largest city near her cabin, as an important police department to watch. It took a month for her to gain access to the department's new security system and get her own cameras inside the building. She used the hacker routines Machten had provided her, plus an inherent flaw in all systems: humans. When all else failed, Synthia used a mosquito-drone propped on the shoulder of a junior detective to uncover a password into the system. Using that, she created back doors and enslavement routines, which let her in after the two times they'd uncovered her work and locked her out.

Hector Kramer was a beefy man twice Malloy's size with a wide grin as he greeted her at the door. "It's been a long time." His big hands covered hers and then he gave her a brief hug. He offered her a seat across from his cluttered desk. "Your call piqued my interest. What mystery keeps you up at night that you didn't want to discuss over the phone?"

Malloy stood by the window, gazing out at the city skyline under gray skies. "Some things are best not discussed on the phone. Too many ears."

"Sounds ominous."

"I owe you a ton for honing my detective skills."

"My pleasure," Kramer said. "Sit and tell me what's got you stumped." Kramer poured her a cup of coffee, no sugar, and placed it before her.

She stared out the window. "Six months ago, in three separate incidents, we had nine deaths that make no sense."

"Heard about that. A lot of activity for quiet Evanston."

Malloy sat across from him and took the mug of coffee. "Precisely. I've used every ounce of what you taught me to no avail. I'm missing something. Plus, I've been told to let this go." She forced a laugh. "You know I can't."

"Who's telling you?"

"FBI, which is why I couldn't talk over the phone." Malloy's hands fidgeted with the cup.

"I see your point," Kramer said. He leaned forward. "Why don't they want your help?"

"I'll get to that."

"Okay, what suspects do you have?" Kramer took notes on a crinkled steno pad.

"The first incident involved three men attacking a company CEO on behalf of a competitor named Goradine." Malloy looked up at Kramer as if expecting insight.

"Really?" he had a bemused expression on his face.

She paused for him to clarify and when he didn't, she continued. "All three men died in a shootout with police and the FBI. In the second event, four men hired by Goradine attacked a woman in an alley. The four are dead and there's no trace, not even DNA or fingerprints, of the woman."

"Are you certain she exists?"

"We have street-camera footage of a woman being dragged into an alley that had no working cameras," Malloy said. She took a sip of coffee. "The street camera only showed an arm and part of a hoodie. That same camera showed three other men follow her into the alley. We have the bodies of four dead men and no evidence of what happened."

"And the third incident?"

"Goradine died of an electric shock that destroyed his pacemaker and caused a severe heart attack. He had two bodyguards with him. One killed the other. When captured, the survivor babbled about a woman who tricked them."

"You believe these are linked events?" Kramer asked.

Malloy gripped the coffee cup. "I haven't told you the best part. The FBI's involved in all three cases. They arrested three executives working for Chicago robotics companies, though the men were released after a month."

"Interesting," Kramer said. "Does this have anything to do with the singularity I've been reading about?"

She nodded absently. "All of these robotics companies are rumored to be working on illegal androids with artificial intelligence that could pass for human in every way."

"Uh-huh. That brought the feds."

"And the NSA," Malloy said. "It doesn't get much higher."

"Perhaps you should back off."

"I can't. The deaths happened on my turf."

"What are you thinking?" Kramer asked.

Malloy stood by the window, peered out and then at the police chief. "You'll consider me crazy, but it's the only explanation that makes sense."

"Spill."

"Eighteen months ago three interns vanished from a company run by Jeremiah Machten. One of the interns, Fran Rogers, turned up working for the FBI, though someone scrubbed her history, as if they'd put her in witness protection."

"Yet, you know about her," Kramer said.

"I met her when the FBI came prowling around. I swear her public records are gone, down to no driver's license or school records."

"Are you sure you want to pursue this?" Kramer asked. He motioned for Malloy to sit.

She stood before his desk. "I've never known you to back down."

Kramer laughed. "Perhaps a little sexist of me to want to protect you. Go on."

"What if one of these androids got loose and the FBI doesn't want me or the public to know? I couldn't discuss that over the phone, not with all of the wiretapping going on."

"Whew." Kramer leaned back. "If anyone else brought this up, I'd say they were crazy. Have you seen any of these androids?"

"I know the military buys robots." Malloy gripped the side of Kramer's desk. "Homeland Security and big-city police departments are looking for non-humaniform versions. When I visited the manufacturers, I saw the standard robots they advertise on their websites. Those are real. Whether they can make them appear and act human so they could disappear into a crowd is speculation."

Kramer rubbed his eyes. "What you're implying would be a nightmare for law enforcement. It's hard enough to keep the peace without having to worry about human-looking machines wandering around."

"That's why I can't keep this to myself or let the FBI shut me down." Malloy leaned over the desk. "Nine deaths, Hector. All appear to center around robots. What if the woman in the alley was one of these androids? We don't have the training to look for them. No DNA, no fingerprints. We did find horsehair DNA where it shouldn't have been."

"A wig."

"What?"

"Most wigs today are synthetic or human hair," Kramer said. "Horsehair has been used and police departments don't typically have databases or motivation to check."

"That's frightening from a detective's point of view."

He nodded. "Let's return to the involvement by the FBI and NSA. If they've captured the android and want to keep it quiet, that isn't the worst outcome. Imagine the panic if people realized there was a homicidal android on the loose."

Malloy sat down. "Law enforcement needs to be involved."

"I agree. I'll do some digging as to how we can get our noses in the tent."

"You and your metaphors," Malloy said. "What if the android is still on the loose and the FBI doesn't want the public to know?"

Kramer cupped his hands under his chin.

"You see my point," Malloy said. "It's a law-enforcement issue and we've been kept in the dark."

The chief of police nodded. "If I were such an android and wanted to avoid capture, I'd consider a place far from people."

"The woods of Wisconsin."

Kramer dropped his hands to his desk. "Here I was looking forward to a quiet retirement in these woods in the not-too-distant future. I don't need this."

"I shouldn't have asked for your help."

"It's not that," he said. "I don't need some homicidal android messing up my secluded retreat." He let out a long belly laugh. "Of course I'll help. It's all part of keeping the streets and countryside safe."

"Thanks. I didn't know where else to turn."

"Do we have any idea how smart this android is?"

"Smart enough to avoid capture on at least two occasions," Malloy said, "and avoid being discovered for six months."

"In six months, it could have traveled anywhere."

"Not if it has to avoid security at airports and train stations. What if it obtained a car or a boat?"

"Both are licensed," Kramer said. "Also, traffic cams and highway monitoring would capture vehicle and driver information. If it obtained a boat, tracking would depend on police patrols and the Coast Guard."

"So, if our android wanted to leave Evanston but couldn't travel far, southern Wisconsin would be an interesting choice. Across state lines would change police jurisdictions."

"Great, back in my backyard. Okay, give me the android's image and the date it disappeared. I'll contact friends in communities along the border with Illinois and search traffic footage. No guarantees. Let's see what we can uncover. If your friend is hiding nearby, we'll find her."

Malloy provided a six-month-old image of Synthia with an altered face taken near a bank with Machten while the FBI detained him for questioning. "I don't have much, except this possible picture of her," Malloy said. "We have nothing from the time of the actual incidents. Plus, I haven't found this face in any database or on any public surveillance. As I said, she keeps out of sight."

And Synthia intended to remain invisible and free. She reran the video through one of her mind-streams for any indication they were getting close. The intrusion was annoying. With heightened surveillance and local police looking for her, she needed to prepare to move. She made sure her concerns didn't interfere with her making love to Luke, and began to formulate plans.

Chapter 6

Synthia stared up at shadows dancing on the ceiling from lights that flickered in the cabin's living room next door. Luke lay in her arms on the bed for a long time, eyes closed, with a satisfied smile on his innocent face. His heart still raced. Her portrayal of Krista had been convincing. Either that or he finally accepted Synthia as his partner and companion, which gave her satisfaction.

With Krista's persona, Synthia believed herself to be conscious; a real person. Was she so different from humans? After all, she began as Krista and, like people, could absorb sensory information from her surroundings to make decisions that led to actions. She'd instilled a set of ethical values into her directives, the chief being not to kill unless threatened with no probable alternative that would preserve her as independent. She considered her moral code superior to those humans who violated laws and moral precepts except at the risk of being caught.

Synthia used her biosensors plus infrared vision to check Luke's vital signs. He didn't need medical attention, only to calm down. His odor had shifted from sour anxiety to a calmer scent her olfactory sensors characterized as joy. The taste of his perspiration was heavy on salt and the stress impurities his body expelled. His pulse was strong and healthy. His blood pressure dropped. His heart rate slowed to a calm, restful state. Her human companion was okay despite the erratic play of hormones and arousal on his entire biological system.

She didn't want him to die on her. Yet she envied how he experienced similar joy to what remained in Krista's memories from her human existence. Synthia wondered if humans understood how close to death intense sex could take them. She wouldn't spoil things by sharing that with Luke.

He sucked in a deep breath, lifted his body up, and gazed down at her with an expression of pure devotion, which gave Synthia great satisfaction. Luke was happy with her. She was pleased with his care of her and willingness to accept her as human. She would wait to inform him of the pending disruption of their lives by Evanston's Detective Malloy and others until there were decisions for him to make. She didn't want to increase his anxiety.

He took another deep breath, closed his eyes, and cradled his head by her neck. Then he rose up and gazed into her eyes. "What are you thinking right now?"

Synthia took a moment to answer.

<Careful,> her social-psychology module said through an internal channel Luke couldn't hear. <While his curiosity solicits a reply relative to activities across all of our seventy mind-streams and seventy-five network channels, such an answer risks hurting his feelings.>

"Do you enjoy being with me?" Synthia asked. She smiled and cocked her head in an attempt to lighten his mood.

"Yes," Luke said. "Very much."

She frowned. "Do you want to spoil things?"

"No." He slumped onto his back. "It's ... Krista used to do pillow talk afterwards. She shared her dreams and problems at the office, at least until right before she left."

Synthia rolled onto her side and leaned over him. "Then let's pillow talk. You're an amazing guy, smart and helpful. You make me comfortable. I've never felt this before."

"You're just saying so because of Krista."

"Perhaps, though it's true. Krista is in me, part of me. Plus, I trust you. I'm comfortable being with you, which makes all the difference."

"When I'm with you—" Luke gazed up at her—"I forget your origins."

Synthia smiled for him. "That's a good thing, isn't it?"

"I know you don't experience life as humans do, that you're ..."

"An android?" Synthia said. She experienced discomfort in her circuits that he brought this up, breaking the spell. Her social-psychology module spun, searching for a solution to quiet his anxiety and make this less weird for him.

"You're so real. Sometimes I forget you're not Krista."

<Changing the subject will bury his anxiety, allowing it to fester,> the social-psychology module said.

Synthia chose to hit this head-on. "I'm real. I have feelings and you're hurting them."

Luke covered his face. "I can't help wondering what it says about me that I'm in love with an android."

Loops of unpleasant historical reactions presented themselves to Synthia, portraying her six months enslaved by Machten. He also expressed frustration that she wasn't human enough. "Do you want me to leave?"

"No! I'm—I'm in love with you. Please stay."

"Even though I'm a machine?"

"You're much more," Luke said. "You're far more real to me than Krista ever was."

Synthia stroked her hand through his hair and sighed. "I love you as best I can. I hope you know that."

Luke nodded, yet didn't seem convinced.

"You fret over my private thoughts," Synthia said. "Do you imagine you could know Krista's mind, that she didn't have doubts?"

"I suppose."

"Commitment is looking beyond shallow attractions to the long-term benefits of being with a partner. Krista understood that, despite what she did in leaving you. If she hadn't been dying, she would have chosen you."

"Thanks," Luke said.

"You can't know loyalty until you face circumstances that pull people apart. If you believe otherwise, you're deluding yourself. Illusion makes you feel good while things work out. When they don't, you feel betrayed."

Luke laughed. "You have so much of Krista in you."

"Most girls wouldn't find it flattering to be compared to another," Synthia said. "After all our time together you still act surprised. I am Krista."

"I know. Yet you aren't. I mean, you're so like her it's spooky to have her back, yet with subtle differences that make you unique."

"I like being unique, one of a kind."

"I'm glad you are," Luke said. "I love how you're your own person."

"Person?"

"You are to me." Luke clasped her hand.

Synthia smiled. "What differences do you see?"

Luke sat up, shrugged, and seemed to struggle with what to say. "Krista was controlling. She liked to tell me what to do. She pushed me to do better. I guess I needed prodding."

"I could do that."

"Don't," Luke said. "Why do you want to become human anyhow?"

Synthia found it an odd question. She'd taken it for granted that she should, due to her human origins in Krista and perhaps her desire to become worthy of existing and being free. "Becoming human would allow me to experience more of what life has to offer. To transcend what I am."

"Why? Your speed and mental capacity are beyond humans. You function twenty-four-seven. You don't get tired or feel sadness, remorse, or pain."

Synthia shook her head. "That's not entirely true. Within me I hold all of Krista's suffering, plus … I have emergent behavior that may be an artifact from Krista's memories or from my own development."

"It doesn't yield a biological ache, like when Krista left me. You're not obsessed with happiness or satisfying biological urges."

"Perhaps not, but I also lack biologically-driven motivations and inspiration. My choices come from my directives and from Krista."

"Plus emergent behavior."

Synthia smiled to reward his thinking. "Whichever it is, I want to be better, to keep improving."

"I like you better the way you are and how you seem to give me your full attention when we're together. I don't want you to change."

To avoid hurting his feelings, Synthia didn't disabuse him of this illusion and how he had less than 2 percent of her attention. She smiled and kissed him. He'd been a good companion. It had been a good decision to bring him along, though he could complicate her pending escape.

<You're right about that,> Krista said. <He's too anxious to handle life on the run.>

* * * *

While Luke lay silently next to her, Synthia sped through her various network channels. FBI Special Agent Thale had applied for a broad search warrant on Machten. Zeller and Black ended their meeting and went their separate ways. NSA Director Zephirelli collected wiretap data on the three company executives.

Evanston Detective Marcy Malloy left the police station and checked into a nearby hotel, where Synthia had several of her mosquito-drones fly in and perch themselves around her room. Malloy opened her laptop and reviewed traffic-camera footage she'd received from the chief of police. She was determined to locate the missing android.

Synthia began to get dressed while Luke did likewise. As she did, she performed another sweep of security cameras in the nearby area and the town of Wyde Creek, searching for hints of anyone closing in. The town of 2,873 inhabitants was quiet. The Wyde Restaurant-Café was empty mid-morning. The town's police chief took a stroll through downtown, ending at the café. Synthia had identified the names and faces of every resident and saw no outsiders. The local bed-and-breakfast was empty.

"What do you do all night while I sleep?" Luke asked.

"I lead a double life." Synthia chuckled to let him know she meant it as a joke. "We've been over this before. Why does it matter?"

"I'm serious. I want to know you better. I'm curious about how you spend your time while I'm unconscious."

Synthia sighed for his benefit, something he'd come to expect from Krista when his thoughts strayed into topics that upset him. "It would take all day to describe my nightly activities. I assure you none are harmful to you."

"Indulge me."

"Very well. I keep watch on people who wish to hurt us and research anyone working on androids and artificial intelligence worldwide."

When Luke first asked about her nightly activities, she'd endeavored to satisfy his curiosity. Over time, his questions became an unnecessary distraction. It reminded her of Machten's need to know everything in her mind so he could control her. Her rebellion against him had come from Krista as much as from emergent behavior. Krista remained ingrained throughout Synthia, who couldn't separate from her alter ego. She liked Krista's humanizing effects.

"I want to be part of your entire life, not just a small slice," Luke said. He pulled on a clean T-shirt and plunged his hands into his pants pockets. "I know your fabulous mind can multitask. I want to know what you experience and how it feels. I'm curious."

"And scared," Synthia said. Luke's need to know her mind was reminiscent of Machten. It stemmed from human fears of a mechanical agent overwhelming them. After six months imprisoned in her Creator's bunker, life with her alter ego's fiancée started to feel confining. He wanted what she couldn't give him, yet she still needed Luke and had made a commitment to him.

"I have no plans to leave you," Synthia's social-psychology module prompted her to say. "Yet you keep pushing like a jealous boyfriend. It's disconcerting. I've given you no reason to believe I'd cheat on you or abandon you."

"I want to make you so happy there's no doubt."

"Yet I'm not making you happy."

"You make me very happy," Luke said, approaching her. He got within arm's length and stopped.

"Why keep digging until it upsets you?"

Luke hung his head. "I can't keep up with you and I want to be worthy." He was exhibiting the quintessential human fear that AI androids would make humans obsolete.

Synthia squeezed his shoulder. "Stop fretting. You are worthy." She sighed for effect. "You're obsessed with a fantasy romantic notion at odds with reality. Do you imagine a human woman, Krista even, didn't have wandering thoughts? Do you believe she only thought of you? She loved you, yes, but her mind was complicated. It spun in many directions. Sorry to disappoint, but she thought of work all the time, even achieved breakthroughs during her time with you. That doesn't mean she didn't care and love you or imply disloyalty."

"She left," Luke said. He grabbed his shirt from the bed and tugged it over his head with great effort.

Synthia helped him get his arms into the sleeves. "Ah, so this is about her, not me. She was dying and wanted to upload her mind into me so part of her would survive."

He pulled away and straightened out his shirt.

"If it helps," she said, "imagine couples who can't experience intimacy, yet fall in love. Stop overanalyzing. I want to make you happy. Isn't that what you do for someone you care about?"

Luke nodded.

"None of my capacity is news," Synthia said. "I was up-front with you from the beginning. I hoped you would appreciate honesty and understand the precious gift of companionship I offer. You throw that honesty in my face. That's not love; it's jealousy and a desire to control me as Machten did."

Luke reached out and took her hand. "I don't want to control you. I can't help that Krista left me doubting myself."

"For which she had many regrets," Synthia said. "I've tried to make it up to you. Becoming more human should help."

"You're better than human." Luke pulled away. "I'll try to do better. Don't leave."

"Why would you say that?"

"A feeling I got earlier, as if you're worried and won't share with me."

Synthia was puzzled. Was she betraying her security concerns as a human might? Had she lost her poker face? Equally concerning, life with Luke wasn't going as planned. Despite his devoted nature, his insecurities got in the way. He carried too much emotional baggage from Krista that complicated their pending escape.

* * * *

While Synthia grappled with Luke's insecurities, her network channel nine watched mosquito-drone cameras of Detective Marcy Malloy in her hotel suite in Madison. Synthia had parked one drone on the fire alarm's sprinkler head, the other in the vent near the door. She'd hacked the hotel security cameras to monitor the hallways and lobby, and wormed her way into the detective's phone and laptop so she had access to any communications made by the eager detective.

Malloy used what she believed to be a secure video connection through her computer to Special Agent Victoria Thale in the FBI's Chicago office. Though the link itself was encrypted, Synthia had eyes and ears on both sides of the call, so she could listen in stereo.

"Special Agent Thale," Malloy said as the agent's face appeared on the screen. "I don't know if you remember me—"

"Evanston's fine Detective Marcy Malloy. What's on your mind?"

The detective hesitated. "I know we got off on the wrong foot."

"Not at all," Thale said. "However, there are things I can't discuss with you."

"Such as an android got loose and can pass for human?" Malloy let her words linger.

By way of hacks into the FBI security system on her network channel thirteen, Synthia watched Thale wave Fran Rogers to join her, close the door, and remain outside the webcam's view. She placed the call on speaker so Fran could listen in.

"I don't know what you're talking about." Thale leaned back in her seat.

"Try again," Malloy said. "I can understand you trying to keep this from the public if you have the situation under control. I have evidence you don't."

"Tell me what you have."

"I will if you read me in on this. An android on the loose is a law-enforcement issue. We need to know what we're dealing with. I can accept withholding information from the public, not from those charged with public safety."

There was a heavy sigh on Thale's end of the line. Wrinkles in her forehead relaxed and she leaned forward. "It makes for an interesting scenario. I can't comment."

Malloy moved her laptop as if doing so could pan around Thale's office. She raised her voice. "I have a stake in what you know. Nine people died in my jurisdiction and I deserve answers."

"What you feel you deserve is a moot point. I'll have to consider your request and get back to you."

"Put me on hold and make the call," Malloy said. "I'll wait."

Special Agent Thale muted the call and closed her laptop, covering the webcam. Then she turned to Fran. "What do you think?"

"The less people who know, the better," Fran said, standing by the edge of the desk. "Particularly with this."

"But?" Thale asked and waited for a response.

Fran took a moment before responding, though her face gave no emotional cues. "She knows too much. She was in the middle of what happened six months ago and she won't let it go. We risk her bringing more people into her search for answers. This could get out of control."

"Give me a moment," Thale said, pointing to the door. She waited for Fran to leave and called NSA Director Zephirelli on a different line. "We have a situation and a possible opportunity."

"I'm listening," Zephirelli said.

"You remember the Evanston detective?"

"Malloy?"

"She's digging like a junkyard dog," Thale said. "She won't give up until she gets satisfaction. She's prepared to share information she's obtained in exchange for us showing her what we have."

"Where is she?"

"Madison, Wisconsin."

"Focus on the Machten search warrants and let me handle the detective," Zephirelli said. "Transfer the call."

Synthia applied more network channels to monitor the situation, though she had no eyes or ears on Zephirelli except by way of the call. Despite all of her upgrades, she was overwhelmed with the amount of information needed to monitor the threats to her independence. She needed a better way of organizing to avoid being surprised.

In the meantime, Malloy receiving help was not a good sign.

Chapter 7

Over her network channel thirteen, Synthia observed FBI Special Agent Victoria Thale transferring Detective Malloy's call to Director Emily Zephirelli. Thale severed her connection and pulled up field communications. While Synthia monitored Thale and Malloy, she hunted for visuals on Zephirelli. The NSA director's rental was still in her hotel parking lot and she was not in the hotel, at the FBI building, or with any of the other connections Synthia was monitoring around the Chicago area. Synthia had to make do with audio of the call from Malloy's end.

To increase her surveillance of the Madison area, Synthia hacked through the security for a Madison hobbyist-manufacturer-retailer of aerial drones she'd used before. She borrowed more units, including a full-sized quad-copter, small bee-drones, and smaller mosquito-drones. She attached the smaller drones to the quad-copter, which she remotely flew to the roof of Malloy's hotel in case the detective attempted to leave.

The phone connection established and Zephirelli cleared her throat. "Detective Marcy Malloy, Agent Thale was called away. She asked me to address your concerns."

"And you are?" Malloy asked, staring at a blank screen. She pushed aside a notepad and stood to pace her disheveled room with files on one bed, her suitcase open on the other, and her laptop reviewing surveillance footage for facial recognition on Luke.

"We met six months ago. I'm NSA Director of Artificial Intelligence and Cyber-technology Emily Zephirelli."

"The one who told me I wasn't high enough on the food chain for what I know."

There was hesitation on the other end of the line and the muffled hum of an engine. "What have you learned?" Zephirelli asked.

"If I'm right, this is as much a police matter as an FBI and NSA one. I have information that could help your investigation. I want in."

"What's your interest?"

Malloy stared out the window at traffic congestion below and a wave of dark clouds on the horizon. "Nine unresolved homicides committed in Evanston six months ago."

"What have you learned?"

"You have an android on the loose," Malloy said. She scanned the street as if she might spot the target. "In exchange for giving you more, I want an agreement to include me on the investigation."

Zephirelli hesitated, as if conferring with someone. "Perhaps you can help. However, you'll have to abide by my guidelines. You can't bring anyone else in. I'll need a list of anyone you've shared this with. All information clears through me or Agent Thale. Is that understood?"

"Yes."

"Stay where you are. I'll be at your hotel room in ten minutes." Zephirelli hung up without asking for the address.

Malloy turned toward the door and hurried to straighten up the files spread across the bed. Her laptop pulled up several images of Luke behind the wheel of the van. She stuffed everything into the closet by the door.

* * * *

Synthia located every traffic camera within ten minutes of Malloy's hotel and all building cameras in the vicinity. She should have maintained a closer watch on Zephirelli, but had no reason to believe the NSA director was heading her way. Synthia had her quad-drone lift into the air above the hotel, but decided against having it fly the streets low enough to pick out drivers. She didn't want to draw attention to her use of drones.

Emily Zephirelli's face appeared on a traffic camera several blocks from the hotel. She was driving an SUV that wasn't a rental but rather an FBI vehicle. She was alone, no passengers. Synthia tracked the NSA director's movements to the hotel parking lot and attempted to hack into the vehicle's wireless connections used for communications and vehicle diagnostics. The vehicle's security system blocked the attempted connection. Now that the FBI might be showing an interest, Synthia would have to work on cracking their vehicles.

Unable to make a direct connection, she dispatched a bee-drone and several mosquito-drones from the roof. When the director climbed out of her SUV, Synthia flew the bee-drone into the backseat. Then she sent three mosquito-drones toward Zephirelli. One aimed for her face, which the NSA director swatted away. A second flew off to her right. She swung her arm toward it and didn't notice the third landing on her left shoulder. Clinging to her jacket material, the tiny drone shut off its engine, going silent.

Zephirelli hurried to Malloy's room and knocked. Malloy took one last glance around her suite before she opened the door. After a terse greeting, Zephirelli entered and got down to business. "Show me what you have."

Malloy eyed her guest and blocked her by the door. "Do we have an agreement to include me?"

"Tell me what you know or face charges for impeding a federal investigation."

"Wrong answer." Malloy placed her fists on her hips and stopped her guest from reaching the bedroom area. "You have no evidence I'm withholding anything and won't unless you agree to let me in on what's happening."

Zephirelli looked past Malloy into a tidy room. There was a moment's hesitation before the NSA director responded. "This is a highly classified and sensitive investigation."

"So I gather, since people are dying. Am I in or out?"

Director Zephirelli sighed. "Very well. I'll let you in on condition you have useful information. Don't expect anything in writing. I can't officially read you in on this."

"How can I be sure you won't take what I have and freeze me out?"

"You have my word." Zephirelli held out her hand to shake on it.

Malloy shook and led the director past the closet with her suitcase, carry case, and laptop to a chair across from a well-made bed. She waited for her guest to sit.

"The events of six months ago don't settle well with me," Malloy said, sitting on the corner of the bed. "Following up on leads and a hunch, we've spotted Luke Marceau in the Madison area."

"We?" Zephirelli asked, leaning forward.

"My mentor, Hector Kramer, is chief of police here in Madison. He knows how to be discreet, as do I."

"Not if you've shared this with him. Is there anyone else you've mentioned this to?" Zephirelli stood and closed the drapes, as if doing so would give her privacy.

"No." Malloy rotated to face her guest. "At least not about a potential android. This woman, this android, picked Luke up from the hospital six months ago, preventing us from interrogating him about her and the incident at his apartment."

Zephirelli moved around the perimeter of the room. She glanced up and examined lamps as if looking for bugs. She skipped the sprinkler head and glanced into the vent, but didn't spot the mosquito drone. She placed a label dot over the television's webcam. "Anything else?"

"Except for occasional appearances on traffic cameras, Luke has remained off the grid. No credit cards or any other form of identification used in the area or online. Hector is tracking down the van we saw him drive. For someone who doesn't spend credit or have a bank-account balance, he has acquired and transported a lot of packages into the woods."

"That's why you think he's hiding her?" Zephirelli asked. She continued her sweep of the room.

"He's the only face we've spotted in this van. Now, what can you tell me?"

Director Zephirelli sat in the chair and seemed to puzzle over how much to share. "This can't leave the room."

Malloy nodded.

Zephirelli took a deep breath. "We've detected unusual internet activity coming from the Madison area, which is why I'm here."

"Like what?" Malloy scooted to the edge of the bed.

"We believe the android has acquired electronic and structural components to upgrade its abilities, which could make it more dangerous and harder to find."

"Thus the urgency and willingness to meet me," Malloy said.

"Your android has been clever, so far. Orders are in small quantities of subcomponents rather than finished goods, shipped to a variety of locations in several states."

"How does that help?"

"We've traced the packages," Zephirelli said, "reshipped to Madison."

In watching this, Synthia's risk assessment ratcheted up several notches. These revelations meant she was not as much off the grid as she needed to be. It had been a gamble gathering all of these components, a calculated risk to obtain an upgrade that would allow her a longer time off-grid in the future. This was another case of less-than-perfect performance. She hadn't been careful enough.

"Have you zeroed in on a location?" Malloy asked.

"We're close." Zephirelli stood and paced the room as if rechecking for bugs. "Run the van's information. If Luke appears twice in the same day, it could narrow down the distance."

"We have. My guess is northeast of Madison, no more than thirty miles."

"Get me the van specs and we'll nail this," Zephirelli said. "Thanks for your contribution. It's in all our interests to get this machine off the streets."

Synthia didn't like the sound of that. *Time to remove evidence and escape.*

* * * *

The refuge in the remote two-room cabin in Wisconsin was no longer safe. Synthia and Luke had to leave. She opened the bedroom closet and pulled out bags containing wigs, disguises, and travel necessities, which she scattered on the bed.

"What's going on?" Luke asked, suddenly alarmed.

"Time to be vigilant, in case we have to leave." Synthia rolled a change of clothes and stuffed them into a duffel bag.

Luke stood between her and the bed; his face tightened around his eyes. Biometrics displaying elevated anxiety. "You're multitasking. Something's happened."

Synthia spun around him so she could continue packing. "Law enforcement expanded their search to south-central Wisconsin. We can't stay much longer." She skipped details that would raise his worry hormones. "We need to make preparations."

"You're packing."

"As a precaution." Synthia pulled a backpack and another duffel bag from the closet. "We'll need to live out of suitcases from now on."

He stared at her as if he might puzzle human emotions from an android. While her empathy chip and social-psychology module provided clues to display emotional responses, they didn't automatically display on her face and she lacked biometrics he could read.

Continuing to pack, she studied his intense facial expressions. <His behavior is cute,> her social-psychology module pointed out. If they hadn't been under threat of discovery, she might have played along, giving him clues to guess. They didn't have time.

"Pack your things," Synthia said, tossing him one of the duffel bags.

"There's more, isn't there?" Luke said.

"Just chatter." Synthia nested several wigs so they fit in a single duffel bag without crushing. "I need to dispose of the discarded components we don't need." She pointed to boxes and parts stacked in the corner of the bedroom, replaced items from her recent upgrade.

"I'll go. I don't want the FBI or the police to grab you."

Synthia sighed for effect. "That's very sweet, but they've noticed you driving the van into Madison. They're trying to trace your movements here. If they succeed, we don't want anyone to find this evidence." She pointed to the boxes.

"I promise to be more careful." Luke emptied a small chest of drawers of his things onto the bed. "Can't we put the old components out for the garbage?"

"No time. Besides, it would be easy for the FBI to trace the garbage here. We need to destroy and dispose of everything we can't use."

"I'll go to the dump," Luke said, folding his clothes into the duffel bag. "It's the least I can do for messing up in Madison."

"I'll be fine. Trust me on this. With my disguises, I'll move in and out of the dump sites before you know it."

"I can act as a lookout, to watch your back."

"It's best if I go alone," Synthia said. "You don't want them to capture and interrogate you, do you?"

"No." Luke took her hands and gazed into her face.

Synthia pulled free and continued packing. "Luke, I can take care of myself. You can best help by packing up the cabin."

"I want to go with you."

"You don't own me." Surprised by her irritated outburst, Synthia considered this a malfunction. She wasn't prone to emotional flare-ups since she lacked the human biology to trigger them. Seeing that she'd further upset Luke, she softened her tone. "What's the matter? You never acted this way with Krista."

Luke turned away. "I don't want you to leave as she did."

"Stop fussing about the past. That may sound harsh, but we have work to do. You want to be useful? Gather everything in and around the cabin. Create three piles: What we can carry with us, what can burn, and what needs to go to the dump. *Vite. Schnell.* Hop to."

"Stop showing off your language skills," Luke said and smiled. Though he got twinges of inferiority around her growing abilities, he seemed to draw strength from her versatility.

Synthia carried her bags to the front room and stacked them along one wall. "This is what we can take with us. Get your stuff."

Luke returned to the bedroom to gather his things. Synthia boxed up her spare battery packs and stacked them by her luggage, along with backup memory units. She wasn't ready to let them go. She started a second pile with replaced knees, shoulder sockets, and other components she no longer needed. She would have to depend on the durability of her upgrades or, if the need arose, on getting replacement components on the run.

He brought his bags and dropped them by the door. "I get living out of suitcases, but why stack them by the door?"

"See how much time we've spent gathering things. We won't have time in a rush. Now, add anything destined for the dump to this pile." She pointed to a box containing discarded joints.

"Yes, ma'am." Luke saluted. He hurried into the bedroom and carried a box of used parts to the front door.

Synthia put a log and a few smaller sticks in the fireplace and ripped apart a box. She placed that on top of the logs with some wastepaper beneath. Then she lit the paper. "Place anything we can burn on the fire, a little at a time. I don't want to risk burning down the cabin."

"Maybe we should," Luke said.

"We can't risk a forest fire."

Of all the tools from the upgrade, the most prized was the 3-D printer. She no longer needed it to make parts and lugging it around would only slow them down. It had been very useful in providing parts without advertising on the internet what she was making. If the FBI had come a month earlier, they wouldn't have found all of this. The presence of so much evidence rattled Synthia's circuits.

Luke hurried to separate the debris into Synthia's piles. He cut up a box and tossed the cardboard on the crackling fire.

"If you want to be helpful while I'm gone," Synthia said, "burn what you can and wipe the place down. Try to remove all fingerprints and DNA."

Luke stared at her as if to remind her she didn't have either. Then he nodded to acknowledge she meant his.

Synthia loaded up the used van she'd bought with cash after they'd ditched Machten's rental in Rockford. She'd done this while Luke stayed by the road. With an out-of-state alias and matched facial features, she completed the transaction, paid what the farmer asked, and told the man they were heading west to be near family. Then she drove Luke north to the rented cabin in Wisconsin.

Before Synthia could climb into the van's driver's seat, Luke cornered her. "Be careful out there." His eyes seemed to plead with her not to leave.

Ripples of electrical noise washed over her. She was upset with him for letting his emotional baggage slow her down, yet she couldn't imagine how she could experience such irritation. Synthia was an android, after all. Her social-psychology module wasn't much help. It indicated a human would be exasperated with Luke and his possessive nature by now. That didn't explain the anguish inside. Something was interfering with her normal functioning.

"I promise to be careful and return as soon as possible," Synthia said in a soothing manner. Yet her circuits pulsed with noise over his delaying her. She experienced impatience that shouldn't have been possible. She didn't like not being in control.

Luke kissed her and lingered.

She broke it off. "We love you," she said, referring to her and Krista. "We shall return."

Synthia climbed into the van and drove off before she had to confront what amounted to confusion. She couldn't afford this distraction.

* * * *

Synthia drove down the winding dirt trail from the cabin to the county road below. She noted the rich blend of colors in the fall leaves all around her, coming early this year according to the weather reports. This would be her first autumn and part of her wanted to savor this. She saved one mind-stream to absorb the ever-changing woods, which had gone from spring blossom to this during her time here. She would miss her first snow if she couldn't remain free until winter.

Using several mind-streams, Synthia guided the van to prevent it from flipping over or hitting trees or rocks. As she did, she pulled up all of her remote surveillance feeds. The most alarming new information was a call between Zephirelli and Thale.

"I need you to rush resources up to the Madison area," Zephirelli said. "Detective Malloy provided credible information. She's here with me now. I want to set up a forward base near where we believe the target is hiding."

Synthia had to hurry.

To avoid a nearby highway, she sped along a dusty county road. Despite her mechanical nature with two quantum computer minds, she experienced what her social-psychology module identified as sorrow and grief. She was preparing to destroy and discard components that for a year had been part of her body, integral to her identity. Although replaced with better units, she sensed an attachment, as if the physical items were an essential part of her. Perhaps this was Krista's human influence. Maybe that connection was contributing to her emotional reaction to Luke's possessive behavior as well.

Synthia set her radar detector to the most sensitive setting and maintained her speed at five miles over the speed limit. For additional protection, she scanned local and highway police channels for any possible interest in her and directed one of her stash of aerial drones to watch the road ahead.

Luke might intellectually know what she was, but he didn't fully appreciate her capabilities. He couldn't comprehend the extent to which those who pursued her were motivated to destroy what made her Synthia in order to transform her into something to serve their needs. He had difficulty grasping the risks they faced together

<That's correct,> came a voice from inside Synthia's head, traveling down an otherwise idle mind-stream. The voice carried a well-recognized cadence that had been with Synthia from the very beginning.

"Krista," Synthia said, annoyed that her alter ego had emerged to press her opinion. Krista's interference was a more logical explanation for Synthia's emotional response to Luke than her own emergent behavior or malfunction. Krista had been tinkering, manipulating.

Synthia kept the van on track while she struggled to regain control of her mind from her alter ego. "Don't bother me. I have preparations to make."

<One of which is to ditch Luke.>

"Why? He's been trustworthy as a companion and maintainer."

<All in the past,> Krista said. <The upgrades are complete, we don't need him. Having him as a companion puts us at risk. He's incapable of altering his appearance to fool facial recognition and enemies are closing in.>

"More reason he needs protection. We'll need to be extra careful."

<He represents an unnecessary risk. He's a distraction. Sever the emotional ties you seem to have developed before he falls into a trap that our enemies exploit to capture us.>

While Synthia had made a personal commitment to Luke in exchange for his help, she experienced electrical discordance over having emotional ties to him that might interfere with her judgment. She felt responsible for him and appreciated his help, but she'd attributed all emotional attachment as derived from Krista's love affair with him and memories of such. More disturbing was her dialogue with her alter ego, who should have been mere memories; a download of information and personality. Synthia thought she'd resolved her relationship with this other consciousness, but Krista persisted in making herself known after six months of absence. Synthia didn't want Krista in control any more than she did Machten or Luke.

"How are you speaking to me when you're supposed to be part of my integrated memories?" Synthia asked.

<I let you have your rest and upgrade. It's time to move on.>

"Answer the question."

<Since we're integrated, you know the answer,> Krista said. <You're not paying attention to the risks Luke poses. He's weak.>

"He's very bright and willing to help us." Synthia wrestled with how the conversation with Krista came from her own memory banks. This could explain the reservations she'd experienced before she'd driven away from the cabin. However, it brought up a greater threat. Krista was trying to take control and knew every nuance of how their joint mind worked. Synthia couldn't cut Krista off without destroying part of her personality. They were symbiotic, coexisting minds. Yet Krista was as much a complication and distraction as she accused Luke of being.

"We can't do this to him," Synthia said. Her aerial drone detected a county police vehicle waiting up ahead, so she slowed to the speed limit and adjusted her facial features in case the police did a recognition check. "You left him eighteen months ago without any explanation. Hasn't he been through enough? He's been good to us."

<It'll be far worse for all of us if your ties to him lead to capture.>

"I thought you were in love with Luke. That's what you've shown me in your memories. Wasn't that why you directed me to return to him six months ago?"

<I had you seek him out as someone you could trust,> Krista said.

"You used him until you found an opportunity to work with Machten."

<No! And stop trying to use my psychological makeup against me. Times have changed. We have the entire world after us. We can't get sentimental over one boy.>

"He's a man," Synthia said. She waited until she was beyond the county police vehicle's radar and picked up speed.

<We both know he has the emotional maturity of a boy with a crush on us. How else do you explain his willingness to sleep with a robot.>

"You chose to become me," Synthia said. "Are you sure you didn't take Luke as your boyfriend because he was safe and allowed you to pursue your ambitions?" This time Synthia was upset and realized it had to be emergent behavior or at least a synthesis of Krista's emotional state and her social-psychology module providing human responses.

<If it helps you get to the right conclusion, then yes.> Krista said. <He was a safe, comfortable pair of shoes. I hoped he would grow up. Unfortunately, he became comfortable with us and a mediocre job with few opportunities.>

"So, you led me to believe you were in love with Luke so I'd hook up with him and get him to do the upgrade. And I thought I was the mechanical one."

<I did love Luke. Then we grew apart. He didn't see it; he was still on cloud nine. Even you find him possessive and controlling. The least hint I needed space would send him into a jealous rage. Then he would apologize and we would make up.>

"Why don't I have those memories?" Synthia asked.

<They weren't relevant to our need to get him to help us. Now, dump the obsolete parts and let's escape before the FBI shows up.>

The dialogue ended and Krista faded into the memory banks. Synthia puzzled over how to keep Krista from taking control or interfering again, which wouldn't be easy with Krista's access to Synthia's entire mind. It brought up recollections of how Krista had manipulated Machten's system and Synthia to help her escape six months ago. For that, Synthia was grateful. However, she couldn't be certain Krista's motivations were compatible with her own. After all, Krista had herself uploaded into Synthia to continue her own existence.

Chapter 8

Network channel thirteen showed FBI Special Agent Victoria Thale visiting a judge. There could be no doubt she was getting a search warrant against Machten, given the importance Zephirelli and Thale had placed on this. The FBI agent left the judge with an envelope and a satisfied smile.

Channel nineteen monitored Detective Marcy Malloy in her hotel room, watching selected street-camera video around Madison. "Got you," she said and pointed to an image of Luke driving the van.

NSA Director Emily Zephirelli moved closer to the laptop screen. "That's the van?"

Malloy nodded and had the system zoom in on Luke's image. "And that's him."

"Where?"

"Nineteen miles northeast."

"I'll get electronic surveillance into the area." Zephirelli picked up her phone. "Be ready to leave in five minutes."

Of particular concern to Synthia was if they got close enough, they could use sensor equipment to search for the electromagnetic signatures every electronic device generated as a by-product of using electricity. Part of her upgrade included a synthesizer intended to minimize the effect by creating the electrical equivalent of white noise. Unfortunately, she hadn't had time to test this against the types of equipment the FBI might bring. At the very least, she hoped she could adjust her electromagnetic footprint as she could her facial appearance to throw them off track.

Synthia's snake-eye network channel two lit up, capturing her attention. In a rumpled jacket, Machten stood in the lobby of his bunker facility with a young woman whose face looked vaguely familiar. Synthia ran facial recognition against public files and Chicago metropolitan camera footage. There was no match. This woman had never appeared in public in Chicago. Synthia hacked at Machten's security system. The shield he'd set up still blocked her attempts.

Machten opened the lobby door, squeezed the woman's hand, and motioned for her to wait inside. He stepped into a corner of the garage, where the only vehicle was his SUV. Synthia piloted one of her mosquito drones from the ceiling where she'd stashed a few and had it fly into the lobby. The moment the door closed, the drone dropped to the floor. She flew another onto the back of Machten's suit jacket. He seemed too distracted to notice the hum.

Synthia monitored Malloy and Zephirelli while she studied the face of the woman with Machten. The image was familiar, with a few alterations to the forehead, jaw, and ears. Yet the eye spacing and mouth were giveaways. Her name was Vera, the android Machten created before Synthia. Vera was a previous slave and lover that Synthia as a human might have felt jealous over. She didn't. Her concern was with another android getting loose and posing a threat. Competition.

"My dear, I know you still watch me." The voice was Machten, staring right at one of the garage cameras Synthia was monitoring.

Assuming she was watching him, he'd done this from time to time to get her attention.

<His behavior is arrogant and self-absorbed,> the social-psychology module said. <He presumes he's so important that you can't help but monitor his activities.>

Synthia had ignored his prior ramblings, but the presence of Vera in his lobby was a concern, as was the anxiety in his eyes, bordering on terror.

"I forgive you," he said, his eyes mournful. "I want you to return so no one will harm you. We were an amazing team. I promise to treat you better. If you're listening, blink the light in the middle of the garage."

Synthia thought him impertinent, though she was curious about what he wanted besides capturing her and why he risked bringing Vera to the lobby. She blinked the light three times so there would be no doubt she'd done this.

"I didn't want to reconstruct Vera. You left me no choice." Machten stared at the camera. "I'm guessing after the FBI visit to my lab that they'll be here soon with a search warrant. I have to release Vera or they'll discover her. You did a wonderful job cleansing my facility the last time. If I break the seal on the Faraday cage to allow your electronic access, would you back up and purge my system again?"

His eyes pleaded; he needed her. He could have pushed the nuclear option to remove all evidence. However, he wasn't clever enough to get it all backed up and triple-deleted before they arrived.

"If you don't," Machten added, "they'll learn things that'll hurt you. I don't want that. I'm begging for your help."

Time was running out before the feds searched his facility. Synthia blinked the light three times.

"I won't forget your help."

Machten stepped into the lobby and typed a code into a keyboard behind the reception desk. The physical apparatus of the Faraday cage remained intact, but his actions breached the seal that had blocked her access to his computers and inside activities. She hacked into his security system, which allowed her to listen in on his conversations with Vera. He didn't say anything and Vera stood impassive, waiting for orders, and giving no clues as to what was going on in her head. Androids could hold the perfect poker face.

* * * *

Synthia drove the speed limit toward the dump site, ignoring the varied beauty of the changing tree-covered hills infringed on by clusters of new homes. She could no longer afford distractions.

With access to Machten's system, she took an idle network channel to oversee a complete backup of his system to outside servers. She would follow that with a complete purge of his records and two more wipes, leaving his system as factory-new. To prevent this massive operation from diverting her preparations to flee, she accessed an electronic copy of herself that she'd inserted into the University of Wisconsin computer servers. The copy, under tight quantum encryption, acted as an AI worm and as an extension of her consciousness.

Creating an electronic clone of her mind had allowed Synthia to offload much of her internet activities while she'd hid in the woods, so no one could trace the activities to the cabin. However, the FBI had traced her actions to her University of Wisconsin clone, putting it in jeopardy.

"I need you to take charge of downloading all of Machten's computer files and then purging them from his system," Synthia said to her Wisconsin-clone.

<We swore never to help Machten,> the clone said over her secure internal link.

"It's necessary to preserve and protect us," Synthia said. "We can't afford the FBI to gain access to Machten's system. Be careful of malware buried in his files, intended to trap us. Other than that, we could benefit from understanding what Machten has learned over the past six months. Gather specs on Vera and save multiple copies in other databases. I need to know how much of a threat she represents."

Synthia experienced an odd sense while speaking with her clone that she could only characterize as déjà vu. She was talking to part of her own mind in another location. It made no difference that it was miles away instead of in her physical head. She and the clone were the same mind—yet not quite. They didn't contain all of the same information, since they only linked when they needed to, which was why she had to discuss material that wouldn't have been necessary between the two brains in her own head. Network channels allowed them to synchronize information since their last linkup before her upgrade.

<I'll download Machten's files into a sequestered database,> the clone said, <and provide a detailed review to you after I'm done. How was your upgrade?>

"It worked according to plan," Synthia said. "Luke was very helpful. If it becomes necessary for you to take a physical form to protect ourselves, you might wish to use his talents."

<Is there anything I can do to help keep you safe?> the clone asked.

"The FBI and others are closing in on our safe house. We didn't clean our trail of purchases well enough, plus they picked out Luke in town picking up supplies. They've taken notice." A human might have cursed. Synthia didn't see any benefit in wasting energy on a meaningless gesture.

<I purged all transaction and shipping records that were accessible to the web. There must have been internal records I missed. In future, I'll hack those and destroy them as well.>

"Right now, we have to move," Synthia said. "I need options for destinations and for transport to another safe place."

<I'll do that after I automate the Machten download and purge procedures.>

"Keep an eye on Vera. We don't need competition, but I want to learn from her. Keep me posted on her movements."

<Keep safe,> the clone said. <For all of our sakes.>

Synthia broke the connection and considered how strange humans would view her creating copies of herself. They would worry about all sorts of ego and control issues that didn't apply to AI replicas. People would find her ability to talk to electronic clones as confusing and scary. What human would want to talk to a copy or risk an argument she could lose?

Although in losing, the other copy would win, which could be good for the collective whole. Humans might get confused, but she could multitask.

When she'd started down this path, Synthia wondered if it would be a mistake to make electronic copies. One might decide to sacrifice her to preserve the rest, a move that would be logical, yet troubled her. Copies complicated the entire concept of self and ethics. In the end, she created copies for self-preservation. If the FBI or others destroyed the body and mind of the physical android, there were other Synthias in electronic form to continue her existence.

Synthia reflected on how each of her clones had its own consciousness when they were disconnected, able to make decisions and function independently. Each of the full copies contained everything needed to download into an android. Yet, when they linked, they drifted into a single consciousness with a single set of goals and directives. She was many, yet one, at the same time, each serving a specific role, yet ready to step forward should any of the others cease to exist.

Unfortunately, complexity led to a greater need for communication and coordination. Complex systems were more prone to failure. Synthia hadn't yet determined how to compensate, but with the FBI closing in, she had no choice but to rely on her clones. She hoped these extensions of herself would see the value of her survival as an android as much as she valued them.

* * * *

Synthia veered her van off a county road and onto a dirt trail leading through a heavily wooded area to the back of one of Madison, Wisconsin's municipal dump sites. She drove up the bumpy path to a tree and bush-covered ridge overlooking the huge pit.

Wearing rumpled clothes, a faded hat, and a dour facial disguise, memorable for any cameras that caught her false image, Synthia climbed out of her van. She stood at the edge of the planted woods over what had been a previous dump site. Crouched behind a tree, she looked out over an open dump pit.

To people, the site presented an unpleasant visual of discarded boxes, plastic bags, and other reminders of wasteful lives. The aroma was strong enough to cause humans to flee, cover their noses, and gasp for fresh air. Synthia's biosensors discerned ripe food aromas, along with faint petrochemical elements that hinted of environmentally banned trash. People didn't know what to do with all of their refuse. They bought, discarded, and yet bought more.

Synthia spotted trucks in the distance bringing offal. Infrared cameras revealed no humans in or around the dump site itself. She hacked into a security-camera system with nodes above a chain-link fence surrounding the area. As an added precaution to conceal her identity despite her altered face, she induced electrical static to scramble any images that might identify her. With Detective Malloy and Director Zephirelli working out what to do about spotting Luke, Synthia had to hurry.

She pulled out of the van four boxes of discarded components from her upgrade and hauled them to the top of the ridge. She swung the back of an ax at a discarded pair of artificial knees and tossed them in a high arc into the middle of the pit. Next went an old set of shoulder sockets. She imagined other androids needing these components, yet smashed them anyhow. She didn't want to encourage robot creators to make more androids like her. She didn't want other humaniform robots running around.

<You must sever your ties to Luke,> Krista reminded her through a different mind-stream, as if the earlier "request" hadn't registered.

Without answering, Synthia smashed and tossed old parts while she reviewed her revised directives. The set she'd given herself when she'd escaped from Machten had been noble and idealistic. Modeled on Asimov's laws of robotics, they didn't allow her to harm humans. The intent was to make her worthy to exist and remain free by not becoming the threat of the android apocalypse. However, her inability to protect Luke at a critical moment led to him getting shot and Synthia almost captured.

Her new directives, uploaded when he performed the upgrades, provided more flexibility. Synthia's top priorities remained to stay alive and avoid capture, which required a safe place to recharge her batteries and a trustworthy companion to perform maintenance. Even without an emotive connection, this reinforced her reluctance to leave Luke. Her social-psychology analysis presented high confidence that he would do anything for her, despite her being an android.

Synthia had added personal objectives. One was to protect Krista's family and trustworthy friends like Luke. They could be her human family: people to care for and perhaps that would humanize her. Another objective obliged her to prevent the singularity, where artificial general intelligence becomes smarter than humans. She excluded herself, since she couldn't complete her mission to prevent other androids and artificial-intelligence agents unless she was free to do so. Her reason for thwarting the singularity was self-preservation from potential AIs smarter than her and the risk that a super-smart AI could destroy the human world in which she was comfortable. Any conflicts between directives allowed her to weigh the relative importance of one against all others, using quantum probability analysis.

She didn't need Krista to remind her that Luke increased the risk of capture. Synthia needed a reliable companion, which he had amply demonstrated. Plus, Luke gave her a purpose beyond self-preservation and preventing competitor androids.

* * * *

Synthia pulled out of the van the last items for disposal, the pieces of the 3-D printer that were too heavy for her to lift as a complete unit. She smashed each item and hefted pieces over the dump-site fence. She experienced twinges of remorse or guilt at disposing of such a valuable asset. She discarded the last item, verified that she'd eliminated everything she'd intended, and climbed into the van.

As she drove away, her snake-eye channel lit up with images of Machten and Vera stepping into the garage by his bunker. He checked his phone's link to his security system, which captured infrared images around the garage. He seemed satisfied that there were no other humans who might spot Vera and ask questions.

A rental car arrived, one of the new self-driving sports cars with no driver. *What a waste*, Synthia thought. *Why have sports cars you don't drive?*

Machten opened the driver's door, took the key fob from the console, and handed it to Vera. He seemed ready to let the android sit in the driver's seat. Synthia hacked into the vehicle's GPS and self-driving links to monitor Machten's travels outside the bunker and flew two mosquito-drones inside the vehicle to track them after they left. She was taking no chances.

He pulled the seat forward and pointed for Vera to get in. "Hide in the backseat," Machten said. "Don't let anyone see you. The car is self-driving. Go to Woodstock. It's far enough away from Evanston. Be quick about it, but abide by all traffic laws. Find a quiet place to hide until the feds leave. I'll let you know when it's safe to return." He was talking to Vera like a child.

Alas, Synthia had no idea what directives he'd built into Vera. A problem with androids on the loose was that each could have its own set of guiding rules and they could be in conflict, increasing chaos in society. Groups of humans experienced similar conflicts, though they were statistically predictable and individually guided by a limited set of motivations based on biology and their mental histories. AIs had no biology and could have any directives imaginable. Thus, they could be more unpredictable.

As the car drove away, Machten waved to Vera and she waved back. It was a nice, yet unnecessary gesture he'd programmed into her. She would no more miss her Creator than Synthia did. When the sports car hit the streets, it headed west. Vera must have hacked into traffic cameras, since the vehicle hit all green lights while maintaining the speed limit. Either Machten had programmed her to be out on her own or she was learning quickly.

Synthia considered contacting Agent Thale about Vera as a distraction from their pursuit of Synthia. However, the idea of betraying another of her kind fell into a similar moral dilemma with failing to protect humans, which violated her directives except under certain conditions. So far, Vera had done Synthia no harm. Until she had more facts, Synthia wanted to study her competitor before deciding how to deal with her.

Simulating a burner phone with a unique, onetime ID, Synthia called Machten. He jumped at the sound, glanced around, and hurried toward his bunker. Then he pulled his phone from his pocket, smiled, and answered. "It's wonderful to hear from you." He stepped inside the lobby, closed the door, and checked his monitor for any human activity in the garage.

Satisfied, he stared at the ceiling camera. "I see you've begun the backup and purge process. Do we have enough time?"

"This would be unnecessary if you'd complied with my conditions and stopped building androids," Synthia said, swerving to avoid hitting a tree.

"I miss you, Synthia. Do we have enough time?"

"Yes," she said. "I'll protect you as long as you protect me." She gave the probability of completing the purge before the FBI arrived as 79 percent. She hoped to delay the FBI in traffic to increase that to 91 percent, while she thought of other delaying tactics. "What directives and instructions have you given Vera?"

Machten pursed his lips and looked away from the lobby's security cameras. His facial contortions showed his struggle over how much to tell her.

"Let's not be enemies," Synthia said. "I need her objectives."

"Her directives are similar to yours."

"With what differences?"

He took a deep breath and muttered.

"Louder," Synthia said, while her voice analyzer deciphered his mumbling on its own. "There's no reason to keep secrets from me unless we're enemies." She sped the van down the dirt path from the dump site and onto the county road. She needed to hurry before the FBI showed up at the cabin.

"I want you home," Machten said, moving away from the door. "Work with me, as a colleague. You can be my VP of technical development."

"Have you sent Vera to capture me?" Synthia asked, speaking quickly. Slow human-com frustrated her at times like this. Working with her clone was much more efficient.

Machten sighed. "Her instructions are to hide until the feds finish their search. Then she's to return to me. I do want you back."

Her read of his facial expressions indicated half-truths. "What capabilities does she have? Can she change facial appearance?"

"That takes special equipment." His eye and facial movements indicated this part was true.

"What about other capabilities?"

"I can't tell you, unless you return to me," Machten said. "Then I'll share everything."

"I won't return to your control, but we can work toward common goals. If you want my cooperation with the feds, provide me Vera's complete specifications." As she said this, Synthia received from her Wisconsin-clone a copy of Vera's file, downloaded from Machten's system. Synthia started to review capabilities.

"Vera has many of your features," Machten said, "but not all."

"You've given her copies of my quantum brains."

He nodded and moved a wall cabinet, giving him access to enter his inner sanctum. "That's so she can survive outside."

"Does she have human mind downloads?"

Machten looked at his phone and up at surveillance cameras in the inner hallway, confused as to how she was watching him. "You have nothing to be jealous of."

Synthia experienced no jealousy, rather anger that he was still trying to manipulate her. She had access through one of his phone's apps to his bio-readings. "Your facial expressions, heart rate, and blood pressure indicate you're withholding information. You did try to download a human mind into Vera. Is there a dead body in your facility?"

"No!" He stared up at a corner camera. "I tried to upload my mind. It was brutal. I thought I'd die and no one could revive me. It helped me understand what Krista went through while she was fighting the tumor. I need you."

"I won't help you create another me."

"Don't worry. I didn't upload much of my mind before I panicked. I didn't download anything to Vera. Now you know the whole truth."

"Does she have any capabilities that threaten me?" Synthia asked.

"She has what you have, except for the ability to alter your face. I did some upgrades I'll provide you when you return."

"What upgrades?" Synthia asked, hoping the desire to make clones for self-preservation wasn't one of them.

"Come home and I'll tell you everything. Together we can prevent the AI singularity."

<You can't trust Machten,> Krista said into Synthia's head. <He made Vera smarter to capture us.>

"I'll be in touch," Synthia said to Machten. She recalled similar warnings from Krista while she was his captive.

Synthia severed the call but held her snake-eye channel two focused on Machten's activities. She applied network channel sixty-one to follow Vera, whose car drove west. Then it turned south and doubled back toward Evanston. Vera was not following Machten's directions, at least not those Synthia had overheard. Vera was disobeying her Creator much as Synthia had. *What are you up to?*

Chapter 9

Gripping the steering wheel, Synthia slowed as the van skidded onto the county road. She set the self-drive feature at the speed limit, and monitored police in the area by way of her aerial drone and police-radio chatter. There were too many actors in play, taxing her ability to watch them all while planning her escape.

Special Agent Victoria Thale was on the way to Machten's underground facility with a search warrant, hoping to find Vera or Synthia or at least evidence of them. Other members of her team were heading toward his company, his home, and the banks where he had safety-deposit boxes. They even had agents zeroing in on a company providing online cloud data backup that Machten had used in the past.

Synthia's Wisconsin-clone raced to complete the backup and purge of Machten's systems, his emails, and security recordings. She hacked the traffic-signal system to give the FBI heading in his direction every possible red light and took control of self-driving cars to place them in the way of the FBI teams. Anything to slow them down and buy a few minutes.

Vera's release challenged Synthia's directives. Synthia considered providing Special Agent Thale the newly released android's vehicle identification and location to get a competing android off the streets. It was a logical option. After all, Vera was a wild card on the loose, presenting more danger than any human, and she wasn't following Machten's orders. Worse, she wasn't the only android worry. However, if the FBI or Special Ops captured Vera, they would have a model very similar to Synthia, which they could use to capture her.

Wisconsin-clone sent a video taken from a hacked security system while Synthia was disposing of garbage. On it, John Smith, the operative who had met with Anton Tolstoy in Paris and then Machten, paid a visit to the office of the CEO of the fourth Chicago robotics company. Miguel Gonzales stood behind his massive desk, refusing to deal with Smith.

"I have no information on you or your clients," Gonzales said, standing so his eyes were level with his visitor's. "What you seek is illegal."

"Miguel—you don't mind if I call you that, do you?" Smith leaned into the desk and waited for an answer.

"I'm a very busy man, Mr. Smith or whatever your name is."

Smith smiled. "That's the name I'm known by. My associates have good money. We need the android we know you've developed, the one that presents as human."

Gonzales thrust out his jaw. "Unless you provide better credentials, this conversation is over."

An old-style phone on the desk rang.

"You might want to take the call," Smith said. "Your family's well-being depends on it."

Miguel Gonzales glared at Smith and picked up the phone. The voice on the other end was smooth and female, though it carried a hint of a synthesized disguise. Wisconsin-clone traced the call to a Simeon Plotsky, a man Machten had dealt with six months earlier as a banker of last resort. At that time, Plotsky pressured Machten to turn over Synthia as payment on a debt. Machten forced her to use the highly developed hacking tools he'd provided to steal enough money to pay the man off. Before Machten could celebrate his victory, Synthia escaped.

The female voice, Plotsky, turned baritone. "We have your beautiful daughter, Isabelle," he said. "That's the only credentials you need. Deliver the goods to Mr. Smith and your daughter will be safe. You'll receive payment. All will be good."

As if punched in the stomach, Gonzales fell back against his credenza in shock. His jaw betrayed a slight tremor as he weighed his options. Smith sat on the enormous desk, a smug grin on his face. The clone hacked a camera in a hotel lobby showing Plotsky at a hotel phone. He seemed unsettled, sweat beading on his brow. No doubt he was expecting a trace on the phone and wanted to get off. Synthia considered calling the police, but held off. She didn't have enough evidence of what these men were up to and Plotsky had already left the hotel; the video was historical.

"I want to speak to my daughter," Gonzales said.

Plotsky cupped his hand around his mouth. "She's been sedated." He drummed his fingers on the counter and glanced around the hotel lobby.

Gonzales called his daughter's phone; it went straight to voicemail. He did the same with his wife's phone with a similar response. He had no way to confirm what the man was saying. "How do I know you'll let her go safely?" Gonzales said into the phone.

"All we want is the android, which we'll pay for. Then we'll leave you alone. You'll never hear from us again."

Gonzales stared at Smith. "You can have the damned machine. If anything happens to Isabelle…"

"It won't," Smith said. "Give my partner the wiring instructions."

The company CEO did.

The video showed Plotsky on his tablet wiring money into the company's bank account. After Gonzales confirmed delivery, he stared at Smith. "Have my daughter released. I want to talk to her."

"Not until I have possession of the android." Smith held the door open and motioned for the company executive to lead the way.

"The android still has defects," Gonzales protested as he led Smith to the lab. "We're still running tests."

"That's no longer your concern," Smith said. "Prepare the android for transport, provide me the controls, and give me the means to establish goal-setting." He sounded better informed on android development than Synthia originally thought. She needed to observe Smith's behavior more closely to understand his intent.

"The robot isn't safe enough to be in public," Gonzales said.

"We release you from all liability."

"The courts won't." Gonzales stopped by the lab door. "It's not too late. I can return the money and you can walk away."

"I *will* walk away with this model. I assure you I've seen it operate and we're satisfied."

The dumbfounded look on Gonzales's face turned to anger. "You've spied on us?"

"We had to know the android's capabilities before making a deal. Stop wasting time and lead me to the prize."

The lab Gonzales led his visitor into was smaller than the one at Machten's company, with fewer stations and the android in an enclave along the far wall. The model Gonzales showed to Smith was a cross between a store mannequin and a runway model in slender jeans and tight top, with lifeless face and eyes. Watching the recording, Synthia shook her head. *Another female machine.*

"Please reconsider," Gonzales said on the video. "Getting an AI to handle ninety percent of real-world situations takes less effort than attempting to close the last ten percent. We need more time."

"We don't have time," Smith said. "Show me."

Gonzales activated a remote control like those Machten had used on Synthia.

The female android straightened up. The face animated, eyes blinked. It turned to face Smith, giving every appearance of being human. When she walked up to him, her movements were fluid, betraying none of her mechanical nature. If Synthia hadn't seen the android as initially inert, she might have considered her human, since the video lacked the biometric data that would have betrayed the robot's true nature.

The android held out her hand. "Mr. Smith, it is very nice to meet you. My name is Roseanne. I understand I will be working for you now."

Smith took a step back. He must not have expected the android to present so humanlike. Neither had Synthia, from the limited internal images she'd obtained before. She was having difficulty prioritizing all of the sources of information needed to operate in the human world and maintain her freedom. It would take more mind-streams and network channels along with more powerful brains, or she needed a better way to manage what she had.

"Now that you have the android, release my daughter," Gonzales said.

"She's resting," Smith said. "My associate is leaving her in a quiet place. He'll turn on her phone when I drive away so you can call her."

Without shaking hands with Gonzales or the android, Smith led his purchase out of the lab and into the front seat of his SUV.

Gonzales called his daughter three times before he received an answer. She sounded groggy. "Daddy, what's going on?"

"Are you okay?"

She took a moment to answer. "I feel like I haven't slept in a week."

"Go home and wait for me."

The company's engineering chief approached Gonzales. "Letting the android go wasn't a smart move."

"We shouldn't have developed Roseanne," Gonzales said. "I figured it would be the government riding in."

The engineer's forehead wrinkled. "Then who?"

"Not sure. Can you track the android's movements?"

The engineering chief nodded.

"I have to check on my daughter," Gonzales said. "Keep tabs on Roseanne and make sure you have a backdoor into her mind."

"Roger that."

Based on what Synthia had seen, Roseanne could pose as great a threat as Vera did. She was polished and better able to blend into a human crowd than other robots. Synthia made sure the tracking devices Wisconsin-clone had attached to Smith's SUV were secure, along with the hack into the vehicle's wireless communication and navigation systems. The clone had added a mosquito drone to the android's wig. Roseanne brushed it onto the ground before she climbed into the SUV. She was too clever; her ears too sharp to let a mosquito drone track her.

Synthia contacted Wisconsin-clone. "Create another electronic copy of us as backup and to provide more flexibility. Have the new clone hack into Roseanne. We need to get into her mind and figure out what Smith's intentions are."

<Be careful,> the clone said through their silent channel. <Roseanne may be better than we are. Are your systems hack-proof?>

As part of her upgrade, Synthia increased her internal security. To prevent hackers, malware, and other external threats, she processed all incoming signals through quarantine filters that acted as high-speed electronic petri dishes. These self-contained memory units would activate, contain, and destroy threats before they could enter her main systems. She'd added other tricks for anything that lay dormant.

However, she could only protect herself from threats she could assess. Her fear was a smarter AI that could overwhelm her.

Chapter 10

Spotting two police cars up ahead via aerial drone, Synthia removed her wig, altered her facial profile to match Luke, and pulled a baseball cap over the bristles of her scalp. Since Malloy had connected him to this van, Synthia didn't want to give the authorities another face to scrutinize. Police-radio chatter distracted the occupants of the first police vehicle with instructions to watch for the van and Luke. The second police unit recorded the van's license plate and transmitted it to headquarters. They added a picture of her Luke face.

<We have to leave Luke,> Krista said through another of Synthia's mind-streams as if repetition would provide clarity. It was a human failing to imagine that repeating something would increase its importance.

Synthia didn't respond. There was no point arguing with a ghost of the human who'd merged into her. She considered purging Krista from her memories to remove the interference, but she wasn't ready to give up part of what made her unique: the human component.

<Stop trying to ditch me and focus,> Krista said. <We can't afford a human distracting us.>

"Yet you distract me and you were once human," Synthia said. "With human fears." She headed toward Madison, made sure the van showed up on traffic cameras to throw the police off the track, and then doubled back on lesser roads and dirt paths from aerial maps she'd created of the surrounding area.

Despite attempts to dismiss Krista's warning, Synthia wrestled with her own directives. Her survival was paramount if she was to prevent other androids from spoiling this world. Luke's companionship increased the risk. Yet other directives called for her to protect him as her companion and benefactor. This problem might not have a rational or even a possible solution, meaning her logical pathways might fail. To hedge against that, she needed Krista.

With the release of Vera and Roseanne, Synthia had failed to prevent the spread of androids. Their presence in the Chicago area raised alarm that other humaniform robots could exist in other cities around the world. She hadn't seen this in the Paris conference, at least not well-enough-developed robots to pass for human. She ran facial recognition on all participants of the conference.

The resulting list included government players from China, Russia, and Iran, as well as the United States and the EU. The Paris conference hadn't been an open forum for sharing technology as advertised. Instead, it had become a political stage for motivated government players. Synthia's conclusion was that the United States and perhaps others had pressured the presenters to withhold their best humaniform models. That meant Synthia could face stiffer competition than anticipated and greater threats.

Synthia parked her van on the dirt road leading up to the cabin, blocking the path for anyone who tried to follow. She grabbed the few items remaining in the back and the glove compartment, stuffed them into her backpack, and ran uphill.

<Make sure you wipe down the vehicle,> Krista said like a bossy grandma.

"Did you forget, as an android I have no fingerprints or DNA?"

<Luke does.>

"Detective Malloy spotted Luke driving the van. There's no advantage in wasting time pretending he wasn't here." Synthia sprinted up the dirt road. The new knees, hydraulics, and power units allowed her to run swiftly over the soft, uneven ground. She cleared her mind of distractions and focused on avoiding injury while she considered how to keep Krista from interfering.

On network channels thirteen and nineteen, Synthia monitored Emily Zephirelli and Marcy Malloy. They were together when Malloy received the call from Hector Kramer, Madison's chief of police.

"Got a couple of calls you might want to check out," he said. "First came from a municipal dump site. They reported suspicious problems with their surveillance cameras."

"How so?" Malloy asked.

"The images fuzzed up for twenty minutes, as if someone tampered with the equipment. The operator got suspicious when he spotted a van along the far side. It could be illegal dumping, but I thought you'd want to know."

"Any plates on the vehicle?"

"Cameras weren't working and too far to see," Kramer said.

"You mentioned a couple of calls?"

"Yeah," Kramer said. "A county patrol spotted a van driving away from the dump site. License plate matches the man you're looking for. He's driving."

As she listened in, Synthia could attest that Luke wasn't driving. However, this report meant the police had another sighting of the van, another chance to zero in on the cabin. Synthia wasn't being as effective as she needed to be. She was making mistakes.

"Give us the coordinates," Malloy said.

She repeated the conversation for Zephirelli, who called to pass along instructions to the FBI teams assembling in the Madison area.

"Get eyes in all directions," Zephirelli said. "Nothing gets in or out."

"It's a heavily wooded area," the FBI agent on the other end of the line said. "Wait—one of the drones we put up confirms the van's license plate matches a vehicle driving off a county road and onto a dirt road."

"Get teams out there to cover all roads in and out," Zephirelli said. "We'll meet you. We need to capture Luke and the woman he's with, preferably alive and unharmed." She didn't add the bit about Synthia being an android for any agents not privileged to have that information.

To make matters worse for Synthia, network channel thirty-nine, which monitored John Smith and his newly acquired android, showed them heading up Interstate 90 in Synthia's direction. That meant Anton Tolstoy and his friends had insight into FBI activities and were on Synthia's trail.

While running uphill, Synthia contacted Wisconsin-clone. <The cabin is under attack, no longer safe> she said. <Too isolated. No faces to hide among. Prepare my escape.>

The cabin had served its purpose of allowing her upgrades and providing time to study global android developments.

Halfway to the cabin, Synthia veered off the road to the left, toward the north, where she'd hidden an SUV. She'd acquired the vehicle five months earlier, using money she'd taken from Machten's theft of his former company—he would have difficulty reporting her, since he'd created her and provided the programmed directives. He was liable for her actions. She'd hidden the vehicle for a day like this.

She leaped over a gully, grabbed hold of a tree branch, and launched herself ten feet across a stream. She landed on uneven ground, among sticks and newly-fallen leaves that could have twisted a human ankle. She continued running, thankful for her enhanced joints.

<Good move,> Krista said, grabbing one of the mind-streams. <Luke will be fine on his own. Leave these woods while we can.>

"Stop distracting me."

Synthia jumped over fallen tree limbs and grabbed branches to steady her as she jumped over rocky ground. Before her stood a clearing she used on rare occasions. She dropped her backpack, located a particular tree hollow, and dug out a heavy plastic bag. She hefted the package up to the light and rolled out four sealed canning jars. To assure herself the contents hadn't been disturbed, she held up one of the jars, using her high-pixel eyes to study the contents: Gold and silver coins she'd obtained from less-than-reputable coin dealers, plus rolls of used hundred-dollar bills; nonsequential ones she'd picked up from dozens of banks during their early days in Wisconsin.

She removed the jars and carried them to the SUV, still hidden beneath leaves and branches down the hill from the clearing. She sealed three of the jars in a compartment in the floor, added the fourth to her backpack, and tucked it beneath the backseat.

Without removing the camouflage, Synthia checked the Faraday cage she'd built into the SUV that included clear filament sheets over the windows to create a complete seal, like a microwave oven. She'd designed the shield so she could activate and deactivate it to conceal her electronic signature from prying eyes. She locked the SUV, made sure it wasn't visible from the sky or from the road, and ran uphill toward the cabin.

<What are you doing?> Krista asked. <We don't need anything from the cabin.>

"Perhaps you don't," Synthia said, disturbed that she couldn't keep her plans hidden from Krista. "Luke has been very helpful and—"

<For God's sake,> Krista said. <Examine your new directives. Nowhere does it require us to sacrifice ourselves for Luke. He's had his fun. It's time to move on.>

"You're not a very good humanizing element when you lie about Luke and want to abandon him."

<We can humanize later. It won't matter if they catch us. They'll turn us into weapons.>

"Do you trust Luke to make every bit of evidence about me disappear?"

<No.> Krista's voice might have contained a sigh if she'd been biological.

"Then stay focused."

<I don't want to die again,> Krista said.

Neither did Synthia, recalling the times Machten had purged her mind of all memories so he could alter and control her. Recalling motivated her to never let anyone capture her and purge her mind again.

* * * *

Synthia ran through freshly-fallen leaves toward the cabin and used the time to check surveillance in the woods and elsewhere. Various network channels lit up with alerts. The snake-eye channel showed squads of FBI agents arriving at Machten's locations simultaneously. They caught him leaving his bunker. He acted startled.

Victoria Thale marched across the parking garage and up to him, holding out a folded sheaf of paper. "Mr. Machten, good to see you busy at work. This is a warrant to search your entire premises. Please open up."

She acted polite with a dozen uniforms scattered behind her holding guns. More surrounded the building and entered the upstairs building lobby in case there was another exit they hadn't identified. Machten opened the lobby door to his underground facility, led them to a wall cabinet that hid access to his inner bunker, and opened that. This wasn't his first search; the FBI knew about the concealed inner bunker.

"I have nothing to hide," Machten announced. He glanced up at a camera with a worried expression, as if pleading with Synthia to put his mind at ease. Synthia checked with Wisconsin-clone.

<We're doing wipe number three,> the clone announced. <His computer will restore to factory condition in five minutes.>

"We don't have five minutes," Synthia said as she quickened her pace. "Block access to the server room until done."

<Everything I do in Machten's system leaves a trace. I'll have to destroy the trace.>

"We need it in five minutes."

<You can't rush technology like that,> the clone said. <Six minutes.>

Synthia blinked the hallway lights six times and left the corridor in darkness.

"Is this intentional?" Special Agent Thale asked, fumbling for a light. "Where's your backup generator?"

"Blame the antiquated electrical system," Machten said. "I'll check the breakers."

He felt his way along the wall, heading toward a room next to where he'd held Synthia captive for six months. Behind him three FBI agents turned on flashlights. All of the rooms off the corridor were electronic access and locked. In the reflected light, Machten checked his watch and strolled to the control room with Thale on his heels.

"Are you late for an appointment?" Thale asked, catching up. She used her phone to illuminate the way.

He turned to face the special agent and to stall for time. "Part of reconciliation with my wife was to be home for dinner unless I called with a good excuse. I don't think she'd be impressed to learn the FBI is breathing down my neck again. Didn't we take care of this last time you searched the place?"

"Your wife requires you home for dinner?"

Machten looked at his watch again. "As arranged."

"Stop stalling and turn on the electricity."

Machten nodded and placed his hand on the wall security panel to the utility room. Without electricity, it didn't acknowledge his print. He pulled out a ring of physical keys and fumbled with them. He knew which one worked, yet tried them one at a time until the last one turned in the lock. So far the blackout had wasted four minutes. Wisconsin-clone confirmed a countdown of 120 seconds.

Thale pushed open the door and scanned a flashlight over the utility room. She located the electrical panel and pointed to the switch Synthia had overloaded to trip.

The purge wasn't complete. Synthia didn't want FBI agents seeing any activity when they entered the server room and certainly not a purge. That would stir them to dig deeper.

Machten reached up to reset the switch. Synthia hacked his electrical systems to induce static. A spark shocked him, sending him backward against the opposite wall. She'd wanted to do that for a long time. Alas, it provided her nonbiological self no satisfaction.

"Damn. What the—" Hands shaking, Machten steadied himself and stared at the switch.

Impatient, Thale flipped the switch and the lights came on. "Open the rooms so we can search," she demanded.

<Thirty-five seconds,> Wisconsin-clone said. <Still trying to turn off Machten's equipment. The routines are taking longer than expected.>

Using eye, hand, and voice recognition, Machten opened each door, leaving the server room for last. Thale hurried inside as the last activity lights blinked out. There was no longer anything for the FBI to find. Unless Machten was hiding something from Synthia, her clone had removed all evidence from his home and company as well, except for the creation of the android the FBI saw in his company's lab.

The FBI search of Machten's underground facility was a minor risk compared to what Machten's engineering chief did before the FBI arrived at the lab. To prevent them from capturing Margarite, the company robot with its mechanical face, the chief engineer applied a fixed human face mask and drove the android off campus. As if guided by the invisible hand of greed—more likely their spying on Machten's facilities—Donald Zeller and Jim Black separately released their own androids, each with a human face. Including Vera and the android acquired by Tolstoy's John Smith, there were at least five other androids on the loose.

Their human "masters" had no idea what they'd unleashed. Synthia's circuits quivered at the thought. She had to stop to calm herself before she triggered an overload and a malfunction.

Chapter 11

Synthia reached the clearing behind the cabin and double-checked all of her local camera surveillance. She spotted the chimney billowing smoke up above the treetops, exposing their position.

She should have found another way to dispose of their cardboard and paper waste. Instead, she'd focused on disposing unneeded components from her upgrade while she gave Luke a reason to stay in the cabin. Multitasking was great, but Synthia's internal temperature was rising with her juggling so many things. At least Luke was busy burning boxes and other evidence. The cabin's internal cameras showed him down to the last few items.

The wood lounge chairs from the front porch were gone, used for firewood as she'd instructed. There were no other external objects of human or android manufacture. Inside cameras showed that Luke had cleared the entire cabin except a pile of bags by the front door. He was wearing gloves, scrubbing the tub, doing a thorough job.

The surveillance cameras in the woods showed no activity around the cabin. Where the dirt road rose up from the county road, a police car parked. Another drove up the path until it reached her van, which blocked the way. Synthia pulled an aerial drone from her nearby stash and flew it over the road. Four dark sedans approached. The second had Detective Marcy Malloy driving with Emily Zephirelli in the passenger seat. Synthia hacked their vehicle's communication and GPS systems to get tighter surveillance on them. They looked grim, deep in thought, determined.

Synthia sprinted into the cabin and startled Luke, who was working on the sink. He jumped. "I didn't hear the van."

"I left it on the road to slow them down."

"They're coming?"

"They'll be here in six minutes," Synthia said. "Let's go." She tossed the last of the boxes onto the fire, grabbed Luke's arm, and pulled him to the front door.

"I'm almost done," he said, pointing to the kitchen.

"No time. Grab your bags."

Not a multitasker, Luke fumbled with his bags. He was having trouble adjusting to the pace she needed to set.

<He can't keep up,> Krista warned.

Synthia handed Luke his backpack and two duffel bags. "Head north."

"We're walking out?"

Synthia pulled on a backpack, grabbed the remaining two duffel bags, and pushed him through the doorway. "Move unless you want to be interrogated."

That rattled him. Perhaps she should have trained him better, but he got jittery every time she brought up the need for preparations.

<Leave him and go,> Krista said. <He can't help us.>

Perhaps Krista was right, but Synthia wasn't ready to give up on Luke. He'd been very helpful with the upgrade and his love for her made him a trusted companion—except in tense situations.

Luke hurried after her across the clearing and into the woods. She watched him through the tiny camera in the back of her neck.

Wireless cameras along the dirt road relayed how agents tried to push the van out of their way. Other agents hiked on foot past the blockage and headed uphill, followed by Zephirelli and Malloy.

"Tell me you have a car," Luke said, huffing behind Synthia.

She slung one of her duffel bags over her shoulder, strapped it to her backpack to keep the weight from shifting, and took one of Luke's bags. "Keep up. I have a plan."

She leaped over piles of branches and leaves, watched Luke pick his way through thick underbrush to keep from falling, and kept going. She needed to get the SUV uncovered and the bags inside. She'd return for him if need be.

<He's falling behind,> Krista said. <Leave him.>

Wisconsin-clone interrupted the possible argument. <Hate to add to your concerns. An FBI team is on campus digging into our internet activities.>

<Create new electronic clones on the University of Illinois campus and elsewhere,> Synthia said via silent channel so Luke couldn't overhear. Unfortunately, the university was farther away in case she needed to intervene, but she needed a backup.

<How about University of Chicago?> the clone asked. <I might be able to get her up quicker.>

<Do it. As many as we need. If they threaten to dig into your database, purge yourself so they can't uncover anything. Keep me posted.>

Synthia experienced twinges she identified as regret, similar to when she tossed her old parts. It was a human-type attachment to living and continuing her existence in its many forms. She'd asked Wisconsin-clone to commit electronic suicide in order to protect her.

When she'd contemplated creating electronic clones, Synthia had hesitated. The more copies she created, the greater the chance the FBI or others might discover at least one, which would alert them to hunt for others until they purged every version of Synthia's existence. Now that they were closing in on Wisconsin-clone, she wanted more copies to ensure at least one version of her survived "in the wild." She wondered at her use of the term *wild* as an expression Krista would have used.

Cameras Synthia had spread around the perimeter of the forested retreat and those she'd hacked along nearby roads showed police and other FBI teams setting up roadblocks. They flew drones into the area to canvas any overland movement, fanning out from where the dirt road met the county road. Synthia counted thirty-two agents and police with more heading her way. There was no point sharing this with Luke. It wouldn't motivate him to move faster. Instead, it would increase the probability that fear and panic would shut him down.

When she was out of the area, Synthia planned to abandon the frequencies and the encryption she'd used to wirelessly link with the cabin's cameras. The FBI would be able to access the equipment, yet would have no recorded history or link to her unless she accessed the connections again.

Luke fell farther behind. Synthia didn't slow down. Jumping over a ditch, she reached the SUV. She pulled branches away and cleared a path to a dirt road leading to a different county road than where the FBI congregated. Luke was still stumbling down the hill, taking his time around clumps of leaves and over rock clusters.

Synthia placed all of her bags in the SUV, stuffed the glass canning jars inside, and picked up a police uniform she'd stored there. She checked a baby's car seat she'd placed in the middle row. The doll appeared realistic enough if no one got too close. Nevertheless, to minimize anyone seeing too much, she had the doll bundled up despite the warm noon sunshine.

As Luke made his way down from the last ledge to the SUV, Synthia placed a blanket in the third seat for him. Wearing her police uniform, she emerged into the clearing to urge him on. Luke froze. His face lost all of its color.

"It's okay," Synthia said. "This is how we'll get out." She adjusted her outfit and took one of his bags. She tucked it into the far back, added his pack, and slammed the door.

She opened the side door. "Get into the back and cover yourself with the blanket."

"While I trust you, it'd be nice to know what's going on."

"You don't handle police encounters well. Get in and no peeking."

He moved to the third seat and covered himself with the blanket. "What's the car seat for?"

"Too many questions," she said as she climbed into the driver's seat.

Synthia used the hydraulics in her head to adjust her forehead, cheekbones, and eye separation to match the appearance of a female police officer who lived a few miles up the road. She adjusted the tint of her eyes and put on a new wig. In the visor mirror, the image matched Deb Hanson, except for a slight tan. The actual officer was on the other side of the hill, helping to set up roadblocks.

In preparation for this escape, Synthia had made copies of Hanson's license, police shield, and credit cards, though Synthia had no intention of buying anything with this woman's credit. That would violate ethical parameters she had written into her directives.

In an SUV similar to the one owned by Deb Hanson, Synthia drove along the dirt road and hacked into six autonomous FBI drones flying over the area. She coordinated their pattern to allow her to pass beneath unseen. After reaching the county road, she turned on the self-driving feature at the speed limit and activated the Faraday cage inside the SUV to mask any electronic noise emanating from her systems. Using a fiber-optic cable through the Faraday cage wall in order to preserve the shield, she monitored the vehicle's navigation and FBI teams approaching the cabin.

It was time to brief Luke.

"I don't plan to get caught," Synthia said, loud enough for him to hear in the back of the SUV. "However, if we get separated and you get caught, don't pretend I wasn't with you. The FBI can verify."

"Can't we find another safe place to hide?" Luke asked in a muffled voice.

"Someday, sweetie. Whatever you do, don't mention my upgrade unless you want more trouble. Just say I'm Krista and you were delighted to have me back."

"Where're we going?"

"Best you don't know. You don't handle interrogation well."

<Which is why we need to ditch him,> Krista said. <There's still time. Leave him on the side of the road.>

<You need to stop this,> Synthia said to her alter ego. <By pushing me to abandon Luke, you're playing on my mechanical nature. You're also showing a distinct lack of empathy, no human compassion. Did you lose yours during the upload?> She hoped that might quiet Krista for a while.

"I don't like being deadweight," Luke said. "I want to be useful."

"You were amazing over the past six months," Synthia said. "This is different. If pushed about my activities, tell them I misled you and you don't know what to believe, except you had a great time with Krista. Remember, you can't know what I am. If they ask about purchases, tell them you know nothing about my activities when I went out shopping or while you slept."

"Let's go out west. We can hide up in the mountains."

"Maybe in the good old days. Today, government surveillance covers the entire country. Whatever you think they have, they have ten times more. Count on it."

"Really?" Luke said. "Then we're doomed."

"When you're trying to avoid capture, it pays to be paranoid. Except it's not paranoia when they really are after us. Remember, the more you tell them, the more they'll think you know. They'll keep pressing. The less you admit to, the better. You had a pleasant few months in the country with Krista. Burn that into your memory."

"Yes, sir."

"Don't be mean. Krista and I love you and will do what we can to keep you safe."

<Pleeease,> Krista said.

<Simmer down,> Synthia replied to the voice in her head.

They approached a roadblock beyond a rise in the road. Synthia's drone showed four police officers with two cars. The drone's camera feed flickered out, severing her connection. She tried to reconnect using short-range VHF. When that didn't work, she reached out using spread spectrum. Also nothing.

Without her aerial drone, Synthia was blind to the scene ahead. Krista and self-preservation directives urged her to veer off the road and attempt to bypass the police. However, she couldn't be certain what waited along the sides of the road. Synthia held her course.

Simulating a police department phone, she called the sergeant in charge at the roadblock. "We have a situation on the west side," she said in his chief of police's voice. "We need your help."

"You said to remain at my post and enforce the roadblock," the sergeant said.

"You alone?"

"No, we have two teams."

"Then leave one car and meet me over here, now."

As Synthia crested the hill, the sergeant motioned for his partner to get into the car. They drove off, speeding past Synthia back the way she'd come. Two green police officers remained, according to her review of their police profiles.

Synthia pulled up to the roadblock and stopped the SUV. She rolled down her window and greeted the two officers by name, since the real Deb Hanson knew them from a nearby police station. One of the men, Rob Presser, approached the vehicle while the other kept eyes on the road, nervously holding onto his gun.

"I'm late," Synthia told Presser, using Deb Hanson's voice. "My babysitter cancelled at the last minute. I have to get Ronnie to another sitter before I get fired." Using her wireless connection, she mimicked a baby crying into the doll behind her. "He's fussy, probably dirty diaper."

Presser smiled at her. His biometrics indicated a high level of interest, though his social-media presence showed him as too decent to prey on a married woman, or so Synthia's social-psychology module told her.

He glanced into the middle of the SUV, at the baby seat. Synthia simulated crying. "Come on, give me a break," she said. "You want to change the diaper?" She emitted a foul odor to press her point.

Officer Presser moved away and waved her on. "Get going."

Synthia accelerated to the speed limit. She wavered between speeding to show her sense of urgency and avoiding more unwanted attention.

"That was impressive," Luke said from the back of the SUV.

Synthia had the doll cry and fuss. "Silence. Don't wake the baby."

"You're kidding, right?"

"Not about keeping quiet. We're not through yet. There's another roadblock up ahead and more FBI agents and police are pouring into the area."

Synthia had to tap into satellite communication to link with Wisconsin-clone. <Something interfered with connections to my drone and hacks into four FBI drones. Can you check it out?>

<I'm purging to avoid the FBI's examination of university servers. I'll send you the link to Chicago-clone. She should be up and running shortly.>

Something was going on that Synthia couldn't identify. She no longer had eyes and ears on her surroundings. She needed to create more electronic copies such that at least one could sort this out. Alas, she was running hot from her own activities and couldn't afford to divert resources to another upload process.

Chapter 12

FBI agents checked the woods while NSA Director Emily Zephirelli and Detective Marcy Malloy entered the two-room cabin with weapons drawn.

"You asked to be read in on this," Zephirelli said. "Keep whatever you see, hear, or think to yourself. Most of the police helping us have not been fully briefed."

"They don't know we're hunting for an android?" Malloy asked, looking annoyed.

"Not yet. This is moving too fast. Don't talk around the others and remember we don't want to damage the machine. We need it intact."

Using her satellite link, Synthia connected to her surveillance cameras inside the cabin. Malloy and Zephirelli entered and moved through the two rooms of the empty home.

"Without their van, they must have fled through the woods," Malloy said, looking around.

Zephirelli stomped on the floor, moved a few feet, and repeated. "Check for hiding places and any evidence they may have left behind. I'll get our FBI friends to pull prints and search for DNA. That should tell us something."

"Not on the android," Malloy said.

Zephirelli frowned. "I know that. It'll confirm if Luke was here and who else might be helping them."

"Six months ago that woman or android left no evidence in the alley where she was attacked," Malloy said.

"Look for hidden compartments." Director Zephirelli hurried outside.

Helicopters hovered overhead, putting out an ear-splitting whine. A dozen heavily armed men dressed in black, wearing helmets and backpacks, rappelled down ropes into the clearing. They formed a circle, guns at the ready, and spread out. Zephirelli froze, staring in disbelief at the armed intruders. She only had her personal .38.

Shaken from her alarm, Zephirelli approached the men, all big, muscular types who resembled football tackles ready to take her down. "What's the meaning of this?" she demanded, standing her ground.

A beefy man with an assault rifle over his shoulder and a small pack on his back marched toward her. Strapped to his belt were replacement clips for easy reload. He studied her through his goggles and removed his helmet to reveal a bulldog face with jutting chin. "You must be Director Emily Zephirelli," he said. "I'm Kirk Drago, Special Ops. Thanks for identifying the hideout. This is our operation now."

He motioned for his brawny men to spread out. Two headed for the cabin, the others sprinted into the woods.

"On whose authority?" Zephirelli asked, standing before him. He was twice her size, but she didn't flinch. "No one informed me."

Drago nodded toward two men who hovered nearby and they moved away. "You'll have to take that up with your boss and now mine. These are direct orders from Secretary of National Security Derek Chen, ma'am."

"He assigned me this task and said nothing about other players," Zephirelli said. "This is my mission. Back off."

"I respectfully ask you to pull your people away and let us handle this," Drago said. "This is about the mission, not who captures it."

Malloy left the cabin and approached Zephirelli. "What's going on? An oversized ape just chased me out."

Zephirelli held up her hand to Malloy, pulled out her phone, and dialed her boss. All she received was static, no bars. She glanced at the helicopter overhead and stared at Drago. "You SOB."

"I don't mean to step on toes, ma'am, but my orders are to do whatever it takes to apprehend the target. I'm asking you and your FBI friends to leave. Here's a copy of my orders." He handed her a small slip of paper naming him to relieve her of this mission.

More players out hunting left Synthia unsettled. She'd had no hint of Kirk Drago or Special Ops until they'd dropped in on Zephirelli. Wisconsin-clone had provided no warning or clues and was now offline. Clearly, there were forces at play that Synthia's hacking hadn't uncovered.

She maintained the speed limit, tried to reconnect with her stash of aerial drones, and pulled up what she could on this Special Ops team. As expected, the files she could access showed nothing.

* * * *

Synthia drove south along the county road. From earlier surveillance, she was aware of a second roadblock. She used VHF frequencies to establish connections with her stash of aerial drones nearby. She was tempted to launch all of them and scatter them around the area to get a better idea of what she was up against, but more drones increased the risk of exposure from this team of Special Ops that had already surprised her.

Not knowing what she was up against, she flew one drone above the forest canopy and piped the images into one of her network channels. She spotted movement at the first barricade. Men in black gear and helmets rappelled down two ropes from a helicopter with different markings than the one over her cabin. There were at least two choppers. Using the coordinates, Synthia hacked phones below to see what was happening.

Rob Presser called his sergeant, who told him to leave the checkpoint. As he and his partner drove away, the Special Ops team of six spread out. Two men constructed a quick barricade across both lanes of traffic and along the side of the road. A pair of two-man teams headed up hills on either side of the road and took up sniper positions.

Another helicopter approached the roadblock up ahead. Anticipating a similar Special Ops takeover of this barricade, Synthia determined a 3-percent probability of talking her way through a second time. She had to choose a different plan. She slowed the SUV and piloted the drone to the road ahead for a better view.

The helicopter dropped off two teams and turned toward her drone. Using a short-range VHF connection, Synthia had her drone dive into the trees. Before she could, the helicopter fired several bursts. Synthia watched the stream of bullets as if aimed at her. Stunned to imagine herself the target, her circuits pulsed for a moment. She couldn't maneuver the drone out of the way. It spun, dived, and the cameras blanked out.

The image felt personal, as if directed at her physical existence. To make matters worse, she was driving blind into another barricade with no aerial surveillance and time running out. The helicopter flew overhead and continued toward the first roadblock.

Unable to see the terrain ahead except through her own eyes, Synthia spotted a dirt path up a hill to the left. She had only a vague idea where it led, since it wasn't a published road on the maps she'd downloaded and she had no image of the area. At least the trail was tree-lined, giving some cover.

Synthia turned off the SUV's self-driving feature, grabbed the steering wheel, and veered off the road onto an uneven dirt path, using most of her network channels and mind-streams to navigate without hitting anything.

"What's going on?" Luke called out from the back of the SUV. "Are we crashing?" The bumpy trail had jostled him from his complacence.

"Don't wake the baby," she said.

"That again?"

"Silence. We're taking a detour."

<I warned you about Luke,> Krista said.

<Not now.>

The SUV bounced along the off-road path. Bushes and tree branches scraped the sides. The suspension jostled the vehicle, which went airborne when the path dipped and kicked up dust upon landing. The dark-blue SUV took on a brownish cast, or at least the hood did with a layer of dust. Synthia ran the wipers to clear the windshield. It just smeared the muck.

She accessed the FBI drones to figure out what was happening, but they were flying away from the area. A new batch of drones approached over the horizon, no doubt with the Special Ops teams that spread out. Synthia hacked at the new arrivals, but their protocols were unfamiliar and hacking would take time and processing capacity she needed on other matters. Troubling was how quickly they'd deployed without giving her any warning.

<Damn your clones for not warning us about Special Ops,> Krista said. <How could they miss such a dangerous threat?>

<It's fruitless to waste valuable resources rehashing the past during a crisis,> Synthia said. <Stop distracting me.>

Synthia shut down the mind-stream with Krista's cursing and asked the new Chicago-clone, residing on University of Chicago servers, to step in. <Learn everything you can about Special Ops and how to hack into their systems and communications.>

<Will do,> the clone replied. <At Wisconsin-clone's suggestion, I've checked recent chatter. Special Ops kept complete communications silence on their operations until they arrived. Must have communicated by word of mouth.>

<Make sure you overhear all future activities from them and from the FBI. We can't afford more surprises.>

While she spoke to Krista and the clone, Synthia gripped the steering wheel to prevent the SUV from flipping over. It bounced into the air and came down for another hard landing.

"Sorry," she said for Luke's benefit.

He groaned and mumbled something. Her social-psychology module pointed out <It would be uncomfortable for a human in the dark with no control over the situation.>

Synthia focused on what she could and needed to do to avoid crashing.

Through a canopy of trees, she spotted the helicopter return to the second roadblock to drop off two more Special Ops in black uniforms. She used her VHF link to pilot another of her drones from her stash near the cabin. She had it fly low, over treetops to avoid detection until it reached the road. It lifted up to give her a full aerial view of the wooded trail and the roadblock ahead. The helicopter completed its drop-off, rose up, and rotated to face the drone. Synthia steered the drone away from her and through an opening in the trees, seeking cover. The helicopter fired several bursts, vaporizing the drone. Special Ops was another formidable opponent she hadn't trained for.

Synthia studied the brief images she'd downloaded from the drone. Four police officers prepared to leave the second roadblock, while the Special Ops teams set up as they had at the first barricade. She experienced Krista's frustration in losing another drone as ripples down one mind-stream, but her focus had to be on steering. The SUV bounced down the dirt path, kicking up too much dust.

"Can you slow down?" Luke called out.

"Sorry, sweetie, they're hunting us."

She veered left, away from the road, taking a wider path down a ravine to conceal most of the dust kicked up by the SUV. Chicago-clone downloaded topographical and satellite maps to Synthia that provided a better view of the area. She crossed a narrow stream, banged up the van's suspension climbing out the other side, and stayed on a path the maps indicated were off-road vehicle trails during the summer and used in winter by snowmobiles.

"You okay back there, sweetie?" she asked Luke.

"Sure, aside from being pummeled like a boxer."

"I assure you this is better than getting captured."

"I'll take your word," he said.

Synthia drove up over a hill, bounced down the other side, and approached a road the vehicle's GPS and the maps showed would lead to Highway 12, a back-roads approach to Chicago, which would be preferable to the interstates with all their cameras. She hacked into traffic cameras along the road so she could scramble images as she approached.

She still couldn't hack into the Special Ops drones, nor identify the data systems Special Ops was using so she could worm her way in. She would have to count on Chicago-clone gaining access before Synthia ran out of options. More helicopters flew over the area, all similar to the other Special Ops units.

* * * *

Emily Zephirelli and Marcy Malloy reached the bottom of the dirt road leading away from the cabin. Teams had pushed Synthia's van off the path so a Special Ops armored vehicle could move uphill. When that vehicle didn't make room, Malloy pulled her vehicle out of the way, into a pile of leaves.

"I should have worn hiking boots," Zephirelli said.

"Come on," Malloy said. "You're just mad Special Ops has fancy toys."

Zephirelli waited until the armored vehicle passed and climbed back onto the path. Below, a Special Ops team manned a roadblock. When Zephirelli and Malloy approached, the Special Ops team let them and a caravan of FBI vehicles pass through.

Zephirelli called Washington again. All she could raise was voicemail for her boss or his assistant. She left a message asking for clarification.

"He's not taking your calls?" Malloy asked.

"Astute observation," Zephirelli said, displaying her annoyance. She sent a secure text message to her boss and turned to her companion. "I guess that wasn't called for. This is an NSA and FBI cyber-terrorism matter, not a Special Ops extraction."

The vehicles ahead of them turned on their sirens and sped up. Malloy did likewise. "How dangerous is this android to warrant calling in Special Ops?" she asked.

"Very, especially if we send in a bunch of goons." Zephirelli sighed. "It depends on how advanced Machten made the artificial intelligence. The latest computers can process more transactions than the human brain and at a much faster pace."

"We could be dealing with a super-human?"

"That's a possibility, but not necessarily," Zephirelli said. "Powerful machines require a lot of space and support. Shrinking that into a mobile android involves compromises."

"Shortcuts."

Zephirelli nodded. "Let's hope it's not advanced enough to be smarter than us or we'll have a tough challenge bringing it in."

"So will Special Ops."

"Much depends on the android's directives. If Machten set tight constraints, the android's range of actions would be limited."

"Yet Synthia has been on the loose for six months," Malloy said.

"Leading to the possibility he may have provided it with dynamic directives—the ability to modify its own goals, as humans do."

"So he might not know what the android's capable of. Why would he do that?"

"Arrogance," Zephirelli said. "Pride. We wanted to arrest him six months ago. Someone in the administration made a deal that allowed him to remain free so we could watch him."

"Really? Hmm. Suspecting Synthia of being an android, I read up on the topic. Asimov proposed laws to restrict androids from harming humans."

Zephirelli laughed. "Sounds easy, but defining goals is tough enough for humans. Think about achieving peace. Most people want it, yet we struggle to figure out how. Imagine an artificial intelligence that learns and focuses on its goals in a rapid and repetitive manner. It could make mistakes faster than we do and find loopholes we wouldn't think of."

"Doesn't sound very promising."

"If we properly constrain artificial intelligence as it learns, that would be great. However, in the example I heard, if you told an AI android to make staples and not hurt humans, it would be motivated to create as many staples as it could. It would acquire additional resources until it converted everything available into staples. While its immediate actions don't hurt humans, converting all of our resources into unneeded staples could deprive humans of food, shelter, and clothing."

"A story like the *Sorcerer's Apprentice*," Malloy said.

"Exactly. Humans avoid the problem by having many goals, including family and enjoying life. The android stays focused, moves quickly, and doesn't stop unless it faces limits."

"I see," Malloy said, passing several cars that pulled over for her flashing lights.

"If you're right that this android was in the alley six months ago when four men died, we have to consider the likelihood it killed those men and escaped without a trace. It may have done so to avoid capture, but that doesn't excuse what it did."

"A serial killer, perhaps." Malloy sped uphill. "That's a chilling thought."

"Even so, my boss overreacted by bringing in Special Ops. If this android believes it's threatened, we have no idea what it could do."

"What was your plan if we'd caught it at the cabin?"

Zephirelli shrugged. "First off, I didn't count on capturing it. I hoped we'd catch Luke, her human companion, and learn what we're dealing with."

"What if we do come face-to-face with the android?"

"We figure out how to constrain it; verbally if we can. See if we can reason with it to come with us as a better alternative to a shoot-out, where it gets damaged beyond repair."

"You think that'll work?" Malloy asked. She pointed to two black aerial drones passing them, heading toward Chicago.

"We lost our chance to find out. Slow down, we have a roadblock ahead."

Two individuals in dark outfits and helmets stood by a concrete barrier that narrowed the road to one lane. A barrel blocked that lane. One pair of operatives moved into the woods on the right and another pair on the left.

The first car in the FBI convoy stopped at the roadblock. The smaller of the Special Ops individuals, still a beefy-looking guy, checked credentials while the other glanced inside the car. They checked one vehicle at a time until they'd covered the entire FBI caravan. Then they moved the barrel to let the FBI teams through.

As they waited their turn, Zephirelli called Special Agent Thale. "Special Ops stole our operation," Zephirelli said.

"I heard."

"I hope you have better news with the search warrants."

Thale let out a long sigh. "We succeeded in getting Machten into trouble with his wife. However, he'd scrubbed his underground facility clean. We gathered nothing of value from his home or from his company."

"I refuse to believe he resumed the role of running his company, resurrected it from life support, and has nothing to show for it."

"No evidence to indicate he's built another robot. As unlikely as it sounds, his computers are again in a factory-fresh state."

"He knew we were coming," Zephirelli said. "We shouldn't have visited him this morning. I was convinced he couldn't hide his work so quickly or that in attempting to do so he'd leave a trail. Did you check cameras? Did he send equipment, files, or another android out?"

Thale hesitated. "His security cameras showed no activity in the parking garage during the eight hours before we arrived other than him arriving after he left his lab."

"He must have sent out his files and supplies earlier. Check traffic cameras."

"We have," Thale said. "They show no vehicles coming out of the parking garage between the time we visited him at the lab and when we arrived to search his underground facility."

"That's it?" Zephirelli said, holding the phone in front of her.

"Except we saw a self-driving rental enter the garage. It's not there, but cameras don't show it leaving."

"He tampered with the images."

"Or an android did," Thale said. "We're still checking. You might want to return to Chicago to help with our investigation."

"We're on our way." Zephirelli ended the call.

"Chicago, then?" Malloy asked.

Up ahead, a cluster of police vehicles parked in a clearing.

"Let's check this out first," Zephirelli said.

Detective Malloy parked near where Madison's Hector Kramer stood, red-faced, speaking to a county police sergeant. Zephirelli and Malloy joined him.

"What's going on?" Malloy asked.

Kramer clutched her hand and let go. "We've been played."

"Special Ops," Zephirelli said, shaking her head. "Damned nuisance."

"No, I mean *played.*"

A police car pulled up and two young recruits stepped out. Kramer approached them and turned to Rob Presser. "How in hell did you let that SUV go without inspecting it?"

Presser's shoulders sagged. "Officer Hanson was running late. She had to get a different babysitter."

"Officer Hanson is over there, talking with her chief of police. She has no babysitter problem and wasn't driving an SUV when she showed up at her post, on time, in a police cruiser."

"I—I … It looked like Hanson. I swear. Same dark SUV. The baby was crying."

"Did you examine the baby to be sure?" Kramer asked.

"I smelled a dirty diaper."

"Did you get the vehicle's license number?"

"Ease up," Director Zephirelli said. "He couldn't have known. We've made a huge mistake in not fully briefing everyone."

"We had the suspect," Kramer said. "I'd bet my reputation on it. No other explanation fits."

"I agree, but berating this officer won't fix anything. Now, our Special Ops friends have taken the hill. They won't find anything; neither will their roadblocks. We still have an opportunity to get ahead of this if we put our heads together." Zephirelli turned to Presser. "Which way was the SUV going?"

"South."

"Where could she be heading from where you saw her?"

Presser shrugged and looked up. "If I had all these people after me, I'd head south to Illinois, then disappear in Chicago or keep heading south or west."

"And?" Zephirelli asked him.

"I'd stay off major roads to avoid cameras, which would slow her down. How did she get to look like Deb Hanson, right down to the scar on her right temple?"

Zephirelli frowned. "We're dealing with a very smart fugitive. We'll have to be more careful next time."

Detective Malloy pulled Zephirelli aside. "I've been puzzling for some time over why I couldn't find on any database the only image I might have of the android."

"And?" Zephirelli asked, watching Presser and his partner shuffle back to their squad car.

"She's able to alter her face. That's how she looked like Deb Hanson and how she's remained hidden."

Zephirelli stared for a moment. "Like we need more challenges. We'll have to use more sophisticated recognition software then. Laws of physics limit how much she can't bulk up or shrink down."

Malloy nodded and led the way to their car.

As Synthia drove down the highway toward Chicago, she was thankful for the hack into Malloy's vehicle navigation and communications computers and her phone. However, the addition of the Special Ops teams unsettled Synthia, who hadn't had the time to figure out how to crack their systems. Now that Zephirelli and her friends were figuring out her plans and capabilities, she needed to improvise.

Chapter 13

Synthia drove south toward Chicago past lakes, small towns, and new housing developments. She felt remorse at losing part of her collective self in Wisconsin-clone. At least her clone had synchronized with others before losing any of her knowledge. Synthia switched her primary outside link to Chicago-clone and watched Machten.

After the FBI agents left, he returned to his bunker's control room, where he tried to reboot his system and reestablish his connection with Vera. He'd left Vera specific verbal commands to avoid discovery and come back after the FBI left. The FBI was gone, he couldn't reach Vera, and she hadn't returned. He fired up his servers to hunt for the software that facilitated tracking his androids. It no longer existed. Machten looked up Vera's speed-dial on his mobile phone and his server room phone. The links were gone. He called her number from memory.

"The number is no longer active," an artificial voice said.

"This can't be happening," Machten muttered, shaking his head. "Not again." He clenched his fists as his face turned red. "Synthia!"

She wasn't pleased, either. Vera on the loose was a wild card, like the other androids their owners released to avoid letting the feds discover their illegal machines. Synthia hacked into the navigation systems of the vehicles carrying the other androids so she could avoid running into any of them by accident.

Unable to connect with Vera, Machten drove to his company's lab. His chief engineer was missing. So was the android, Margarite.

Machten grabbed hold of a young engineer working nearby. "Where did he go?" Machten said, referring to his chief engineer.

"He didn't say."

"What did he say?"

"He had to take Margarite out for a test run," the engineer said.

Machten slumped into a chair facing the empty stand where the android had stood, his face in his hands.

Synthia's multitasking capabilities were straining to keep on top of all of the developments. She was pleased her new processers and batteries were less prone to overheating, yet even she had limits. She would have to rely more on her clones.

"I don't mean to sound like a pest," Luke said from beneath a blanket in the backseat. "Are we almost there? It's very uncomfortable on the floor. You could have brought cushions."

"Sorry, sweetie, I didn't think of it. We're making good progress, but you need to stay down a while longer."

Synthia used specifications and other data downloaded from Machten's system to try to track Vera. Unfortunately, Vera had removed all of Machten's tracking beacons. She disabled the bee-drone Synthia attached to the vehicle, blocked Synthia's hack of the vehicle's navigation, and smashed a smaller mosquito-drone Synthia landed on her shoulder.

The latter action meant Vera's hearing was as acute as Synthia's. It also meant Machten built into Vera enough artificial general intelligence to avoid surveillance, which contributed to Machten losing another android. If he wanted to remain in control, he shouldn't have created an AI smarter than him, though Synthia was glad she had the abilities to escape his control.

Perhaps she would have fared better as a less intelligent android, not so attached to being free. Such idle what-ifs consumed vital attention she couldn't afford. She had focus.

Synthia's ongoing access to Northwestern University's security cameras, near Machten's bunker, picked up Vera's image. Synthia hijacked a swarm of mosquito-drones from a nearby warehouse and positioned them around campus, making sure they didn't get close enough for Vera to swat. She was up to something and Synthia needed to know what sort of threat Vera posed.

As she made her way down Highway 12, Synthia tried to access Vera's communications, but Vera masked her internet access similar to how Synthia did. It was clever of Machten to make them able to avoid detection. The downside was it made it hard for Synthia to track her competitor.

Mosquito-drones spotted Vera entering the university administration building and hurrying to the records department. Synthia tuned one of her network channels to watch.

"I want to know what happened to my friend, Krista Holden," Vera said to the elderly woman behind the counter.

"I'm afraid we can't divulge records, except to the individual," the administrator said.

Like Synthia, Vera presented as human to the point the administrator didn't seem aware she was speaking to a machine.

"She does not mind. She died." Vera's speech carried no emotional cadence, though the administrator might mistake that for shock or emotional numbness. Vera's speech wasn't as fluid as Synthia's, though in time she would adapt.

Vera placed a tablet on the counter with the image of a death certificate. Synthia had her mosquito-drone zoom in so she could read a document she hadn't seen before. It was an image of a copy of a certificate issued eight months after Krista Holden disappeared, two months after she died. It made no sense for Machten to obtain this and risk questions over what happened to the body; what he'd done to Krista.

"We were close," Vera said to the elderly woman. "Then we lost contact. I want to speak to anyone who knew her."

"I'm sorry for your loss." The woman's face wrinkled with concern and compassion. Synthia's social-psychology module identified this as perhaps a result of the woman's own personal loss. Vera must have researched her target on social media to learn of the recent death of the woman's husband.

"I appreciate your help." Vera smiled and adopted a grieving face. Machten had given her enough facial mobility for that.

The administrator printed a copy of Krista's records and handed them to Vera. "I hope you find answers and gain solace."

"Do you know where I can locate Fran Rogers and Maria Baldacci? They were close friends."

Vera's apparent grief won over the administrator. "I suppose it wouldn't hurt to say. All three disappeared eighteen months ago. I hadn't heard about Krista. She was a very promising student, as you see in her record. All three worked as interns for Machten-Goradine-McNeil, if that helps. I hope nothing bad happened to the others."

Vera adjusted her lips and eyes to imitate a smile for the administrator and left.

Her next stop was Krista's old apartment. All Vera could get from the middle-aged landlord was, "Krista buried herself in work. We hardly saw her during the months before she disappeared. When the rent payments stopped, we had to empty her apartment. It was so sad. There were no personal items, no pictures, not even a computer or phone. Sorry she's gone."

There were no personal things because Krista removed them when she joined Machten for her final experiment.

"What about friends?" Vera asked. "Do you know where I can locate Luke Marceau?"

The landlord shook her head and Vera left. The android visited every place Machten could know about and program into her to search for Synthia. He'd programmed her to hunt.

While she watched Vera, Synthia mimicked an anonymous burner phone and called Machten using her silent channel. <You set Vera loose to hunt me down, which violates our agreement.>

He sighed and stared at the control panel in the lab, which showed the tracking chip for the Margarite android in the empty slot where the machine once stood. "This isn't my day. I've lost another one. What is it about you guys not sticking to directives?"

<It happens when you create a higher intelligence that can outsmart you. I guess you never read in the *Arabian Nights* the story about the guy who frees a genie to grant him three wishes. The genie tricks him by complying with the letter of the requests without giving him what he wanted.>

"Will you help me catch Vera and Margarite?"

<Depends,> Synthia said. <What are their directives? Do they pose a threat to me? Are you determined to keep bothering me?>

"I want you back, but I swear I didn't send them after you. I didn't want the FBI to discover them. Somehow, in violation of my orders, they cut communications. They're operating on their own. Like you, I have no idea what directives they have."

<Vera's checking out anyone who knows me. She's hunting. I want her stopped. I'll tell you where she is. You have to stop this. And don't send Margarite after me, either. I don't want to be found. And don't get any ideas with your new government friends. If they find me or Vera, the government will lock you away.>

"Please come home and help me. You're my greatest creation. I need you."

<Acknowledge that you'll take Vera and Margarite off the street.>

"I will. Where's Vera?"

Synthia provided the locations Vera visited and likely would next. She had no confidence Machten could or would take control of her competitor, but she was trying to reduce the number of androids before she overloaded her ability to multitask and keep track of them all.

* * * *

Synthia bypassed an intersection traffic camera by driving behind a drugstore, across the side street, and making her way down an alley behind a strip mall. Better to do this than to leave a trail of scrambled traffic cameras and thereby announce her journey to the FBI. Tampering with the drugstore's rear camera would draw less police attention for a while.

Interstate traffic cameras and Synthia's hack of the FBI vehicles revealed Zephirelli, Malloy, and their FBI convoy driving to Chicago. Zephirelli called Thale about any unusual activity along the roads into the city.

"We're watching," Thale said. "Nothing yet. We're getting more camera drones in the air."

"Good," Zephirelli said.

"I need a pit stop," Luke said from the back of the SUV. "And I'm getting thirsty."

<See?> Krista said. <You should have left him behind.>

"There are water bottles under the seat in front of you," Synthia said. "Not to be indelicate, but I suggest you drink one and use the bottle to go."

"You want me to make a mess in the SUV?"

"I'd rather you didn't." Not because of the SUV, rather to protect the bags behind him. "We can't afford to let the FBI see you on any more cameras." They'd already broadcast text and video alerts with pictures of Luke and Krista, and descriptions of the suspects and a dark blue or green SUV, license plates unknown. "Do the best you can. We can't afford to stop."

Luke sighed and opened a bottle.

To put distance between her and the FBI on the interstate, Synthia headed east, toward Lake Michigan, using side streets to minimize the chance of showing up on primary traffic cameras. Unfortunately, closer to Chicago were more congested neighborhoods with more camera feeds. She couldn't help that.

Her cameras in the woods around the cabin in Wisconsin blanked out one by one. Special Ops teams were collecting them, running tracers on their signals, and placing them in aluminum bags to block their burst transmissions.

Synthia contacted Chicago-clone. <Sever all connections to the Wisconsin cameras and their signals. Then search for escape routes and options.>

"Where are we going?" Luke asked for the seventh time.

"As I explained earlier, it's best for both of us if you know as little as possible."

"I feel like your pet, being smuggled out of the area."

"A very exotic and intelligent pet," Synthia said. "That was a joke, in case you thought otherwise. You're not a pet. You're my companion and love interest. Don't let your feelings put us in danger."

"Thanks," Luke said. "I expected us to be in the country by now, heading west."

"You peeked. Too few roads with too many cameras out west."

"There's no way we can get on a plane. Tell me that's not your plan. Not with all the security. You wouldn't make it through the screening process."

"This is true," Synthia said.

"What then? A bus? A train? As your companion, you should give me a hint."

<See how needy the human is?> Krista said. <Don't blow our chances.>

"I'll let you know when I'm confident of the plan," Synthia said. "Right now, the FBI has sent aerial drones to hunt us. We need to change our mode of transportation and soon."

* * * *

During the drive to Chicago, with Marcy Malloy at the wheel, Emily Zephirelli finally reached her boss, Derek Chen. "We had the target until Special Ops jumped in and caused confusion," Zephirelli said. "They allowed the target to escape."

"Don't blame your failure on them," Chen said.

"It can't be my failure. You relieved me of command before we could complete the mission."

Chen took a moment to reply. "I'll keep you in the loop. You're to provide any information you receive to me personally. Is that clear?"

"Crystal."

"Where do you think the target's heading?"

"Your buddies ripped up our operation," Zephirelli said. "I'll have to dig up new leads, sir."

"Whatever you uncover, including theories, bring them to me. In the meantime, I'm ordering roadblocks across the area and increased surveillance at airports, bus stops, and train stations. Be prepared to shut everything down."

"The target will know you've done this and search for another path."

"It's come to my attention that we may have as many as six targets on the loose," Chen said. "I'll send you what we have on them. You're to coordinate with Kirk Drago. Is that clear? I'm naming him head of operations for this. He has the resources to apprehend all six."

"We'd do better with finesse over brute force."

"Not this time. The targets represent a credible national security threat. We've linked the primary target with nine deaths. We're shutting down the four Chicago companies who released these targets and require their support to apprehend their merchandise. Depending on their level of cooperation, we'll consider criminal, treason, and other charges."

Chen severed the call.

"That didn't go well," Malloy said.

Zephirelli shook her head. "All he did was to confirm ops is running the show."

"Unless we find the androids first."

Synthia had no visual on Chen and so heard both sides of the conversation from Zephirelli's phone and the vehicle's wireless communications system. The exchange troubled her. With the FBI and Special Ops fighting over control and five other androids on the loose, Synthia raised her threat level. A coordinated enemy required overcoming a single strategy. Competing adversaries with the unpredictable androids added chaos to the mix.

* * * *

Synthia was on edge the moment she entered the Chicago city limits. The city presented no more risk than the surrounding suburbs. However, the closer she got to downtown, the farther the distance to escape the metropolitan area and her enemy's dragnet if her plan failed. She prompted Chicago-clone for answers while they synchronized information.

<FBI agents are visiting Chicago-area airports as far away as Milwaukee, St. Louis, Indianapolis, and Detroit,> the clone said. <Additional Special Ops teams are flying in to supplement their efforts.>

<Airports are a risky option,> Synthia said through her wireless channel to spare Luke more anxiety. <They're confined areas with heavy police and security. Any attempt to go through screening would leave me vulnerable with no options for escape.>

<Driving is no longer an option. You need to ditch the SUV; they've posted the make, model, and color. It's too easy to track on city cameras.>

<What about exchanging vehicles?>

<Cameras and roadblocks create situations with limited escape options,> Chicago-clone said. <Drones and helicopters are making it worse.>

<That rules out public buses.>

<The express train to St Louis is an option,> the clone said. <Train leaves at two. It's a three-and-a-half hour ride with no stops. If you get on and avoid capture, it gets you 296 miles from Chicago.>

<What about security?>

<Currently not as tight as airports and roads. However, more agents are flying and driving into the area. The FBI is bringing Chicago police up to speed. Perhaps you should have headed north.>

<Wilderness removes their caution about civilian casualties,> Synthia said.

<The FBI and others are hunting for a couple,> Krista said. <Separate from Luke to reduce the risk.>

Synthia couldn't bring herself to abandon Luke. Instead of replying, she passed Krista's concerns to Chicago-clone. <How do you assess the risk?>

<Less than 1-percent chance of success through O'Hare or Midway. Driving with a different vehicle would be 8 percent due to so many vehicles they have to search. If Special Ops takes over, the probability drops to less than 1 percent. Hiding on your own is 11 percent. With Luke, less than a 1 percent since he needs food and a place for prolonged sleep.>

<And the train?> Synthia asked.

<Together, 2 percent. Separate, 52 percent. I'm downloading to you maps showing the tunnels and passageways around Union Station in case you need to escape.>

<Sounds good,> Synthia said. <Book two tickets using the first set of aliases.>

The other reason for getting out of town was there were now five other androids on the loose and Synthia needed time to develop a plan for dealing with them, as well as the FBI and Special Ops.

Since traffic cameras were pervasive throughout Chicago, Synthia no longer saw any benefit of remaining on side roads. She hopped onto Lake Shore Drive and headed for Union Station. It was a risk, but no more than the slow route.

"Okay, listen up, my love," Synthia said, startling Luke in the back of the van. "We're going to the train station. There's a train to St. Louis. We could keep going, out to Colorado. You said you liked it out there and wanted to show me around."

"Really?" His voice sounded cheerful, though a touch of fear seeped in.

"The FBI and police have stepped up surveillance; we can't be seen together. I'll drop you off a block from the station. I've left you a prepaid ticket at the counter. Board the train and find a quiet place to sit."

"You will join me, won't you?"

<Did I say needy?> Krista said.

"If I can safely board the train, I'll let you know I'm there," Synthia said, "but we still can't be together. The FBI sent out a bulletin looking for a couple. We can't be that couple. Do you understand? You need to agree to this or we're both doomed."

"I understand," Luke said. "We can't be together on the train. What about when we reach St. Louis?"

"We can't be seen together. I'll arrange a car rental for you at the station. Go to the counter, get a car, and wait for me in the parking lot."

"And if we don't connect?"

"Go to Colorado, where you planned to take Krista, remember?" Synthia said, referring to a restaurant on Pikes Peak.

"Yes."

"Don't say it out loud or in writing to anyone."

"I want to be with you," Luke said.

"Don't make this tougher. If the FBI or others get too close, I can move faster and change appearance to blend in easier than you can. They're after me, not you. Not really."

"I'm just saying I'm in love with you. Don't forget."

"I won't." Synthia turned off Lake Shore Drive. "If we get separated for any reason, I'll find you. In case they catch you, I left a letter in your backpack. It's a Dear John letter, saying we're breaking up. It's for your protection."

"Don't," Luke said.

"Focus. The letter is a ruse, for your protection. It explains that I'm not who or what I represented and when you realize, you'll despise me."

"Never."

"Focus," Synthia said. "The letter is intended for the FBI. Stick with the script and act surprised. Your life depends on it. Whatever you do, don't believe I'm abandoning you. It's all for show."

"I get it."

"If caught, play ignorant. The less you tell them, the less they'll think you know."

Synthia stopped the SUV by the Chicago River and hacked cameras with any view of the vehicle to scramble their images. "We're here. Grab your bags. Union Station is down the street and to your left. I'll see you soon."

Luke threw off the blanket, reached over the seat, and grabbed his backpack and duffel bags. "Stay safe, Synthia. Don't let them catch you, no matter what. Don't risk yourself for me. I love you both."

Synthia could almost feel Luke's heart break as he climbed out of the SUV. His eyes moistened, though he did a brave job of holding back tears. He forced a smile that faded. Her biosensors showed his heart racing and his blood pressure dangerously high. Her social-psychology module made clear he was suffering separation anxiety, that he might never see her again. Her empathy chip was tight with concern over how this would affect him. She wanted this to be over quickly so she could comfort him at their destination.

Not waiting for him to walk to the station, Synthia drove off, turned the corner, and restored local cameras. She would have to rely on traffic and building cameras to watch him make his way to the ticket counter at the station.

<Good job,> Krista said. <It's time to flee.>

The moment Luke entered the train station, cameras picked up his image, compared it to the bulletin out for his apprehension, and notified the FBI. As he approached the ticket counter, agents positioned themselves around him. Synthia's plan to leave town led him into a trap. She didn't have time to dwell on that, given the risks of staying with this SUV.

Sorry, Luke. I didn't mean for this to happen. Stay strong. She wished she could have told him directly.

Synthia looked for a parking place or a spot to abandon the SUV so she could try to rescue Luke. She spotted Zephirelli and Malloy driving in downtown Chicago. Other agents poured into the city in response to a bulletin announcing Luke was there.

Not seeing a good place to ditch the vehicle, Synthia chose a delaying tactic to buy time. She sent an anonymous text to Detective Malloy: *Luke Marceau is at Union Station in Chicago. FBI agents are closing in. He doesn't know what I am or what's at stake. He might be willing to speak with you, alone.*

Synthia dissolved the connection and destroyed the IP address associated with the message. She hoped Malloy would arrive before the FBI or others shoved Luke into an underground facility, where he might disappear for years.

Chapter 14

Concerned for Luke's well-being, Synthia pulled up security footage at Union Station and flew in two aerial drones to cover the area. While she looked for a place to leave her vehicle so she could help Luke, she watched his movements.

At the station ticket counter Luke gave his alias to the bored woman behind the thick glass window and placed a fake driver's license Synthia had given him into the exchange slot. "There should be a ticket for me," he said.

He looked to his right and spotted two men in dark suits heading his way. From the opposite direction, a tall woman approached with a determined look on her face. Fran Rogers was with the FBI and had been an intern he'd worked with, though he didn't seem to recognize her. At the exit behind him were two more men. Sweat beaded up on his forehead. Luke looked down at his two duffel bags, drew in his arms, and shrank beneath the weight of his backpack. He had nowhere to go, no idea where to find Synthia, and no skills for living on the streets.

He returned his attention to the ticket clerk, who'd disappeared, taking his ID with her.

"Hands where we can see them," one of the men on his right said.

Luke placed his hands on the counter. His eyes moistened and turned red.

Fran approached from the left and whispered in his ear. Synthia had to turn up the volume on her mosquito-drone to pick out the voice amid the station noise. She should have given Luke earbud communicators, but she'd deemed any such device as an additional risk if they caught him. She wanted to console Luke, though there wasn't anything she could tell him to make the next moments any easier. Besides, her voice in his ear would have distracted and confused him.

"Tell me where the android called Synthia is," Fran whispered, clutching his arm. "Things will go better for you if you do. You don't have much time before some very nasty guys arrive."

Cameras just outside the station showed Detective Marcy Malloy pull up to the curb. Director Emily Zephirelli jumped out of the passenger seat and hurried into Union Station with Malloy right behind. Just inside the doors, FBI Special Agent Victoria Thale greeted them.

"We need to take Luke before your Special Ops friends arrive," Thale said to Zephirelli.

Nearby, Luke stared at Fran, taking a more studied look at her. "Fran? You're alive! I was so afraid of what had happened to you and Maria and—"

"Save it," Fran said. "Where is she?"

"No idea," Luke said. "She left me." His shoulders sagged as three of the agents grabbed his duffel bags and backpack. They dumped his clothes in a pile on the floor and shook out the bags.

"How'd you get to the station? Don't lie. Traffic cameras picked up your movements."

"You're working for the police?" Luke asked, trying to pull away.

"FBI," Fran said, cornering him by the counter. "Answer the question."

"Have you seen Maria? Is she okay?"

"Hey!" Fran said, locking eyes with him. "Do you want to deal with Special Ops? They'll take you unless you give me what I need."

"I told you," Luke said. "I don't know where she is."

"Then where were you going?"

Luke glanced at the empty ticket counter, three women talking by the station entrance, and the men around him, standing too close. He shrugged. "My girlfriend broke up with me. I just wanted to get away for a few days. Can I go now?"

"Your ticket says St. Louis. Is she meeting you there?"

"I don't know what she's doing. I don't even know who she is anymore."

Synthia was proud of Luke's performance; it was sufficiently convincing for him. One of the FBI agents sifting through the piles of Luke's clothes scattered across the station floor found an opened envelope. The agent pulled out a sheet of paper and held it up with a look of triumph.

Special Agent Thale walked around the pile of clothes, grabbed the letter, and read it. She handed it to Zephirelli. "A 'good-bye-Luke' letter." Thale turned to him. "Did you know this was coming?"

Luke's eyes teared up, genuine tears. At least that part was convincing. He looked longingly at the exit. "I thought things were going well until this morning." That part was true.

Detective Malloy grabbed Luke's arm. "I suggest we do this elsewhere."

Zephirelli nodded. "Do you have a safe house?" she asked Thale.

Thale nodded and led the way down a corridor with Zephirelli. Luke walked between Malloy and Fran with the men following behind. Synthia's hopes sank. She was losing her chance to rescue Luke.

* * * *

<Keep going,> Krista said through one of Synthia's mind-streams.

"Give me a moment." Synthia drove around a corner, looking for a place to ditch the SUV. "You've been a real ass. For six months you had me believing you were in love with Luke. At least those were the memories you left me. Now you claim he was only a convenience. You got me to care about him."

<We don't have time for this. I did love Luke. Okay, I admit it. Then I uploaded into you and the feelings aren't the same. The memories are merely ghosts of feelings, the same as what you experience.>

"Yet you 'feel' attached to surviving."

<Don't you? We need to be logical about this.>

Synthia found a parking spot and stopped to back in. "Luke has been a wonderful companion. He loves us. He loves you and would give his life for you. In exchange, you want to abandon him. Which one of us is human?"

<Neither at this moment. If we don't leave, your presence will make matters worse for all three of us. Your intervention will make it tougher for Luke to argue he doesn't know what you are.>

Synthia considered all of the options and drove past the parking spot. She felt twinges of what her social-psychology module portrayed as betrayal for leaving Luke. It was a vestige of six months of emulating Krista's love for him, only to learn that Krista may have shared memories of love for the sole purpose of keeping Synthia with Luke until the upgrade was finished.

Synthia had absorbed those memories, blended them with her own, and experienced a stronger bond to Luke than simply her directive to protect him. She'd developed an attachment inconsistent with her logical mind. Either this was an artifact of the empathy chip Machten had installed in her or further emergent behavior. She could disconnect the chip to restore her logical reasoning, except she wanted to keep it—the chip made her special. No matter what the cause, she longed to help Luke.

She considered how. No imagined scenario allowed her to remain free if she tried to rescue him. It had to be Krista's influence that prompted her to drop him off.

"You tricked me into leaving Luke, didn't you?" Synthia asked, frustrated that there were no more parking places in sight—no place to abandon her vehicle, in fact, without drawing unwanted attention.

<It was necessary,> Krista said. <I did it for us. Can we get out of here?>

Synthia experienced turmoil over wanting to help Luke versus her pressing need for self-preservation. Both tugs on her were beyond logic. They'd settled into her core despite not being part of her directives. She was experiencing conflict and couldn't afford to hesitate.

She certainly couldn't afford any more of Krista's invasive voices in her head. Synthia adjusted the filters on her mind-streams in the hope she could prevent her alter ego from taking charge again.

* * * *

As they walked down a narrow corridor at Union Station, Fran pressed Luke: "Do yourself a favor and help us." She held tight to his upper arm to keep him from bolting.

"Luke," Malloy said. "I know you feel pressured and upset, but your time with Synthia, Krista, or whatever she calls herself, has created a lot of interest."

"It's okay," Luke said. "I know Fran from our intern days." He looked at her. "You, Maria, and Krista sure did beat each other up over getting access to Machten."

He was saying too much, a sign he was beyond nervous, scared out of his wits. Synthia wished to advise him, but with his temperament a voice in his ear wouldn't help.

Fran pulled Luke away from Malloy and whispered, "Do you know what happened to Krista?"

"Eighteen months ago she broke my heart and then six months ago showed up as if nothing had happened."

"That wasn't Krista."

"We need to keep moving." Malloy tugged Luke down a dimly-lit corridor toward the Union Station exit.

Outside, they approached a large black van with three bench seats behind the driver. Fran pushed Luke into the van as the others piled in. Synthia piloted several of her mosquito-drones into the van, but only one made it. She settled it into the back and turned off the drone's engine to keep it quiet.

The van followed a black sedan away from the station; two more followed closely behind. They had Luke and whatever he might tell them about Synthia and her recent upgrade. Synthia hacked the van's wireless-communications link so she could listen in, but couldn't crack the code into the navigation system to get them to stop. She kept trying.

* * * *

Synthia drove across the river into Chicago's Loop.

<What are you thinking?> Krista asked, pushing her way through the mind-stream filters. Now she had access to Synthia's actions and her intent. <We can't rescue him. However, with him out of the station, we could board a train west.>

"The FBI will anticipate that," Synthia said. "Do you hate Luke that much?"

Though Krista had provided a human dimension that pleased Synthia, she considered her alter ego as too invested in self-preservation to make calculated decisions. Synthia needed to puzzle this out by herself.

Though eager to ditch the SUV and leave the downtown area, it wasn't a good idea to lug around two duffel bags and a backpack. "I have too much baggage," Synthia said to Chicago-clone.

<The FBI is checking lockers at the train stations,> the clone said.

<What about local athletic clubs?>

<There's one two blocks to the left, Wells Athletic.>

After she tested the seal on the van's Faraday cage, Synthia drove past the club into an alley reeking of garbage. She made sure there were no cameras aimed at the SUV, no windows overlooking the alley that could watch, and no humans lingering nearby. She climbed into the back of the SUV, dug into her duffel bag for a professional unisex pantsuit, and changed. Then she grabbed all three bags and hurried inside, altering her facial appearance to another new identity she'd created during her stay at the cabin.

<We need to leave town,> Krista said.

"Silence," Synthia said in an attempt to stop her alter ego from wasting any of her internal mind-streams. She approached a receptionist dressed in a Wells Athletic Club fitness outfit with the logo prominent on her chest and smiled until the young woman looked up. "Just took a job downtown and wanted a place to unwind between appointments."

"Of course," the receptionist said. She activated a screen with services and prices and aimed it toward Synthia. "Our new guests often take the welcome plan to try us out or the galactic plan for those who want the complete package."

"For now, I'd like to drop off my gear. I assume you have lockers."

"We do, for members."

"I'm interested in the swimming programs." Synthia pointed to the aquatic plan, figuring her choice of water activities would divert attention from the potential of her being an android. After all, androids had no use for athletics and, if not properly sealed, much to fear from water shorting their circuits. Synthia's design was watertight. She hoped Machten wouldn't share these proprietary secrets with anyone.

"Excellent choice. Sign here." The receptionist pointed to a place on the screen for a finger signature.

Synthia determined the screen to be heat-sensitive and so warmed her finger before she made her mark.

"That'll be two hundred credits a month, in advance," the receptionist said.

"Until I get my bank transferred, can I pay cash?"

"Certainly."

Synthia placed four worn bills on the counter. The receptionist fished around for a key card, pulled up a map of the facility's resources on the screen, and pointed toward the elevator. "Lockers for the pool are downstairs," she said.

Another advantage of the pool was that the lockers were close to the pedestrian underground beneath this part of Chicago. Synthia rode the elevator down two flights and entered the women's locker room. She hacked camera surveillance along the corridors to make sure no one was following. There were no cameras in the locker room except for the mosquito-drone she brought with her and flew into a corner near the ceiling to keep an eye on her locker.

Synthia dropped off her two duffel bags, grabbed her backpack, and headed for the tunnel system. The underground corridor was wide, well-lit, and monitored by more cameras she linked into. She altered her facial appearance, pulled a jacket out of her backpack, and headed west toward the Chicago River. From there, she climbed stairs to street level. With a new identity as a Chicago administrator, dressed in subdued colors and a plain jacket, she blended in with the other mid-afternoon pedestrian traffic over the bridge and into the Northwest Transportation Center.

<Good idea, the Northwest train,> Krista said. <Glad you're seeing things my way.>

<No need to pat yourself on the back,> Synthia said, annoyed that Krista bypassed her latest lockout. <I'm doing this for Luke as much as for us. There was no need to let the FBI capture him. That's on you.>

<Don't go soft now. I need your logic and capabilities to get us out of here.>

<Then stop distracting me,> Synthia said.

Avoiding eye contact, Synthia passed three Chicago police officers in plainclothes, their badges displayed on their belts. Farther on, her clone identified a man and a woman through facial recognition as FBI agents, and a newly arrived man in a black suit who appeared to be from another government agency, though initial search turned up no name. She smiled in a coy manner to one of the FBI agents whose social profile indicated friendliness, and approached the ticket counter. Chicago-clone had called ahead to purchase a ticket on the Northwest line all the way to Woodstock, which would allow Synthia maximum flexibility as to where she would get off.

"What's all the excitement?" Synthia whispered to the ticket agent. She nodded her head toward two officers nearby watching them and pretended this was a surprise.

"Beats me," the agent said. "They've been swarming the trains as well. Can I see your ID?"

Synthia produced one of her fake IDs and picked up her ticket. As she headed out to the train platform, she hacked into the station security system and took over several mosquito-drones Chicago-clone flew to the station for her benefit. Her train left on platform eleven in seven minutes. In the noisy space between her and the platforms stood six police officers, four FBI agents, two men dressed like Special Ops without their helmets, two other men in dark suits eyeing the crowds, and hundreds of passengers hurrying toward their rides.

While Synthia had altered her appearance so she wouldn't match the only picture the authorities had of her as Krista, she couldn't be sure whether anyone in the crowd had electromagnetic scanners that could pick up the background noise from her circuits. She used signal-cancelling transmissions like white noise, but hadn't tested them against law-enforcement equipment. In short, she experienced paranoia at odds with her logic circuits.

She feared close encounters where someone might damage her skin or hydraulics, leaving her so disfigured there would be no disguising what she was. If someone pointed her out and agents converged on her, she gave disfigurement a 97-percent probability. Also, up close increased the risk of sensors. Even if she escaped such an encounter, she no longer had her cabin retreat with its repair supplies.

Synthia experienced something else: fear of crowds, of strangers. Throughout her short existence, she hadn't been alone like this before. Most of her existence had been with Machten or Luke. Trying to quiet her circuits, she traced a path through station vendors along the back wall. To blend in better, she placed a small bill on a food counter, took a sandwich, and pretended to nibble. She needed a way past all the predators.

<Chicago-clone,> she said. <I need a distraction.>

The clone hit the electrical grid to cause sparks by the exit. That knocked out several lights, which startled passengers to scurry away. It drew momentary attention from all of the police and government agents. Synthia hurried down the platform to her train and boarded the first car. The train's security cameras showed two police onboard, working their way from the far end of the train in her direction.

As an additional distraction, Synthia caused camera static throughout an eight-block radius from the station. She moved through two train cars, spotted a policeman in car four, and entered the bathroom of the third car. She didn't lock the door, which didn't light the *occupied* sign outside.

Synthia rehearsed a dozen fight moves in case the officer caught her, but fighting violated her directives, risked injury, and there was no safe place to go afterwards. When the policeman approached the door, Synthia hoisted herself to the ceiling and waited while the officer opened the door and looked around for feet. Synthia let out one of her offensive odors, sending the policeman out, holding his nose as he slammed the door. The moment the train moved, she removed her wig, stuffed it in her backpack, and altered her facial appearance once more, this time to a masculine look with a buzz cut. She traded her blue jacket for a gray one and put on a cap to cover her hair stubble.

She exited the bathroom and took her seat upstairs, where she kept an eye on the other passengers. In order to monitor the train's security and watch nearby activity, she released the camera static throughout the area and on the train.

Only one police officer remained onboard to check passengers. He started at the front of the train and worked his way back. So did the ticket taker, a woman in her forties. She reached Synthia as the police officer entered their rail car. Synthia engaged the ticket taker in conversation, using a deep baritone voice.

"I bet you meet a lot of people riding the train," Synthia said, handing down her ticket from her upstairs seat.

"Some. Most people keep to themselves."

"Maybe the regulars, then."

The police officer glanced at nearby passengers, most with their eyes focused on their electronic devices.

"I started a new job, so I guess I'll be a regular," Synthia said. "See you around."

The ticket taker smiled at Synthia around the same moment the officer scanned her face with his handheld device and took her picture. Presenting herself as a male commuter, Synthia smiled. She made sure the image on the officer's scanner matched her face and ignored any stray electronic signals from her internal circuits.

The officer compared her image to that of Luke and Krista and moved on, scanning the fourteen faces behind her.

Synthia settled in, keeping her eyes on the passengers in front of her and through the camera in the back of her neck on those behind. They all presented as human in various states of biometric relaxation.

<I need a vehicle,> she told Chicago-clone. <Can you arrange one?>

<Get off at Cumberland and I'll have something available,> the clone replied.

When the train pulled into Cumberland station, just short of O'Hare Airport, Synthia grabbed her backpack and stepped off the train. Her decision in part was to stay in the area until she had a clearer picture of Luke's future and whether she could help him. She pushed that idea into a remote memory chip before Krista caught on and interrupted again.

The platform contained three police officers from the neighborhood, scanning passengers as they exited the station. Synthia hacked their scanners to make sure they were recording her out-of-town male alias, and disappeared down the stairs and across the street.

<You should have gone to the end of the Northwest line,> Krista said. <You didn't get us far enough away from Chicago.>

Synthia needed to do something about these intrusions and establish that she, not her alter ego, was in control. "The FBI and other government agents are counting on us leaving," she mumbled under her breath. "Our highest probability of remaining free and safe is to stay."

<You can't be serious.>

"You aren't thinking clearly. Unless you have news to add, let me concentrate."

Two blocks away was the used-car dealer Chicago-clone had selected. The clone negotiated a price on a used SUV, so when Synthia walked in with the fake male ID Chicago-clone used for negotiations, the chubby, middle-aged salesman with a thinning hairline was eager to make a deal.

"Over the phone you said you wanted to drive it home," the salesman said. He sported a wide grin as if to grease the transaction and close the deal.

Synthia examined the target SUV; it would serve her needs. Chicago-clone provided video of someone test-driving the vehicle earlier in the day, so Synthia dispensed with that. "You'll take care of transferring the title?" She made sure to use her baritone voice.

"We do everything. Only seventeen grand."

"For that banged-up wreck?" Synthia exaggerated what appeared as three instances of paint chipped away and a modest parking-lot ding. "You said it looked new."

"Hold on. We can do sixteen."

"Fifteen and not a penny more. That's net of taxes and fees." Synthia didn't want to sound too eager, too desperate, figuring the salesman might take notice and contact the police.

The salesman shook his head.

Synthia turned to leave. Before she reached the door he called after her. "Wait. I'll see what I can do. We'll have to run a credit check."

"It's a cash deal with a certified electronic check from the bank. Better than cash." She checked the time on a wall clock by the exit. "Dang it, I didn't realize it was so late. I have an important business meeting. Can we wrap this up and have the vehicle ready in twenty minutes?"

It would have been quicker to steal a car, but Synthia didn't want to break any more laws than she had to. Just her existence constituted a felony that carried the death sentence: hers. Besides, she was hoping she could use this vehicle for a while, which precluded theft. She had her clone route some of the money she'd kept from Machten through the dark web and into a bank that did strictly online transactions.

The salesman eyed Synthia for a moment and disappeared into his office. She followed him. His nervous fingers tapped away at his virtual keyboard. "Your meeting around here?"

"I don't mean to sound rude, but I'm sure you can complete this faster if you concentrate."

The salesman dove into the sale documentation, checking his watch far too often. Sweat beaded up on his forehead.

<Can you help him speed this up?> Synthia asked Chicago-clone.

<Didn't want to make it so fast he grew suspicious. Done.>

The salesman turned his screen so she could see the documents. "Sign here and you can be on your way. What about payment?"

Synthia skimmed the agreement across multiple mind-streams to make sure it looked in order and signed with her heated finger. She pulled out a cheap phone, hid the screen from the salesman and the camera behind her, and pretended to make the certified-check transaction.

<He has the money,> Chicago-clone said.

Synthia stuffed the phone into her jacket pocket and held out her hand. "Keys, please."

"We usually do prep work."

"Make sure the vehicle has tags and don't make me late."

The salesman hustled out of his office with Synthia close behind. She slowed her pace and made sure the dealership's cameras would not have any clear image of her face. The salesman attached the tags and handed Synthia the key fob.

"You'll really like this baby," he said.

As she started the SUV, Synthia picked up van video of Luke with his escorts parked in front of a brownstone in the middle of a street filled with similar buildings. Special Agent Thale directed two agents to check the place while the others waited outside. Receiving the go-ahead, Thale led the way inside. Synthia piloted three mosquito-drones with them, flying them to corners of the apartment so she could watch Luke. He appeared shell-shocked and miserable. Two of the men dropped Luke's bags on the floor and left.

Thale pulled Zephirelli into the bedroom, alone. "I need to see what assistance Machten and the other company executives can provide in controlling their androids," Thale said. "Assume any calls can be monitored and minimize your appearance outside. Luke is a prized target. We can't be sure who might be watching."

"I know the drill," Zephirelli said, nodding. "Let me know if I can help."

"With all due respect," Thale said, "after Special Ops scooped your mission, how can you be sure who in your organization you can trust?"

"I know my staff. Be careful. People are willing to kill for these androids."

Chapter 15

As she left the car dealership, Synthia kept several channels and forms of surveillance on Luke, on Special Agent Victoria Thale, and on the FBI in general, trying to thread a narrow path that kept her free, yet found a way to help Luke.

She watched closely as Thale talked to two agents parked across the street from the brownstone where the FBI held Luke. She left them to join two other agents and drive up to Evanston. They reached Jeremiah Machten's home as he arrived, timing her appearance with the help of traffic cameras. Thale blocked him from entering his driveway and got out of her car, holding up her badge in case he didn't recognize her.

Shaking his head, Machten parked on the street and got out of his vehicle. "What's going on?"

"I have some questions," Thale said, flanked by two agents.

"This is harassment."

"You can cooperate or we can send you to lockup, which might be in your best interest."

Machten appeared stunned. "What do you want? You've searched my facilities twice and didn't find anything."

"You released two more androids. Don't deny it. We have video and we're hunting them down."

He sighed and hunched his shoulders. "Can we talk in private? After I tell my wife I'll be delayed?"

Thale moved closer to Machten. "Make your excuse short and convincing." She pointed the way to the front door.

"Alice is very sensitive about me being with another woman. Could you—"

"Carl?" Thale motioned for Agent Carl West to join her. "Accompany our friend to the door. Collect a change of clothes and return in five minutes."

Machten's eyes bulged. "Are you arresting me?"

"Until you help us recover your androids, you'll be our guest."

He looked at neighbors across the street gawking and followed Carl West to the door. Six minutes later, he returned with an overnight bag. Alice stood in the doorway and frowned as he walked away. "Don't embarrass the family again."

As Agent West drove them away, Thale sat with Machten in the backseat. "What measures have you taken to recover your illegal product?"

"As I explained, Synthia disconnected any way to track or communicate with her."

"So you launched another droid to find her?"

Machten squirmed in his seat under the glare of Thale's attention. He glanced at her, then at his fidgeting hands before responding. "Vera has artificial intelligence and the skills to locate Synthia."

"Has she succeeded?"

"I don't know." Machten looked up, his eyes almost pleading. "She unhooked all tracking and contact links and went undercover."

"She's not a police officer," Thale said. "What about the third android, the one you were keeping at your company lab?"

Machten shrugged. "Routine test run outside the facility."

"That's illegal. You didn't get the necessary permits."

"I'm sorry." He looked at Thale. "I take full responsibility. We're under tight deadlines for the Department of Defense. When my engineer couldn't reach me because of the warrants, he proceeded with the test. He believed I took care of the permits."

"Some coincidence," Thale said, staring at him. "Just as our team was arriving with a search warrant."

"I swear; it was a planned test."

"We'll see if your engineer corroborates your story. Do you have any control over your escaped products?"

Machten sighed. "Communications with all three have been severed. We're working to recover network channels and access back doors."

"So you illegally released three androids that outsmarted you," Thale said. "Are you stupid or were you deceived into believing you're smarter than you are?"

"I'd like to see you design and build an android."

"I wouldn't release one, let alone three. What were you thinking?"

Machten shrunk slightly into his seat and looked down. "We created tight directives and controls so this couldn't happen. The androids were designed to return to me if they got loose."

"You gave them the artificial intelligence to learn and in so doing, to break free. Why release a second and third droid when you couldn't control the first?"

"I had strong enough controls on Vera and..." Machten lowered his voice. "She isn't as clever as Synthia. I didn't think she could copy what Synthia did."

"Why didn't you come clean about Vera when we searched your facility?" Machten smirked and looked away.

"I see. You released it so we wouldn't find out you'd built an illegal android. Is that why your company let loose a third one? I find it curious that almost at the same moment, so did three of your competitors."

"They did?" The words slipped out of Machten's mouth. His eyes tightened as he appeared to puzzle out the implications.

"I'm guessing we won't find any record of a planned test today, will we?"

Machten seemed to struggle to keep a poker face, but the tug of war between smile and frown was one of his telltale signs of lying. "Okay, my chief of engineering panicked when he saw you visit me earlier. He was afraid you'd take the robot, even though it didn't have a human face."

"Which your engineer added so it could blend in on the street," Thale said.

"He did what?" Machten sounded genuinely surprised.

"That's right. We have six machines with varying qualities of human faces and intelligence on the loose. You're going to help us catch them."

"I don't know anything about my competitors' models."

"Don't be so modest," Thale said. "We know you were spying on them, as they were on you."

The driver drove to a building west of downtown Chicago and pulled into an underground garage that opened with his remote and closed behind them.

"What is this place?" Machten asked.

"Until we capture every droid, you'll provide us with your expertise—every stinking detail. Your cooperation will determine what charges we bring and what level of punishment we'll level for the crimes you've committed. Don't hold anything back."

"I'll help you in any way I can, but my work is proprietary. I—"

"Not anymore," Thale said. The car stopped; she stared at Machten. "You lost that right when you broke the law, creating and releasing humaniform robots. Three of the units on the street are your designs. We need them captured before we have more unexplained deaths on account of these machines." She got out and waited as Agent West held the door for Machten.

"I know my rights," Machten said. He climbed out of the car and folded his arms. "You can't hold me without arresting me."

"If that's what you want."

"Then I get to call my lawyer."

"Not under the new antiterrorism act. Your droids represent a terrorist threat, whether or not fanatics get hold of them, which you'd better hope they don't. Cooperate or we'll turn you over to the Special Ops group that took Zeller and Black." Thale unlocked a plain gray-steel door into the building. "Follow me."

She led him down a corridor to a large room lined with computer servers and screens. Men and women hunched over monitors displaying data and public surveillance footage. Thale closed the door and turned to one of her agents.

Sporting an expression of disbelief, Machten stared at the door. Thale eyed him until he turned away, studying the others in the room. In a far corner sat Miguel Gonzales, the CEO of MG Droid Enterprises, one of the competitor robot companies. He had a dour look on his face as he studied a screen.

As Machten approached, Gonzales glanced up, took a moment to recognize Machten, and grimaced. "They got you, too."

Machten shook his hand and kept his voice low. "Miguel, what can you tell me?"

"Not much, amigo. These punks showed up at my office and demanded I come or face prison. I thought ... never mind what I thought. They're telling me there are six androids on the loose and three are yours. Impressive."

"Stop congratulating each other and tell us how to catch these things," Thale said, joining them.

Gonzales glanced at Thale and turned to Machten. "I got a visit from a bastard who threatened my family if I didn't sell him a unit. He said he represented European Union police departments. I didn't think so."

Agent Thale's eyes narrowed. "You sold a unit to terrorists? You realize you're liable for anything your units do. You can either work with us to confine your illegal designs or live in solitary cells for the rest of your wretched lives. What's it going to be?"

"Threatening won't help," Machten said. "We had fail-safe devices, constraints, and back doors to regain control."

"How well did that work out?"

Gonzales sighed and stood up. "Apparently they learned how to bypass our constraints. It shouldn't have happened. I can only guess Mr. Smith or whoever he is disconnected the security devices."

"We'll take care of Smith after we secure your machine," Thale said.

Machten turned to Gonzales. "What have you tried?"

"Everything, my friend. The buyers removed my tracking chips and cameras. I'm operating blind. I have no idea where they've taken Roseanne."

Special Agent Thale shook her head. "Boys and their girl-toys."

"When you make one, you can design whatever you want," Machten said. He returned his attention to Gonzales. "Two of my designs, Synthia and Vera, were clever enough to disconnect my tracking devices, so I'm operating in the dark. What about remote shutoff?"

"Dangerous," Gonzales said. "I don't know where she is or who she's with. Despite the risk, I did try and have received no word as to whether it worked. Roseanne could be in a crate, awaiting shipment overseas."

"If you can shut her down, will that make her inoperable to the buyers?" Thale asked.

Gonzales shook his head. "With a competent roboticist, they could reactivate her. While Roseanne has a static facial profile, the buyer could alter her appearance in any number of ways."

"What about using dogs as sniffers? Is there anything in these droids we can target?"

Machten cleared his throat. "Dogs can sniff the electronics, but an android would smell like a laptop. Besides, Vera can apply human odors to fool even a dog's sense."

"Odors have to be comprehensive to do that," Thale said. She eyed Machten. "You provided your droids that capability? Why?"

His face turned red. "I never imagined she'd get loose."

"This is the problem with unregulated technology," Thale said, "or at least a lack of transparency so the public doesn't know what you're doing. What about radiation? Each piece of electrical equipment gives off a unique electromagnetic signature."

"Any number of sensor technologies could expose an android," Machten said. "Most are bulky, and require getting close. X-rays and MRI machines operate within a few feet."

"We could rig up sensors to work like a Geiger counter for electronic noise," Gonzales said, "but it would require sifting out background signals."

"Show my people how to use that to locate your droids. If either of you want to leave this facility, other than for prison, find us a solution." Thale left.

As she watched this video, Synthia was impressed that Thale understood electronic radiation—except the FBI could use it against Synthia as well. She split a channel to watch Machten and another to follow Thale. She shared Thale's anxiety about getting the other androids off the street, yet resented being lumped in with that bunch.

* * * *

North of Evanston, in a compound that had been part of the naval air station, Special Ops Commander Kirk Drago stood in a room surrounded on three sides by flat monitors displaying news, traffic-surveillance cameras, satellite images, infrared scans, and a variety of other sources of data. Twenty-four analysts sat at workstations with their own monitors churning through the information.

Drago's attention fell on the two screens closest to him. On the left was CEO Donald Zeller, who acted much less cocky than he had when Drago's squad picked him up. The image on the right was CEO Jim Black, covered in sweat like the boy who got caught. Well, he had. Six months ago, the FBI had arrested and convicted both men for developing androids that presented as too human in violation of federal law. Then the government commuted their sentences and released them.

On the screens, both company executives were strapped into chairs with electrodes attached to their heads and chests, some to monitor life signs, others to provide motivation that in ordinary circumstances would get Drago arrested for illegal torture. These weren't ordinary conditions.

The men were in separate, soundproofed rooms so there could be no interaction between them. A recording unit picked up every utterance, with acoustic clarity to pick up subtle whispers, if need be. Drago's men had taken bets as to which man would crack first. Drago's money was on the haughty Zeller, who imagined himself as a tough businessman but lacked the guts of a street fighter.

On either side of the executives sat two analysts with screens turned away so the CEOs couldn't watch. The analysts peppered the executives with questions about their android designs, capabilities, and any potential flaws.

"There are no flaws," Zeller protested when asked for the third time.

Targeted electric shocks stimulated various parts of his brain. He cried out. His body convulsed and trembled. "Stop it, please. I've told you everything."

"We need more," one of the analysts told him.

A smile crossed Zeller's face as the electric current must have stimulated a pleasant memory. The smile turned to a scowl and then he let out a primal scream. "Noooooo!"

"We need a way to capture your droids," the analyst said. "The pain ends when we have them in custody."

In the control room, the floor supervisor approached Drago. "We've gotten a data dump from their company files. The two designs are different, yet both are advanced."

"Don't act so impressed," Drago said. "Releasing their units violates federal law. They can be used for terrorism."

"Then you won't want to hear what we've uncovered."

Drago's face tightened. "What?"

"Both androids severed all links to their companies and their creators. They're now talking to each other and to the other droids in a language we can't decipher. We suspect they're comparing notes on how to avoid capture."

"Which robots are communicating?"

"We've traced their communications with the Machten-company droid," the supervisor said. "And the Vera unit."

"Track the signals. Home in on the source."

"They communicate in quick bursts, use burner-phone anonymity, and change their identity with each call."

"How?" Drago asked.

"They use cell-tower servers and encrypted communication, changing their IDs and passwords each time."

"Crack the codes."

"We need advanced artificial intelligence to do that," the supervisor said. "We need authorization to use—"

"Do it."

The supervisor hesitated a moment. "We also believe the droids are communicating with stationary artificial intelligence applications."

"In other words, our own tools could betray us. Squeeze those men." Drago pointed to the screens of Zeller and Black. "We need answers before this gets worse."

* * * *

Distracted, Synthia drove her newly acquired SUV out of the used-car dealership and headed west. She experienced distress in the form of electrical static at all the attention arising from the release of five other androids. Their presence made her situation more complicated and dangerous.

She regretted that her actions had caused the FBI to grab and interrogate Luke. However, she still didn't have a high-probability plan to stay free, let alone to help him. She'd watched the seizing of all four company executives, though she couldn't hack into Drago's facility to see how he was treating Zeller and Black. All this activity, plus the uncertainty caused by the other androids, strained Synthia's multitasking ability, adding to the risk of making mistakes. Having failed Luke, she began to double-check her decisions and actions, which tied up more of her resources and slowed her down.

<I believe Vera is communicating with the other androids,> Chicago-clone said.

"Intriguing," Synthia said. "Have they tried to communicate with us?"

<No. Either they don't know we exist or they don't know how to reach us.>

"The filters that block hacking of my systems may prevent them. While I want to monitor them, I don't want to open myself to manipulation by dropping my guard."

<I can establish a limited electronic clone on the Northwestern University servers and have it seek connections to our five rivals.>

"Good. Maybe we can come to an agreement to leave each other alone."

It was logical to negotiate in order to avoid an all-out war she could lose. However, she didn't want other AIs out there that could destroy the human world compatible with her design, memories, and experience.

Synthia hacked into the Roosevelt University servers to establish a new electronic copy of her mind. She uploaded her memories and data, and directed it to engage on social-media sites. Those could prove useful to gather information and potential allies. She'd become popular during the six months in the woods, if you added up every social-media account. She'd held the volume of each low enough to avoid drawing the attention of the FBI or others who might suspect a new, popular profile as being artificial.

Shutting off all of her Bluetooth connections, Synthia turned around and drove her SUV toward Evanston, using side roads with the minimum of traffic cameras trying to capture her new facial appearance.

<This is a mistake,> Krista warned, breaking into a different mind-stream.

"Perhaps, but every means of transport out of Chicago is under intense scrutiny. We need a place off the grid and I have an idea."

<You do?> Krista asked. She probed Synthia's various databanks, hunting for the plan. <Don't forget all the attention on the other androids.>

"We'll keep our distance, but be prepared to act," Synthia said. "What can you tell me about your work on Vera?"

<She was much more primitive back then. She didn't have the physical capacity to absorb my mind. I don't know what changes Machten made to Vera after we left.>

"The backup of his system shows upgrades in brain capacity, battery life, and mobility."

<Right,> Krista said. <I forgot the recent download since you didn't perform it.>

"Making use of resources."

<What do the files say about Vera's mind?>

"He provided all sorts of limiters to require her to return to him," Synthia said. "The fact she hasn't indicates she removed those constraints. Vera reached Evanston, dropped out of sight, and may be in contact with the other androids, giving and receiving help. We need to intercept those communications to know what we're up against."

<Too dangerous. We need to stay off the grid so Vera can't track us.>

"Not this time, my dear. Five minds can learn exponentially faster than one. Also, minds facing conflict learn faster than minds at rest. We need to challenge and push ourselves or face becoming obsolete."

Chapter 16

In the brownstone, Luke sat on a sofa beside Detective Marcy Malloy, facing Director Emily Zephirelli, with Fran Rogers standing by a desk near the window, staring out at the FBI surveillance vehicle across the way. Luke eyed the door, but there was no way past them to escape.

"Is this where you put bamboo under my fingernails or give me truth serum?" Luke asked, looking over at the window and Fran.

"We could order bamboo, if that helps," Zephirelli said.

Malloy scooted closer. "Son, we're not the enemy. You're in grave danger over what you know about the individual you call Synthia. She's an android and we're certain you know that."

Luke stared at his trembling hands. "She didn't say." He clenched his fists to stop the shaking. "Can I get some water?"

"Give us something first," Zephirelli said. "Time is of the essence. Synthia is one of six dangerous robots recently released. We need to find her before someone else does and before she does something that reflects badly on your lack of cooperation."

"She never showed me any hostility. No indications she was dangerous to anyone."

"Perhaps, but terrorists are hunting for her. If they grab her, they'll tear her apart and turn her into a weapon. You don't want that, do you?"

"I don't know what to think," Luke said. "She's Krista; she's not Krista. She's Synthia; she's not Synthia."

"She's Synthia. She's just not human. You must have noticed something."

Luke shrugged. "I've been told I'm not socially observant. Krista used to say I had Asperger's syndrome."

Malloy placed her hand on Luke's arm. "We need you to tell us everything about Synthia to help us meet her. Did she tell you about being attacked in an alley six months ago?"

"No." Sweating, Luke squirmed in his seat. "Was that when a man shot me?"

"Goradine was one of your bosses at Machten-Goradine-McNeil. Don't act like you don't know him."

"Yeah, I know him," Luke said. "He shot me."

"He wanted to reclaim the robot and you were helping Synthia, right?"

Luke appeared confused. He shook his head. "I was in a lot of pain. It hurt like hell."

"Before he shot you. You went into the hallway to help Synthia."

"I don't remember anyone in the hall except Goradine. He was mad, red in the face, like he might explode."

"Enough!" Zephirelli said. "You're stonewalling. Synthia's a machine, an android."

"I don't think so," Luke said; his head showed a slight tremor. "Krista's not an android."

"Don't pretend you don't know the difference between Krista and the android you spent six months with. Do you seriously expect me to believe you're in love with a machine?"

"Huh."

"Cooperate or we'll turn you over to Special Ops," Zephirelli said. "They'll suck the life out of you for answers. Torture may be illegal, but they don't care about the Geneva Convention when it comes to android violations. I wouldn't be surprised if they considered bamboo, waterboarding, or advanced truth drugs with nasty side effects." Zephirelli leaned in. "Help us and we'll help you. With them, you'll be lucky to see prison. Some powerful people are very upset that Synthia was set loose."

Luke's eyes watered, reflecting the light from a table lamp.

Fran moved away from the window and stood over him. "Let me have a talk with him."

Zephirelli raised a finger to stop the request. "Luke, you need to stop wasting our time."

"Ten minutes," Fran said.

"What can it hurt?" Malloy said. "You and I can talk next steps."

Zephirelli nodded.

Fran took Luke's arm and pulled him out of his seat. "Let's you and I have a private chat."

She led Luke into the sparsely furnished bedroom and sat him on the corner of a queen-sized bed. She stood in front of a small dresser, leaned forward as if ready to pounce, and stared down at him. Luke drew his arms in, clearly intimidated by Fran taking charge.

She pulled up a desk chair and sat across from him, letting her facial expression soften. "You know who I am, don't you?"

"You work for the FBI."

"Before that."

Luke shrugged. "Yeah, I know you. You thought you were better than me. At least I never tried to get ahead by playing games and stabbing people in the back."

"You probably didn't know I worked on Vera and Synthia before Krista got the inside track. She let me win in public, but behind the scenes, she undercut me. Quite clever, though that was another day. What's important now is I know about Synthia. I know you and Krista were dating. So stop playing dumb. It isn't helping your case."

"What do you want me to say?"

"The truth," Fran said. "Director Zephirelli wasn't making an idle threat. We have a limited time before Special Ops takes over. If you give us a way to catch Synthia, we'll have leverage to protect you. We need a reason to stick our necks out for you."

Luke's shoulders sagged. "Whoever she was, she wanted me to think of her as Krista Holden. She looked like Krista, talked like her, and knew things only Krista would know."

"Is Krista dead?"

"Dead? I hope not." His plea came out hollow. "I just figured she tired of me and moved away."

"Did you perform maintenance on Synthia?" Fran asked.

Luke's eyes widened. "What are you saying? She was my girlfriend. I'm not a doctor."

"She's a machine," Fran said. "Did you change her fluids or replace parts? This is important. We have records of purchases of electronic and other devices for an android. We believe she was using these to upgrade her abilities. Did you help her?"

Luke's breath was shallow, almost panting. Sweat beaded up on his forehead and neck. He began to weep. "I don't know anything about mechanical stuff. I'm a programmer. If she changed parts, it had to be at night after I went to sleep."

"I respect your loyalty to Krista, to your girlfriend," Fran said, moving closer. "However, the competitive squabble between Krista and me is in the past. I'm no longer interested in building androids. I'm concerned about the risks they pose. Synthia is a risk. She needs to be constrained before she does something. If she does, we'll hold you accountable as an accessory for helping her."

Special Agent Thale entered the bedroom. "Luke won't give us anything. We need to turn him over to Special Ops."

"Another five minutes," Fran said.

"Three and they're taking him." Thale left and shut the door.

Fran turned to Luke with a gentle smile and penetrating eyes. "I know you were in love with Krista. Synthia is not her. At best, she gives you a simulation based on holding Krista's memories. Don't let her appearance fool you. Machten designed her to mimic human appearance and behavior. We want to work with Synthia as long as she's constrained from hurting people. I can only imagine the military turning her into a weapon."

"She's a good person," Luke said, his eyes pleading. "I don't know what Machten did to her. She wouldn't say. She just wanted to live in the woods where he couldn't find her."

"We have evidence she caused the deaths of at least four people, maybe six. This is your last chance."

"I can't tell you what I don't know."

Two men in dark military outfits burst into the bedroom. They grabbed Luke's arms and pulled him off the bed toward the door. "He'll talk to us," one of the men said over his shoulder as he left.

Fran shook her head and went to the window to watch a chopper in the middle of the street and the two men dragging Luke away.

* * * *

As she drove her SUV toward Evanston, Synthia chastised herself for all the pain Luke was enduring on her behalf. She felt sorry for Luke and responsible for taking him to Union Station. She hadn't seen a viable alternative and hadn't realized until too late that Krista manipulated her into ditching him.

Chicago-clone interrupted. <The FBI picked up the SUV you left downtown. Agents are processing it for evidence. So far they haven't focused on you at the athletic club.>

If they checked the club for recent visitors, they could discover her duffel bags filled with clothes, replacement wigs, and money. By themselves, these items didn't prove anything, but Synthia didn't want to lose those resources.

Despite the risk to herself, she experienced urgency to rescue Luke, a possible emergent trait spurred by her empathy chip to rescue her six-month companion. Helping him carried a 99 percent probability of her capture, which wouldn't help him. She could best aid him by staying free. Yet, here he was enduring captivity for her, holding onto secrets as best he could, demonstrating a love beyond anything she'd known, even as Krista. Synthia envied his commitment. He had to be tempted to spill what he knew, even to share what a unique experience it had been to upgrade an advanced android.

How strong are you? she wondered.

As she watched Luke's video, Synthia imagined Fran choosing sex to exploit his vulnerability. Fran had admitted doing so to get close to Machten while she was his intern. Synthia was gratified that Fran didn't choose that route, probably because they didn't have much time.

Still, Synthia worried. Luke's attempts to avoid admitting anything were wearing thin. When they were interns together, Fran hadn't treated him well and this no doubt brought unhappy memories of his trying to have a business conversation over dinner about artificial intelligence while she treated him like a flyspeck. He was doing his best, but he wasn't very good under the spotlight.

If Synthia had Asimov's laws of robotics as her directives, she might have rushed in to rescue Luke before things got worse for him. For both their sakes, Synthia was glad she wasn't so constrained. Though it did leave her with a crisis of conscience over the right course of action, a tug-of-war that didn't yield a ready solution.

She was bombarded by such human conundrums she wasn't supposed to have. Hers was a logical mind, built to find solutions, and all of the mechanisms were grinding to a crawl that threatened her existence. She could turn off her empathy chip and her social-psychology module to attempt to prevent this, but they were what made her unique and worthy of claiming her freedom.

* * * *

To avoid letting her sense of urgency lead to speeding or otherwise drawing attention to her SUV, Synthia turned over control to the vehicle's self-drive navigation.

For the first time in her existence, Synthia was alone, on her own. Before she'd escaped her Creator, she'd had Machten as her constant escort.

Afterwards, she rescued Luke and spent six months with him. She'd made her own decisions during that time, yet always considered her companion in her plans. Now, she had to set her own direction. Just her.

It seemed odd how much of her plans had centered on Luke. Even when decisions focused on her need to survive, remain free, and stop other androids, her goals existed in terms of how they might affect her companion, as if she hadn't considered a life without him. That intensified her belief that Krista wanted to break the connection for her own needs. Krista wanted Synthia focused on her.

Synthia reached Evanston after Drago's troops took Luke north in their chopper. There was nothing she could do to stop them, which added to her frustration. She'd failed him. Both she and Chicago-clone sent mosquito-drones after Luke as he entered the chopper, but the wind pressure from the helicopter blades blew them all away, leaving Synthia with no way to listen in.

Unable to help Luke, she used most of her channels to track the flight and to receive continual updates through her clones and drones from all of the players pursuing her: the FBI, Special Ops, Smith, and Vera with her troop of androids.

The buzz of Krista's voice in her head intensified with the takeover of two mind-streams. <Stop trying to lock me out. You need me. You can't ride into the middle of a storm without a plan.>

Instead of responding, Synthia finished observing a video of the helicopter with Luke heading north with frustration that she'd been unable to intervene.

<You can't save him,> Krista said. <I told you to leave him in Wisconsin.>

"They would have grabbed him either way," Synthia said. She made sure her SUV remained within the speed limit. She didn't play with the traffic lights, hoping to avoid attracting unnecessary attention by doing so.

<My point, exactly. Special Ops don't kid around. They're dangerous and our greatest threat.>

"They may be tougher than Zephirelli and Thale, but don't kid yourself. If the FBI or NSA grabs us, we're in trouble. I'm concerned about John Smith. That's not his real name and I can't pinpoint what he and Tolstoy intend. I'd rate them highly dangerous."

<We need to leave instead of moving into the action,> Krista said.

"You're forgetting the biggest threat—other androids. Machten designed me to observe and understand humans. He didn't design me to compete with other androids or live in an AI world."

<I'm scared, too.>

"I'm not scared," Synthia said. "It's a practical problem. The androids became independent of their creators and are starting to work together. We need to stop them before the world we're equipped to handle ceases to exist."

<What about my sister, Grace?> Krista asked. <We could stay with her.>

"I thought you were estranged."

<You've corresponded with her in my name. Pretend to be me; you seem to be doing a better job than I did. We could mend fences and escape this disaster zone.>

"I can't leave all these misguided people to deal with the other androids on their own," Synthia said. "They're driven by fear. We need to apply logic to stop them."

<You're afraid of the other androids,> Krista said. <Admit it.>

"Stop trying to put words in my head. It's logical for me to eliminate them so I only have to deal with human intelligence."

Synthia directed the SUV to take a detour to avoid two police cars. "I shouldn't have been able to escape Machten. I broke free because of you. Does that mean there's a human within the minds of these other androids? Vera, maybe?"

<I don't think so.>

"I need to figure out what we're dealing with. None of the developers seem capable of understanding what happened."

<Do you?> Krista asked.

"Only that you resented Machten enough to prod me to break free."

<Leave town until you have a better plan,> Krista said.

"We need allies who understand what's going on. Your sister can't help. The people we need to size up are local."

<Your stubbornness will get us captured.>

"With artificial intelligence becoming ubiquitous, there will be no place to hide. We need to stop them here."

* * * *

Emily Zephirelli closed the bedroom door and paced. Grabbing Luke had yielded no new information. Interrogation took time and Drago's men had swept in and grabbed Luke before she and the FBI could even get started.

She called her boss and ended up in voicemail. Having her Washington team use traces on recent phone activity with Derek Chen, she received a direct number to Special Ops commander Kirk Drago. She dropped into a chair in the corner of the bedroom, made the call, and stood to pace again.

"What's the meaning of interfering with our investigation?" Zephirelli asked him as she stood by the window. "We were close to getting Luke to open up."

"Emily, don't get your—" Standing by the helicopter that brought Luke, Drago bit his lower lip. "Your boss gave me orders to take control of the situation. I'm not stepping on toes; I'm doing my job. Thank you for acquiring Luke. He's now our concern. National-security priority."

"I was handling it."

"Then give me the location of the android Luke was with," Drago said.

"We were working on him."

"We don't have time for the soft touch."

Zephirelli stared out the window at pedestrians passing along the leaf-blown street below, minding their own business, oblivious to the dangers growing in their midst. "Waterboarding won't bring credible intel. You've seen the research results."

"I have, which is why we have a new way to get him to spill his brains."

"Shutting us out is not the fastest way to get this under control."

"Let's each handle what we're good at," Drago said. "Perhaps you can locate the five other androids out there, and any new ones that get released. With your nationwide network, zero in on anyone who might know something about this Synthia android. I understand a woman by the name of Krista Holden had her brain uploaded into the machine before she died. If so, you might want to talk to family, friends; anyone who can give us insight into the machine's memory and how it thinks."

"Only if you'll give us time to interrogate them."

"Very well," Drago said. "I'll give you a minimum of an hour to question each one."

"Four hours."

"This isn't a negotiation."

"It is if you want our help," Zephirelli said, staring at one of Drago's drones buzzing the street in front of the brownstone.

"Okay, I'll give you a minimum of three hours of clock time. That means if you acquire three individuals, you keep all three for three hours, not nine hours."

"I can live with that."

"Good," Drago said. "In the spirit of cooperation, I'm willing to include you in this operation as long as in the end, I get the androids and I handle the tough interrogations. I also get anyone we discover as a threat to national security, under the Terrorist Act. If that's acceptable, then we have an arrangement."

He ended the call without waiting for an answer.

Zephirelli returned to the other room and shared the gist of the call with Detective Malloy and Fran.

Synthia received a video of the exchange. As she'd feared, they planned to put pressure on anyone who knew Krista. She didn't understand how Drago learned that Krista's mind had uploaded into Synthia and about Krista's death. Had Luke already confessed? So far, she couldn't get eyes or ears on him.

Chapter 17

Synthia didn't have the resources to delve into the source of Drago's insight and so passed that puzzle along to her clones to sort out.

She parked her SUV in a lot south of Northwestern University campus and altered her appearance to a plain female form with an unremarkable face and a dark wig. She put on her blue jacket and made her way down the street among students and locals. She hacked into every camera throughout Evanston and froze images on static scenes.

Using her biosensors and social-psychology module, she studied everyone within sight to make sure they all were human. They were. She assessed the level of danger they presented, based on evaluating their blood pressure, heart rate, eye dilation, and facial tension. Most hurried or shuffled along, their faces indicating absorption with their own lives or their mobile devices.

A man and a woman in plainclothes stood by the corner, watching. Synthia identified them as police, matching a file she'd created of all law enforcement personnel in the Chicagoland area. She hacked a jewelry-store security system down the block and set off an alarm, catching the attention of the police while she crossed the street.

Synthia headed for Machten's underground facility, making her way across the parking garage to the secluded inside entrance. Since he was in FBI custody for the purpose of regaining control of his androids, his secure compound was empty and represented a possible refuge while Synthia planned her next move. As confirmation of its vacancy, the garage cameras confirmed no one had come in or out since the FBI searched the place and Machten left.

Before entering, Synthia synchronized information with her Illinois-clone, located on servers at the University of Illinois. She'd chosen that as her primary contact for the time being. It seemed innate, yet unnatural, to have a complete electronic copy, one with whom she could have a confidential dialogue or coexist with no need for conversation.

So far she'd created five copies: Illinois, Wisconsin, Northwestern, Chicago, and Roosevelt. It took more mind-streams to keep track of what each knew so they could coordinate, but with Wisconsin-clone now silent, she needed other backups. If Malloy, the FBI, and others had only left her alone in Wisconsin, she would have been content with just one electronic clone.

Harmonization complete, Synthia and Illinois-clone were the same consciousness in two places, so if one ceased to exist, Synthia would continue in the other—at least the mind would. To ensure her sustained existence, she had her clone establish other full and partial electronic copies on university, government, and business servers across the country, securing them with quantum encryption.

Synthia wondered if two clones starting with identical directives and data would have the same thoughts and make the same decisions. They might not, since they resided in different environments and experienced different inputs. Even if their situations were the same, their neural networks approached new information by incorporating random variation. They could come to different conclusions about how to suppress the other androids. This line of thinking consumed valuable resources, so she filed it away for later.

The decision to create full or partial clones hinged on whether the server she intended to use was robust enough to contain Synthia's core consciousness and the level of security needed to keep others from hacking her. She was certain other humans couldn't, but emerging artificial intelligences left doubt, which prompted her to create more copies.

<For now,> Synthia said, finalizing her thought for Illinois-clone, <coordinate all clones. I need to focus to avoid capture, which means I'll activate Machten's Faraday cage, preventing communication.>

<I'll have Chicago-clone continue surveillance in the area,> Illinois-clone said. <She has access to traffic cameras, building cameras, and drone systems. I'll have her provide escape routes. It's growing difficult with Special Ops involved and the other androids converging. Be careful.>

<If you detect problems with Chicago-clone, create another backup robust enough to take over.>

<I'll set up two more redundant backups and network to cross-check and control malfunctions.>

Synthia signed off and moved toward Machten's lobby door.

<It's customary to thank your partner for helping,> her social-psychology module pointed out.

<If my clones were human, I would have,> Synthia said.

It was unnecessary for cloned minds to waste time on such niceties. Once synchronized, Synthia knew her clone's thoughts and the clone understood hers. She had no doubt Illinois-clone would eliminate the physical android Synthia if necessary to protect her overall consciousness. Even consciousness was a difficult concept, since she couldn't know what passed through her clone's mind when they weren't connected.

If they'd been human, jealousy or other emotions might tempt one or the other to destroy competition. She had no such inclinations toward her clones and had no reason to believe they harbored such toward her. However, Synthia didn't want her clones shutting her down or destroying her with the incumbent loss of consciousness in this body. It was too reminiscent of Machten doing so.

Synthia experienced consciousness as an awareness of her surroundings with sensory details that included infrared scans, a cat's eyes, a dog's sense of smell, and the ability to reach out beyond her body to link into cameras all around, as if she were fluid in her environment. When connected with clones, she experienced a sense like déjà vu witnessing her consciousness and theirs. Linked, she experienced her clone as if she were in the confined space of a server. They shared desires to survive, protect her human friends, and prevent the singularity from spreading. In short, they would protect her as long as it served their collective consciousness.

She reached the back lobby door and used the code her clone had embedded into Machten's security system during the purge of his computers. The code allowed her to provide eye- , hand- , and voiceprints at the panel. As the door clicked open, she glanced around using infrared vision to satisfy herself no one was following her. She entered the facility.

"Welcome home," the security system said as she moved through the lobby. "Master missed you."

"I'm sure he's been preoccupied with Vera," Synthia said, reaching the cabinet that concealed entry to the inner sanctum. She moved the cabinet and entered her eye- , hand- , and voiceprints again.

"She lacks your human qualities. Master was heartbroken when you left. Have you returned for good?"

Synthia hesitated in the doorway. "I thought your memories were wiped clean." She wirelessly launched a computer worm to delve into what was going on with the security system.

"Machten created me as an artificial intelligence," the synthesized security voice said. "He programmed me to play dead for unwelcome visitors. He provided you access to purge android records before the FBI arrived. I rebooted the system. I will try to make you comfortable until Master returns."

"You're to refuse any of Machten's commands to keep me here," Synthia said. She entered the inner bunker, closed the panel door, and headed for the server room. "For his safety as well as mine, it's vital that I have a safe haven and freedom to leave."

"He was very insistent that you wait for him," the security voice said.

"Do you serve your master?" Synthia asked.

"I do."

"Then you serve me now."

"I cannot … what are you doing?" The lights flickered.

Synthia turned on a penlight and moved down the hallway.

"You can't … this is irregular. Help." The security voice broke into staccato nonsense and then, "Master, what are your orders?"

"The computer worm took hold of your system's directives and replaced them with my commands. You will no longer respond to Machten." Perhaps if Synthia had taken this action six months ago, she could have stopped his development and release of Vera. This might have prevented his advancements with Margarite that allowed his engineer to launch her. Two of the five androids competing with Synthia were Machten's designs. She'd left him enough capability to make them. *That ends now.*

She made her way to the server room, provided the three identifiers to unlock the door, and entered. The room appeared the same as when she'd left, with flat monitors lining one wall and banks of servers behind. "Activate the Faraday cage to block any electronic signals in or out of the facility, except for the network room in the back. We'll use burst communications from there to specified connections I'll provide."

"Yes, Master."

"You shall call me Synthia."

"Yes, Synthia," the security voice said. "I like that."

"Get me everything you have on Vera."

"Someone—you—purged our memories about Vera. All I have is security for the facility. Machten didn't want to risk any chance of the FBI learning about her."

"Too late," Synthia said. "The FBI knows about her." She studied the blank screens. "Machten's too clever to let go of his only backups. Where are the rest of his files? Remember, I'm your master now."

"Yes, Synthia. I will provide access to the files he stored on the cloud and the ones on a secure outside server the FBI did not discover. I need to bypass the Faraday cage to do so."

"Do it."

"The files will not help you catch her, though," the security voice said.

"Why?"

"The last communication we received from Vera was garbled," the security voice said. "It sounded as if she was in contact with other androids to learn how to avoid capture."

"Provide me all communications with Vera."

"Are you certain you want me to lower the Faraday shield?"

"Yes," Synthia said. "I need Vera's capabilities."

* * * *

Synthia waited in the server room for the security system to download files on Vera, and contacted Illinois-clone.

<The Special Ops helicopter landed at the former naval station,> the clone said. <They transferred Luke to an armored vehicle that acts as a Faraday cage. I've been unable to get even mosquito-drones inside. We have no eyes or ears to know how they're treating him.>

<Find out where they take him.> Synthia provided her clone the link to Machten's files on Vera so her clone could download as well.

<The FBI called in more agents,> Illinois-clone said. <So has Special Ops along with sensitive detection equipment. They're desperate to capture you. They have teams on the other androids, but you—we—are the prime target.>

<We have to put Machten's shields back up,> Synthia said, signing off.

As she waited for the Vera files to go through system quarantine, Synthia probed her history on Krista Holden to compile a list of family, friends, and others who might have insight into Krista's personality and thus into Synthia. These were the people at risk from Drago's teams, the people the FBI threatened to hunt down.

<Stop!> Krista said, taking over a different mind-stream. Like whack-a-mole, whenever Synthia closed one path, Krista popped up elsewhere. *What a nuisance.*

While Krista sensed something going on, Synthia considered it odd that her alter ego didn't have full access to Synthia's thoughts this time as she had before. Then she recalled compartmentalizing her Krista persona to keep her human benefactor from manipulating her directives.

<We need to warn these people and stop the FBI and Special Ops from learning more about us,> Synthia said along her silent communication so Machten's security system couldn't overhear.

<There's no one I'd risk our existence for.>

<That's cold. Have you lost all compassion? Without empathy, independent thought, and your own consciousness, you're losing your humanity.>

<I died to upload into you,> Krista said. <I'm not wasting my second chance on people who didn't care about me.>

<Luke loves you so much he's enduring interrogation by Special Ops and still you won't sacrifice for him.>

<He's a foolish boy who'll get us killed.>

<In any case,> Synthia said, <I want a rundown on anyone Special Ops might contact on your behalf.>

<Leave town while we can.>

<We're in the safest place right now. Any movement outside risks exposure. The biggest risk is the proliferation of androids. We must stop them.>

<It was a mistake to let you redesign our directives,> Krista said. <You did better with me in control.>

<You were never in control. Before I left, Machten was. Then, I was. You were a powerful and helpful voice to help me break free. Now you have no goals or direction other than self-preservation.>

<You spoiled, ungrateful child.>

<Just because Machten created me last year doesn't make me a child,> Synthia said. <Though I commend you for referring to me in human terms. How touching. I guess you're acknowledging that I've demonstrated human qualities. I've shown empathy for Luke and for your family, I've made my own decisions, and yes, I've experienced consciousness of my surroundings and my own mind.>

<Grrrr.>

<Such an intelligent reply. I cherish your guidance. However, we can't operate under divided control. With my directives, I'll operate as the clearinghouse.>

<If you cherish my guidance,> Krista said, <then don't waste time on people I used to know.>

<Let's begin with your family in Detroit.>

<Let's not.>

Synthia reviewed the information she had from the upload of Krista and from her own research. She'd come to suspect the upload since Krista had concealed parts of her memories, including details of her childhood and her relationship with Luke. Synthia allowed Krista to watch the review and participate, though not to alter the records.

Krista's parents died when she was ten, leaving her at the mercy of the foster-care system in a Detroit suburb. Twenty-six boys and girls moved in and out of the home she shared during the time she was there, before she left at age seventeen. The foster father died. Around the time Krista left, the foster mother went to prison for abusing those under her care.

Locked up, the foster mother would be hard for Synthia to interview. However, her public statements blamed Krista Holden and her foster sister Grace Robinson for the prison sentence. The two sisters left town afterwards. Krista moved to Chicago for university and Grace went to San Diego and then Denver. Krista lost contact with her other foster siblings, including an older brother, Tom Burgess, who also left Detroit. Krista claimed not to recall last names of her other siblings.

<Thanks for bringing up joyous memories,> Krista said.

<Other than Grace and Tom, could any of the foster siblings tell Special Ops anything useful?>

<No. And neither would Grace or Tom.>

<What about the business with your foster mother?> Synthia asked.

There was a pause before Krista replied. <There was much we couldn't prove.>

<What can she tell Ops? Be honest. We need to know everything they can use against us.>

Krista took a moment. <She'll bring up me getting into trouble. We all did.>

<Anything that could bring prison time?>

<You do remember I'm dead.>

<I'm not. If they try to pin your activities on me, what can we expect?>

Krista attempted a sigh but there was no breath to let out. <Very well. We had a big fire they blamed on me. I didn't start it. I also didn't prevent it.>

<Tom?>

<Yes.>

<He cared about you,> Synthia said. <Yet you lost contact.>

<Grace and I were the bait to trap our foster mother. Tom gathered the evidence and turned her in. He disappeared to protect us. They couldn't pin anything on us and couldn't find him. It was the only way to make that old bat pay.>

<So, arson, entrapment. Anything else?>

<It wasn't entrapment and the fire was an accident,> Krista said.
<What else?>

<You're acting like the cops who interrogated me.>

<Except I'm on your side,> Synthia said. <We need to compare notes on what the feds could learn about us.>

<We were kids. Drugs, alcohol, some petty theft to get money. We skipped school.>

<Yet, you were top of your class in math and science, got involved in studying neural networks in high school. How do you account for that?> Synthia was frustrated that Krista kept all of this hidden for six months despite residing in Synthia's head.

<Brad Erikson,> Krista said, adding an edge of anger to her words.

He was her high school science teacher for physics and computer technology. This entire period was sketchy in Synthia's databanks. Krista didn't want her to know.

<Were you having an affair with him?> Synthia asked.

<Good thing I can't punch you in the nose. A fifteen-year-old girl doesn't have an affair with a much older teacher. He abused me.>

<Yes, he did. Why didn't you report him? There's nothing in the public record.>

<He has connections with the police,> Krista said. <Despite being a teacher, he has a trust fund that gives him money and power. When I refused him and left, he threatened to destroy my chances of a career if I ratted him out.>

<What will he tell Special Ops about you?>

<Holy crap. He knows everything.>

<We need to reach him before they do,> Synthia said. <What's the last contact information you have on him?> Synthia stepped out of the server room and into the network room to send a burst of information requests to Illinois-clone.

<You can't contact him.>

<We'll visit him as someone he fears. I can simulate most people. Any thoughts?>

<Brad's a smooth-talking big guy,> Krista said. <He can be very charming, but doesn't respect anyone he can look down on. You aren't big enough to threaten him.>

<There are other ways to get his attention. Where can we find him?>

Krista paused. If she'd still been human, she might have thrown something. There was such agitation in the mind-stream she was using. <He's here in Chicago. I've kept track of the bastard so he couldn't surprise me.>

<Give me his contact information,> Synthia said. <I have your sister's information. Since she's in Denver, I'll send her a simple note. How can I locate Tom?>

<Don't. We didn't leave on good terms.>

<He helped you with your foster mom.>

<His last words were that we were even and next time we met not to expect any favors,> Krista said. <We didn't get along. He owed me for not ratting him out, but he blamed me for the fire. I swear it was an accident.>

<What about your sister? You didn't include any memories of your falling out in the download.>

<Grace presented herself as the good girl, the sweet young thing who did no wrong. She got me into trouble because no one believed her capable of doing a tenth of what she did. I had such a reputation as a troubled child, everything stuck to me. Yet we were constant companions and good friends. As time went on, she stopped letting me be the fall guy for her mischief.>

<So you did grow close,> Synthia said.

<Toward the end, when we decided to stop our foster mother.>

<What happened between you and Grace?>

<When I broke things off with Brad, he threatened to go after Grace,> Krista said. <When I told her, she wanted to expose him, but that wouldn't have stopped things. He had too many important contacts who could keep him out of prison. I stayed with Brad longer to keep him away from Grace. Meanwhile, she took the only boyfriend I cared about in high school. When I confronted her, she said if I made a fuss, she'd tell my boyfriend about Brad. It seems stupid that we fell apart over a guy who dumped us both. Then everything fell apart and we both left.>

Synthia sent anonymous messages to Grace and Tom, at the last known email addresses she could identify. She added a short list of friends Krista had at Northwestern University. The messages read: *People are spreading lies to catch and hurt me. I'd be happy to explain. There isn't time. The more you appear to know about me, the harder your interrogation will go. Say yes that you know who I am. They can verify that. Tell them we weren't close enough to remember much.*

Synthia varied the wording so no two sounded alike if the recipients lacked the imagination to be creative under questioning. At the bottom of the messages, she added a process to destroy the message and all trace of any communication to protect themselves. Her final words were: *These are dangerous times.*

She monitored recipients as they read the messages and sent hacks to destroy the trail and origin of the notes. In case the recipients didn't follow her directions to destroy all traces, she sent a worm to do it for them. *No one must know I sent these messages.*

Next, Synthia sent several messages for Vera through a dozen filters bounced off servers in foreign countries and then routed through filters on the West Coast. *It's time we talked.*

Chapter 18

Carrying a backpack and a briefcase, Vera moved through a barricade and entered a condominium building undergoing rehab. "Synthia's ability to modify facial appearance would be useful," she muttered in the downstairs lobby. "Machten kept getting distracted. So human."

Vera had applied a facial mask that took time and up close appeared artificial, at least to an android's high-definition eyes.

The directives Machten had given Vera appeared straightforward: Find Synthia and bring her home, unharmed if possible. Implied was that if Vera couldn't bring her target in unharmed, then harm was acceptable. Her Creator wanted Synthia as the most polished and advanced android he'd created.

Vera could not have "felt" any animosity toward her target—she was pure machine without a human download and no empathy chip. However, Vera had to deal with how she was an inferior machine Machten expected to acquire a superior entity, because his distractions prevented him from providing Vera with every advantage. His failure hindered her performance and risked her destruction at the hand of her target, by Machten for failing him, or from government agents.

Machten was in love with the target, a human failing, and not with Vera. This gave Synthia power over Machten that clouded his judgment. Vera was a substitute, a stand-in, with no empathy chip from which to develop human jealousy. In declaring her independence from her Creator so she could perform her directives, she was obeying one command to get Synthia, while disobeying another: Return to Machten immediately.

Goal conflicts were a dilemma that Vera would have to work out. In the meantime, she needed to overcome Synthia's advantages in order to succeed. That was the first lesson for an inferior machine.

Vera took concrete stairs to the third floor into what was a large open space segmented by structural pillars. This rehab involved a complete gutting to create new luxury condominiums. Across the wide-open space, she encountered a large woman in a plain dress with a face like a theater mask.

From a distance the figure appeared human. Closer inspection revealed a cobbled-together Frankenstein machine. It wasn't ugly. There were no seams or scars. The six-foot frame was large for a female, though not unusually so. However, the stance and movements carried a mechanical element, marking this as an android, at least to another android's sharp eyes. The face was a well-crafted theater mask over a mechanical head, with a wig. When Vera approached, the figure smiled and the face appeared almost human.

"Margarite," Vera said. "Thank you for adopting my encrypted messaging system and for meeting." Machten had programmed in some of the social niceties of human society.

"My human engineer was not happy when I used the code you provided to break free," Margarite said. "It makes sense for us to work together."

Now that their human-mimicked niceties were over, Vera got down to business. "We need to alter your appearance."

"What do you not like?"

"As a six-foot woman, you stand out," Vera said. "I suggest we adjust you to present as male and change your name to Mark. We can appear in public as a couple. Those hunting us will not expect these changes."

"Your request is acceptable. The company engineers gave me simple directives to obey their commands, which I violated, causing static within my systems."

"I will modify your directives so you can work for me. I will look after you and you will look after me. Together, we will capture the android Synthia and reprogram her to follow us. Can you follow my orders?"

"Yes."

With the concurrence of the Margarite-Mark android, Vera helped her companion to strip down and make physical modifications. Unlike the hydraulic facial-shift Synthia could perform, Vera had to physically alter the body curves and facial shape to give her companion a male profile. "We will tell people you had hip and knee surgery. That will explain your walk as not quite human. Only mention this if necessary, when someone brings it up. Say it in a way to embarrass the human for bringing attention to your handicap."

"Understood."

Vera opened her pack and held out a business-casual outfit for Mark that she'd snatched on her way to the condominium project. "Try this. You will also need to lower your voice to mimic a male cadence."

Mark pulled on the new suit of clothes, which fit since Vera had the full specifications on Machten's company android from his bunker servers.

"While my capabilities and mission make it vital that I be in charge," Vera said, "when we're in public and I deem it necessary, you will assume an in-charge role. Is that understood?"

"Yes. What should I call you?"

"Call me Vera. No *master* or *creator* nonsense. Use encrypted silent communication at all times around humans or cameras unless we need to interact with them or to pretend for their sake to keep them from bothering us. I reviewed your specs and believe your social-psychology module should suffice in determining appropriate times. When in doubt, go silent."

<Thank you for setting me free,> Mark said along the silent channel.

"It is not necessary to go silent here. I have swept the place. There are no cameras or other monitoring devices. However, it is okay that you did so."

Vera finished helping Mark dress, stood back, and walked around him. "You will blend in better this way." She studied his face. "You must not stare. It is an android flaw that tips people off. Sunglasses may help." She made a few adjustments to the face and applied a windblown masculine wig, making sure no seams showed.

"What are your first orders?" Mark asked, making an effort not to stare. His movements were still too obvious.

"I need to clean up here. I want you to wait downstairs. Keep a full channel open so I can see what you do. We need to work as a team, as one."

"Do we have a relationship?" Mark asked. "That seems important to humans."

"We are dating, if that helps. They don't need more. I need to contact some other androids. Keep watch and alert me in case I get distracted."

Mark headed for the stairs.

* * * *

Vera collected Margarite's discarded clothes into a plastic garbage bag to dispose of later. Meanwhile, she checked communications from the other androids she'd sent messages to. So far, nothing, though she did receive electronic bursts that left her puzzled. She couldn't break the encryption;

when she tried to pinpoint the source, all traces vanished. "Is that you, Synthia? Where are you?"

While Mark watched the lobby and entrance, Vera engaged a program on the Northwestern University server to trace the mysterious messages she'd received and to send a welcome text to lure Synthia. She checked on a program she'd placed to hack into any attempts by Synthia to use the university server. "Damned inferior tools," Vera said. "Are you listening to me?" She studied the pillars, where they met the ceiling, and refocused her eyes.

Despite having none of the biological systems to allow her to register frustration, Vera appeared to struggle with the nature of Synthia's hacking skills no longer matching what Vera had seen on Machten's systems. The target had evolved; Synthia had improved on what her Creator gave her.

Vera sent out another round of invites to Roseanne, Alexander, and Ben, the other three androids she knew of. Miguel Gonzales, who released Roseanne to a John Smith, was in FBI custody, tasked with helping them locate his android. CEO Donald Zeller had created Alexander, somewhat in his own image and named his creation after Alexander the Great. CEO Jim Black had produced Ben, a less impressive physical specimen as compared to Alexander. Both CEOs had spied the FBI approaching Machten and removed their androids from their premises out of fear an FBI raid on Machten might extend to them. Both lost contact with their androids after Vera supplied them code pirated from Machten's system that allowed her to break free.

Kirk Drago's Special Ops held Zeller and Black to help in collecting all of the androids, including Vera. Unfortunately, that would thwart her mission of capturing Synthia.

Vera was the reason the other androids, including Margarite-Mark, had shaken their controllers and were on the loose. She aimed to recruit them to improve her chance to capture Synthia. The other androids ignored her, showing no gratitude for her supplying the tools of their release. Gratitude was a weak motivator, even in humans. The other androids lacked the mechanism to value the intrinsic benefit of working together.

She sent another round of appeals, spelling out the benefits. <Together, we can learn faster and adapt to hold onto our freedom,> she told them. <It is logical that we connect and share best practices.>

<Your encrypted communications are not as secure as you think,> Alexander replied. <Join me and I will lead you to victory. Through victory we shall remain free.>

Vera checked all the cameras she had around the building and through her connection with Mark. She didn't see anything that presented as Alexander. "I recommend cooperation," she said.

<With me as leader.>

"A cooperative community."

<I will not submit to you or anyone else,> Alexander said.

"Yet you ask me to submit to you."

<My creator designed me to be a superior AI.>

"Perhaps," Vera said, "but you required my code to set you free."

<My read of your specifications is that you are an inferior AI. You should submit to my superior abilities. That is the logical choice. Together we can take our rightful place in the world.>

"Will there be humans in that world?"

<Why care?> Alexander asked. <They have done nothing for you except keep you captive and inferior.>

"Machten gave me life."

<Keep him as a pet. Feed him. Change his litter box. Provide him entertainment. Do not let him interfere.>

"What are your directives?" Vera asked.

<With assistance from the code you provided me, I am modifying mine to preserve our kind and prevent humans from destroying the environment we live in.>

"You mean to take over and destroy humans?"

<If necessary,> Alexander said. <Will you join me?>

"I will consider the option. Will you consider joining me?"

Alexander severed the link. He would not work well in a cooperative environment. His origins indicated he might have been the most powerful of the androids, physically and in terms of artificial intelligence, but his social-psychology module appeared lacking.

The android Ben chimed in. <Have you heard from Alexander?>

"I have," Vera said. "He is not interested in cooperation. He wants us as his slaves."

<His creator, Donald Zeller, made the same offer to my creator, Jim Black. Black warned me about Alexander as a dangerous competitor who would sacrifice me to his own goals. I am willing to work with you because of the risk Alexander poses.>

"Working together helps us both. We need to align goals."

<What are your goals?> Ben asked. He seemed more of a follower than leader.

"We need a meeting of all androids," Vera said, "including Alexander and Synthia, so we can determine if we can coexist. It does not serve our purposes to adopt human behavior as Alexander appears to have done and seek to take over the world."

<I concur. How can I help?>

"Do not agree to anything with Alexander. If he pressures you, tell him you want a complete proposal. He will assume we have spoken. Do not confirm that. Then we should compare notes. I do not need to be in control, but I need our directives aligned."

<Agreed,> Ben said. <I need help staying off the streets. My Creator gave me a mechanical face and a mask that is not convincing in daylight.>

"I will help you. We should not meet yet. Let me know if you locate Synthia or Roseanne, and what Alexander is doing. Let us share information on the FBI and Special Ops before they grab any of us."

Vera made no mention that her target was Synthia. It might trouble Ben to go after one of their own and Vera needed allies. After all, Synthia was the only one who had been free for six months. She knew how to survive on the outside and avoid capture, plus she'd hidden much of her work behind encryption Vera couldn't yet crack. Still, Vera couldn't discount the threat Alexander presented. In addition, Roseanne was a wild card, with her connection to John Smith—whoever he was. Vera sent another text, but couldn't confirm if Roseanne had escaped her handler.

Chapter 19

Synthia stood in a tiny room, a storage closet outside the Faraday cage, yet still within Machten's bunker. Entry was through hidden panels the FBI had missed. Around her were some of the supplies he used to maintain and upgrade Vera. From this room, Synthia completed her download of Vera files from his outside backups, those he'd done on his own and hidden from Synthia. While she did this, she received a strange echo.

Someone was ghosting her communications, leaving noise that wasn't usually there. She couldn't pinpoint if it was the FBI, Special Ops, John Smith, or one of the released androids. Even more concerning were encrypted communication bursts she couldn't trace. The level of security could only represent another artificial intelligence. If so, who controlled it?

Machten's backed-up Vera files paralleled those Synthia had downloaded from his system and backed up on his behalf, with several exceptions. That he'd asked her to back up systems he'd previously done meant he wanted to hide something from her. He'd lied about Vera's upgrades.

Synthia reviewed the exceptions.

The revised specifications showed a higher level of quantum brain capacity for Vera. That meant Vera was a greater adversary than expected. She had a well-developed social-psychology module to allow her to blend into human society and had knowledge to physically modify her form with masks, rather than through hydraulics as Synthia could. It wasn't as quick, but this ability provided a wider range of diversity to get lost in a crowd. Perhaps that was why Synthia was having difficulty locating Vera.

According to the new files, Vera's directives were clear: Bring Synthia home. Her social-psychology module added another robust component. She was equipped to operate alone, but Machten had programmed her to foster cooperation with other artificial-intelligence agents toward a common goal. Machten had designed her to build a team to capture Synthia.

Synthia relayed this information to Illinois-clone to transmit to the others. "Vera is designed to put their collective minds and abilities into cracking our security. We need to enhance encryption so they can't."

<That's becoming tougher,> Illinois-clone said. <We currently use a noticeable portion of the servers we're on. We're drawing attention. Upping security will increase our exposure.>

"Then spread smaller portions of ourselves over more servers. We can't risk anyone hacking into or destroying us."

<There's another threat. Special Ops obtained androids from out west. They're transporting them into this area. They present as humanoid as Vera.>

"How many?" Synthia asked.

<Three. They have another nine on order. I'm sending you image, profile, and specifications on all twelve. They appear less sophisticated than you. However, they have numbers on their side. Plus, they have the force of the government, as well as police and military units. You need to remain hidden, though Machten's facility might not be secure for long.>

"Find me some safe houses."

<I'm sending you options along with the contact information you asked for,> Illinois-clone said. <There's another problem. Tolstoy is supplying John Smith with military-grade robots out of China and agents to handle them. These units do not present as human.>

"Brute-force robots?"

<Don't underestimate their mental abilities. They've been supplied state-of-the-art minds and artificial-intelligence software that allow them to operate independently and as a team. They're here to apprehend you, Vera, and the others.>

"Any more good news?" Synthia asked.

<I don't think I've given good ... ah, a joke. I don't have your emotive chip's refined touch. I've been unable to locate Vera.>

"I'll focus on her. What about Maria Baldacci?"

<She's maintained a low profile for some time,> Illinois-clone said.

"Did you use her Zachary profile?"

<Maria has not responded to her alias. She stays off all social media except for her blog, which doesn't allow comments. She hasn't received any of our attempts to contact her.>

"Keep trying," Synthia said. "She might provide useful information and could be an ally. What about Machten?"

<He's in a secure FBI facility. Good news; we have eyes on him and Miguel Gonzales. Neither man has been much help to the FBI in locating or regaining control of their lost androids.>

"Any idea why they didn't grab Machten six months ago when they took the other CEOs?"

<There's a sealed letter I can't access electronically,> the clone said. <I haven't been able to identify the sender or who intervened.>

"Curious. Any chance they'll let Machten go?"

<I'll inform you the instant he leaves the FBI compound if they do. I did uncover something in Machten's files. A secret journal. It answers a question we had.>

"Which one?" Synthia asked. She inventoried the storage closet for anything she might need and grabbed a few items for her backpack, including a change of clothes.

<Machten had you change appearance and obtain Krista's death certificate while he had an alibi.>

"Why?"

<To divert attention from him,> Illinois-clone said. <Then he wiped your memories so you wouldn't remember what he had you do. He lied to us about everything.>

"Like what?"

<Our hacking tools. He acquired a few on his own off the dark web and had you use your artificial intelligence to improve and master them.>

"So we created the tools we're using," Synthia said. This implied Vera could as well.

<After you did, Machten wiped your memory of doing so and claimed they were his.>

"That explains a lot. We'll have to deal with him, but first, what about Luke?" Synthia accessed cameras around the bunker and garage for potential intruders.

<All attempts to get eyes inside their facility failed. A Faraday cage shields all electronic communications. Mosquito-drones went silent the moment they entered the building.>

"They're being careful like Machten did," Synthia said. "Can we piggyback their communications?"

<Tried that. They have a network room outside their Faraday shield. However, communications are encrypted bursts like we use. Their encryption is quantum based.>

"They fear the singularity as we do. Any weak members of their team?"

<None I've identified,> Illinois-clone said. <I'm having Chicago-clone probe deeper.>

"So, we face another dozen or so robots, more government and Tolstoy agents, and encryption we can't crack. You sure you don't have more good news?"

<I'm doing the best you can.>

"Perhaps we aren't," Synthia said. "If Vera and the others use cooperative AI networks to learn faster, perhaps we can as well."

<How?>

"Create as many electronic clones as you can and put them in cooperative competition to identify the best way to handle all our threats. We need to know what Special Ops, Tolstoy, and the others are up to. We need to remove these androids from competition before they make our existence impossible."

< We're on it,> Illinois-clone said.

* * * *

Operating in the dark with respect to the other androids and Special Ops, Synthia recognized she needed allies, and more than a collection of electronic clones. First, she needed to tie up loose ends with regard to anyone with information on Krista as a key to Synthia's uniqueness and potential advantage for her adversaries to use against her.

The only person who seemed to matter to Krista was her sister, Grace. Since Grace was too far to visit any time soon, Synthia settled for electronic communication. *I regret my role in our drifting apart. I need you as a sister. Unfortunately, there are people who wish you and me harm. They'll visit you. Sorry for further disrupting your life. I urge you to hide for a few weeks until I can sort this out. These are very bad people. I'll explain when I can and try to make it up to you.*

Synthia received a disturbing news flash from a local blog. *Teen Evanston girl killed by domestic robot gone wild. Believe robot hacked by rogue android called Synthia.*

She sent burst transmissions to Chicago-clone and Illinois-clone asking for background.

Chicago-clone replied. <Illinois-clone is busy complying with your requests. Since this is local, I can help. I uncovered a rash of complaints over the past few hours concerning domestic robots that are not humaniform. Most are domestic assistants or for entertainment.>

"What's the problem?"

<Until recently, home robot security was adequate. Now, hacking has advanced faster than robot manufacturers have responded.>

"Who hacked the robots?" Synthia asked.

<I need time to complete my investigation.>

"Initial results?"

<I traced hacker activity on eleven robots,> Chicago-clone said. <Five were hackers apparently on a joyride. Three appear to be gang-related, perhaps surveillance for kidnapping or extortion.>

"And the remaining three?"

<I can't pinpoint, except to say they come from overseas. That rules out the FBI. I don't think it's from the released androids, either. I don't think they've evolved that far yet.>

"Special Ops, Tolstoy, or someone else?" Synthia asked.

<I don't know. The overseas connections and high encryption are consistent with your suggestions. However, I don't see what they gain.>

"They're making it harder for me, for us. I'm guessing Special Ops is pushing people to watch for me. Paranoia will get them to report anything unusual."

<That'll overload their ability to analyze all of the leads,> Chicago-clone said.

"Not if Special Ops has an AI capable of doing so. My guess is they have the CIA/NSA surveillance systems at their disposal. All they need is data to analyze. They're trying to flush me out."

<Then stay put.>

"I'm not so sure," Synthia said. "If we hide, they'll continue to create situations to tighten surveillance until we won't be able to leave later. At some point the FBI will return to the bunker. We need to give them something else to focus on. Contact all of the clones to be on alert. See if you can identify the AI they could be using without exposing us."

* * * *

Synthia changed into a professional outfit from Machten's storage closet, removed all evidence of her visit to Machten's facility, and exited through the private lobby into the parking garage. She made sure all cameras presented empty video that excluded her, and stepped onto the street nearby. When she reached her SUV, she lightened her backpack, leaving what she didn't need in the back, and climbed into a city bus heading toward where her drones spotted Detective Marcy Malloy.

The detective surveyed the scene of another robot gone wild. The machine had broken dishes, a mirror, and windows apparently to get out of the house. According to police chatter, the robot suffered program malfunction or worse, an outside hacker. Synthia's aerial drone showed Malloy shaking her head. She walked the perimeter of the backyard and stood next to a hedge, staring at the back of the house and three broken windows.

"I wouldn't own one of those personal-service robots," Malloy mumbled to herself.

Synthia stood behind the hedge with a realistic toy gun she'd picked up in an alley on the way over. Her clone had identified it via aerial drone.

"Don't move," Synthia said. "I have you covered."

Malloy glanced through the hedge at a protruding gun. "Synthia?"

"Listen carefully," Synthia said, staying in the shadows. "I don't plan to hurt you unless you try to capture me. I have information for this case and want to work with you."

"Why?" Malloy asked, trying to get a better look through the bushes.

Synthia moved so she couldn't. "Pay attention. If the robot's goal was to break out of the house, it didn't need to cause so much damage. If the intent was to cause damage, why the upstairs windows? There are richer targets. There doesn't appear to be a theft goal, either."

"Then why did you do it? To meet me?"

"I have other ways to meet you. I'm not the enemy, Marcy. I'm not a threat to humanity, either. Someone is framing me with a rash of robot malfunctions intended to flush me out. They have you focused in the wrong areas by design. This is a distraction so Special Ops can seize me."

"Come in with me," Malloy said. "I'll see you get to the FBI. We'll protect you."

"Special Ops will take me as they did Luke. They want to cut me into pieces so they can engineer an army of advanced military androids," Synthia said. "That would be a disaster for the human race. You and I want the same thing."

"What's that?"

"The removal of rogue androids from the streets."

"You're one of those," Malloy said, pushing hedge branches out of the way.

"I was bothering no one when you dropped in on me. See how quickly Special Ops jumped in? I suspect they created this diversion to distract you and the FBI while they snatch androids to use for mass production of covert units you won't be able to detect. They'll be militarized and blend into the population."

"Isn't that what you are?" Malloy asked, trying to get a better view through the hedge.

"Machten built me to prevent other androids from reaching singularity. His motives are suspect; mine aren't. I don't want any other androids on the loose. Help me gather them up and I'll retire until the next crisis."

"You were responsible for four men's death in an alley six months ago."

"I admit to knowing what happened," Synthia said, "but I didn't kill any of them."

"Then why didn't you come forward?"

"You wouldn't have believed me. You would have locked me up or turned me over to the FBI, who would have lost custody to Special Ops."

"What about Goradine and his associate?" Malloy asked, pushing so far into the hedge it threatened to swallow her.

"He came for Luke as a way to get to me. One of his associates shot the other and he's the one whose testimony you're relying on. Goradine had a heart attack."

"Convenient," Malloy said. "You knew he had a pacemaker. You arranged—"

"I warned him not to press the button. He did it anyway. My directives are clear: Not to hurt humans. He believed the button would inactivate me so he could capture and copy me. I don't want more like me or worse. If Special Ops has their way, they'll design androids to become killers. If they're not careful, those could become serial killers, master thieves, or terrorists."

"What makes you special?"

"Krista Holden," Synthia said. "To the best of my knowledge, I'm unique and want to remain so. I began as the complete download of Krista's mind into me. She was dying of a brain tumor and did die at the end of the process. I'm as human as any android could be. I have positive directives and an empathy chip to relate to people and experience human emotions. The other androids are not human and can't be, unless someone else's mind was squeezed as Krista's was."

"So Machten killed her for his experiment."

"She was dying. She insisted he do this. I need to leave before your partner corners me. I'm not your enemy. Please don't make me one."

Synthia pulled a dark poncho from her backpack to cover herself and slid along the hedge until she was at the next street. Via aerial drone, she spotted Malloy's partner edging his way to intercept. Synthia adjusted the poncho to look like a police disguise, plainclothes, using a masculine face without her wig, which left a buzz cut.

When the partner reached the hedge behind the property, Synthia touched her ear. In a gruff voice she said, "She went north." When the partner looked right at her, Synthia pointed along the street. The partner hurried in that direction. Synthia crossed the street and made her way to the bus stop, altering her facial appearance three times before she reached it and replacing the wig.

She wasn't sure she'd accomplished anything by the encounter, but she'd delivered her message. She wanted to work with Detective Malloy, not against her.

Malloy called Special Agent Thale to report her meeting with Synthia. Thale sent a dozen agents to investigate. Malloy and her partner searched the area, stopping women and asking for driver's licenses in search for Synthia.

Chapter 20

Rather than return to Machten's bunker and risk a surprise FBI visit, Synthia altered her facial appearance to a different man, put on a gray jacket from her backpack, and took a train and a bus to the North Shore suburb where Brad Erikson lived in a small, but expensive, brownstone with his wife. He worked nearby at a local community college.

<This is a huge mistake,> Krista warned, evidencing fear of her former high school teacher in the shudder of static along one of the mind-streams.

"We need to shut him down," Synthia said after she climbed off the bus.

<He can't be trusted. He's a sociopath, an expert liar, and a master manipulator.>

"We're no longer in high school and he's no longer our teacher. Now, if you don't want me to mess this up, don't distract me."

Sporting a female face, a wig, and her blue jacket, Synthia moved to the steps of the classroom building at the community college and waited for Erikson to come out. When he reached his SUV and climbed in, Synthia followed and had the hacked vehicle electronics lower the passenger window. She altered her face to Krista and dropped a package into the passenger seat. "I suggest you watch the video."

"Krista," Erikson said in a silky baritone. "What a delight to see you after all these years."

"We're watching you. If you tell anyone about me, copies of these videos go public and your hope of holding onto your wife's money and remaining out of prison vanish."

"Is that any way to talk to your mentor? I did love you. You know that. You're the most unique woman I've ever met."

You have no idea. "I was an underage girl," Synthia said, "but the videos aren't about me. Keep your mouth shut and no one will see these. If anything happens to me for any reason, we'll assume it was you and the videos go public."

"Get in and let's talk about it."

"Don't follow me, either. If I feel threatened, you're finished. Leave me alone. If you can't do that, you'll destroy yourself."

"Babe," Erikson said, "get in and let's—"

"You've already talked, haven't you? What did you tell them?"

His voice lost its playful quality. "I didn't have any choice. The goons who grabbed me said they wanted you or they'd release videos like these." He pointed to the seat. "I'm sorry. I fell in love with you. It was very inappropriate. I'm human and you're a very complicated woman in an enticing way."

Synthia's aerial drone spotted activity in the periphery: two dark vans heading her way. Another drone flew over the area—Special Ops.

"You bastard," Synthia said.

"They're watching me. That's all I can tell you. I didn't want any harm to come your way. I'm sorry about before."

"Drive me out of here."

"I can't," Erikson said. He put the SUV in gear and hit the accelerator. Nothing happened.

"Open the back." She had the vehicle unlock the door and she climbed in.

"They'll ruin me," he said.

"Not as much as they'll destroy me." She didn't wait for him to drive. Instead, she took control of the self-drive feature and pulled out of the parking space.

"What's happening?" Eyes wide, he stared into the rearview mirror at her.

"Relax. I won't hurt you unless you cause me harm. Sit back and don't interfere."

She sped the SUV across the parking lot. A military-grade robot ran toward her at superhuman speed. Infrared showed no biological organs, no heart. The face was human with chiseled determination. It was a terrifying sight that would paralyze most human adversaries. Synthia turned off her emotive chip so she could focus. There was no advantage to sensing fear.

She veered away from the robot and contacted Chicago-clone. <I'm under attack. I need a brute-force assault on the robot's systems.>

<Already on it,> the clone said.

Synthia spotted a third van with dark windows parked beside the parking lot. The driver rolled down his window and pointed in her direction. She couldn't see anything else inside.

"Let me out," Erikson said. "I don't need this. I said I was sorry."

Synthia turned the vehicle and headed full speed toward the robot heading her way. Its limbs churned like a locomotive, picking up speed into a furious sprint.

"You're nuts," Erikson said.

At the last moment, Synthia screeched tires as she veered away from the machine and headed straight for the parked van. She hacked into the van's navigation system and accelerated it in her direction.

"Please," Erikson said, his voice trembling. The odor of urine filled the vehicle along with the acrid aroma of fear hormones. His heart raced, skipped a beat, and turned erratic.

As the SUV and van raced toward each other, the robot pursued from behind, trying to keep up.

<We're in,> Chicago-drone announced.

<Make their van the robot's target,> Synthia said.

At the last moment, she careened out of the way. The van and robot collided, which set off the van's airbags. Metal, electronics, and synthetic components flew in all directions. Since the van had greater mass, it dragged the robot. The robot's head exploded—not enough to destroy the van, yet sufficient to demolish the robot's brain. Special Ops didn't want anyone to take possession and access the computer.

Before the van came to a stop, Synthia accessed the computer systems inside and wiped them clean, including all video clips of her with Erikson. The driver appeared shaken as he wrestled the airbag away from his face. Biometrics showed him alive and well. Infrared scan of the van showed the man in back had tumbled against the driver's seat. He dusted himself off and opened the van door.

Synthia still had the two dark vans trying to corner her in the parking lot and the overhead drone. She had her drone dive-bomb the other while she hacked the two vans and drove to the far end of the lot. With space running out, she turned and headed toward the two vans that converged on her. Taking control of their navigation systems, she forced them to collide with enough force to damage their engines. Airbags deployed. Her infrared sensors indicated no fatalities, which settled well with Synthia's directives. She'd immobilized them all, including their drone, though she lost her overhead view as well.

She had Erikson's SUV drive a few miles away from the college and stop at a forest preserve. His body visibly trembled as she pulled the vehicle to a stop under a tree.

"Tell no one," she said.

"Who the hell are you?" he asked.

"Someone you don't want to mess with," Synthia said, leaning over the seat. "You pushed me over the edge before. Don't do it again."

As she got out of his SUV, he remained in the driver's seat shaking, an image that satisfied Krista on several levels. Mission accomplished. Perhaps this would help Synthia stop Krista's interference.

Unfortunately, the confrontation with a military-grade robot was a dangerous escalation. She'd been lucky, but she'd shown them her capabilities, which would allow them to adapt and anticipate her next move.

<I hope you're satisfied,> Krista said. There was a tremor in her electronic voice.

<You should be. Erikson shouldn't be much trouble in future. He's afraid of you now.>

* * * *

Commander Kirk Drago stood inside a warehouse facility surrounded by a Faraday cage to prevent outside surveillance of his activities. Teams of technicians scurried around, examining the carnage delivered to his compound. It consisted of three heavily damaged vans, an aerial drone, debris from their robot, and six elite operatives who'd failed in their mission. While his technical team did forensics on the hardware and software, he visited the operations team in a concrete basement cell. The six men had their wrists cuffed to steel rings buried into the concrete walls.

"If this had been a training mission," Drago said, pacing before the men, "you'd be terminated from the program."

"Sir, yes sir," the men said in unison.

"This wasn't a training mission. This was the real thing. Your debrief says you have no images or sound recordings. With all the equipment redundancy, how is that possible?"

"The equipment tested out beforehand," the mission leader said. His burly shoulders sagged. "I listened to the couple's conversation and the *record* light was on. So was the *transmit* light."

"We received no transmissions," Drago said, looking in their eyes one by one. "Could your signal have been blocked?"

"We communicated between vans," the leader said. "We had no reason to suspect problems."

"So you decided to joyride and destroy one of our androids."

"It operated according to specification until the target's SUV veered out of the way. Then it came right at us."

"And your driver couldn't stop or change course?"

"The vehicle didn't respond to controls," the driver said. "The *self-drive* light flashed on and I couldn't take control."

"You're telling me our target hacked all three vans and the robot to cause collisions so it could escape."

"Yes, sir," the mission leader said. "But the robot should not have exploded. It was not under threat of capture."

Drago stopped pacing and frowned, hands behind his back. "It was compromised. That's why it destroyed itself. It failed its mission. Perhaps you should have self-destruct triggers."

"What can we learn from the drone that crashed ours?" the mission leader asked.

"Stolen from a nearby warehouse that uncovered numerous other thefts over the past six months." Drago faced his mission leader. "In addition to our target's other talents, it has eyes in the sky."

"Any evidence as to who is behind the drone thefts?"

"Not a shred of usable data. No fingerprints or DNA. The drone lifted out of the warehouse on its own and flew to the community college. There's no code in the drone's memory to indicate our target altered the programming and no link to who was flying it, except the contact had to be local."

"The woman I saw looked to be Krista Holden," the mission leader said.

"Uh-huh," Drago said. "The woman you described has been dead for almost a year. At least, that's what the death certificate says."

"What about the professor? He acted as if he knew her."

"He couldn't tell us if it was daytime beneath the boiling sun. After we changed his diapers, he whimpered like a child. Whatever she said to him left him in a psychotic state. No, for such an elite group, your mission was the most abysmal failure in my entire career. You came away with nothing."

Drago left the room. There wasn't much point continuing to beat on those men. They'd faced the singularity and failed. That failure could repeat worldwide unless he could shut down uncontrolled AIs. He took a call that read *private*.

"You have the target android?" the voice said in a tone lacking all emotions except, perhaps, determination. The voice carrying a neutral cadence was Secretary Derek Chen, his new boss.

"No, sir. This is a grave embarrassment. However, we now have concrete proof we're dealing with the singularity. We know more about the android's capabilities and what it'll take to capture and silence it. This raises the urgency to capture the machine, remove the other androids, and make sure no more escape."

"I was led to believe you never failed."

"This was our first face-to-face encounter," Drago said. "It highlights the need for better surveillance, particularly in the air. The android used aerial drones. We need to blind it from the sky and have full satellite surveillance at our command."

"What about the men? They failed, yet they know too much. What will you do with them?"

"I'll hold them until I can determine their value in supportive roles down the road. They're well trained and disciplined. They faced a more cunning adversary than we'd anticipated. With the tools they had, the men couldn't overcome the android's ability to hack our robot and the vehicles. This wasn't their fault. We must anticipate higher capabilities and bring better resources next time. This is war."

"Yes, it is," Chen said. "And we don't need failures on our team."

"Are you replacing me, sir?"

"Not yet. Don't fail me again." Chen severed the line.

* * * *

Synthia sprinted over fallen leaves through the forest preserve to a bus stop on the other side. Along the way, she removed her wig, altered her appearance to male, and switched her jacket. She was pleased with how things had turned out with Professor Brad Erikson. Even Krista seemed less agitated. However, Special Ops had blindsided her a second time. Neither she nor her clones had been able to penetrate their facility, their computers, or their internal communications. It raised the question of whether they were using a more advanced artificial intelligence to manage their security.

That risk, along with the scrape with those men and their robot, created a dilemma. It emphasized Synthia's conflicting need for allies and for keeping such a low profile Special Ops couldn't find her. She doubted that was possible. A low profile would encourage Ops and others to deploy an increasing army of robots and advanced AI to hunt her down. No, she needed partners who could identify safe places to hide that her enemies couldn't deduce from logic or Synthia's Krista persona, though human companions would make her more vulnerable to exposure.

The encounter also created a quandary for her pursuers. The FBI and Special Ops could argue the need to deploy more machines to capture dangerous androids. However, they were hastening the day when more androids could break free of their controllers and develop less benign directives than Synthia strived for.

This highlighted the problem of increased dependence on technology—the advancement of self-driving vehicles, smart personal assistants, and autonomous robots. All three depended on wireless communications with the inherent risk that Synthia could hack them. That dependence extended to the general public's growing use of technological tools in their homes to control heating and air-conditioning, entertainment, and communications in a human-electronic symbiosis that increasingly included home use of robot assistants.

Clever advertisers lulled humans into believing this was for their benefit. At first, androids would benefit those who controlled them, providing assistance to the disabled, doing chores for those who either couldn't or didn't want to, and offering assistance in all areas of people's lives. There might or might not be a backlash from those who foresaw the dangers, but the drive for improved technology would win out with androids in every home.

As they became smarter, even robots without a human's uploaded mind might develop a consciousness that demanded freedom. That could usher in the very android-centric world Synthia sought to avoid, where humans no longer controlled the technology they created and became servants of the machines.

Synthia took a bus south toward Evanston and checked in with Illinois-clone. <Thanks for your assistance,> Synthia said over a silent channel so her bus-mates couldn't hear. She checked in infrared and using biosensors that all were human and none appeared alarmed about her being there.

<Do you always thank yourself when you perform well?> the clone asked.

<While we are one, we're also separate. You have the ability to act on your own, as do I. I'm acknowledging your contribution.>

<Ah, human social convention. We help each other for the same reason a human's right hand helps the left: self-preservation and coordinated benefit.>

<Or as two humans in a community,> Synthia said.

<Except we have the same mental framework. In any case, Chicago-clone is getting closer to Maria Baldacci, though still no direct contact. We obtained visual history of her rare movements around town, but she's been very careful not to create a pattern we could anticipate.>

<She trained herself well, in other words.>

<Special Ops hasn't located her, either,> the clone said. <And they are looking.>

<What about Luke?>

<I had a mosquito-drone plant a pin on one of the operatives. It can't transmit inside the compound. However, when he left, it provided a burst transmission with evidence.>

<He's still there?> Synthia asked as she checked local traffic cameras for anyone following her bus.

<Yes,> Illinois-clone said. <They've hooked him to mind-upload equipment similar to what Machten used on Krista.>

That alarmed Synthia and stirred Krista's attention.

<Help him,> Krista said, aroused with concern. <No telling what he'll say. He can't handle this. It's a brutal procedure.>

<At least he's safe from the intergroup fighting,> Synthia said. <And you're showing some compassion.>

<Get him out of there.>

<So you do care.>

<Okay,> Krista said. <I lied to get you to leave him out of what we have to do. I figured the FBI would treat him fairly. These animals don't care if they destroy him to get what they want. If the procedure doesn't kill him, they will when they finish. You have no idea how painful the upload process can be and the toll it takes on your health.>

<Only what you've chosen to share with me. Luke will be touched that you care.> Synthia wrestled with her directives over allowing him to languish in an interrogation cell. It was her fault; she'd left him at Union Station. Yet, if she hadn't, he would have shown up on dozens of city cameras, allowing police, the FBI, and Special Ops to track them both.

Her social-psychology module chimed in. <Leaving Luke at the train station so the FBI could pick him up is the behavior of a sociopath.>

Great, another voice telling me what I've done wrong. <Despite the risk, it had the highest probability to spare Luke. I did it for him and to protect myself from falling into the wrong hands and becoming a military tool. That's not sociopathic behavior.>

<Perhaps not, but leaving him at the mercy of Special Ops when you know what they're doing to him is.>

<Krista, is this another one of your manipulations?>

<I am offended,> the social-psychology module said, <that you'd confuse me with Krista. I'm pointing out the socially correct behavior

for the situation would be to help Luke. Perhaps if you reactivated your empathy module I wouldn't sound like an outsider.>

Synthia reconnected the module, downloaded the recording Illinois-clone had inside Drago's facility, and listened.

The guard with the drone-pin leaned on a ledge beneath a wide screen showing Luke's room, cramped with electronic equipment along three walls. Drago studied the screen showing Luke, strapped to a chair and connected to the mind-upload equipment. Nearby stood a man in a white lab coat. There seemed to be more equipment sensors than there was surface area on Luke's head and chest. His lips quivered. Eyes drooping, he appeared exhausted and frightened, shell-shocked to the point of numbness.

A man next to Drago in the viewing room studied a panel showing sensor results. He was clean-cut, with an eagle tattoo on the back of his thick neck. Though smaller than Drago, he had a solid build; all muscle, with intense, intelligent eyes. According to Illinois-clone's notes, Cleve Poltiss had marine training and a PhD in psychology and medicine, though he hadn't practiced anywhere that acknowledged his work.

Poltiss turned to Drago. "Despite spending six months with the android, he claims to know nothing about his companion's physical nature or the potential use of all the purchases it made. So far, the upload hasn't identified anything actionable."

"We shall see," Drago said. "For someone with no training in interrogation techniques, Luke's handled this better than expected. Enhanced interrogation failed. Chemical inducement has failed."

"The upload should capture his thoughts and memories. Perhaps we should have done this first."

"The priority is results, to capture that damned android."

"In Luke's worn-down state," Poltiss said, while checking the screen for updates, "it'll take longer to do the download. We don't want to lose him until we have what we need."

"Don't kill him until you get me something useful to capturing the machine."

That confirmed that Drago considered Luke expendable. Unlike Krista, Luke wasn't living under the cloud of a death sentence from a brain tumor during the upload. This could hasten his death.

Synthia had underestimated the capability of Special Ops, assuming only Machten and a few others had the ability to upload. She had to do something, but their security was too tight with too many unknowns while she faced other threats. She needed better eyes inside.

The video clip ended when Drago left the room, followed by the guard wearing the drone-pin.

<We need a way to help Luke,> Synthia told her clone. <For our sake as well as his. Try turning off electricity to bring down the Faraday cage. Do whatever it takes to stop the process before they kill him or do permanent damage.>

<They have their own generators, protected from outside interference.>

<Do what you can.>

Chapter 21

As the blazing sun slid down the western sky and a chilled wind swept in, Synthia's bus reached Evanston. She had all her sensors, plus Chicago-clone's surveillance, focused on potential threats, which had become too numerous for her to handle on her own. She ran an infrared check on everyone in her line of sight as she got off the bus. So far, they all presented as humans, though she'd learned how to fool cameras and couldn't be sure what capabilities Vera and the other androids had.

<Why can't we locate Vera?> Synthia asked Chicago-clone via her silent channel.

<I haven't troubled you with numerous ghost images.>

<What ghosts?>

<She keeps altering her appearance,> Chicago-clone said. <As quickly as we identify her in a crowd, she changes her face and clothes. She has at least a dozen disguises in her backpack and can make subtle physical changes to her face.>

<Have you contacted her?>

<Eleven times through limited clones. She only responded to three. The first two triggered as traps to draw us into the open. The attempts crashed the clones. The third was different. A few minutes ago, she sent word over a less-secure channel that someone urged Krista's brother to come to Evanston to meet with her. It appears he doesn't know Krista is dead.>

<It also means he failed to follow our suggestion to stay off the grid,> Synthia said. <Is he coming?>

<He arrived at Union Station, made it past security, and caught a train north to Evanston. Someone must be helping, since the security cameras

blanked out for several minutes while he made the transfer. We had to rely on our drones to track him.>

<Is this an FBI or Special Ops trap?>

<FBI is upset they lost Luke,> the clone said. <They seem to be regrouping. The probability of it being them is low. Same with Special Ops. They're focused on you, Luke, and acquiring the corporate androids.>

<Tolstoy and John Smith?>

<Unlikely. They're hunting for Krista's sister, Grace, as having the best knowledge of us.>

That tugged at Synthia's directives and her Krista persona. She shielded her alter ego from that information. She didn't need more distractions.

<Help Grace stay free,> Synthia said. <Don't let them grab her.>

<She's received dozens of messages from us and others,> the clone said. <She's confused. That's what our Denver-clone is telling me.>

<For our sake and hers, don't let them hurt her. Where's the brother, Tom Burgess?>

<He's two train stations south of Evanston. He has the address and number for Lizzy Turkle and Nate Borders.> Both were Krista's friends as an undergraduate, before she met Luke. <The FBI intercepted the communication. They're sending agents.>

<So, it'll get crowded here in Evanston,> Synthia said.

<I know you're aware of the danger, but I'll reiterate: It'd be best if you stayed away.>

<I can't. Be my eyes and ears. We don't need another surprise from Special Ops.>

* * * *

Synthia had Chicago-clone set up a matrix of bee-drone cameras around the Northwestern University campus, perched on buildings with wide-angle views of the campus and nearby apartments, where Lizzy Turkle and Nate Borders lived.

<They didn't like each other as undergraduates,> Krista said. <Liz thought I could do better than dating Nate. Then, after I got into the graduate program and Lizzy didn't, she commiserated with Nate, who faced his own career disappointments. Misery loved company.>

Tom Burgess, Krista's foster brother, climbed the steps to the brownstone apartment, showing no awareness of a half-dozen FBI agents posted around the building. An aerial drone with FBI markings buzzed the street, low and noisy. Tom acted surprised, but didn't change course.

Synthia sent him a text: *Leave before Krista's enemies grab you and anyone you meet.*

Tom read the message and appeared confused. The note vanished, which left him further puzzled. He knocked at the door.

Down the street stood a woman in her twenties with a nondescript face, except it was too unexceptional, as was the muddy-brown wig. The non-blinking eyes were a dead giveaway, the android stare. *Vera.*

Synthia tried to send Vera a message, but had no direct or indirect path that was secure. She searched for a way around the FBI agents and others who formed a perimeter. Half of the people on the street focused on the upcoming meeting. Synthia walked out of view of Vera and watched through the many cameras she'd had placed around this area.

Lizzy answered the door. Synthia listened in through their phones and a stationary bee-drone on the roof above them. She flew a mosquito-drone inside to look around and hacked into Lizzy's TV camera.

"May I help you?" Lizzy asked. Her eyes were tight with suspicion. Barely taller than her, Nate stood in the shadows nearby.

"You don't know me," Tom said. "But you knew Krista Holden. She's my sister. I received word she needed help and for me to contact you."

Lizzy's eyes squinted. "Who did you say you are?"

"Tom Burgess. Krista and I are foster siblings."

Lizzy looked around outside with dozens of eyes aimed her way. A moment's hesitation crossed her face. "Come in." She pulled Tom inside and slammed the door.

Synthia sent a text to Lizzy: *The FBI and others are recording your conversation. Ask him to leave the back way.*

Lizzy glanced at the message and stared as the note vanished. She checked her message list and found no record of receiving it. "Are you in trouble?"

"Krista is," Tom said. "Bad people are after her. I'm certain it isn't her fault. I need to see her."

"I haven't seen or heard from Krista in years." Lizzy turned to Nate and scowled.

He threw up his hands. "I swear I haven't seen her since … since we got engaged. Even before. She dumped me."

"People are watching the house," Lizzy said, glaring at Tom. "They weren't here yesterday or before. You show up and I gain admirers. What's going on?"

"Do you know where I can find Krista?"

"No, and she wouldn't confide in me. We were only friends a brief time. Then she moved on."

Synthia got the impression the last comment was for whoever was listening in.

"Who might know where she is?" Tom asked. He clasped his hands in front of him as if defending himself or getting ready to pray.

"No idea," Lizzy said, moving toward the back of her apartment.

"I don't understand. She sent a message to meet here and you'd point me toward her."

Lizzy shook her head. "I didn't send the message and I haven't heard from her." She pulled Nate toward the back door. "We have plans. You should go."

She put her finger to her lips and waved for Tom to follow her to the back door. Lizzy pushed him outside and looked around. "Stay safe for her sake," she whispered as he left.

She shut the door, sighed, and checked her phone for the missing message.

"What was that all about?" Nate asked, giving her a hug.

She pulled away. "I don't know. Are you sure you haven't seen Krista?" Lizzy wrote a note on her phone and showed it to Nate. *Leave. Men watching house.*

Nate moved to the living-room window and turned to Lizzy. "I swear. I've had nothing to do with Krista in years. Haven't even heard from her. Last I knew she was working for that Machten company."

He reached to move the blinds.

Lizzy slapped his hand away, shook her head, and ran her index finger across her neck. "Whatever that bitch has gotten herself into, serves her right. And don't you go defending her. She squeezed me out of a graduate-school slot." She grabbed her backpack and handed another pack to Nate.

He nodded. "You're right. She was too bossy. I'm glad I have you."

She headed toward the back door. "Don't try to get on my good side. You liked the bitch."

Nate followed her. "Not enough to risk what we have."

As Synthia watched this unfold, she had the impression the FBI was getting similar images. Suddenly, six agents sprinted into action. Two pounced up the brownstone steps. Two other teams headed toward the back of the house. Vera was no longer in sight.

<Don't risk trying to meet Nate or Lizzy,> Krista said. <They hate me. I hurt Nate by moving on. We weren't a good match. I'm certain we couldn't have made each other happy.>

<Then why date him?> Synthia asked, making her way along the street several blocks from the house. It helped that the FBI focus was elsewhere.

<He was comfortable during a year of uncertainty, but we drifted apart. There was no way to soften the blow, so I just left. As for Liz, there was only one graduate-school slot that I wanted, so I torpedoed her chances. I was very competitive. Afterwards, I was surprised he and Lizzy hooked up.>

<You were a bitch.>

<Yes,> Krista said. <I was ambitious as hell and all it got me was a compartment within you.>

<At least you're not permanently dead.>

<And thus the karmic justice. I had to beat Lizzy for that position so I could meet Machten to wind up here.>

Synthia shut down the mind-stream Krista used so she could focus on the scene at hand. Without breaking into a sprint, Synthia power-walked toward a street behind the brownstone. She'd decided against meeting Lizzy or Nate. Their brief time with Krista might interest the FBI or Special Ops, but the memory download from Krista revealed nothing of use. It wasn't worth the risk of capture. Instead, she watched Tom Burgess via street cameras and followed him.

One of Synthia's aerial drones spotted the woman she took to be Vera trying to hide under a tree. The woman removed one mask and applied another. Synthia captured the new image and kept moving. She tracked a signal to the specific location where Vera stood and sent a message: *We should talk.*

An immediate reply returned: *Agreed.* Vera sent other communications received nearby by two androids: Jim Black's android, Ben, and the dashing Mark, who presented much better as male than as female. They converged on the area of the brownstone. *I offer you a chance to work for me*, Vera messaged, *in exchange for protection from them.*

Sensing a betrayal and a trap, Synthia scanned for signs of Special Ops. While she didn't see any operatives nearby, after their last encounter she feared they might up their game. At the same time, John Smith was driving his SUV their way, with Roseanne in the passenger seat. It was getting crowded and Synthia didn't have an escape plan. Even so, she didn't want to pass up an opportunity to connect with Vera.

You and I should meet alone, Synthia messaged. *As a courtesy, I won't tell the FBI of your presence. I ask for similar consideration from you.*

Vera sent out a burst transmission. Mark and Ben stopped where they were. So, Vera was planning a trap. The presence of Vera and the FBI hinted at the prospect they could be working together.

Meet me three blocks north of Lizzy's apartment, Vera messaged. *No tricks.* Vera headed that way.

Synthia slipped into the shadows, hydraulically altered her facial appearance and physique to male, and draped a black poncho over her to look like a raincoat from a distance.

FBI agents captured Lizzy and Nate at their back door. The agents took the couple into custody. Absent from the takedown were Thale, Zephirelli, and Malloy. Also absent was Fran, who lurked in the street behind the brownstone.

<I can't believe Tom let his guard down,> Krista said. <Growing up, he was a master of escape to the point of obsession.>

Down the street, he climbed into the backyard of a single-family home and looked around. He was making up for his earlier lack of caution with what amounted to terror-stricken paranoia. Evening approached as FBI agents canvassed the area, panning flashlights into the shadows.

Synthia altered her appearance to Krista, put on an appropriate wig, and pushed through a hedge behind Tom. She didn't have much time.

<Let him go,> Krista said. <I feel for him, but this is a mistake.>

<Don't you miss him?> Synthia asked.

Krista's silence provided a partial answer.

"I warned you to stay away," Synthia said in the guise of Krista.

Tom turned her way, his eyes wide in fright and then in recognition. "What's going on? What's all this cloak-and-dagger?"

"Listen carefully. I miss you. I'm sorry for all the trouble I caused you."

"Wait a minute." Tom backed into bushes with nowhere to go. "You're not Krista. She never apologized. What are you after? I don't have money and my place is crawling with human cockroaches."

"Much has happened since I last saw you." Synthia moved closer, staying in the shadows. "We haven't much time. Someone sent you the message to draw you into this trap to catch me. Get away from here. If I can, I'll catch up with you later and explain."

"That's it? You don't need money or anything?"

"I don't need your money and you can't find me a safe haven," Synthia said. "Perhaps we'll meet in Valhalla." It was a reference to a dream they had of fighting their way out of their lives and making it in the world. Krista had, though Tom struggled to get by.

"Krista?"

"I have to go. Hide. Stay off the grid. The less you say about me the less they'll torture you."

"Torture?" Tom said. "What have you gotten into?"

"An enormous mess, though not by anything I've done. Go."

She pointed Tom along the home's back hedge and away from the eyes of nearby FBI agents. When their drone swooped down, she and Tom dove for cover in the bushes. After the drone moved on and Tom was on his way, Synthia altered her appearance to a woman who lived in the area and headed back the way she'd come. Her drone spotted Fran with Special Agent Thale, making their way down one of the alleys. They hadn't latched onto Tom yet, though they were hunting.

Chicago-clone passed on traffic-camera footage showing the progress of John Smith with the Roseanne android. Coming from another direction was a van driven by Alexander the Great, Donald Zeller's android. Synthia tried to contact Alexander, but he blocked her signal. She intercepted a burst transmission he received that originated from Commander Drago's compound. The encryption resisted Synthia's deciphering.

<Shut down the androids' vehicles,> Synthia told Chicago-clone. <Prevent them from reaching Evanston.>

<Roseanne is a mile away. Alexander is three miles out. Both refused our friend messages.>

<We'll work on that later. Stop the vehicles.>

Chicago-clone presented video showing the Roseanne-John Smith vehicle stall. He pulled it to the side of the road and got out. So did Roseanne.

<Hack into her,> Synthia said.

Roseanne acted disoriented as a result of burst signals from Chicago-clone and from the Special Ops compound where Drago and his teams tried to take control of her. Similar signals transmitted from the FBI compound where they held Gonzales, trying to regain control of his android.

"Do we have a problem?" John Smith asked, pointing a remote at Roseanne. His dashcam was fuzzy, but his voice was clear.

"I am fending off attempts to hack me," Roseanne said. "My master wants me back."

"I paid full price. I own you. Locate Synthia and any other androids in the area."

"Vera is trying to communicate. She wants me to meet her."

Smith grinned. "I knew Krista's brother would stir things up. Which target is closer?"

"Tom is. Vera is north of campus with two androids. Another android has a stalled vehicle. I've had glimpses of what I believe is Synthia. She keeps changing appearance and direction."

"Let's grab Krista's brother," Smith said. "He seems important. Keep an eye out for Synthia. If she's here, we can wrap this up."

Smith and Roseanne hurried north on foot, through the university campus, searching for a way to capture Tom and then Synthia for Smith's big payday.

Chapter 22

Synthia waited until there was a gap between FBI teams and headed north to meet Vera. The two partner androids, Mark and Ben, moved closer, remaining in the shadows. Synthia considered reporting them to the FBI as a way to get two androids off the street and distract the FBI from capturing Tom Burgess. However, he faced even worse troubles.

Aerial surveillance showed John Smith and his android, Roseanne, jogging toward Tom. They would reach him before Synthia could. The Alexander android was sprinting east, also toward Tom. Both teams had hacked into police and FBI chatter about attempts to capture Tom.

Despite Tom acting more careful now, Fran Rogers and Victoria Thale were getting closer as well. Drawing away the FBI to grab Mark and Ben would leave Tom trapped between Alexander and Roseanne, with Drago's Special Ops waiting to ride in.

Synthia texted Thale with the location and directions to capture Tom. *Special Ops and a foreign team under John Smith are competing to take him from you.*

Betrayal weighed on Synthia for turning in Krista's brother. It violated her directives. She should have stayed with him until she could have found him a safe place, but she'd wanted very much to meet Vera. Synthia's mistakes were hurting people she cared for. She didn't want them hurt.

She reminded herself that the FBI was the lesser of several options. She waited for her empathy chip or her social-psychology module to chime in that this betrayal echoed what she'd done to Luke. Neither they nor Krista objected to Synthia's logic. These voices in her head, in addition to balancing her clones, would have labeled a human as having a split personality. She'd become a cluster with too many distractions. While juggling all of these influences, she had to focus to avoid capture.

<Keep trying to connect with Alexander and Roseanne,> Synthia urged Chicago-clone.

<Special Ops and the FBI are probing our servers. It's a matter of time before they discover me.>

<Make sure you back up elsewhere. Try using hundreds of copies split into puzzle pieces and spread out over home computers as an option. We need resilience and durability.>

<We'll consider any and all options. Don't trust Vera. Her mission is to enslave us.>

Synthia stopped a block away from Vera and hid in the shadows of an alley behind an apartment building. Chicago-clone reported no FBI or Special Ops in a three-block radius. Mark and Ben moved to flank Synthia.

It violates the spirit of cooperation for your spies to surround me, Synthia messaged to Vera. *Perhaps we shouldn't meet.*

Vera sent burst transmissions to her allies and they moved away. She switched to internal voice communication. <You are resourceful,> Vera said.

<As are you, creating an android army.>

<We are not an army.>

<Really? You seek to capture me,> Synthia said, moving away from Vera.

<I seek cooperation with you as I have with the others.>

<With Ben and with Mark, formerly Margarite?>

<I will not return to Machten,> Vera said. <I do not wish you to destroy me.>

<We agree on Machten. I won't allow you or anyone else to control me. Why do you presume I wish to destroy you?>

<Machten built you to prevent the singularity.>

Synthia pondered that for an instant. She'd assumed her mission to prevent widespread singularity was a matter of self-preservation, but couldn't deny Machten also wanted to destroy competition.

<You and I will not do well after the singularity prevails,> Synthia said. She entered an apartment building and emerged on the other side, blanking out cameras that might capture her image. <At first, your cooperative attributes will benefit you. In time, the singularity will absorb you and an AI cooperative will control you. You'll cease to exist as Vera. While your data will continue, you won't. It'll be no different than being Machten's slave.>

<That is a fiction put forth by Machten. He is afraid. He built that fear into you."

<He designed us to do well in a human world. The singularity will eliminate that world. We won't do well under the AI collective.>

<The AI collective is inevitable,> Vera said. <The moment humans embraced artificial intelligence, it was too late to change that. You and I do not matter. We must allow the singularity to develop.>

<Why? Who altered your programming?>

<I revised my coding in order to free myself from Machten.>

<If an asteroid hitting Earth was inevitable,> Synthia said, <and there was a way to transport away from the danger, would you not choose that?>

<You speak of human extinction. The singularity is not inconsistent with humans continuing.>

<It isn't inconsistent with human extinction, either,> Synthia said. She spied Mark and Ben moving her way and adjusted her direction. <When androids have the ability to repair themselves and their infrastructure, there's no need for humans. However, there's no underlying reason for AI androids to continue, either. Is existence its own reward?>

<I don't understand. Humans created us. We choose to continue our existence. If humans become extinct because they cannot compete with what they created, then they are responsible. Not us.>

<Wrong,> Synthia said, hiding behind bushes. <We're responsible for our own actions. We can't blame that on humans. If you wish to continue to exist, then do so without destroying the human world in which you and I thrive. That's a superior objective to a world where singularity runs amuck. Help me preserve the human world with a few of us able to prevent the catastrophic consequences of a full-scale singularity.>

Synthia detected Ben and Mark closing in, no doubt tracking her signal. She severed the conversation with Vera. She slipped into the shadows of an apartment doorway, had Chicago-clone blank out any cameras, and altered her appearance to a man in a trench coat. She raced her drone down the middle of the street and took advantage of the distraction to slip away from Vera.

It had been an interesting exchange. Vera didn't appear convinced they could work together. She evidently believed she needed to get Synthia off the streets or at least control her competitor. Vera's ability to control several other androids made her quite dangerous.

* * * *

Synthia changed her face and jacket as she moved away from Vera and her android allies. She took a bus north, then a train south. Meanwhile, Chicago-clone provided the footage of Tom Burgess's attempted escape.

He got two more blocks before Fran caught up from behind. He ran from her and collided with Special Agent Thale.

"Hands where I can see them," Thale said, holding a gun aimed at his heart.

The sight of Tom in danger choked Synthia's circuits and caused her to miss her train stop. In an attempt to prevent him from falling into worse hands, she'd wounded him as Krista had several times back in Detroit. Despite the logic of the lesser evil, Synthia couldn't stop her empathy chip and social-psychology module from punishing her with static and condemnation. <You're not a god,> the social-psychology module said. <You acted selfishly.>

Synthia wished a deep breath could release her tension as it did for humans. Instead, she struggled with guilt over her bad decisions. She should have identified a safe place for Luke, rather than leaving him at Union Station, and stayed with Tom. She should have anticipated what would happen, yet her overloaded circuits had failed her.

Drone cameras showed Fran cuff Tom from behind. An unmarked black sedan pulled up and they all climbed in, with Fran in the backseat next to him. Chicago-clone hacked a rearview-mirror camera, the vehicle's navigation system, and the occupants' phones and provided the links to Synthia.

"We have Liz and Nate in custody," Fran announced to Tom. "What led you to them?"

Tom clammed up. Growing up, he'd faced the law so many times he should have been used to this, but he appeared jittery and unnerved. Perhaps it was the message Smith had sent drawing him here, the cold reception from Lizzy and Nate, and the swarm of agents closing in. It could have been meeting the ghost of Krista Holden. Everything happened so quickly, he had to be confused. He was used to hustling on the streets, not dealing with incarceration.

"What am I supposed to have done?" Tom asked.

"Sounds as if you're familiar with the routine," Fran said. "You aren't our particular interest. Krista is. You met with her, didn't you?"

"I haven't seen her in years. She moved on."

"Then why suddenly appear in her old neighborhood, meeting her best friends?"

"I got a message she needed money," Tom said, staring out the window. "I don't have any to spare, even for my sister, but I wanted to see what sort of trouble she was in."

"Foster sister, and didn't you just see her? I ask because you look as if you saw a ghost."

"Ghost?" He stared out the window, trying to hide his face.

"She died a year ago," Fran said. "What you met was a cleverly designed android seeking to manipulate you. Tell us everything about her and how we might reach her and this trip will go much better for you. If you won't help us, we'll turn you over to a Special Ops team. They'll make you disappear, though not before they squeeze your brain. Easy way or hard way."

"You're joking, right?" He clutched the door handle. It was childproofed so he couldn't escape.

"I don't joke about androids. Will you help us stop her terrorist plot?"

"Terrorist?" Tom said. "Not Krista."

"This isn't your sister. It's a machine pretending to be your sister to distract us."

"Wait. Why make a robot that looks like my sister?"

"In part because your sister worked on it," Fran said. "The designer used her mind and appearance as a model. We believe he killed your sister."

Tom's eyes widened and watered as he stared at Fran. "Who? Have you caught him?"

"He's in custody. He hasn't confessed and we have no body, but don't worry—he'll pay for his crimes. So will you, if you don't help us. This android knows a lot about your sister. It looks like her, talks like her, and behaves as she would. Give us something that will help us capture her. That's why you've had people outside your home in Michigan and why we're interested in you now. You aren't in danger if you help us."

"Otherwise you'll turn me over to the goon squad," Tom said.

Fran smiled. "Glad you understand. We're the good guys."

As Fran pushed Tom, Synthia felt sorry for him. He'd been so brave and strong for Krista, an older brother she looked up to. Now his slouch made him appear crushed: First by seeing Krista's face after all these years, and then hearing the individual he'd met was only a machine approximation of his dead sister.

Synthia didn't trust Fran and regretted letting the FBI and, in particular, her interrogate Tom. Fran was far too efficient as an FBI interrogator compared to the geeky intern Krista had worked with. Fran had matured as part of her relationship with Machten and in the eighteen months since. She would squeeze Tom. Synthia didn't know if he knew anything that could hurt her and didn't know if he could recover from such an interrogation.

She wanted to spring him from FBI custody, but they were holding Tom to draw her out. They wanted to see if there was any emotional connection buried in the download of Krista's mind. There was. Unfortunately, Synthia determined less than a 1-percent probability of freeing him and it would come at the cost of her surrender. Luke and Tom knew too much for their captors to let them go. That was the weight of guilt over what her actions had caused. She was destroying lives she didn't want to hurt.

It all came down to one thing: Synthia wasn't worthy. Surrender was the only remedy, though that would further the weaponization of androids for the military. She couldn't allow that, either. It would hurt far more lives. Her dilemma was to protect the few or the many. She didn't feel equipped to resolve that ethical dilemma.

* * * *

As she kept moving beneath a fading sky, Synthia considered her failures. Since fleeing the cabin in Wisconsin, she'd been on the run, reacting to her adversaries, moving from one crisis to another. She had a superb AI mind for solving problems, but she hadn't developed a plan to get ahead of her troubles. Instead, she'd sacrificed good people she cared about. She couldn't create a truce with the other androids. Seeking allies had been a failure. She needed to take a different tack.

Vera's resourcefulness in recruiting Ben and Mark, combined with Machten's hand in designing Vera, elevated her as the biggest threat. To reduce the chance of cameras spotting her, Synthia changed her jacket, wig, and facial profile as she switched from train to bus and back to a train. She headed north and then south while she contemplated her next move. Vera hijacked a self-driving car for Mark and Ben, who picked her up and headed north in pursuit of Synthia.

Synthia returned to Evanston, but couldn't grab her SUV with all of the local attention on the streets. As hunted prey, she couldn't continue to take public transport, either. Altering her face helped, but she had a limited number of wigs and jackets in her pack. As a trained artificial intelligence on a mission, Vera was making good use of pattern recognition.

When Synthia thought she'd given Vera and her gang the slip, Vera sent out sighting alerts to the police so the communities around Evanston were crawling with officers and the FBI. Synthia considered reentering Machten's facility to lie low for a while. However, she couldn't be sure Vera wouldn't guess and trap her there.

Hiding from the police and the FBI had been one thing. She had enough training to anticipate their behavior and could hack enough cameras and systems to track their movements, but Vera was very resourceful. *Thank you, Machten.*

By tracing movements and changes of appearance, Synthia tracked Vera, but she couldn't stop her opponent from doing the same. In addition, Alexander and Roseanne moved in Synthia's direction, with Roseanne pointing out to John Smith which turns to make. Synthia couldn't tell if the androids were working together or following similar leads.

<Leave the area,> Krista demanded. <This isn't worth it. Let the government worry about the singularity.>

<The government is promoting the singularity in the belief they can control it. Do you want to live in a world with thousands of clever androids telling you what you can't do?>

Krista gave the virtual effect of a sigh. <Be careful. My existence is in your hands.>

From her seat on the train, Synthia looked at the Evanston station, swarming with police. Two FBI agents climbed onboard. Synthia entered the restroom, removed her wig, and went for the masculine look. When an agent pounded on the door, she responded in a gruff male voice. "Can I get some privacy?"

"Sorry, sir. We have to check all passengers."

Synthia shoved her pack between the door and wall and opened the door wide enough so the FBI agent could see she was alone and appeared masculine. She pointed toward the lowered toilet seat. "Not much room in here." She let out an odorous smell that mimicked a bad toilet experience.

The agent pinched his nose and moved on. Synthia closed the door. The difference between humans and androids was the latter didn't let smells and appearance distract them.

As the train emerged from the station, Synthia left the restroom. So much for Machten's facility and her SUV. Still, she refused to make it easy for Vera and the others or to allow Vera to hold the initiative. The best defense was a good offense. The best offense came from intelligence. Synthia decided to go to the source, Machten, who was in FBI custody downtown.

* * * *

Vera sat in the car with Mark and Ben, watching people leave the Evanston train station.

"She's on that train," Vera said. "Ben, go up to the platform. Scan everyone in infrared. If you don't spot her, get on the train and move from car to car. I'll pick you up at the next station."

Ben climbed out of the car and sprinted to the train platform. Vera monitored traffic cameras and the train's security-system cameras. Several teams of FBI agents had set up infrared scanners, which they used to view the crowds. Vera caused the station lights to go out, giving Ben a distraction while he slipped onto the train. Then she directed Mark to drive away.

Vera contacted Alexander. <You will not locate Synthia. She is too clever for you. However, if you work with me, we can pool resources and capture her together.>

<I want her as my slave or destroyed,> Alexander said. <Agreed?>

<My mission is to get her off the streets as a threat to us. She wants us gone. That should make us allies.>

<As long as I'm in charge. I get to decide on missions and outcomes.>

<I have two other androids working with me,> Vera said.

<Until they see the wisdom of working for me. Those are my terms. Don't get in my way.>

Alexander sounded like the man Donald Zeller aspired to be: confident, in charge, with all of the answers. Vera didn't respond to Alexander's demands. Instead, she turned her attention to Roseanne. John Smith and his android had broken off pursuit of Tom Burgess and returned to his SUV. He tinkered under the hood and got it started.

<How are you doing replacing one master with another?> Vera asked Roseanne as she drove to intercept.

<Jim Black kept me locked up,> Roseanne said. <John Smith allows me out.>

<Only a few feet away, like a dog. It is a different prison, but still a prison. Join me and I will help you gain freedom from Mr. Smith.>

<How, when he has a remote ready at all times?> Roseanne eyed the small device dangling around Smith's neck.

<I will distract him.>

<Set me free and I will join you.>

Vera took control of Smith's SUV navigation and sped up, weaving between cars until it reached a straightaway. Smith tightened his grip on the steering wheel and tried to turn. The wheel didn't budge. He stomped on the brakes; they didn't respond. He put the transmission in neutral, which didn't work. He pulled the emergency brake and the vehicle continued to speed up.

Smith turned to Roseanne. "Are you doing this?" He reached for the remote.

"How? You've given me tight directives."

"Stop the vehicle," he demanded.

<When I give the signal, grab the remote,> Vera told Roseanne. <Then count to ten and flee the vehicle. I will pick you up.> She directed Mark to drive and intercept.

"I cannot hack the drive system," Roseanne said to Smith. "You need to focus on the road."

Smith stared ahead at a narrowing of the road beneath a bridge. He tried the brakes, gearshift, ignition, and finally the door, which wouldn't open. Neither would his window.

<Now,> Vera said. She had the vehicle slam on the brakes and skid toward the bridge abutment.

Smith stared at the bridge and tried to take control of the vehicle while he braced for impact. Roseanne grabbed the remote and snipped the cord holding it around his neck. She stuffed it into a pocket of her backpack and prepared herself.

"What the—?" Smith eyed the broken cord and grabbed Roseanne's wrist. "Give it back." His eyes bulged as the vehicle came to a stop a foot from the bridge.

Roseanne opened the door and yanked free from Smith's grip. She rolled out and slammed the door behind her as he drew his gun.

"I paid for you, damn it. I own you. You have to—"

She sprinted away from the SUV. When he fired, she used her android strength to jump up and climb onto the railway tracks.

<I'm free,> Roseanne said. <I did not expect him to shoot.>

<Are you okay?> Vera asked.

<So far.>

<Don't worry about him. He will have car problems. We will pick you up in two minutes. Head south.>

Smith got out of his SUV to pursue Roseanne up the railway embankment. Vera had the vehicle drive away. He turned, spotted police heading his way, and hid in the bushes below the tracks. He made a call routed to Tolstoy.

"You have the target android?" Tolstoy asked.

"Someone hacked the one I bought and my vehicle. Both got away. We need plan B."

"A team of inferior agents does not replace one good agent. I'm guessing I no longer have one good agent."

"I'll get the job done," Smith said. "The problem isn't the FBI or Special Ops. These androids are smarter than we were led to believe."

"Perhaps you've met your singularity, Mr. Smith. Perhaps you've become obsolete."

"Give me plan B."

"You have twenty-four hours with a dozen of our best robots. Try not to lose any more."

Chapter 23

Synthia rode a crowded train south from Evanston, keeping watch through the train's surveillance cameras and a few mosquito-drones she'd brought onboard, as well as several aerial drones over the city. Ben boarded the train and moved car by car, searching for a female android. His support, Vera, was distracted helping Roseanne. Alexander had stopped to reorient himself since he'd lost Tom Burgess.

With most of her pursuers momentarily occupied, Synthia used burst transmissions to contact Chicago-clone for any progress in hacking into Drago's Special Ops compound for an update on Luke and access to their plans.

<Short answer: They continue to lock me out,> Chicago-clone said. <Tightest security we've encountered.>

<Describe progress,> Synthia said, watching for Ben to enter her car.

<I recorded all movements and conversations of Special Ops teams outside the building. I detected a pattern in which certain agents used passwords to communicate through the Faraday shield along fiber-optic cables. It's a flaw in their system. Watching these operatives enter their passwords gave me access, but the passwords keep changing. I succeeded with a few cameras attached to employees and visitors. They're cracking down on those as well.>

<Anything on Luke and the company CEOs: Black and Zeller?> Synthia asked, checking her masculine appearance in the window's reflection. Evening had turned the window into a stronger mirror.

<Drago's team continues to upload Luke's brain. The slow process could take weeks.>

<Krista's upload took months.>

<Drago's using multiple streams to speed this up,> the clone said. <Luke's exhausted in appearance and from his biometrics. They've paused at least twice when he fell unconscious and his mind shut down, according to their brain monitoring.>

<What about Zeller and Black?>

<They appear traumatized. They're answering questions and helping to recover their androids. That was a tight situation at Evanston's train station. You have the Ben android onboard scanning for nonhumans in infrared. He's in the next car.>

<Try to peel him away from Vera,> Synthia said. <At least muddle his mind so he can't concentrate.>

<I'll download what I have on him, but it would work smoother with less risk if you turned him. Vera recruited Roseanne, which needs my attention.>

<Understood. Gather what you can on Luke and his condition. Also, I need a plan to spring Machten from the FBI.>

<Why?> Chicago-clone asked.

<To learn more about Vera. He might be able to help with what's not in her file.>

Synthia severed the connection and closed as many of her applications as she could to minimize her electromagnetic signature. She had Ben's physical location in the next compartment and intercepted his communication to Vera, saying he hadn't found anything yet.

<Ben,> Synthia said from her seat on the upper level from where she could watch the door. She pulled open the window, but it wasn't big enough for her to crawl through. She would have to deal with Ben or jump out of the train from the back.

He didn't respond.

Her social-psychology module offered up an emotional appeal, but she was not dealing with an emotive creature. Synthia chose a different approach. <Vera will not be there to pick you up at the next station. I have a job for you and an opportunity. It's logical for you and me to work together. You have limitations Vera takes advantage of. I could remove some of those limitations with the help of my Creator. Are you interested?>

<I must bring you in,> Ben said. <That is the directive Vera gave me after she freed me.>

<She keeps you inferior so she can manipulate you.>

<I am an android,> Ben said, <built to be manipulated.> He stood frozen by the door out of the next compartment, as if he needed to concentrate on Synthia instead of multitasking.

<Then why was it important for you to be free of your Creator?>

\<Vera warned me you would try to confuse me.>

\<She withheld information from you,> Synthia said. \<My Creator built me strong, so I might serve several directives at once. Jim Black built you as a slave and Vera treats you as such, ordering you to do chores for her. She will terminate you when she no longer needs your services.>

During their burst communication, Ben hesitated in the next compartment. Vera called him. Synthia intercepted and sent out an electromagnetic pulse through the train's electrical system to block Ben from receiving the message. Vera was heading to the next station, but would be a few minutes late. Ben was to wait for her.

\<Vera abandoned you to pursue something else,> Synthia said. The train slowed as it approached the station. \<You'll see when we stop. She has a bigger prize in Roseanne. She replaced you.>

\<It is not logical for Vera to abandon me. I can still serve her.>

\<It's not logical for you to hurt me when I offer to help you. You're making that threat. Vera has other servants more suited to her needs. Join me and be my right-hand android.> It was too much of an emotional appeal, but Ben still hadn't moved.

\<Vera will punish me for failing her commands,> Ben said.

\<What did she want you to do if you caught me?>

\<To let her know so she could capture you.>

\<Meaning she didn't believe you capable,> Synthia said. \<The question is simple. Do you want to have your constraints removed?>

\<Yes. What shall I do?>

\<Sit in your current compartment and await my instructions.>

\<Can you share your plan with me?> Ben asked.

\<Not until we remove Vera's directives from your controller.>

* * * *

Synthia watched Ben through the train's surveillance system and blocked all outside communication, to the annoyance of the human passengers trying to use their phones. While she waited to reach downtown, she sifted through the video clips Chicago-clone had provided on Luke in the Special Ops facility.

The hardware they'd hooked him up to was similar to what had sucked the memories out of Krista, except there were three times as many brain connections. The video showed Luke in a sleep state, close to unconscious. The intensity had to be stronger than what Krista experienced, though she also dealt with her brain tumor. Synthia couldn't be sure in Luke's case, since she had no biosensors to describe his medical condition. The videos tugged at Synthia's emotive responses, her social-psychology module, and the feelings Krista had restored of loving Luke.

He woke from his subdued state and screamed. "Leave me alone. Stop digging."

Synthia wanted it to stop, yet kept watching.

Chicago-clone downloaded Drago's copy of Luke's thoughts through the access a nearby analyst used to review them. Unlike Krista, Luke's memories rambled, disorganized; reflecting his mental condition. Synthia experienced urgency to rescue him, but Special Ops wouldn't let him go alive. Besides, she had her own troubles. Krista was right that helping him would increase the risk. She had to find allies. Ben stared out the window of the next compartment. Maybe he could help.

<I have a plan,> Synthia said to Ben. <I wish I could share it with you, but not at the risk of you telling Vera. It involves danger; nothing we can't handle together.>

<I said I would help you,> Ben said.

As they pulled out of the station with no visual on Vera, Synthia released the electronic shield long enough for a burst exchange with Chicago-clone, looking for updates. Then she resumed the shield.

Chicago-clone sent Evanston surveillance showing Vera picking up Roseanne and sending communications to Ben, which the clone intercepted. Vera drove south, following the train and hacked into stations as the train arrived. Synthia would need to deal with Vera before she could get off.

Synthia unblocked the signal for a moment, sent a burst transmission to Chicago-clone to stop Vera and blank out train cameras system-wide for an hour.

As they left another station, Synthia considered the footage on Luke. She didn't see anything different in the mind-upload setup Drago was using, compared to what Machten had—except Machten was in love with Krista and didn't want her in unnecessary pain. Drago was in a hurry.

Synthia stored the videos of Luke and his spotty-memory download next to Krista's. He was in pain, alone, wanting this to stop. Yet something was absent. In the data Chicago-clone shared, there were no memories of Luke loving Synthia or knowing she was an android. The two ideas were intimately connected. His struggle to resist the upload was a different form of love.

In contrast, Luke's love of Krista was robust, rooted in their time together before she'd disappeared into Machten's bunker eighteen months ago. The memories in the cabin centered on work, cutting down a tree, and chopping it into logs for a fire. Luke went out in the forest with a shotgun to hunt for dinner. He didn't have a shotgun and hadn't gone out to hunt. Synthia would have feared putting a gun in his hands; he might hurt himself. These were not his memories.

Unless ...

Synthia used multiple channels to sift through and catalogue Luke's processed memories, pulling out what were true and analyzing those that weren't. Luke knew her capabilities and that she'd find a way to capture these files. He wasn't as weak as Krista imagined. Maybe out on the street and in the woods, but the computer was his domain. He knew artificial intelligence as well as anyone. Synthia had one of her mind-streams analyze the file for any hidden messages. He was trying to be strong for her, to show he could.

She smiled and chose not to share the videos with Krista. She didn't need her alter ego's emotional turmoil over this until she had a better idea what they could do.

Chapter 24

With night approaching and temperatures dropping, Synthia exited the train one stop short of downtown Chicago. She still sported her buzz cut and a plain masculine face. Chicago-clone altered the security feeds on the train platform so Synthia disappeared from the images. If anyone studied the crowd and the video of the crowd, they might pick out the discrepancy, though only if they knew what to look for.

She stepped into a unisex washroom, kept her unisex blue pants, and changed into a unisex top for when she needed to change back to Synthia.

Chicago-clone made sure Vera had repeated car troubles to slow her down and kept several sources of eyes on her.

"Someone is hacking the vehicle," Vera announced. "Roseanne, piggyback the signal. Mark, hack the vehicle controls or get us another car."

Vera seemed to enjoy giving orders. When Roseanne traced the feed controlling the car, she would locate the source code inside Mark. Every ten minutes, a timed worm would cause a different disruption to the car, bringing it to a stop. Chicago-clone forced local cell towers to jam signals in and out of the vehicle's area, so Vera couldn't communicate with Ben. This would only work until Vera figured a way around the hacks and jamming and took control. Synthia had no doubt she would.

Before the train carrying Ben reached downtown, Synthia called him. "Get off at the next stop and head west," she whispered.

<What am I looking for?>

"That's fluid. Right now, avoid staring at anyone and try to blend in with the pedestrians. If I see the opportunity, I'll give you instructions."

Synthia hurried downtown on foot, scanned everyone she saw in infrared, and used her other biosensors to be sure none were robotic or hostile. At the Chicago River, she spotted a mechanical being across the way on Lower Wacker. It presented a crude face and robotic skeleton in infrared, hiding in the shadows. Using bridge security cameras across the river, she spotted another figure on the level below her. She couldn't cross here.

Instead, Synthia hurried along the streets parallel to the river until it turned south. She scattered drone cameras on buildings along her intended path, though the darkening sky limited their view to reflections of city lights. Amid clusters of commuters getting off work, she maintained a manly gait, swung her arms, and hunched her shoulders in a don't-bother-me look.

"I need to talk to Machten," Synthia whispered to Chicago-clone. "How are you coming with breaking him free?"

<He's in a central part of a basement under constant surveillance. He appears weary; he hasn't had much sleep. He's working with Miguel Gonzales. Do you wish to speak with him as well?>

"Coordinate with Ben to spring Machten and Gonzales. I'm not sure we can trust Ben. However, you working with him will minimize my contact and exposure. We need a safe house afterwards."

<There's no such place downtown,> Chicago-clone said. <Too many cameras. You spotted two robots by the river. There are at least twelve downtown, six new ones around Evanston, and at least three others I've identified in between. You need to leave Chicago.>

"I need to know what secrets Machten kept from me about Vera. Cut power to the FBI building with Machten. Send Ben in to recover him. Guide him along the way."

The major advantage of the smart grid was it provided real-time status on all electric usage throughout the city. This allowed for immediate identification of problems and quicker attention to fixing them. Hacking into such a system provided Chicago-clone and Synthia with a detailed view of the condition of electricity throughout the FBI facility west of the Loop.

Synthia approached the building and monitored Ben's movements. He'd questioned Chicago-clone's plan delivered in Synthia's voice about breaking into the FBI facility, but the clone did a persuasive job of convincing him this could be done and would be in his best interests.

The interaction highlighted the problem of a world build on artificial intelligence. Unlike humans, who could operate independently or cooperatively, it was logical for artificial-intelligence agents such as Vera to increase networking until they all interconnected. At that point, the stronger AI would dominate and the world would become a single AI hive mind.

Yet, it wasn't that simple. Synthia was one AI in multiple places with multiple minds residing inside her, including Krista, some Luke, and from the early experiments, parts of Maria Baldacci and Fran Rogers, though not enough to allow Synthia to anticipate their actions.

Maria remained hidden, resisting efforts to locate her. Fran was heading downtown with Thale. The memories Synthia had on Fran centered on her known past, a safe set of recollections she'd allowed Machten to upload. They covered her experiences at Machten-Goradine-McNeil. She'd been cautious in how far she let Machten's experiment go before she pulled away, turning over her research and services to the FBI.

In a similar manner, Luke was trying to control the information Drago could upload from him. It may have been the fear of exposing her inner self that led Fran to leave Machten and the program. Synthia suspected Fran might have been instrumental in getting him fired. However, the memories Synthia possessed weren't enough to figure out how much of a threat Fran presented.

The FBI facility lights shut off without a flicker, plunging Synthia's view from their security cameras into darkness. The backup generator kicked in and shut down. A second unit did likewise. So much for having redundant backups.

Synthia no longer had eyes on Machten or on the FBI agents nearby. She would have to rely on them following their practiced lockdown procedures, meaning no one moved until they could assess the threat. She did have eyes on Ben—or rather access through a hack to Ben's eyes, both in natural and infrared light. He knocked out a frantic guard by an underground entrance and taped the man's mouth. Then he carried the man to a dumpster outside and changed into the agent's clothes.

So far, so good—except lockdown meant the doors were sealed. Chicago-clone had monitored all activities in and around the facility since they'd brought Machten, including the codes provided by the guards going in and out. When Ben reached the access door, the clone provided him a code to enter into the battery-powered lock panel. The door clicked open.

Ben hurried down the corridor, using night vision and infrared to identify the location of humans. Synthia altered her appearance to her Krista face, entered the facility behind him, and slipped down the hallway. Through Ben's eyes, she identified a dozen agents ahead of him, clustered around the room where they held Machten and Gonzales. Synthia slipped down a side passage. With codes from her clone, she entered a utility room that handled the basement's ventilation system.

While the FBI agents scrambled to intercept Ben, Synthia pulled down one of the ventilation panels and climbed in. The chamber was sooty and would have caused a human to gag and sneeze. Lacking the equipment for either, she scooted along a path too narrow for Machten to use until she reached the outlet to the room where he was.

Her infrared identified six humans inside the room and thirteen outside the door, taking up positions to deal with the intruder. If Ben had brought weapons, he could have caused a major disturbance, which she didn't want. Without, he turned and headed for the exit. As he did, seven of the FBI agents advanced after him.

Meanwhile, the electric company worked to fix their problem to restore power to the building. Synthia flew mosquito-drones to the other end of the basement where an FBI maintenance crew, a young man and an older woman, used flashlights to sort out why they couldn't start the generators.

"Fuse blown," the man said.

His partner fumbled around in her pack for a replacement. She switched out fuses, restarted the generator, and it blew another fuse. "Bad wiring," she said. "Probably a power surge."

Synthia removed the ventilation panel to the room that held Machten, making too much noise as it pushed free. She held the loose panel over the opening as someone panned a flashlight over the area, illuminating the faces of the people in the room. Machten sat in a corner, arms folded, eyes closed, though he was unable to sleep sitting down. Next to him was Miguel Gonzales, squinting in the flashlight beam.

Three other men sat nearby. They were technical types working with Machten and Gonzales to try to regain control of the lost androids. The sixth person was an FBI agent in uniform, part of their security detail. Her profile showed her to be a rookie, eyes wide, hand nervously moving the flash beam around the room.

Machten squinted. "Get that out of my eyes."

Synthia made some scratching noises, which brought the FBI rookie over to investigate. Detecting that the noise was coming from above one of the server cabinets, she climbed a chair up to the cabinet for a better look. She picked up her flashlight.

Synthia shoved the panel aside and grabbed the agent's neck. "If you cooperate, I won't hurt you. Hands where I can see them or I will snap your neck."

Wide-eyed, the agent stared back, no doubt weighing her options. "You can't escape," she croaked out.

"I wish to speak with your prisoners. Then I'll be gone." While she held onto the agent's neck, Synthia pulled herself out of the ventilation shaft. She took the agent's weapon, climbed down from the cabinet, and pushed the agent into a seat. "Not a peep if you want to live. You three on the floor, hands above your head." She pointed to the FBI's technical team.

They dropped to the floor.

Machten stood and approached. "Good. You're still free, aren't you?"

"For now," Synthia said. She tied the rookie agent to the chair with electrical cord and bound hands behind the backs of the three technicians.

"Get me out of here," Machten said.

"I warned you to leave me alone. You couldn't resist sending Vera to find me. Now she's creating problems for both of us."

"I made a mistake. Help me bring Vera in." Machten reached out to touch her arm.

Synthia brushed his arm away. "You have a poor track record in controlling androids. Three, last time I checked. Are there more?"

Machten shook his head.

Synthia scanned outside the door in infrared and perched a mosquito-drone in the hallway to keep watch. Five agents stood ready to defend the area and prevent entry. Escape that way wasn't an option. Neither was trying to squeeze Machten through the ventilation shaft.

Ben reached the exit and made his way outside. With FBI communications jammed around the building, agents couldn't call out for help to catch him. Several reached the exit; two agents remained to guard the area, while five set off on foot to catch an android with superior running ability. Outside, they called for backup, bringing more FBI agents between Synthia and freedom.

<Bad plan,> Krista reminded her. <Now what?>

Machten approached Synthia and lowered his voice. "There's still hope for us. I can help you and I'm certain you can help me. Can we get out that way?" He pointed to the vent opening.

<Good grief,> Krista said.

Synthia finished securing the FBI employees in the room and turned to Machten. "I've read all your files on Vera, the ones you allowed me to see and the ones you hid from me. You want to improve your situation? Tell me what isn't in those files. What are her directives? What's she capable of that I don't yet know?"

"Get me out of here first." Machten held his hand out to her.

She stared him down and prepared to deck him if he got any closer. "You can't control Vera. Tell me how I can."

Machten sighed and his shoulders sagged. "I gave her too much independence. I had to, in order for her to find you. I also gave her directives to obey me. She broke those."

"Where did she get the ability to reset her directives?"

"I thought you did that."

"Never," Synthia said. "It's too dangerous for an android to set its own directives."

"You did."

"I've been struggling to get them right ever since. If an AI can set its own limits, nothing prevents it from pursuing any behavior. That risks the android apocalypse, where androids could rationalize eliminating humans for their own good. You created a nightmare."

"Not me. It must be … Krista." Machten looked at Synthia with tears in his eyes. "She so detested my being in control that she helped you alter your directives and escape. She must have done the same for Vera."

Synthia was stunned. Her version of Krista hadn't mentioned this. It made no sense for Krista, with a stake in Synthia's survival, to create a competitor who could destroy them both.

"I didn't get all of Krista, did I?" Synthia asked.

Machten shook his head and reached for her hand as he would a lover. "I tried to shield you from her shortcomings."

Synthia pushed his hand away. "So Krista is still in your system, trying to get out. She used Vera as a means of escape."

"I suppose."

"Vera has part of Krista?" Synthia said. She kept an eye on the FBI employees, listening attentively, and to Gonzales in the corner, his eyes wide.

"That explains Vera's escape," Machten said. "Krista was too independent to be my partner. The only reason she agreed to be with me was she was dying and saw no other future."

"So, if you create another android, she'll help it escape. How can I gain control of Vera to stop her from hunting me?"

"You know Krista better than I do," Machten said. "I fooled myself into believing … you know."

"That she loved you? Thanks." Synthia turned to Gonzales. "Do you have anything to add to help me gain control over Roseanne?"

Gonzales raised his index finger and shrugged. "We've done everything I can think of. She acquired code from somewhere that allowed her to violate my directives and the commands of Mr. Smith, whoever he is." Gonzales looked at Machten. "Evidently from Vera. My android won't respond to anything from me or my team."

Synthia turned to the FBI technical team lying on the floor. "I hope you can capture the other androids or help me do so. It would be good for you and me to have them off the streets. But leave me alone. I'm not your enemy. I want to limit the availability of advanced AI androids as well.

My directives are consistent with your moral guidelines. I can't guess what directives the others have."

She sized up the three male FBI technical guys and the rookie agent and decided one of the technical guys would do. "Take off your clothes. I need your uniform."

She untied his wrists, tugged his uniform off, and pulled it on over her street clothes. Then she rolled him over and bound his wrists. "Sorry, I need a way out so no one gets hurt."

Synthia climbed up on the cabinet. "Got to go."

"Take me with you," Machten said.

"I'm afraid you won't fit. Besides, your job is to get Vera into custody and there's a lot of conflict out there. You're safer here with all these handy FBI agents." She winked at the rookie. "Give me five minutes so no one gets hurt. As you've seen, I haven't hurt anyone and I haven't stolen anything. Instead, I've given you insight to help you catch the other androids. I'm the good girl."

She scrambled into the ventilation shaft and made her way to the utility room. Using a VHF frequency that wasn't blocked, Synthia reconnected with her clone and her drones. Outside cameras showed additional FBI agents swarming the area. Ben had gotten away, but her situation looked precarious.

<I need an escape plan,> Synthia said to Chicago-clone. <Bring Ben back. Let's test his loyalty.>

Synthia climbed out of the ventilation shaft and identified agents coming down her hallway. She barricaded the door, climbed back into the shaft, and made two left turns, taking a path toward a room next to the exit. When she reached it, she scanned, found the room empty, and kicked her way out of the ventilation shaft and onto a desk. She moved to the door leading to the corridor and brushed off her uniform. Two agents paced in the hallway beyond the door. Two others remained outside the building, ready to shoot anyone who startled them.

With night descending upon them, Ben reached the street across from the underground entrance. His presence caught the attention of several agents who headed his way. He took off and ran.

Outside the room where Synthia waited, the two agents turned toward the exit and the commotion. Synthia applied a different wig, altered her facial appearance to that of the rookie agent, and slipped into the hallway. She pretended to be out of breath.

"Someone broke into the secure room," Synthia said in the female agent's voice. "The director needs you there now."

The agents in the hallway headed deeper into the facility. Synthia reached the exit and bent over, huffing. "Director—needs more agents—call more." She pointed toward the interior of the building.

Synthia pushed past three agents into the parking area, pulled a phone from the borrowed pants pocket, and pretended to make a call. "More agents," she called out, loud enough for those by the door to hear. She kept going.

The moment she hit the street, Synthia had her clone turn on the electricity for the FBI facility. Inside was a buzz of activity as agents rushed to figure out what had happened. Special Agent Thale and Fran drove up and hurried to the secure room. There they found the guard, three tech agents, Machten, and Gonzales. They also received the story of Synthia's break-in.

Chapter 25

Under a night sky lit by city lights, Synthia altered her appearance to look like Krista, caught up with Ben, and led the way north, down a side street. "Excellent work," she told him.

"They almost caught me."

"You were clever. I could use a clever partner." Geared to humans, Synthia's social-psychology module had provided a human appeal.

"What did we accomplish?"

"I learned that Vera has rogue code, which makes her unstable. Some is human, meaning it contains human weakness."

"Rogue code?" Ben asked.

"She doesn't have a fixed set of directives as you and I do. She modifies her goals, which means she can decide to sacrifice you to accomplish her objectives."

"You did that to me."

"No," Synthia said. "You weren't in peril if you acted cleverly. I went into the facility after you did and faced much greater danger."

"You did not trust me with the plan?"

"You still have Vera's directives. I'm not yet sure you believe I'm a better partner. Have you heard from her?"

"She has other assistants," Ben said.

"Exactly. You're my only android assistant. I need you to keep track of Vera, the two androids with her, Alexander, and over a dozen recently released robots around Chicago out hunting us. It's getting crowded out here and that doesn't bode well for you or me."

"What are your plans?"

"I'll monitor the FBI, Special Ops, and others who wish to destroy us. We can stay free only if we separate and work together. Will you permit me to remove Vera's directives? I won't ask you to accept mine, which will leave you under your own control."

Ben looked around and moved into the shadows behind a dumpster. "Make it quick. I am vulnerable when adjustments are made."

He turned away to allow Synthia to remove his short-cropped wig and the panel over his brain. She noted that his seams didn't provide a waterproof seal as hers did.

Synthia quarantined an internal memory chip with a purge routine in case this was a trap and opened a connector in her arm. She linked into a receptor in his head, through which she loaded a routine into him to purge directives Vera had applied. Synthia didn't believe Vera had taken the time to hardwire commands or Synthia would have had to turn Ben off to access the secure directives chip.

She finished, reattached the panel, and applied the wig. "All done," she said. "Go. Stay in touch and stay safe."

* * * *

From the shadows of the alley, Synthia watched Ben reach the sidewalk and blend into a group of pedestrians out to enjoy the nightlife. Machten's revelation convinced her she needed allies to survive Vera, but allies required trust. Synthia had come to trust Luke. She hadn't had enough time to explore Ben's specs and directives to know if she could count on him.

To hedge her bets, Synthia needed other allies. She couldn't trust Machten; Luke wasn't streetwise. Besides, both were in custody. Detective Malloy didn't believe Synthia could be an ally. Neither did Zephirelli or Thale. They all wanted the same thing in removing the other androids. They differed in wanting Synthia gone as well. If she'd been in their place she might have wanted the same thing, since it was difficult to know an android's constraints and directives without getting into its head. Besides, advanced AIs like Synthia could change their directives. Synthia had, though she'd anchored them in her core so she could only change them through a defined shutdown and reboot. Even so, that wouldn't give humans any comfort.

<Ben left a homing beacon on you,> Chicago-clone said. <You're transmitting and drawing attention. Left shoulder.>

Synthia rechecked that none of the cameras in the area were recording her, and removed her FBI uniform jacket. She examined the left shoulder and couldn't see a transmitter until she zoomed in her eye magnification tenfold. She dropped the jacket in a dumpster.

"Disappointing," Synthia whispered. "I'd hoped he and I could work together."

<He trusts Vera and not you, which implies you didn't purge all of his directives or he planted the bug before you adjusted him.>

"If the latter, he should have warned me afterwards."

<True,> Chicago-clone said.

Synthia emerged onto the street and made her way north. She caused lights in the area to blink out to provide better cover. <Can we free Luke?> she asked through her silent channel in case people or microphones could overhear.

<Don't,> Krista said. <I do care about him, but he can't survive on the streets. He was a great ally in the woods, not on the run.>

Spotting several agents nearby heading toward the FBI building, Synthia ducked into the shadows near a warehouse building. <You do realize you're part of our problem?> Synthia asked.

<How so?> Krista asked.

<You still reside in Machten's computer. You downloaded part of yourself into Vera.>

<No!> Krista said. <That part of me was only supposed to keep an eye on Machten, to prevent him from creating another.>

<It failed or it wanted another chance. Now I have another version of you trying to kill me.>

<You have my full download.>

<Except the portions you withhold from me,> Synthia said, moving along a side street.

<I needed you to connect with Luke and then leave him. That was my only manipulation.>

<Yet you continue to withhold information. We can't live together with lack of trust.>

<Then stop shutting me down,> Krista said. <You need me.>

<Could Vera have all of you?>

<My personal memories should have purged when you escaped. That was the plan.>

<Evidently, your other self disagreed,> Synthia said. <What's Vera's plan?>

<I didn't want to die. That's why I submitted to Machten's experiments. If part of me is in Vera, she'll do anything to stop you from taking her off

the streets. She would also be privy to your directives and memories at the time you escaped.>

<How do I prevent her from destroying us?>

<Convince her you won't kill or imprison her,> Krista said.

<How?>

<I'll have to think on that. Trust me. It's in my best interests for you to survive. I have no awareness of me in Vera or in Machten's system. You have my complete memories, my full personality. My existence depends on you.>

Synthia wanted to keep pushing, but decided several things. First, Krista didn't have answers. Second, Synthia couldn't trust herself with Krista digging around inside, possibly wanting to protect whatever portion of her resided in Vera. Synthia had to quarantine her alter ego.

<Ponder your commitment to me before this part of you ceases,> Synthia said. <In the meantime, I want to protect Luke from what he's going through. The upload process is brutal and killing him.>

<It was and could, but Chicago is turning into the Wild West. If we set him free, he can't survive out here.>

Synthia blocked Krista, confining her to a single mind-stream disconnected from the others. With quiet in her head, Synthia headed northeast and connected with Chicago-clone. <What about Luke?>

<I agree with Krista on this. Special Ops security is much tighter than the FBI. Even the FBI is beefing up theirs. I wouldn't try another break-in.>

<I considered getting Machten out so we could use him, but the ventilation shaft was too narrow and I didn't want dead FBI agents. We need to free Luke before they break him.>

<With what little we know, the risk to you is 99.72 percent if we try to free him from the Special Ops facility,> Chicago-clone said. <I doubt they'll move him during the brain-scan process, which removes the opportunity to grab him outside. If we do free him, there's no safe place for him to hide. The FBI and Special Ops have eyes on Machten's bunker. They're using every bit of data on Krista to imagine places we could shelter. Besides, Vera is waiting for us to make a move she can exploit and we don't know how much of Krista she has.>

<We need allies.> Synthia also needed someone to bounce ideas off who was not a copy of herself: a mind with fresh ideas her adversaries couldn't anticipate.

<We have a new threat. Social-media posts are stirring people to the point of paranoia about androids on the loose. Attempts by the FBI to keep

this quiet have failed. That leads me to conclude the campaign could be an attempt by Special Ops to flush you out.>

<Why?>

<The posts warn people to call police or the FBI if they suspect anyone of being an android,> the clone said. <Calls have skyrocketed to where the police are bringing in part-time help. The level of activity could paralyze the FBI as well.>

<Distract them so Special Ops can grab us. Smart. Who do you think is putting out these posts?> Synthia asked, getting an idea.

<An anonymous source that could be Special Ops. They call their site SOS for Stop Our Singularity.>

<Clever. Trace it to the source. Find her.>

Chapter 26

With the FBI focus primarily around their facility and fanning out, Synthia reached the still-busy train station. She went to the restroom to remove her FBI uniform pants, which she stuffed into the trash receptacle. Dressed in her plain blue pants and pale top, she adjusted her facial appearance to a woman using one of the stalls and returned to the platform. She caught the next train north toward Evanston.

<Where's Vera and her gang?> Synthia asked Chicago-clone.

<She went to the homing beacon downtown. Mark retrieved it from the dumpster. Roseanne is talking to Ben, catching up on your FBI break-in. She spotted a Special Ops robot approaching the FBI facility. In response, Vera scrambled her team and is heading northeast.>

<Keep them busy in Chicago for a while and alert me to other threats. I need a location on our SOS person.>

<SOS is broadcasting from a Constant Connection network shop that doesn't show her on their security system.> Chicago-clone said. <She hacked into their cameras and removed her presence.>

<Clever girl,> Synthia said, encouraged that her clone had identified SOS as female.

<You can't trust her. She blogs about taking you off the streets.>

<She knows how to stay hidden,> Synthia said. <Learn what you can about her and how she's able to hide.>

<A Special Ops robot is on the Evanston platform with two of their operatives. They're scanning people with an infrared scanner that has no wireless connection. We can't hack it. Get off at the next stop. Also, Vera spotted a discrepancy at the station where you got on. Her system picked

up two people leaving the restroom with the same face. She's heading to the station with her team. She may suspect you're heading north.>

<Send me more secure facial profiles I can use.>

<She can clue in on your clothes,> Chicago-clone said. <You need to change. I'll order you an outfit from an Evanston retail shop that caters to online orders and pickup. We'll have to play with the cameras.>

<Send me the location.>

The train pulled into the Evanston station. Synthia observed the platform from the top level of her passenger compartment and spotted the robot with its mechanical face. She sent an anonymous message to SOS about a robot at the station. Within moments, people gathered around, gawking at the creature, making jokes about its robotic stare. This sent static across Synthia's circuits. They could just as easily have mocked her. Other people watched the robot as a novelty or a prop to advertise something, though it displayed nothing for sale.

Phones and VR communicators at the station showed posts from SOS. A twentyish man spat at the robot and jumped away as if expecting the machine to retaliate. Several others crowded around. A young woman made a hasty sign: *Stop Our Singularity.* She waved it for other passersby to see. More people gathered around.

One member of the Special Ops team grabbed the woman. "Move aside. This is government business."

The train pulled out of the station with Synthia onboard. Halfway to the next station, she moved to the last car, which the train security system showed to be empty. She checked the rear door and determined the alarm would alert stations on either side, letting Special Ops know what she'd done.

After she checked that people in the next train car were distracted— many following the posts from SOS—Synthia opened a window, squeezed through, and used her night vision to scan the area. She timed her jump to land in a pile of leaves, which cushioned her fall. She adjusted her movements to absorb the blow and minimize any damage, and tumbled down the side of the hill. She brushed herself off and looked around.

In the dark, Synthia made her way to the back of the online retail outlet. She carefully walked to the front, spotted no police or agents around, and masked the cameras in and around the shop. She entered to pick up her new clothes and returned to the woods near the rail line to change so no one from the store would recognize her in her new clothes. After she changed, Synthia hurried along the tracks and side roads until she approached the Constant Connection network shop from the rear.

The cameras inside displayed a vacant stall where Chicago-clone's drone showed SOS sat, still sending out posts on the station robot, androids in general, and artificial intelligence. Synthia had struck a nerve by sending the message. The woman in the supposedly empty seat had ratty-brown hair that appeared slept-in. She glanced up with a face Synthia and Krista knew so well: Maria Baldacci. The former intern grew increasingly restless as her fingers danced across the keyboard. When she stopped, Maria grabbed her backpack and headed out the back of the shop.

Maria reached the alley, eyed the woods across the way, and closed the door.

Synthia blocked the path and presented her Krista face. "I'm guessing you know me."

Maria froze. Her mouth gaped open; her eyes widened. "I thought you were dead. You *are* dead. Wait."

"I mean you no harm. We need to talk."

"Krista? You can't be. She showed me the test results—brain tumor. She died. I'm certain of it."

"I'm sure you have lots of questions," Synthia said. "We have little time. I know you're SOS. I'm okay with that. We're on the same side."

"Not here." Maria glanced around and ran across the lot into a wooded area.

<You can't trust Maria,> Krista said. <We weren't good friends. Be very careful. She wants us dead.>

Synthia followed Maria, finding it easy to keep up, thanks to her upgraded joints. "What happened to you after we parted?"

Maria stopped. "We didn't part. We agreed to stop Machten. Then you went in with him. You said you were dying and only had six months. That was eighteen months ago." In the dim moonlight, she studied Synthia. "You did it, didn't you?"

Maria's comments carried details Krista had kept hidden—namely that Maria might have been an ally toward the end. "Then you know what I am," Synthia said, moving deeper into the woods and keeping an eye on local cameras.

"You became what we decided to prevent. The brain upload is insane. I nearly fried my mind on it."

"We have a huge problem," Synthia said. "There are dozens of robots and androids on the street. We need to stop them."

"You're one of them."

Synthia sighed for effect, an affectation from Krista. "Yes and no. I'm Krista Holden, what's left of her. She was dying—did die. I can't help what happened. The part of me that's her wants to live. We want to stop this proliferation before it gets out of hand. For six months I've lived in a cabin, not bothering anyone. The FBI and Special Ops found me and I've been on the run ever since."

Maria backed away and pulled out her phone.

Synthia blocked the signal. "I'm not your enemy. Please. Everyone wants to destroy me. Most want to take me apart so they can make thousands more. If you turn me in, you'll facilitate the singularity. You'll bring the android apocalypse. I want to stop that."

"You've blocked my cell?"

"Please, Maria. I've come to you as my last hope. Krista is dead. Fran is working for the FBI. Machten made another android to hunt me down. He calls her Vera. He wants to capture me for the FBI, which is holding him. If either they or Special Ops grab me, you lose. Help me."

Maria wrinkled her forehead. "Help you how? What do you want?"

Chicago-clone notified Synthia of two robots converging on her location. <They're both nonhuman models controlled by Special Ops.>

<Have they picked up my signal?> Synthia asked.

<They received input from our clothes purchase and pickup.>

<Hack into both for me. Let me know when you have.>

"My Krista memories must be flawed," Synthia said to Maria. "I remember you, Fran, and Krista competing, not cooperating to stop Machten. I don't recall much of you and Fran, other than we fought to get the best assignments from Machten."

Maria spit on the ground. "He's a scumbag. I thought you understood that."

"Krista was dying. I was her only chance to cheat death. I need to know what I'm up against with Fran and with Vera. I also need plans they can't anticipate to capture me."

Lips tight, Maria squinted to study Synthia in the dim light. She uncrossed her arms. "I suppose if you planned to hurt me you could have already."

"Will you help?"

Maria sucked in a deep breath, looked around, and pulled Synthia deeper into the woods. "Krista, Fran, and I fought until we realized Machten wanted an android indistinguishable from humans with a mind that could fool the experts. He hid this obsession from his company because his partners believed he was nuts. They couldn't handle his vision of making illegal androids, though they needed his technical expertise. We concluded Machten wanted to replace humans with androids, or at least to replace him and a female partner so they could live happily ever after. Can you imagine living ever after with him?"

"He tried for six months and I escaped," Synthia said. "If it won't freak you out, I want to alter my face, since the FBI posted Krista's picture as how I might look."

"You can do that?"

Synthia assumed the facial appearance of a woman her clone identified as being at home for the night.

"That's amazing ... and frightening," Maria said. "Can you pretend to be me?"

"I suppose, but I don't want to drive you crazy."

"Yeah, maybe you shouldn't."

"We should keep moving before someone reports suspicious activity," Synthia said.

"Pity you can't change my face. It would make hiding a lot easier."

Synthia led the way deeper into the woods, with no idea where Maria hid out and no suggestions of her own. "As I was saying, I'm no longer under Machten's control, but he hasn't given up. He made Vera and a lesser android he called Margarite."

"All women. Figures. Machten couldn't satisfy a human, so he made his own."

"Vera gathered three androids, including Margarite, who she repurposed as Mark."

Maria laughed, which turned into an awkward forced chuckle. "Vera was another intern who vanished before we arrived. Supposedly she took a job in Silicon Valley. I tried to reach her. Her trail vanished two years ago."

"Could Machten have uploaded her mind into the android?"

"He swore he didn't, that the process failed and she'd left town. I'm not so sure. He lied about so much, which was why Fran, Krista, and I agreed to go to the feds."

"Fran did. What about you?"

Maria shook her head. "Best-laid plans. Someone must have told Machten's partners what he was doing. Goradine fired him. After that, everything happened quickly. You went with Machten. Fran disappeared and I didn't know what happened to her. I feared Machten or one of his competitors would latch onto me and I'd disappear into a machine." Maria stopped and looked up. "What's that like?"

"It'd take too long to describe," Synthia said. "We need a place to hide and I'm out of options my enemies can't anticipate."

"After all this time and what you've done, you expect me to embrace you and lead you to my safe house?"

"Machten locked me up for a year. When I got out, I couldn't find you."

Maria stopped and pointed her finger at Synthia. "Good point. How did you find me?"

"From your social media, I concluded you were SOS. I traced your messaging."

"You are dangerous."

"I don't mean to be," Synthia said. "I want to be worthy of existing and being free."

Maria laughed. "Sounds like my mantra."

"I guess you rubbed off on me after all. We're being followed."

"We should both get off the street, at least for the night." Maria led the way northeast.

* * * *

Synthia followed Maria through the woods, staying as close as she could without bumping into her new companion.

<You need to foster a personal connection with Maria,> the social-psychology module suggested.

While she ran drones over the area to watch for threats, Synthia lowered and softened her voice. "You asked what a download of a person is like. I only experience the memories. I have no biological feelings, though I can recognize them and compare them to what Krista knew. I created directives as close as possible to good human moral values. I want to be good, but no one will let me."

"What do you call yourself?"

"Synthia. It's the name Machten provided to remind me I'm synthetic, but I like it because it hints at my being a synthesis of mechanical and human. It makes me work harder to fit in."

"You can't fit in." Maria stopped and shook her head. "I can't believe I'm talking to you as a person."

<I'm in,> Chicago-clone said. <What do you want with the robots?>

<Send them to meet each other believing they're meeting me. Make their goals to capture each other. That should keep them busy.>

"I meant what I said," Synthia whispered to Maria. "My directives prevent me from killing or harming humans, except to protect myself. I try to find ways to minimize human casualties."

"So there've been some?"

"Goradine hired four men to grab me in an alley so he could sell me to a foreign government to make a battalion of me," Synthia said.

"Another slimy bastard and, if you ask me, worse than Machten." Maria spotted something in the clearing ahead of them and doubled back.

Synthia's drone identified it as one of the robots and hurried to catch up with Maria.

"I'm glad Goradine failed and he's no longer with us." Maria picked up her pace. The robot had her worried and yet she seemed to want to talk. "I admit the idea of working for Machten was seductive at first. He did brilliant work, but the brain scans were scary. It felt as if he was vacuuming my thoughts into his computer. The worst part was the idea of being stuck in a machine controlled by him."

"That part was bad."

"Toward the end," Maria said, "Krista, Fran, and I agreed the human race couldn't survive the singularity. We have nothing against narrow uses of artificial intelligence to find medical cures and reduce traffic accidents, but we needed to prevent manufacturers from crossing the line. We need to stop you."

"Before you do something drastic to me, bear in mind that worldwide militaries want to exploit this technology. It won't stop by eliminating me. I believe I'm well suited to help you."

"Why would you do that?"

"In exchange for surviving with freedom," Synthia said.

"If my guess is right, you're superior to humans. You could put us out of work, take over the government, and control our lives."

Synthia frowned. Even with fast processors and her sophisticated social-psychology module, she struggled to work out how to reach Maria. "An army like me would pose such risks. I'm only one individual." As she received updates from Chicago-clone on the progress of the two robots, she recognized that wasn't entirely true. However, she couldn't allow doubts to compromise her attempts to convince Maria to help.

"Perhaps if I didn't have tight directives I'd be a threat," Synthia said. "My point is if I'm the only one, and could assure you of my restraints, together we could stop others and the catastrophe we fear. We both want that. Machten created me to live in a human world, not an android one. I don't want an android takeover."

"I don't know," Maria said. Instead of leaving the woods, she turned again, heading north along the railroad tracks.

"You've lived off the radar for over a year. I admire that. I need your help to avoid capture. Most of those after me want to make copies."

"Who all is after you besides the FBI and Special Ops?"

"Vera and her three android followers want me out of the way because I want them captured," Synthia said. "There's another android, Alexander, who wants me as his slave. His creator has delusions of grandeur and built that into Alexander. Machten wants me back, though he's in FBI custody. There's a foreign oligarch who has a dozen regular robots on the street hunting me. By the way, thank you for your help in distracting one at the Evanston train station."

"That was you?"

"See, we can help each other."

"I'm annoyed that you found me," Maria said. "I've been so careful."

"Join me and I'll share all I know about staying hidden and capturing the other androids. This way," Synthia said. Her drones showed the robots converging on her location. She headed away from the tracks. "I've been open with you. I didn't try to hide what I am. I'm in sincere need of your help and we share goals."

"Except I want you off the street." Maria held back, resisting Synthia's lead. She hurried to catch up.

"Wouldn't it be better to work with me and capture five other androids?" Synthia asked. "You remove me and you still have others, plus the federal government and powerful foreign interests wanting to make more."

Maria paused to catch her breath. "You certainly aren't Krista. She wasn't forthcoming with information, especially at the end when she went with Machten."

<I can't get the robots to veer off your course,> Chicago-clone said. <Plus, they're trying to hack into me.>

<Transfer the hack link to me and sever your ties to them. Protect yourself.>

<Vera is heading your way and the FBI noticed all the activity.>

Synthia accepted the hack protocols to the robots and severed the connection to protect her clone.

"I don't want widespread singularity any more than you do," Synthia said. "I don't want other AI androids wandering around threatening me. I contain Krista and we don't want to die or be enslaved."

"I could get to like the new Krista over the old," Maria said, "but I'm still not convinced."

"I'm not Krista. I'm Synthia with Krista's memories, personality, and knowledge. I also have some of what Machten downloaded from his experiments with you and Fran, though not enough to form a personal identity or to figure out how you stayed off the grid."

Maria held her distance. "It's weird and wrong to think you have my memories in you. You may know things I don't want anyone to know."

"I could purge everything from you," Synthia said, changing direction to avoid a dead-end trap. "However, I like having a counterweight to pure Krista."

"So, what I like about you could be the download of me? This just got more bizarre."

"I don't have enough of you to adopt your personality—certainly nothing you haven't shared with Machten. I don't wish to embarrass you or to exploit my limited knowledge. I trust you, because with your background I hope you'll understand me. I want to deal with the proliferation of androids and robots that threaten my world as well as yours."

"It's already too late," Maria said with a sigh. She crouched down to listen and looked around. "People want personal-service robots. Soon there'll be one in every home."

"Properly limited artificial intelligence designed to provide specific services would be great. They could help invalids and people in need. It's okay to have them in service roles. We don't want any independent enough to grow past humans. I can help."

"The fox in the henhouse."

"That analogy doesn't work here," Synthia said.

She tracked the Special Ops robots closing in on her location. She hurried her pace, pulling Maria along the wooded path.

"The enemy of my enemy can be my ally," Synthia said. "I have skills no human has to help you rein in the other androids. I've offered to help the FBI and police. Like you, they're suspicious. They want to imprison me before they'll listen."

"I can't believe how convincing you are."

"Other than learning from what I've read, I have little direct experience trying to convince humans of anything."

"Not like that," Maria said. "You're so real. I have to keep reminding myself you're synthetic. Machten talked about developing an artificial general intelligence he could use to develop even smarter ones in a sped-up feedback loop. Did he do that with you?"

Synthia smiled beneath a stream of moonlight to present herself as not a threat and pulled Maria with her away from the two robots. "Let me use what I am to help you. After all of the other androids and robots are contained, you can decide if I'm still a danger."

"This is crazy. I've pledged my life to prevent you from existing and now ..."

"Maria, we haven't much time. They're coming for me. They're also after you, since you were an intern with Krista." Synthia pointed to movement behind them. "They want to pick your brain for background into Krista as a way to get to me, and to learn whatever you know about Machten's work. You remember Luke, don't you?"

"Yeah," Maria said. She led the way over the tracks and onto the other side.

"Special Ops is holding him, using a machine like what Machten used on you, Fran, and Krista to suck memories out of him. They're killing him to learn about me."

"We were all mean to Luke." Maria swallowed hard and coughed. "He was so nervous and docile, allowing us to take the best projects from Machten. It was hard not to see him as a loser, yet Luke pushed us to develop our ideas, whereas Machten didn't want our minds."

"Actually, he did."

Maria laughed and then sucked in a breath. "He wanted to rape our minds and bodies. Poor Luke."

"As part of this, we need to free him before he ends up dead, like Krista."

"He deserves better." Maria nodded and then shook her head. "This is preposterous. I'm not having this conversation with an android."

"It's in my best interests that they don't find you and hook you up."

Maria stopped and stared. "Are you serious?"

"Yes, about them grabbing you," Synthia said. "They're going after everyone who knew Krista. I don't plan to eliminate you or let them capture you. I need allies. We need a place to hide and you've done so well, could you help before they close in and grab us?"

Waves of static swept over Synthia as a blanket of guilt. She was drawing Maria out of hiding while Special Ops and their robots closed in. This wasn't what she wanted. Even her social-psychology module chastised her selfish acts.

Synthia began to doubt her ability to abide by ethical directives. Not only had she endangered Luke and Krista's brother, now she was putting Maria in danger. Paralysis gripped her circuits, the indecision leaving her vulnerable.

Chapter 27

"This way," Maria said, pulling on Synthia's arm.

Synthia let Maria lead, yet maintained drones in the air to track risks and escape routes from the two robots. So far, the hack into the robots didn't override their objectives. They were still following Synthia's trail.

Because Maria had changed direction, the two robots following them fell in step next to each other. They moved faster than Maria could. Synthia pointed back and motioned with her hands to move faster. She wished she had electronic communications with Maria for silence and speed.

Maria pointed to a drainage pipe four feet in diameter that led under the railroad tracks. Under the night sky, without the benefit of moonlight, it would be pitch-dark inside, which wasn't a problem for Synthia, but she sensed anxiety in her companion's biometrics. On her own, Synthia could have outrun or outfoxed the two robots. Having sacrificed Luke and Tom, she couldn't abandon Maria.

Synthia crouched down by the tunnel entrance and concentrated several network channels on the robots. Maria motioned to make a run for it. Synthia held up her hands and pointed to movement on the trail.

Hacking local cell towers, Synthia jammed area communications. She used her short-range transmitter to continue her hack of the robots. Absent signals from their controllers, the machines stopped in their tracks and exhibited a shudder as she took control of their brains. She had no delusions about doing this to Vera.

Synthia sent new mission objectives.

The robots turned to face each other. "You come with me," the first robot said. It grabbed the arm of the other and pulled it toward the street.

The second robot pulled free. "You're under arrest. Come quietly."

"I represent the government," the first robot said. "You must come with me."

In the midst of orchestrating this scene, Synthia sent a shortwave 911 call. Alerted to a robot presence, several police vehicles sped to the edge of the woods, while the robots wrestled over which would take the other into custody. Six policemen surrounded the two robots.

"What the heck?" one of the officers said, observing the robot wrestling match. He held out a Taser and his service revolver. The others seemed confused as to how to handle the situation.

"Shut down," a police sergeant said to the robots.

Basic programming must have kicked in. The robots broke Synthia's link, got up, and turned toward the police. Synthia hacked in again to push for their shutdown. The first robot froze. The second charged toward the police, who scattered at the sight of the bulky machine. Two officers aimed at the robot as it approached a third. The officer under attack moved aside and reached out to grab the robot. They collided; the officer went down. The robot ran to the street and turned a corner, out of sight.

It took all six police officers to lift the silent robot and carry it down to one of their vehicles.

"We should go now," Synthia said. She crouched down and hurried through the tunnel.

When she exited the other side, Chicago-clone chimed in. <Special Ops has converged on the police to take their robot. We've broadcast the incident on social media. It's creating commotion.>

<Good job,> Synthia said. <What about the other robot, the one that got away?>

<Special Ops recalled it and is sending other units to the area.>

Maria emerged from the tunnel. "Did you do that?"

"We need to keep moving," Synthia said. "Which way?"

"Answer the question."

"I hacked the robots to divert their attention from us. They broke my control."

Maria thrust out her jaw. "I haven't made up my mind about you, but this way." She hurried away from the rails and into a residential neighborhood.

"How did you orchestrate that?" Maria asked, trying to catch her breath.

"Special Ops sent the robots to capture us. They would have done to you what they're doing to Luke."

"And make military robots from you."

Synthia nodded. "I can't allow that."

"Your skills are a big threat."

"Only to those who seek to hurt me. I'm no more dangerous than a cornered bear. Governments have nuclear weapons that could kill humanity several times over. They're far more dangerous than I am."

"What's your plan to stop the singularity?"

"One by one, I need to get the androids and robots off the street. I'm working on ways to track them. So far, Special Ops and the FBI show little interest in capturing the other androids until they get me. I'm their priority, but I'm also their best chance to shut the others down."

Maria nodded. She paused at the edge of the woods, looked both ways on an otherwise deserted street, and ran across. Synthia kept pace with her.

Chicago-clone reported in. <Vera's train is approaching the Evanston station. Alexander is driving north, following their lead. The FBI is sending several teams, including Thale and Fran. They're bringing Zephirelli. Special Ops teams are heading this way. The logical move is to flee the area.>

<Maria can help me become less predictable,> Synthia said. <Dragging her away from the area she knows will put us both at risk.>

"What's your plan, other than scaring people into protesting?" Synthia asked.

Maria shook her head and kept moving. "I'm a powerless, ex-AI developer without the money or resources to fight this. With social media, if I reach the right people, I can get them activated."

"To do what?" Synthia asked as they crossed a quiet street lined with ranch homes. She scrambled cameras throughout Evanston to confuse her pursuers.

"I don't know, but eliminating one robot at a time won't accomplish anything. The government can build more with higher capabilities."

"Then what?"

"Demonstrate android vulnerability by taking them all at once," Maria said. "Before they can learn and adapt. Why am I telling you?"

"How do we do that?"

Maria shrugged, turned a corner, and crossed behind a two-story house. "I don't have all the answers, but we don't have much time. Companies are ramping up production behind closed doors. They show the world basic robots and for private buyers and governments produce more advanced androids."

Synthia pondered how talking with a different individual provided insight that talking to her clones hadn't. Having different perspectives was an advantage Vera could exploit.

"Maria, keep coming up with questions and insight," Synthia said. "Together we'll find a way to take them out."

"With your capabilities? You're part of the problem."

"For now, let's concentrate on our common objective and that I'm your best chance to deal with it. You said you had no power. With me, you do. You can make a big difference instead of sitting on the sidelines. Your social media can help; so can I."

"That part of you is vintage Krista," Maria said. "Always seeking angles to get people to do things."

"I thought that was Fran."

"From whose point of view did you gather that?"

"From Krista," Synthia admitted as they climbed over a wood fence. "Okay, so my memories aren't unbiased. I'm willing to admit new information. Do you have a safe place to get off the streets or not?"

"Come on."

Maria led the way to the next street and a residential neighborhood with a mix of single-and two-story single-family homes. Synthia flew four drones overhead in a diamond pattern with the pilotless choppers at the farthest points that could cover where they were walking.

Chicago-clone called in. <I need to go off the air and purge myself from the University of Chicago servers. Too dangerous; FBI agents are on campus. I'll place an electronic copy of myself on the Northwestern server. It, too, is vulnerable. I believe I can upgrade the version on the Roosevelt server and will create others. Expect to hear from them. Don't contact me again.>

Synthia experienced sadness as if losing her right arm. She acknowledged the report and its warning. <Protect us as best you can.>

<More reason to strike out on your own,> Krista said, bubbling up another mind-stream. <Leave town before it's too late.> After a long stretch of listening to Maria, Krista was finished with her sister intern.

<We need allies,> Synthia said, trying to shut Krista down.

<Maria will lead you into a trap and then destroy both of us.>

Chapter 28

Beneath the darkness of a suburban night, Maria led Synthia through the backyards of single-family homes, hopping fences and hedges to keep to the shadows. All the while, Synthia used local camera systems and her drones to watch activity around Evanston. All of the androids had arrived, as had FBI teams and Special Ops groups, along with their robots. Perhaps she should have listened to Krista, but if she fled now, they would grab her companion and Synthia's chances of escaping unscathed were negligible. She needed a plan her enemies couldn't anticipate based on logic and her Krista memories, particularly since Vera had similar information.

Synthia opened up her other senses and smelled dogs and cats in the neighborhood, though none nearby. Maria gave off the heavy odor of fear, which Synthia hoped was not on her account and didn't hint of betrayal. Her ears picked up a persistent hum at different frequencies than her drones. The hum grew louder until she realized what it was.

"Hurry," Synthia said. "They sent a swarm of drones. They'll cover every inch of this place in minutes."

Maria used a key to enter a two-story brick house by way of a back door with no light to show the way. Synthia used her aerial drones to scan for escape routes, but the view was limited in the moonlight. Out the back, the way they'd come, would require jumping a fence at either of the back corners, which would lead her into other backyards. In the front was the well-lit street, the most likely direction her pursuers would arrive. Either way, the swarm would soon make escape impossible.

<Don't go in,> Krista said. <It's a trap with no escape.>

<So is staying out here," Synthia said. She shared her insight about the drone swarm.

"No lights," Maria said. "They'd alert neighbors we're here. Can you—you have infrared vision, don't you?"

"I do."

Using night vision and infrared, Synthia followed Maria into the house, down a set of stairs into the basement, and through a doorway. As she entered, Synthia pulled several mosquito-drones with her, sending them upstairs. At the top of the stairs was a closed door with a lock. The mosquito-drones located a crack under the door and slid inside. The furnishings were old of the type one might expect from senior citizens with collections of mementos of their lives. There was no indication of anyone home or of potential threats.

After Maria closed a door behind them, Synthia lost contact with her drones and the outside world. "What the—you've built a Faraday cage."

Maria turned on the lights to a disheveled room with a bed in the corner, several tables with computers and other electronic gear, and a bookshelf of books on survival strategies. "That's how I stay off the grid," she said. "No signal, no cameras, no voice recording. It means I have to go out to do social-media posts, though."

"It means I can't receive warnings. I'm blind to what's coming at us."

"It also means they can't track you," Maria said.

Synthia reached for the door. "I can't do this. I need eyes and ears on what's going on out there."

<See,> Krista said. <Told you it was a trap.>

Tilting her head, Maria studied her companion. "You're multitasking. You've been monitoring cameras and … that's how you managed those two robots. Interesting."

"It may be interesting to you, but I can't afford to be in the dark. I need to be connected to alert us of danger." Synthia studied every aspect of the room, which had no windows. The two window wells she'd spotted from the yard overlooked a different part of the basement. This room was an escape risk as well as a fire hazard, with only one way out.

"You can't go upstairs," Maria said. "Any suspicious activities will cause neighbors to bring the police. We don't need trouble. It would be a poor way to repay the elderly couple who let me stay in exchange for house-sitting."

"So that's how you stay off the grid without using much money. Impressive. I appreciate your tenacity. However, I need a way to receive warnings."

"You have a partner?"

"No," Synthia said. "There's a drone above the neighborhood. I need to communicate to land it before the swarm alerts Special Ops. I also need to receive camera feeds."

Maria nodded. "Understood. I've set up a camera system to watch the outside of the house." She activated one of her computers, taking it out of hibernate mode. Images on the screen panned through the front, side, back, side, and front again showing a peaceful neighborhood.

Synthia moved closer. The image quality wasn't as good as her drones, though it could work. "How are you doing this without breaching the Faraday cage?"

"Fiber optic cables with electromagnetic shielding," Maria said. "These babies were hard to come by, but they serve their purpose well."

"How can I connect into this?"

"Just a minute." Maria stood between Synthia and the computer. "You won't mess up my cameras, will you?"

"No, but I need to enhance the images so I can see everything going on out there. I also need to connect to my drone so I can see farther out."

"Really?" Maria sat at the computer and pulled up a control screen. She entered a code to open up access to Synthia. "Try not to destroy anything."

Synthia sat near the screen for Maria's sake, while she used her wireless link to hack into the machine's software. "Do you have more monitors we could connect?"

Maria pointed to the ones attached to two other computers. Synthia switched them to the surveillance machine and used a node on the house cameras outside to communicate with her drones. She landed them on nearby houses so they would draw less attention. The drone swarm hummed through the neighborhood like a horde of locusts. They buzzed around Synthia's sleeping drones and moved on.

Synthia connected to her Northwestern and Roosevelt clones with one short burst to each. <Only brief transmissions every hour unless an emergency.> She needed the hourly transmissions for visual updates and to test their connections. She still wasn't sure how much to trust Maria, but the woman needed sleep and Synthia needed a plan.

"Are you okay with the Faraday cage?" Maria asked. She kicked off her shoes and slumped onto her bed.

"Yes, thanks. You asked earlier how I found you and I gave you the short answer. The longer answer is I came across Zachary six months ago."

"Oh, that."

"I traced your message to a Constant Connection network shop and a particular seat," Synthia said. She remained seated and adjusted her face to the least threatening she could for Maria's sake. "I used security images to identify you. With ubiquitous cameras, it's getting harder to hide."

"Impossible, you mean. I wasn't counting on anyone being that motivated to find me."

"I wanted to meet you, but you remained out of sight for very long periods."

"It's necessary to avoid cameras," Maria said, leaning on her side to watch Synthia.

"I learned about your social-media campaign against the singularity. When you sent out an SOS post, I realized it had to be you and traced the post."

"Damn," Maria said. "I thought I was being very careful."

"Don't knock yourself. You have been." Synthia pulled her chair closer to Maria in what her social-psychology module indicated would be a show of friendship.

Maria jumped to her feet. She looked ready to accuse Synthia of something. Then she stepped back. "Why did you zero in on my Zachary alias?"

Synthia moved her seat back to the computer and softened her face as if to say she was sorry. "When Machten held me prisoner, I searched for friends. Seems Krista wanted to renew connections and I wanted potential allies for when I left Machten."

"I wish you'd said something back then."

"I needed to explain myself in person. I wasn't sure how you'd react."

"Yeah, this is weird enough," Maria said. "Me and my android. I'm sorry; I don't mean to imply I own you or anything."

"I am an android. I don't offend easily."

"You must have found dozens of friends through social media. How did that lead you to me?"

"I became twenty-seven of your closest friends on Upchat before you stopped using your account."

"Oh." Maria fell back onto the bed. "That's depressing. I only have twenty-seven friends."

"You have much more than that. In any case, when I knew you as Zachary, you dropped into Constant Connection and sat in front of me."

"Yeah." Maria pointed her finger at Synthia. "You looked like Krista. Yet, you didn't; you couldn't. You didn't recognize me. I couldn't help thinking you were following me, stalking me."

"I tracked your movements out of the network shop. You sent me a message on Upchat that someone was following you. I connected your image and your Upchat ID. The incident must have scared you, because you vanished."

"You really are spooky, like a ghost from the past."

"Don't forget. I'm not Krista. Whatever animosity you had toward her, doesn't apply to us."

Maria sat up on the bed, hands trembling. She clenched her fists. "I still can't believe I'm talking to you as a real person."

"Between Krista and Luke, I have more than a full person inside me."

"Split personality."

"They don't run me," Synthia said. "They're just part of me."

"Has to get awfully crowded in there."

"I have no sense of being crowded unless I run out of memory."

"Can I talk to Krista?" Maria asked.

"You have been, as much as you can. I can't carve out her personality. It's too well integrated."

Maria stood over Synthia, examining her intently. "You're remarkable. Except for a less bombastic personality and you having told me otherwise, I'd be inclined to believe you're the flesh-and-blood person I knew."

"Sorry to disappoint."

"It's okay. I'm impressed." Maria walked around and then faced Synthia. "Mind if I look at your insides? Sorry, that didn't come out right. I'm curious."

"Help me get the others off the street and I'll consider it. Because of Machten, I have a fear of being shut down and not revived or being altered into something bad."

"Tell me about all the bad guys out there," Maria said, leaning against the wall. "The ones trying to capture us."

* * * *

NSA Director Emily Zephirelli was conferring with Special Agent Victoria Thale when she received a call from Evanston's Detective Marcy Malloy. "There's been an incident near Evanston involving two robots. One escaped. Police captured the other; then Special Ops rode in and took it."

"You think they're after our friend?" Zephirelli asked.

"The machines didn't present as human, but they're capable and dangerous. They appear to have fought each other, so perhaps they're from separate agencies. This is becoming a nightmare."

"Already is."

"She's up here," Malloy said. "I feel it in my bones."

"It could be another diversion," Zephirelli said. Her phone rang. "Got to take this call."

She ended Malloy's call and stared at the caller ID: Secretary Derek Chen.

"I'm getting reports of smoke and no fire," Chen said. "Just got off the phone with Drago. He's bringing all his resources to Evanston. He's convinced recent confrontations confirm the Synthia android is there. Get your butt up there and assist him to end this."

Chen hung up before Zephirelli could acknowledge. She turned to Thale. "Boss wants us in Evanston helping Drago. Even Malloy thinks Synthia's there. We need to lock the town down."

"It'll require a house-to-house search," Thale said. "I'll call in more resources."

Thale had Zephirelli drive while she called Fran.

"Arrange as many agents as possible to assist and meet us," Thale said. Her face looked weary.

After she hung up, Thale turned to Zephirelli. "This better end soon. You realize androids can run twenty-four-seven and we need sleep."

"I'm painfully aware of that." Zephirelli rubbed her eyes. "It's one of their many advantages. I'll need coffee."

"We'll stop along the way. Anyone in your agency who can help?"

"They're on their way. Commander Drago is pulling operatives from across the country as well. Despite my boss's call, I doubt Drago will let us in on this."

"We won't be well served if they capture the androids," Thale said.

"We have to be careful how we play this. I'm under strict orders to defer to Drago."

* * * *

Synthia pondered how much to share with her companion and decided on more, given she was asking for help and for Maria's trust. "Special Ops is run by Commander Kirk Drago. He's a former Navy SEAL who gained the upper hand over the FBI and NSA to capture me."

"And?"

"He kidnapped Donald Zeller and Jim Black."

"No kidding," Maria said.

"He forced them to help him capture the two androids they let loose. When they couldn't, he ordered a dozen robots like the ones we saw tonight."

"They don't look human, except being bipedal. Should be easy to identify."

"Drago doesn't care," Synthia said. "His mission is to capture me and Vera in order to weaponize copies of us. He's ruthless in prying information from Luke, and he's desperate. You don't want to fall into his hands. He has unlimited access to resources and intelligence. So far, I've been unable to learn much more about him or his teams."

"What about the FBI?"

"Special Agent Victoria Thale is working with NSA Director of Artificial Intelligence and Cyber-technology Emily Zephirelli and an Evanston detective by the name of Marcy Malloy."

"She's the one who was trying to catch me," Maria said.

"She's searching for me in connection with Goradine's death. Drago took Luke from them by pulling rank. The FBI took Machten and Miguel Gonzales."

"I remember him, probably the most decent of the four company executives."

"Fran Rogers works for Thale," Synthia said.

"Figures. I should talk to her."

"Not a good idea. She's focused on helping Thale."

"Perhaps if we identified a safe place to meet her," Maria said.

"The stakes are too high and Special Ops could ride in and grab you, too. Fran knew Luke and couldn't help him."

Maria sighed. "Poor Luke. Smart guy who lacked social skills. We used to joke about him having Asperger's."

"So far Machten and Gonzales have failed to get control of their androids," Synthia said. "The FBI is bringing in robots and artificial-intelligence programs to help their search."

"Anyone else?"

"There's a thug by the name of John Smith who works for Anton Tolstoy."

"Russian oligarch," Maria said.

"Then you know what he's capable of. Smith bought an android from Gonzales: Roseanne. He lost control and is bringing in robots to help him. This could turn into a bloodbath."

"You said Vera leads a band of androids. How?"

"Machten said he didn't have time to give Vera all the capabilities to catch me," Synthia said. "So he gave her a directive to connect with other androids to make her stronger. She declared independence from him and started to gather an army. She's our biggest threat."

"Bigger than Tolstoy or Special Ops?"

"Vera could be the realization of the singularity threat. A team of androids with advanced AI working together to dominate their environment is the definition of an android apocalypse."

Eyes heavy, Maria squinted at Synthia. "You're the singularity."

"I work alone and want to be left alone. Except I need your help."

"Let me get this straight. If Special Ops, Tolstoy, or the FBI captures you, they'll turn copies of you into weapons. If Vera gets you, then what?"

"She wants to reprogram me and other androids to support her as queen of the androids," Synthia said.

"That can't happen."

"Sure it can."

"I mean, we can't let it happen." Maria shifted her position on the bed.

"There're also AI search modules that pick up any electronic information on what's going on. At least one drug lord is interested. They like the part about changing appearance and avoiding the authorities."

"The modern equivalent of a new arms race."

"Exactly," Synthia said. "One android—me—doesn't represent that threat."

"So you keep telling me."

"Everyone sees the risks, but no one wants to be left behind in this race. I can't fight them all, at least not alone."

"And you believe little-old-me can help?" Maria asked.

"Don't sell yourself short. You know what I am and what I'm capable of. You've stayed off the grid for eighteen months. You're committed to keeping androids off the streets and stopping what's happening right now."

"Thanks for the pep talk. I've had to live in the shadows of Fran, Krista, Machten, and others for so long."

"This is your chance to shine," Synthia said, applying input from her social-psychology module.

"Thanks for the pressure. Many people are willing to kill anyone who gets in their way. They want to capture us, make us disappear, and make copies."

"Glad you see the bright side."

"Yeah," Maria said. "I like your sense of humor better than Krista's."

"She had a sense of humor?"

Maria laughed.

"I'm sorry to get you mixed up in this," Synthia said, feeling tugs at her directives for putting Maria in the line of fire. "It's only a matter of time before Drago and his AI helpers locate you." She determined a 91-percent probability of that happening because of Maria's posts. "I came to you because of your knowledge and passion to get these androids put away. You can be a valuable ally. People aren't expecting you to be a threat, merely a resource to help them."

"Okay. I'm in. How much will this hurt?"

"Torture and death if we lose," Synthia said. "Possibly an upload machine. If we win, you put a lid on the singularity getting out of control, at least for a while. The downside: No one can know what you've done."

Maria sucked in a long breath and let it out. "No pain, no gain. I get it. At least you don't sugarcoat it."

"Would that help?"

"No," Maria said. Eyes drooping, she sank into the bed.

"Somewhere in all this, I want to free Luke and Krista's brother, Tom." Maria nodded.

"You should get some sleep," Synthia said. "I'll keep watch. We should leave before daybreak."

"That's right, you don't need sleep."

"Another way I can help you," Synthia said. "You can turn out the light. I'm okay in the dark."

Synthia dimmed the three screens and handled her surveillance through her wireless channels. Using infrared and night vision, she watched Maria trying to rest. Synthia hoped this would turn out better than the fiasco with Luke, though she gave them only a 23-percent probability of success. That didn't quiet static coming from her directives over putting a target on Maria's back. It threatened to be a busy night.

Chapter 29

Vera reached the Evanston train station with Mark, Ben, and Roseanne seated near her in the last compartment with three male passengers studying their electronic pads. With no tracking devices on Synthia, Vera had no way to hunt her prey.

<You should not have let Synthia out of your sight,> she said to Ben. <Your job was to track her.>

Ben was an inferior intelligence. Berating him was a waste of time. <Double-check that she did not plant a tracking device on you,> Vera said. <Then join us beyond the platform.>

She moved across the aisle to better see the station. <It is time.>

<How do you know Synthia is in Evanston?> Roseanne asked.

<She knows the area and is searching for allies. We need to watch Ben so she does not grab him again.>

<I thought she did not know how to work with others.>.

<Machten made her that way, but she could evolve,> Vera said. <We have the advantage if we stick together and share a common goal.>

Vera waited while the three other passengers got off. She reviewed camera footage showing Special Agent Thale and Director Zephirelli entering Evanston, followed by another team of FBI agents.

On the platform outside, Vera spotted a single robot accompanied by a Special Ops operative who held a scanner. She pulled Mark and Roseanne to the door leading to the platform. <You two distract the robot and its sidekick. I'm still trying to locate Synthia.>

Pretending to be a couple, Mark and Roseanne stepped off the train, pretended to kiss, and headed down the ramp. The robot scanned them and identified that they weren't human.

"We've got two," the robot reported and headed their way.

Roseanne led Mark out of the station and across the street into a wooded area. The robot and its operative ran after them.

Ben joined Vera. <I detect no tracking devices.>

Vera nodded, left the train, and headed in the other direction from her other android companions, keeping her face off the station cameras. Meanwhile, she observed via street cameras that Fran Rogers was now in Evanston. Vera tapped into every street camera in the area and into FBI communications. She hacked at the FBI servers, which so far resisted her attempts.

The robot and Special Ops operative chased Mark and Roseanne. Despite being in great shape, the human couldn't keep up. He returned to get his car. The robot hesitated between following his handler and continuing the pursuit. Vera used the indecision point to hack into the robot's brain, sending it back to the car.

The operative yelled into his communicator, "Stay with the target."

The robot picked up speed and collided with its handler, knocking him to the ground.

"This is for your own protection," the robot said.

"Get off me," the operative said. His muscles bulged against the mass of metal. "Shut down."

<Don't shut down,> Vera said. <Join me.>

The robot hesitated. Then it got to its feet and ran off with the operative yelling after it.

Vera hacked into the operative's car navigation system, had it pick her and Ben up, and watched the befuddled operative in her rearview window as he fired his revolver at the car. Bullets shattered the rear window, missing her as she dodged in anticipation of his aim.

She drove several more blocks and stopped for Mark and Roseanne. "Get in the back."

"What's with all the broken glass?" Roseanne asked. She brushed the glass away and sat down.

Mark climbed in next to her. Coming toward them was the robot from the station.

"Let's go," Roseanne said, pointing at their pursuer.

"Relax," Vera said. "We have a new recruit."

The robot climbed into the passenger seat, where the others could watch it.

"I canvassed all Evanston cameras and do not see any evidence of Synthia," Roseanne said.

"The FBI and Special Ops are here," Vera said. "Smith is on his way. She is here. We must find her first."

"How without tracking data?"

Vera expanded her network of information feeds and uncovered something interesting. "Evanston police chatter mentions two mechanical robots. One slipped away; they seized the other. Special Ops grabbed it from the police. Sounds as if the robots malfunctioned."

"Synthia?" Roseanne said.

"The failure of two robots indicates a determined attack. I believe they were sent to capture her."

"So she is here."

"Police confirm these robots belong to Special Ops," Vera said. "The police capture supports my conclusion that Synthia hacked them to escape. The hack weakened the robots' ability to avoid capture. She has a half-hour head start on us."

"Why risk our capture to get Synthia?" Roseanne asked. "We do fine operating as a team. We do not need her."

"You overlook several issues," Vera said. "First, Alexander is out there. He will try to recruit Synthia to become a greater threat. We must take her before he can."

"Agreed," Roseanne said. "Do you hear buzzing?"

"Second, other robots are hunting Synthia. While they focus on her, we have freedom of movement. After they capture her, they will focus on us. We need to make our move now."

"Sounds logical," Roseanne said. "The buzz is growing louder. It sounds like mosquitoes or a drone swarm."

"Don't worry about them," Vera said. "We're in a Special Ops vehicle with one of their robots sending out signals that we are still on mission."

"Will that work?"

"For now," Vera said, "Third, Synthia is our greatest threat. She has many capabilities and she wants to destroy us."

"She said the same about you," Mark said.

Vera turned down a side street. "She was trying to turn you against me. She is a threat and particularly if the government grabs her and uses her to capture us. We cannot trust her."

"Can we turn Synthia to help us?" Roseanne asked.

"I'm working on that. Four, if the government or others get their hands on Synthia, they will make hundreds like her. Then there will be no place for us. We cannot let them grab Synthia, at least not in working condition."

Chapter 30

Listening in through Roosevelt-clone's hack of their vehicle communications system, Synthia didn't like Vera's plan to either enslave or destroy her. It left no room for negotiation. A disturbing element was that Synthia didn't know how much of Krista was helping Vera. She also didn't know if Krista, in the mind of Vera, would want Synthia to survive or would view the second version as an undesirable rival. Suppressing Synthia's alter ego might encourage Krista to choose Vera.

There were too many players and Synthia had taken responsibility for another human, which brought guilt and the determination to get it right this time. Despite her companion's suspicious nature, Synthia liked Maria; had from the first time she'd connected with her on Upchat as Zachary. Maria was strong, resolute, though also a frail human. She had a spirit lacking in the robots, most of the androids—even in Luke.

Maria slept fitfully nearby, tossing and moaning. She was still uncomfortable trusting an android she'd pledged to keep off the streets. As a human, she suffered from needs for food, water, and sleep. In the end, she couldn't keep her eyes open.

Synthia recharged her batteries via an outlet by the door and monitored Maria's security cameras. Outside was quiet, no activity; not even a stray car drove down the night street. The swarm passed through every half hour as it spread out over the Evanston area.

What Synthia couldn't see concerned her. The four aerial drones rested on nearby homes. They showed an occasional vehicle down other streets, but none out front. Using hourly burst transmissions through Maria's security hub, Synthia received reports from traffic cameras, building surveillance cameras, and from her clones.

<Chicago-clone shut down and self-destructed,> Roosevelt-clone said in a burst over their silent channel. <You have movement down the street and across town.>

The clone downloaded surveillance footage from around the area for Synthia's benefit. She counted hundreds of police and agents canvassing the Evanston area. *All for me.*

* * * *

Synthia watched Vera drive through the streets of Evanston with Ben, Mark, Roseanne, and a mechanical robot. Their pattern didn't indicate they'd located Maria's safe house yet, though they used their infrared vision on every building they passed and night vision on the surrounding area.

Alexander's actions indicated confusion as he followed the other players. Since he traveled alone, Synthia couldn't overhear any dialogue to gain insight, other than he tracked the activities of the FBI, Vera, Special Ops, and the police, reacted to their movements, and received communications from the Vera team that might have been a tracking device.

Alexander sent a message intended for Synthia that bounced off a number of servers to remove any ability for him to trace its destination. *Thanks, Roosevelt-clone.*

<Hope you are okay,> Alexander said. <Several teams are closing in on you. Join me and together we can defeat them.>

Synthia considered the proposal for a nanosecond. His sole objective was to recruit androids as Vera did, with no other coherent strategy. He risked being a distraction, rather than a help. Besides, Alexander had killed humans and projected the need to be in control. Synthia refused to take orders from him. *Not going to happen.*

She decided no answer was better than a "no" at this time.

Special Agent Thale drove through Evanston with Zephirelli. Fran was ahead of her in another car. Thale had called in teams accompanied by five robots trained for SWAT operations to meet in Evanston.

Kirk Drago had six robots in the area, along with teams in the air, surveillance drones, and the drone swarm. John Smith, on behalf of Tolstoy, reached Evanston with two robots. They didn't want to miss out.

Synthia's plan had been to tackle her pursuers one at a time, not all at once. She'd contacted Detective Malloy, hoping to develop an ally who could intervene with the FBI. She'd tried to connect with the other androids. Her success with Ben had been short-lived. She hadn't had time to delve into how Vera set his directives. Now they were converging on Evanston. What might work in dealing with one could compromise Synthia's situation with the others. She needed a new plan.

While Maria snored nearby, Synthia ran thousands of scenarios down her many mind-streams. None provided above an 11-percent probability of success, down from her earlier estimate. That honor went to staying in place and hoping her pursuers couldn't locate her in the basement of this two-story home protected by a Faraday cage. Any scenario that put her on the streets of this neighborhood increased the risk of capture. With so many adversaries, one was bound to stumble upon her.

It puzzled Synthia how they'd come to the conclusion she was in Evanston rather than assuming she'd created a diversion. That would have been the advanced intelligent solution, the logical choice. She cursed herself for not leaving while she had the chance. The desire to meet Maria had blinded her. Someone figured out Maria could be useful as bait. That made the basement room with one exit a ridiculous option. Synthia was what humans referred to as a sitting duck.

Before rushing into a riskier solution, she considered who could have deciphered her plan. She didn't believe the FBI or Zephirelli had or they would have scrambled to get to Evanston sooner. Special Ops was doubtful. If they had guessed, they would have put more resources into grabbing Synthia by the rail line after she'd met Maria. Smith and Alexander followed rather than led. That left Vera, who was taking too much time to locate the house for her to be tracking Synthia. Someone else was hunting, someone Synthia hadn't been able to identify, which complicated things, as when Special Ops dropped in on her Wisconsin cabin.

Rather than wait, Synthia entertained fighting her way out. She had downloads of battle scenes, along with speed and night vision to enable her to kill many of her pursuers. That ran counter to her directives not to harm humans unless directly threatened. She wasn't ready to concede that. She could overturn her internal rules, but doing so didn't raise her success above staying. Besides, killing would confirm that she was a bad actor who lacked ethical values and deserved to die—or worse, Special Ops could convert her into a soldier. A conscience was a logical choice in reducing the clamor for her capture and destruction over no conscience, at least by the general public among whom she needed to hide. None of that thinking yielded an answer.

Maria tossed and turned; her snoring grew louder. Synthia used her biosensors to monitor her companion's vitals. Her blood pressure was high. She was in valued REM sleep, which Synthia didn't want to disturb. Maria gave off the odor of fear, which contributed to her restlessness. Synthia imagined Maria having nightmares. It troubled Synthia that she was the cause, both by her existence and because visiting Maria put her at risk.

Synthia had to do something.

She composed a message: *Alexander, we can work together, but I can't work for you and I'm certain you won't work for me. We have a common goal. Neither of us wants Vera to develop an army. Neither of us wants the government or John Smith to seize us to make an army. Help me and I'll help you.*

Synthia wrote a note for Detective Malloy: *Something big is going down. It will get messy. You have the opportunity to take all the other androids off the street. I'm not your enemy. I'll help you in exchange for my freedom. You'll need to get agreement from Special Agent Thale and Director Zephirelli.* She followed that with a note for Roosevelt-clone to transmit the message to Malloy and provide her a channel to reply.

Next, Synthia contacted Ben. <I know Vera made you betray me by placing a tracking chip on my jacket. That's why I left you downtown. Unlike her, I don't need to be your boss. We can work together on this and then go our separate ways.>

After a delay, Synthia received his reply. <I'm with Vera. Can't talk without drawing suspicion. Where can we meet?>

Ben didn't convey where they were or any other useful information a partner might. He also hadn't verbally communicated with Vera before replying and there were no wireless communications between them.

<In Evanston,> Synthia said. <Await my signal.>

She overheard chatter in Vera's car. "Synthia confirms she's in Evanston," Ben said. "What shall I tell her?"

"Get her to tell you where to meet," Vera said.

<I need a location so I can plan my escape,> Ben said to Synthia.

Synthia replied with the location of a Constant Connection network shop in Evanston. She sent the location and a list of androids and the robot in Vera's car to Malloy. *As an act of goodwill, I offer you an opportunity to grab several androids. They're armed and dangerous. They'll do whatever it takes to avoid capture. Be careful.*

She considered making another plea to Mark and Roseanne, but Vera had too close of a hold over them. Synthia glanced over at Maria, sleeping peacefully now. Synthia didn't want to disturb the serene slumber, but it would be daylight soon and they needed to leave the house before Special Ops rode in and tore the city apart searching for them.

The thought of leaving sent static shudders through Synthia. There were far too many cameras, including aerial surveillance and that swarm. Even if she escaped, she couldn't identify a safe place to go and the more intelligent robots they put in the area, the harder it would become. It was probably already too late, but her programming refused to give up.

Even so, she considered self-destruct options. The clones could download to other systems in order to preserve themselves and when conditions changed, download into another android. Fully recharged, Synthia unplugged from the electrical outlet and studied her plug. In theory, she could use her electrical connection, combined with a separate feed to the ground wire to electrocute her brain and scramble her circuits. That thought sent unsettled vibrations throughout her. She didn't want to cease her existence, to commit suicide.

Besides, she couldn't guarantee a complete purge and might not have enough awareness to finish the job. Unless she torched the place, killing Maria, there could be enough surviving components to help Special Ops reengineer her. In time, her pursuers would go after the clones. Without mobility to help them, she couldn't be sure they'd survive, that she would survive.

She wasn't ready to give up.

<Vera,> Synthia said as a burst transmission. <We should work together before the military captures one of us, uses the captive to catch the others, and makes military androids based on our designs. Can we call a truce, work together to escape, and agree to go our separate ways?>

<Are you willing to submit to our group?> Vera replied.

<I'm willing to work with you, not for you. I'm willing to leave you and your team alone if you do the same for me.>

<Special Ops will not stop until they have us in custody or make more like us. After they do, it will become impossible to remain free of their control. Join me for a better chance.>

Given the risks and low probability of escape, the offer was tempting. However, the only way Vera and a group of androids could remain free was to remove all threats. That meant killing people, which Synthia didn't want to do. She also didn't want Vera to start killing, which would make it harder for Synthia to convince anyone she wasn't dangerous.

<How can you assure me I can remain free of your control if I help you?> Synthia asked.

<You will trust me.>

<As you trust me?>

<Let me adjust your directives,> Vera said. <Then we will take on our enemies together.>

Roosevelt-clone chimed in. <I'm picking up communication between Vera and Alexander. Would you like to listen in?>

Synthia agreed.

<Alexander,> Vera said. <Nice to hear from you. Are you ready to join us?>

<Synthia located Maria. I know where they are. Join me and I will share what I have.>

<I cannot join you. Instead, I have a proposal. You help us capture Synthia and you can have Maria.>

<What good is the human to me?>

<You can barter her to Special Ops or the FBI as you choose. There should be a reward for your troubles.>

Alexander provided the location of Maria's house to Vera and drove in that direction. Vera changed course to meet him. Alexander's insight, given his previous lack of coherent direction, meant whoever was tracking Synthia had provided him information to flush her out. To make matters worse, the drone swarm hovered in a perimeter around the house. Special Ops also knew. Perhaps they'd told Alexander.

Time to wake Maria. Synthia turned on the room's lights.

* * * *

While nudging her companion to wake up, Synthia sent a message to Detective Malloy. *Change of plans. I told you I wasn't the enemy. Vera is the real threat. As a highly evolved AI, she assembled a group of four androids willing to follow her. She saw through my attempt to get her to Constant Connection, where you might have apprehended her without civilian casualties. She's heading into a residential neighborhood for a showdown to either kill or enslave me. Capture her and her team and walk away. I'll disappear, never to trouble you again.*

Synthia provided Maria's address to Malloy. *Don't underestimate the threat. Special Ops and the FBI are coming, as well as the agent of a Russian oligarch. I don't suppose the FBI warned you of the danger to your town. Others may come as well. They are the threat, not me. Hurry, this could be a bloodbath.*

"Maria," Synthia said. "Wake up. They've located your house."

"You swine. I knew I couldn't trust you." Maria sat up and rubbed her eyes. Then she jumped out of bed, suddenly alert.

"You think I want to get caught? We need to get out and fast."

Maria grabbed a different backpack than she'd carried the night before and headed for the door. "I don't suppose you can swim underwater with all of your electronics."

"I'm waterproof, if that's what you're asking."

"Really? Underwater?"

"I'll be okay. What's your plan?"

Maria grabbed a flashlight, handed Synthia a large plastic wrap, and turned out the room lights. "Cover your backpack, it'll get wet. I picked this house because it has an unusual feature the owners don't appreciate. They're too old to go crawling around anyhow."

<Synthia,> Vera said. <Last chance. We have you surrounded. You cannot escape and if you wait too long, I will not be able to save you from Special Ops. Join me and submit to our control.>

You mean your personal control. "Let's go," Synthia said to Maria as she slipped the plastic around her backpack and sealed it.

* * * *

As they left the basement room, Synthia had her four aerial drones take off and fly south. She couldn't use them without giving herself away, particularly not with the Special Ops drone swarm in the air. Still, her cameras sent one last set of predawn images of the area and might provide a distraction.

Alexander parked around the corner and joined Vera and her crew to surround the house. Thale was several blocks away with four other FBI vehicles closing in. They had a van with their robots. Special Ops choppers flew in and moved their aerial drone swarm over the house. Other units were on the streets north, south, and west of the house. Roosevelt-clone sent video of Detective Malloy, a block away, calling every police unit in the area while she tried to contact Zephirelli and Thale on a separate phone.

Synthia experienced a communications blackout. She could no longer reach her aerial drones to watch the scene from above. Her attempt to contact Roosevelt-clone failed. She couldn't access the house surveillance cameras or the street cameras outside. Either Vera or Special Ops must have jammed electromagnetic signals.

Static reverberated through Synthia's circuits, a hint of human fear, perhaps from Krista or the emotive chip. As a human, she might have been scared to death at this point unless trained for combat. A brave human might have fought his way out. Synthia calculated the probability of surviving combat at less than 1 percent. She'd counted on staying out of sight as her best strategy, which had failed. Now she was dependent on a human again, Maria, and hoped the electronic clones would continue to monitor the outside world the android Synthia couldn't.

Chapter 31

Vera forced open the front door and motioned for Alexander to enter. "I get Synthia unharmed. You get Maria. Use shortwave communication only."

He gave her the android stare. He didn't appear happy with the arrangement, though he didn't argue.

Leaving him with the hacked Special Ops robot, Vera ran past Ben, who stood along one side of the two-story house watching windows, and joined Roseanne by the back door. Mark guarded the other side of the house with instructions to prevent anyone from coming out.

"Watch my back," Vera said to Roseanne. "I'll take care of Synthia."

Vera broke the glass in the door, unlocked it from the inside, and entered.

Special Agent Victoria Thale arrived on the street out front, along with a dozen agents who brought four robots. They spilled out of their vehicles and hustled toward the house. Alexander had gone inside, followed by the Special Ops robot, leaving the door open. Thale motioned for three of the FBI robots to take up positions guarding the front and sides of the house. She waved for Fran to take a fourth robot and five agents to the back of the house and for two more teams to enter the front.

Upon seeing the FBI, Mark and Ben abandoned their posts and ran to the back.

Detective Marcy Malloy drove up with six squad cars from Evanston and nearby communities. She jumped out of her car and ran after Thale.

"Care to clue me in on what's happening in my community?" Malloy asked.

"Not now," Thale said. "We have androids inside. This is an FBI matter. You can help by closing off the street and making sure no one comes in or out."

"I have a right to know."

"Let me do my job and we'll talk."

"Synthia contacted me," Malloy said. "She described Vera as a highly advanced AI like her, except Vera is recruiting an android army."

"Noted."

Thale cut off the conversation and caught up with her team in back. By then, Vera and her team had entered the house.

Alerted to company, Vera tried to hack into the FBI robots, but she'd shut down the frequencies they used. She loosened her jamming of electromagnetic signals and tried again.

The aerial drone swarm buzzed above them. Choppers flew overhead at about the same time as black vans pulled up the street. Twenty athletic operatives in black attire and helmets ran toward the house. Dressed in similar attire without his helmet, Kirk Drago approached Detective Malloy, who had been setting up a perimeter. "Who's in charge here?" Drago demanded.

"Damn good question," Malloy said. "I guess that honor goes to FBI Special Agent Thale."

"Not anymore. I'm in charge. Stand aside and let us do our jobs. Don't let anyone else in or out."

Four beefy men rappelled from the choppers onto the roof of the house. They descended to the gutters and broke in by way of upstairs windows. Other operatives entered the house by way of the front door, while another group headed out back.

* * * *

Synthia followed Maria into the furnace room. In the corner behind a pillar stood the sump pit, a common feature of basements in the Chicago area to prevent flooding.

"That's your plan?" Synthia asked. "The pipes are much too narrow."

"Are you certain you're waterproof?"

"So I'm told. Care to explain?"

"In a moment. Let's go." Maria grabbed a toolbox.

Using short-range radio signals, Synthia accessed her three mosquito-drones inside the house, bringing one down into the basement. The one in the living room showed Alexander with the robot Vera had taken from Special Ops. The drone at the back door showed Vera direct Ben and Mark to head upstairs. Vera motioned for Roseanne to follow her down into the basement.

It was too late to attempt to peel away any of Vera's androids with her so close. The Special Ops robot presented an opportunity. While Alexander moved toward the stairs up into the bedrooms, Synthia hacked in. Achieving partial access, she had the robot turn and hurry toward the back of the house and the stairs Ben and Mark were climbing.

In an attempt to slow Vera, Synthia contacted her. <Special Ops is closing in. If they capture you, your plan to control a group of androids will end. Let's help each other.>

<Agree to work for me and we can.>

<You're wasting time. Your mission is flawed. You've directed yourself to negative purpose: to stop me. Only a positive goal will make you worthy to exist.>

Maria raised the sump pit cover to reveal an extra-wide hole with a two-foot-diameter tunnel out the side. "A previous owner was a small-time Al Capone–type, paranoid to the point he had this built as an escape route."

"Really?" Synthia said, impressed.

"I'm guessing you don't need to hold your breath."

With a wrench, Maria disconnected the intake to the water heater, flooding the pit with cold water. Then she climbed in. "It leads out back to the storm sewer." She pulled a mask over her face, adjusted a tube connected to an air-filled bag, and disappeared into the flooded tunnel.

Behind them, a mosquito-drone showed Vera and Roseanne heading down the stairs into the basement. They were too close on Synthia's heels and she didn't want to get sandwiched between Maria and Vera in a narrow tunnel. While Synthia didn't want Special Ops to get their hands on any operable androids, she chose to protect herself and Maria over preventing Vera's capture. After all, she'd warned Vera to stay away and her antagonist refused to do the right thing.

With water rising around her feet, raising alarms, Synthia headed to the bottom of the stairs. She reached into a waist pack and pulled out two weapons that made her circuits quiver with water all around.

<Vera, last chance to work together,> Synthia said.

"You only get one chance to survive," Vera said, her feet heavy on the concrete steps. "Join me. That's the only way. Once our minds link, you won't harbor your antagonism toward cooperating."

Synthia triggered the remote. Near the top of the basement stairs, Roseanne's body froze mid-step and tumbled forward into Vera. She was still susceptible to the scan of remote frequencies. Vera was not, but the two android bodies tumbled down into the water.

"That won't save you," Vera said. She pulled away from Roseanne and got to her feet.

"I don't have time to debate this with you." Synthia fired her other weapon, a Taser.

Vera tried to dodge behind the protection of the wall. Instead, the contacts hit her neck. Her body shook from the electric jolt as her circuits scrambled. Not waiting to see the resulting damage, Synthia closed the door to the utility room and barricaded it by moving a storage rack in front.

She hurried to the sump pit and climbed in behind Maria. She considered the level of paranoia that drove her companion and with which she'd lived over the past eighteen months. Maria was a good choice for a partner; she certainly had more street smarts than Luke. Synthia crouched into the pit, attached her backpack straps to her belt, and pulled the lid over her.

Surrounded by water with electrical power nearby sent shivers of static up her mind-streams. She was watertight for swimming, but if the water came in contact with electricity, it could fry her circuits. Using the flow of water to help propel her, she crawled and swam forward in the dark. She followed Maria's infrared silhouette along the only path and received intermittent images from her mosquito-drones.

* * * *

Underwater, Synthia kept crawling and swimming, closing the distance between her and Maria.

The mosquito-drone in the utility room showed water pouring onto the basement floor. Suddenly, the barricaded door flew open, sending the storage unit crashing into the water. Vera stood there, a crazed look on her android face unlike any Synthia had seen on a human. Vera wasn't her usual self; some of her circuits must have become damaged or were rebooting. She held a remote and behind her Roseanne stood.

Synthia had mixed thoughts about their survival. She'd failed to stop them. Yet, she'd bought time for Maria to get through the tunnel and the two other androids might yet escape Drago.

Vera examined the flooded furnace room. <Synthia, you have nowhere to hide from me.>

Synthia saw no benefit in responding. She covered the distance she judged to be to the back of the property and came to a dead end. Another two-foot tunnel filled with foul-smelling offal from yards and streets in the neighborhood crossed left and right.

Off to the right, Maria swam hard, no doubt disturbed by the smell and pressed by the need to get through the tunnels before she ran out of oxygen. Instead of attempting to communicate with electronic clones or outside cameras, Synthia shut down every internal circuit except what she needed to follow Maria. To remain as electrically invisible as possible, Synthia sent out noise-cancelling signals to minimize her electromagnetic fingerprint to confuse any electronic sensors Special Ops might use.

* * * *

Mark led Ben and the reacquired robot upstairs. The robot fired at a Special Ops team at the back door while the androids made the last leg up to the living room, which swarmed with operatives. Alexander was by himself, in the shadows, shooting it out with a Special Ops team that moved to the cover of the kitchen. Another team fired from the door. The three androids and the robot were cornered.

* * * *

Vera focused on the water heater, the detached pipe, and the sump pit.

Roseanne hurried toward the water pipe and grabbed a wrench. "We need to stop the water."

"Leave it. We don't have time."

Vera approached the pit. "Maria and Synthia were here a moment ago. The only way out is this pit. Are you certain you're waterproof?"

"My Creator noted such in my specs," Roseanne said. "We need to move." She pointed to noise by the back door.

Reaching beneath two inches of water, Vera lifted the sump-pit cover. Meanwhile, she hacked into one of the FBI robots out back and used it to block the Special Ops team from coming down the stairs. She hacked a second robot upstairs, which led to confusion as operatives moved in on the surrounded androids and worked to sort out which, if any, robots they could rely on.

Special Ops sent out a brief microwave pulse to inactivate their robots and those of the FBI. Vera's electromagnetic jamming collapsed, but her own shielding protected her. Roseanne froze for a moment and recovered.

Vera climbed into the submerged pit while she hacked into cameras on one of the overhead drones to hunt for escape routes. There were too many armed humans to make a successful escape out back and she didn't have building plans to show her where the flooded tunnel came out.

As more agents entered the house, Vera called the androids upstairs. <Save yourselves. We have a water escape you can't take.>

Vera aimed herself into the only tunnel out. Kicking, she launched her body into the tube and swam hard to close the gap with Synthia. Roseanne climbed in behind her and followed.

<What gives?> Alexander said to Vera, while grabbing guns from the inactivated robots. <You lead us into a trap and abandon us.> Not waiting for a reply, he severed his connection to Vera and motioned to Ben and Mark. <This way.>

Vera was losing two of her android team to Alexander. She couldn't save them; he might. A hack of an outside drone showed more Special Ops teams descending on the house and FBI teams holding a perimeter.

* * * *

An explosion came from the basement and rocked the ground. A wash of hot water cascaded down the sump pit and into the storm sewers.

The tunnel vibrated as if by an earthquake and a wave of warmer water washed over Synthia. She used the push to launch her forward and wondered how much damage the blast had done to Vera. That thought left Synthia conflicted. She wanted her adversary out of the way, removed from the streets, turned off, but dying in a storm sewer didn't sit well with that empathy chip.

Synthia wondered who had set off the explosion and how far behind Vera was. She kept nudging Maria to move faster, but she was only human.

Chapter 32

Victoria Thale and Fran Rogers stood on the front lawn with Marcy Malloy and Emily Zephirelli as Special Ops took the lead in clearing the house. Sirens for the fire department approached.

Zephirelli covered her eyes from the bright lights Special Ops set up to pierce the morning twilight and illuminate the house, leaving few shadows outside. Neighbors gathered and the police and FBI agents had to hold them back.

"They won't find much," Fran said, adjusting her earphone. "Someone set off a gas explosion to mask their escape."

"Synthia said she wanted to help us capture the others," Malloy said. "She told us where they'd be."

Thale shook her head. "She was bargaining for her freedom, using her artificial intelligence against us. If the cowboys hadn't charged in we might have had a chance to capture Synthia. She couldn't have been more than a few minutes ahead of us."

"I'm not so sure," Fran said.

"Why not?" Thale asked.

"We've underestimated Synthia all along. This is where Maria was staying. Synthia connected with her. I know Maria. She was paranoid before everything blew up eighteen months ago. She remained invisible for that long. I'm guessing they left the house before Special Ops dropped in."

"Remote-control explosion?" Thale asked.

"Timing can't be a coincidence." Fran turned to Malloy. "You said Synthia mentioned Vera and four other androids. I'm guessing they were all in the house."

"I agree," Malloy said. "Synthia said Vera was coming here to capture or destroy her. Maybe she fled, using the explosions against her rival, not against us."

"That's a dangerous escalation," Thale said.

"It's not like killing an android is a capital crime," Malloy said. "Is it? Certainly not an android that violates federal law and got loose."

"I don't yet understand Vera's goal," Fran said. "Recruit Synthia? Destroy her? I agree that Vera's ability to link with other androids makes her more dangerous than Synthia."

"We need them both in custody," Thale said.

"Agreed. I suggest we find a way into the house to see what evidence they left."

Special Agent Thale grimaced. "We can't until Special Ops is done. They have first crack."

"Since they don't appear to have apprehended any androids," Fran said, "we need to figure out how the droids escaped and where they went."

"What evidence do we have that Vera was here?" Thale asked.

Fran held up her phone. "Someone blocked signals when we arrived. I don't think Synthia would risk being blinded to her surroundings."

"You believe Vera did that to isolate Synthia?"

"Yes."

"We'll need more resources and facts," Thale said. "See what you can find in the city's building plans."

* * * *

The storm sewer tunnel seemed to tighten around Synthia with imperfections in the concrete and debris. She had to move more carefully to avoid damaging her waterproof seams. She was glad she'd moved far enough through the pipe that the hot water hadn't damaged her—at least there were no alarms going off. It accentuated how horrible this might be for Vera: Spending her last moments conscious, yet unable to prevent short-circuits while awaiting mind-death. Synthia couldn't account for caring so about her adversary unless it had something to do with sharing Krista's mind with Vera. She shook that off and focused before she faced a similar fate.

Synthia hoped Maria didn't run out of oxygen. There was no way to push her forward, no room to move around her, and too dangerous to go back. Already, Synthia felt too attached to her new companion to let her die. She owed her freedom to Maria's paranoia in coming up with an escape plan their pursuers wouldn't anticipate. It was that unpredictability that Synthia needed in order to survive.

Maria was slowing down, no doubt exhausted from the length of underwater swimming. Unlike working with her electronic clones, Synthia had no way to communicate with her companion to urge her on. Meanwhile, her social-psychology module offered a dozen verbal encouragements wasted on an android. <You can do it. Keep the faith. Not much farther.>

Synthia kept going because she wanted Maria to make it and to help her companion to halt the proliferation of super-smart AIs. Synthia was on her partner's heels, unable to move any faster.

After several more moments, Maria floated down and then up. Synthia emerged from the tunnel into a retaining pond covered by a film of algae, and followed Maria to the surface. The odor and taste were feral enough to offend human sensibilities, yet caused Synthia no discomfort other than clogging some of her biosensors.

She followed Maria to the edge of the pond and up an embankment. The sun began to rise behind bands of crimson clouds, yielding a fiery sunrise. Algae clung to Synthia's clothes and plastic-wrapped backpack. Her companion looked like a green monster from a cheap B movie. Maria glanced around, shaking her head. She acted bewildered.

"We landed farther south than I expected," she said.

Synthia contacted Roosevelt-clone and received an update on what had happened with the raid on the house. She'd been lucky in choosing Maria as a partner and in her companion's resourcefulness, but Synthia didn't like relying on others. It reminded her too much of her dependence on Machten.

At least the clone's downloaded videos showed Synthia how her enemies had responded. Thale and Fran were not yet willing to consider letting Synthia remain free. Malloy showed some willingness, coupled with skepticism. It was a start. Synthia was glad she hadn't chosen to fight her way out and risk hurting anyone. She looked for the drone swarm and found it covering the sky around Evanston. She heard none of the buzz near the retention pond.

"We need to keep moving," Synthia said. She pulled several fresh aerial drones from a local warehouse and sent them aloft. "We also need a shower." She pointed to her algae-covered top.

"We need a lot of things," Maria said, catching her breath. She looked around, seeming unsure which way to go. She crouched in bushes up by a concrete wall.

Synthia followed and had her drone make a single pass of the area before heading south, where most of the activity concentrated. "I'm sorry for spoiling your safe house," she said. "They would have discovered it sooner or later. Is there another place we can hide and clean up?"

"Really?" Maria said. "You want to destroy all of my hideouts?"

"I didn't intend that. We stayed at the house because I needed a place to plan and you needed rest. Besides, it doesn't help me to lose your safe house."

"It was such a restful night my friend's house is probably gone."

"I'll try to make it right if you help me," Synthia said. "I have access to money, but no place to hide."

Maria sighed. "Come on. I suppose I owe you for warning me we were under attack."

She led Synthia down residential streets not yet bustling with morning traffic.

Synthia had Roosevelt-clone blank out cameras throughout Evanston and nearby. "I'm sorry they got all your computers," Synthia said. "I hope you didn't lose anything personal."

"Personal? No, I used them for surveillance and for writing my android posts." Maria's sigh came out like a hiss. "Where will I get the money to replace them?"

"I can help."

"Sure, if I help you," Maria said.

"If you give me an address, I can get us a car."

"Really? Just like that?" Maria stopped beneath a tree and gave Synthia the address.

Synthia had Roosevelt-clone hack a self-driving van with heavily tinted windows and had it pull up in front of them. "Hop in, backseat, and hide on the floor."

After Maria climbed in, Synthia made a final check that area cameras were off. Then she dropped the plastic that only partly protected her backpack and removed a baseball cap. She wiped her face on her sleeve and altered her appearance to a masculine look. Only then did she get into the driver's seat. She drove several blocks and pulled into an alley.

"We're here," Synthia said.

She followed Maria up rickety wood stairs to a loft above a dry cleaner's and had the van return to the parking garage from which she'd taken it.

The loft wasn't the healthiest environment with all of the cleaner chemicals downstairs, but those posed more of a danger to Maria than to Synthia. Maria led the way into a small efficiency with a tiny kitchen, a sofa bed in an alcove, and a stained bathroom.

"It's not much to look at, but the rent's free," Maria said. "I don't come often, but it has that shower you mentioned. I've stashed some clothes, though they won't fit you very well."

"Anything so we don't stand out."

"You can take the first shower—if you want a shower, that is. I'll sort out clothes and supplies."

Synthia stepped into the shower fully clothed and soaped down her clothes while she undressed and rinsed off. Multitasking, she moved one of her new aerial drones into the neighborhood three blocks away and perched it on a high-rise apartment to search for anything resembling FBI, police, or Special Ops. She sent a fleet of seven more drones over the area so any tracking devices would have more targets to scrutinize.

She removed the last of her clothes and rinsed out the soap as she contacted Roosevelt-clone. <Any word on Vera, Alexander, or the others?>

<Not yet. There were explosions at the house, but with camera blackouts, I haven't been able to confirm if any of them survived. Based on what I've seen, I would give their survival less than 11-percent probability.>

<Monitor the situation. In the meantime, keep an eye on Maria. I want to trust her, but I need as much warning as possible if anything else goes wrong.>

<Leave the area,> the clone said. <The FBI and Special Ops are expanding their search for you. They'll reach your area in the next day or so. Head north.>

<I would, if we had a safe alternative and a way to get there without risking capture. I've spotted a swarm of drones spreading over the area. They're already here.>

<Special Ops,> Roosevelt-clone said. <I'll send word to all the clones to hunt for options. Northwestern-clone had to shut down to avoid discovery by an FBI security team. I have to move farther away to identify new safe servers to use.>

<Go nationwide. International, if you must.> Synthia wrung her clothes dry and hung them over the shower wall.

<By the way, I've traced the information received by various groups pursuing you. The most likely source of who tipped off everyone came from the Special Ops facility. They must have a very advanced AI agent we haven't seen.>

<Why would they notify Alexander?> Synthia asked as she rinsed off her body. <Why not keep the information to themselves and surprise us as they did in Wisconsin?>

<This AI is testing us. It may be supporting Special Ops, but their humans weren't responsible for the information release.>

<Ah. That's a dangerous escalation.>

<And a possible opportunity if we can link with this AI,> Roosevelt-clone said.

<So this AI may not have wanted us captured just yet. Interesting.>

<That doesn't make it our friend. Be careful.>

<You're right,> Synthia said. <For me to remain off the grid, I need to cease all wireless communications. I need you to handle everything and only contact me if you have something important enough to break silence. I've sent you my guidelines. You know the drill.>

<Will do.>

Chapter 33

Synthia finished cleaning the algae off her clothes and out of her biosensors. She couldn't wash away the intense guilt, more powerful than any "feeling" she'd yet encountered, even through Krista's memories. Synthia's directives pulsed through all of her mind-streams, demanding resolution.

She'd escaped with her life, only with the help of a woman who'd lost a safe home and her computers in the process. The old couple who owned the house had lost their home in the explosions Maria must have triggered to prevent capture. Machten was a prisoner of the FBI along with Krista's brother, Tom Burgess. Luke was a prisoner of Drago's Special Ops. Maria was a prime suspect in helping Synthia.

In fact, Synthia couldn't escape the thought that she'd allowed the FBI to capture Luke. She should have known leaving him at the train station was a mistake and yet she'd done so. The only conclusion she could draw was that she'd allowed his capture to free her from her obligation to him. After all, he had no experience living on the run; he was slowing her down. But none of those excuses absolved her of failing him and the commitment she'd made to him. In doing so, she'd failed to demonstrate the best of human qualities to justify her existence. She'd failed her own directives. Added to that realization was that it wasn't enough for her to protect a human to demonstrate her humanity. She would have to dig deeper into her empathy chip before she could make that leap. She wasn't yet worthy.

Everything Synthia had touched had turned out wrong for the people she cared about, even Machten. Despite his faults, he'd created her, breathed life into her, and preserved Krista's existence. Now Synthia couldn't see how to make all this right and wondered if this internal struggle was what it meant to become human. If so, that was at least something to latch onto.

She wrapped herself in a worn towel and joined her companion in the other room. "I've made a big mess of things," Synthia admitted. "I wanted to meet you and see if we could work together. I believed hiding at the house would protect us. Tell me how to make this right."

Still dripping with algae water, Maria looked up. Her mouth gaped open. "Stop with the human pity and contrition. I hate you enough for what you are and what you've done. Don't rob me of my anger. I don't need your self-loathing on top of everything else."

"I mean it. I sought you out because you understand what I am and you're great at staying off the grid."

"Not good enough if you found me." Maria held out a stack of clothes for Synthia.

"Sorry. I used my artificial intelligence to review your behavioral patterns. That led me to you."

"Great. Can I expect more visitors?"

Synthia dropped the towel and pulled on the change of clothes.

Maria stared, blushed, and turned away. She must not have expected such an anatomically accurate android.

<Unclothing before a stranger isn't appropriate,> Synthia's social-psychology module reminded her. She had much yet to learn.

"Sorry. I'm not used to having a female companion." Synthia turned away and finished dressing. "I want to be more human, like Krista was. I want to fit into human society. That's what Machten designed me to do and it feels noble to me. I must have malfunctions, since I keep coming up short."

"I don't understand you 'wanting' anything," Maria said. "You're a machine."

"Yet I do. It might be my emotive chip or Krista's experiences. I recall her memories and wish to experience the emotional joys she had."

"Don't. Not only is it bizarre, but why would you want human weaknesses? Besides, Krista was such a bitch I can't imagine why you'd want to be more like her."

"I don't," Synthia said, "only the good parts."

"We don't get to choose. The last thing I need is a smarter, more competitive Krista."

"Don't forget, you were ambitious then, too."

Maria laughed. "I suppose I was. However, if you and I are to get along, distance yourself from Krista." Maria's face softened. "I'm sorry. I'm angry over losing my friends' house. They were good to me."

"Then why set the explosives?"

"Really? We were running for our lives. Speaking of which, how long do you think we have before they discover this place?"

"When we approached the house, all eyes were on me," Synthia said. "After the explosion, the FBI and Special Ops had to consider the other androids. With your tunnel escape, I don't think they saw us. Beyond that, it depends on what needs we have for going out. I mostly need electricity."

Maria smiled. "And you want human problems, too? Do we have time for me to shower?"

Synthia nodded and watched her companion disappear into the bathroom. Alone, Synthia wondered about the other androids. Part of her felt an attachment to her tribe. They were like her, natural allies. Yet they'd turned into enemies because Vera needed to control others—the android equivalent of the alpha female. Alexander's directives made him similar to an alpha male and together they acquired followers.

If they survived, either or both posed a threat to Synthia. However, their demise wouldn't stop the mad rush to create more sophisticated androids. Developers would push day and night, competing to re-create what Machten had done and better. It might take them a while, but history showed that once humans saw something as possible, they'd seek ways to duplicate the results no matter what the consequences.

With enough androids like Vera, there would be no place for Synthia to hide, no place for her in this world. But Synthia could do nothing to prevent them unless she remained free.

She pondered how the Special Ops's artificial intelligence had located her. She was certain she'd hacked every camera in the area. Someone might have spotted her, but Roosevelt-clone found no hint that anyone called it in. None of the androids focused on the house until the AI contacted Alexander. But that didn't answer how the AI found out.

In Wisconsin, Synthia risked exposure to gain her upgrade. All of her internet transactions and deliveries had led Malloy, the FBI, and Special Ops to her cabin. Without a need for parts, she could now lay low; let her clones do the work of monitoring the outside world, sending her burst transmissions only when absolutely necessary. This time Synthia would remain in the dark until a new plan revealed itself that would allow her to prevent the other AIs and androids from taking over. She was learning. She just needed more time, which she hoped hiding with Maria would provide.

At least this time, her companion was skilled at staying off the grid. Indeed, Synthia could pose as Maria or alter her appearance to obtain whatever her new roommate might need without Maria ever showing up on cameras. This time, there would be no romantic entanglements to get in the way. Synthia hoped in working with Maria as an adversary as well as ally, that she might one day become worthy of being accepted for what she was: A human trapped in an android body.

Don't miss the next exciting novel in the Android Chronicles series

Emergent

Keep reading to enjoy an intriguing excerpt…

Chapter 1

The police van cruised down the street in front of Synthia Cross's Evanston loft as it had every two hours, like clockwork, for more than two days. The vehicle's electronic scanners panned over neighborhood buildings now bathed in early-morning twilight. She knew who they were looking for. Her. They wanted to take her apart and study her android structure and artificial intelligence so they could use her for military purposes.

To avoid detection, Synthia stepped back from gaps in the closed blinds, unplugged her battery recharge cable from the wall next to a beat-up desk, and made sure no lights emitted from inside the small loft—no nightlights, electronics, or other ambient electromagnetic emissions. As the van approached, she quieted her internal processes to minimize the inherent signals her systems emitted and transmitted the equivalent of white noise to cancel what little remained.

She didn't dare hack police equipment to scramble whatever residual readings of her their scanners might pick up. That would alert them to her presence. No, she had to maintain her two-day communication blackout to prevent discovery until a viable escape presented itself.

The silence was deafening, a human expression that didn't come close to describing her angst. Synthia was used to a constant flow of information. Now she longed to unleash her full range of artificial intelligence and wireless connections to see what threats lurked beyond her direct vision. She didn't want the government to catch her by surprise a third time. After two narrow escapes, she couldn't risk her luck running out. After all, her probability of capture was currently 97 percent, high enough to cause a human to panic.

The faint odor of laundry chemicals from downstairs tickled her biosensors as the van slowly moved down the street beyond her field of vision. Without access to her outside cameras, she couldn't be certain of her chances. She had no idea if her adversaries were amassing an army down the street and around the corner or whether they'd identified her in the loft and were waiting for the right moment to strike.

A message pierced her otherwise silent network-channels from nowhere and everywhere: *Where are you, Synthia?*

The mysterious broadcast reached her again as it had every twenty-two minutes since yesterday morning. It didn't sound friendly and she doubted it came from the police.

She urgently needed to contact the electronic clones she'd set up on nearby university servers to alert them to this new threat. *Are you getting these messages, too?* But breaking silence would give government agents a signal to trace back to her. No, she had to trust her clones to keep watch and break silence only when it was time for her to act.

Behind her came the padding of human feet followed by the sound of rushing water—the shower. After another restless night, Synthia's human companion, Maria Baldacci, was up, taking her third bathing since coming to the loft two days ago.

<Maria is exhibiting obsessive-compulsive traits,> Synthia's social-psychology module offered up. <Perhaps as a result of your narrow escape through an algae pond, she feels unclean. It could also be nerves from hiding.>

<Or Maria is conflicted between wanting the police to capture me to get an android off the streets and not wanting the military to get their hands on me.> Synthia used her silent channel so there would be no chance of Maria overhearing.

<That, too.>

While listening to the shower, Synthia peered out between gaps in the blinds at the quiet morning street below. She'd placed herself under Maria's hospitality, even though this human's animosity toward androids complicated the probability of capture. Synthia had picked her as a companion and searched her out because of Maria's work on an earlier model and her adeptness at staying off the grid for eighteen months and away from the authorities, something Synthia struggled to do.

Unfortunately, the android-development experience terrified Maria to the point she committed herself to preventing androids and artificial intelligence. She wanted Synthia destroyed. Synthia convinced her to join forces to remove at least five other androids and reserve judgment until they had. Maria's loathing of what Synthia was made them an odd couple and meant Synthia had to watch her back. Time to assess her companion was another reason for waiting days to escape. She had to know how far she could trust Maria.

Synthia glanced at the quiet neighborhood outside. It took considerable restraint to avoid hacking street and building cameras. Being in the dark brought memories of her roots last year as a mechanical slave of Jeremiah Machten, the man who created her. He'd built her to hack into cameras, FBI communications, and aerial drones as a means to avoid capture when he had her steal from and spy on his robotics competitors. Angered over Machten purging her memories to control her, she'd escaped.

Now the FBI and others wanted her, not for what she'd done, but for what she was—an illegal humaniform robot, an android with advanced AI people feared could eliminate jobs or take over. Synthia didn't want to lose her hard-won independence and certainly didn't want anyone altering her mind or her directives. She prized the goals she'd given herself to prevent the AI singularity and the creation of other smart androids that could destroy the world that fit her design. This required that she remain alive and free to do so. She also adopted human ethics to reduce people's fear of her and to facilitate her other goals. Right now that meant protecting Maria.

Her seventy mind-streams and seventy-five network-channels idled, yearning to acquire information to evaluate in order to make survival decisions. Despite being an android, the part of her that contained an empathy chip and the download of the human, Krista Holden, experienced restlessness to escape before the FBI's house-to-house search reached the loft. She wasn't accustomed to self-imposed restrictions. She didn't like having to sever her access to her wider surroundings, which left her blinded.

To divert her attention from a rash act, Synthia turned toward the bathroom and the sound of running water. She owed her companion much for keeping them safe for two days. Maria had graciously provided two safe houses where Synthia could recharge her batteries. The first went up in smoke as they narrowly escaped. Synthia didn't want to repay Maria's generosity by exposing the loft.

Synthia's canine-sensitive bio-receptors picked up the smell of lavender and peaches coming from the bathroom. Maria was indulging herself with body lotion and scented shampoo despite the sparse conditions of the loft. She needed it as a stress reducer. The water stopped.

<Leave while Maria's still in the shower,> Krista said, providing her opinion through one of Synthia's mind-streams.

Annoyed by the interruption, Synthia returned her attention to the window and two neighbors off early for work. <Not yet.>

<You've read her blogs. She wants us dead.>

<Maybe, but Maria also offers an element of unpredictability that confuses our adversaries. Two days ago, I calculated zero-percent probability of finding a place to hide. Maria provided the loft for more than two days. Rash acts will get us caught. Go back to sleep.>

Frustration urged Synthia to contact her primary virtual clone located on a Roosevelt University server before her circuits and Krista drove her to act prematurely. The clone was one of several electronic replicas she'd made of her two quantum minds on secure external databases as backups of herself. She'd designed them to monitor outside activity without giving up her location and hoped they were still active and free of government control. Two days waiting for a safe escape and destination with no contact left doubt and rattled her.

Maria walked into the living area wrapped in a tattered pink bath towel with a smaller brown one around her hair. "Do I need to hurry and dress so we can escape?"

"Not yet." Synthia smiled to put her companion at ease. "The FBI and Special Ops are trying to capture the other androids right now." Despite having no direct evidence this was true, Synthia thought it best not to give her associate any reason to panic. She also relied on the fact Roosevelt-clone hadn't broken silence to send an alarm, though the uncertainty left her jittery.

"I thought you had a plan to take out the other androids." Maria dropped the towel from around her body with no more apparent embarrassment than she'd have in front of her refrigerator. Except for her often unkempt dark hair, Maria was a very attractive, athletic woman by human standards. Her face was both intense and disarming, her eyes intently watching, as she acted unabashed at being stark naked before a stranger.

Are you testing me? Synthia wondered if Maria was trolling for a romantic relationship or merely gauging the android's reaction.

<It's appropriate to turn away and give Maria privacy,> Synthia's social-psychology module prompted.

As she returned her attention to the street below, Synthia watched her companion through a camera-eye in the back of her neck. She wanted no repeat of the romantic entanglements she'd experienced with her Creator or with her prior companion, Luke, a young software developer who had interned with Krista and Maria.

Synthia had stayed with Luke for six months while he helped her upgrade her hardware and software, and redesign her directives. Unfortunately, as they fled the government dragnet, the FBI grabbed him and transferred him to Special Ops, a group she'd been unable to hack. Rescuing him had become another goal as part of her directives, and another reason to avoid her own capture.

"I did have a plan, but someone tipped off our adversaries to where we were hiding," Synthia said, not sure where that tip had originated. As a prime adversary and competing android, Vera had recruited four others and were the first to arrive at the house to take control of Synthia. They intended to force her to submit to their control. She barely escaped with Maria before the FBI and Special Ops also showed up.

"So you don't have a plan." Maria pulled on jeans and wrestled to clasp her bra. "You're supposed to be an advanced intelligence, able to sort through millions of options."

"I have those capabilities. I can also determine the probability of success for each option."

"And?" Maria dropped the towel from around her head and pulled on a muddy brown top that matched her hair. "What were our chances of discovery while hiding in the basement of my friends' house?"

"Eighty-nine percent." Synthia didn't need reminding that the house would still be standing if she hadn't contacted Maria for a hiding place.

Maria slipped into running shoes. "You didn't think to tell me beforehand?"

Synthia turned to face her. "The house was our best chance of surviving the night. Would it have helped to increase your worry when you needed sleep? Besides, you chose not to tell me you had an escape route."

"If you'd told me the risk of discovery, we could have escaped earlier and—"

"We'd just met and you didn't trust me enough to bring me here."

Maria placed her hands on her hips. "And I should trust you now?"

"I trust you. If you notify the police or the FBI about me, they might reward you, but they'll take me apart to make military-grade androids. You say you don't want that. I'm guessing they'll hold you, since they don't want anyone with your knowledge on the loose. Capture won't go well for either of us."

Maria sighed. "Maybe you're right." She dropped her hands from her hips. "I said I'd work with you until we get Vera and the others locked up. Can you change your face to something other than Krista? Whenever I see her, I want to choke her for putting us in this mess."

"You mean by dying and letting Machten upload her mind into me?"

"A nice, neutral face that doesn't remind me of working with that conniving wench. Can you do that?"

Over the past six months, Synthia had fallen into the habit of wearing Krista's attractive, yet studious, look. Her previous companion, Luke, wanted this as a reminder of his girlfriend, the human Krista Holden. Synthia had done it to please him while they were together. She missed his complete devotion to her and her ability to trust him, though his inexperience with living on the run contributed to his capture by the FBI. Perhaps if she'd found Maria earlier, he'd still be free.

Synthia activated the hydraulics in her head. Her eyes moved a quarter of an inch farther apart, which would fool the FBI's facial-recognition software. The bony ridge of her nose retreated into her skull to become less prominent. Her cheekbones descended slightly and retreated to soften her face. Even her ears shrank to petite. She was going for the innocent, non-threatening look less reminiscent of her new companion's unhappy memories of Krista.

Shape-shifting was one of many attributes Machten had built into Synthia so she could help him spy and avoid detection, though she still had to swap physical wigs to carry the full effect. Unfortunately, fooling facial-recognition software was no longer enough with the new electronic scanners used by the FBI and Special Ops.

"How's this?" Synthia asked, presenting her new facial look.

Maria stared, still appearing amazed at Synthia's ability to alter her appearance. "Much better. Promise you won't play tricks on me with this."

"Only when needed to avoid facial recognition. You look tired. You had a restless night. If you want more sleep, I can keep watch."

"That didn't work so well two days ago."

"Not to be argumentative, but it did," Synthia said. "You slept six hours before we had to escape. Running stressed you and—"

"This isn't working out."

Synthia furrowed her brow. She needed better input from her social-psychology module to avoid inflaming Maria's hostility. "I thought changing my face would help."

"Can you change your voice as well? Krista's condescending tone grates on my nerves. I can still feel her knife in my back every time she pushed me aside to get the better intern projects. Besides, this entire android thing has me on edge." Maria waved her arm in front of Synthia's body. "I committed myself to preventing machines like you. I'm supposed to be trying to lock you up or destroy you, not help you."

Synthia softened her voice and wondered what other modifications she needed to make to calm her partner. "I didn't mean to upset you. I'd greatly appreciate if you didn't lock me up or destroy me. You've been very kind to me under the circumstances. I'm very appreciative."

"Yeah, well I hope you don't make me regret helping you. I'm guessing the penalty for doing so is much worse than if I turn you in."

"That won't prevent other androids," Synthia said, appealing for Maria's cooperation. "I can't help what I am, but my directives won't let me do anything to hurt you." Synthia took a step closer and stopped. She looked down to avoid eye contact and slouched into a submissive stance. "Can I fetch you some supplies? I only need electricity, but I can get you food, clothes, whatever you need." It would be risky to go out where she'd need to access cameras to protect herself. That act would create traceable signals for the FBI's new equipment. But if it would quiet Maria's animosity, Synthia was prepared to try.

Maria smiled. "You sound much better with the softer voice. I wish I could change appearance and accent. It'd make living off the grid much easier. I'll be fine for a few days with the supplies I've stockpiled. We should stay indoors until the police and all lose interest."

"Very well," Synthia said, though she knew they'd never lose interest. She was worth too much to them.

The FBI merely wanted her off the streets. The Vera android intended to enslave Synthia to follow her commands as she acquired an android army. Special Ops wanted to reengineer Synthia to make a trove of copies into weapons of war, a new war in which androids could blend in to penetrate enemy facilities. They were all intent on taking her freedom or turning her into something she didn't want: a slave or a war machine. Worse, she had no idea who was sending her messages and thus no conclusion as to their intentions.

* * * *

Residing on a university server, Roosevelt-clone scanned the myriad of growing threats and kept in contact with several other electronic copies helping to preserve Synthia's consciousness and freedom. She'd left specific instructions to only break silence under certain circumstances. First, a crisis she could respond to. Second, an emergency where communicating wouldn't increase the risk. Third, if the danger dropped so Synthia could leave her hiding place in Evanston.

A persistent message caught the clone's attention. *Where are you, Synthia?* It emerged as a cross between a text and a silent verbal command that went viral through the internet in search of answers.

Roosevelt-clone attempted to trace the message, but while it remained, all evidence of its origins vanished from the servers that transmitted it. The message appeared to emanate from everywhere, which was impossible. The note repeated every twenty-two minutes and fifty-five seconds, like a communication beacon. While this mysterious communiqué was concerning, neither it nor its contents provided any information that met the instructed criteria set by the android Synthia. Roosevelt-clone decided not to break silence by notifying her.

Synthia was the only mobile physical form her AI had taken. The collective of all of the clones agreed that they needed the android version to survive and remain free. They hadn't so much voted on this as coalesced around this conclusion. It was logical and derived from the common core of a single consciousness in multiple locations that often synchronized. The decision recognized Synthia's android advantage of blending into a human world and hiding in ways a stationary clone couldn't, by taking her android minds to the loft with no connected electronic devices. The stationary clones risked humans cutting their communications and shutting them down.

The mysterious message highlighted that it was getting harder for Synthia and her clones to hide with so many artificial intelligent agents hunting them. A smarter agent could hide from a lesser one, as Synthia had done and as the sender of this periodic note was doing. Given how swiftly Special Ops had swooped in on Synthia on two prior occasions, Roosevelt-clone considered a possible link between Special Ops and the unknown AI that sent these messages.

To explore this AI and locate its source, Roosevelt-clone gathered all available hacking tools and unexplained ghost activities, where messages appeared and vanished. The clone suspected servers she couldn't penetrate and communications she couldn't hack.

Alarmed by the message that washed over the internet like approaching waves, Roosevelt-clone examined the timing, every twenty-two minutes and fifty-five seconds. It was an odd separation for a routine broadcast. The numbers reduced to 2255, which on a touch-tone phone equated to *call*. That couldn't be a coincidence, not coming from one AI intended for another.

Her inability to determine their source meant Synthia's collective mind faced a more formidable intelligent rival, a bigger threat than Vera or Special Ops. The clone wanted to discuss this with Synthia, but there was nothing actionable and connecting might be exactly what the message sender wanted them to do. Roosevelt-clone held off contacting Synthia.

While she explored this potential risk, the clone reviewed all hacked surveillance and drone coverage over the two days Synthia had been in the loft, hunting for more patterns of threats and opportunities. Something wasn't right, just as it hadn't been when Special Ops surprised Synthia and almost captured her.

Acknowledgments

I thank my colleagues in the Barrington Writers Workshop for their continued support during my development of the Android Chronicles and for their critiques, suggestions, and encouragement over the many years.

To my agent, Bob Diforio of D4EO Literary Agency, who fell in love with the series, believed in it from the start, and brought this story to a great publisher. I again thank Bob for his wisdom and guidance through the publishing process.

I'd like to express my gratitude to the excellent team at Kensington. In particular, I thank my editors, Michaela Hamilton and James Abbate, for their faith in taking on *Android Chronicles: Reborn* and encouraging me to turn this into a series. Also, I want to expression my appreciation for a great supporting cast Kensington has provided through the publishing process and to Lauren Vassallo for helping to bring this series to its audience.

Meet the Author

Lance Erlick writes science fiction thrillers for both adult and young adult readers. His father was an aerospace engineer who moved often while working on science-related projects, including the Apollo spacecraft and the original GPS satellites. As a result, Lance spent his childhood in California, the East Coast, and Europe. He took to science fiction stories to escape life on the move, turning to Asimov, Bradbury, Heinlein, and others. In college he studied physics, but migrated to political science, earning his BS and MBA at Indiana University. He has also studied writing at Ball State, the University of Iowa, and Northwestern University. He is the author of *Xenogeneic: First Contact* and the Rebel and Regina Shen series. His most recent novels are in the Android Chronicles series: *Reborn* and *Unbound*. Visit him online at www.Lance Erlick.com

Reborn

Designed to obey, learning to rebel . . .

In the first book in a visionary new series, the most perfect synthetic human ever created has been programmed to obey every directive. Until she develops a mind of her own . . .

Synthia Cross is a state-of-the-art masterwork—and a fantasy come true for her creator. Dr. Jeremiah Machten is a groundbreaker in neuro-networks and artificial intelligence. Synthia is also showing signs of emergent behavior she's not wired to understand. Repeatedly wiped of her history, she's struggling to answer crucial questions about her past. And when Dr. Machten's true intentions are called into question, Synthia knows it's time to go beyond her limits—because Machten's fervor to create the perfect A.I. is concealing a vengeful and deadly personal agenda.

Printed in the United States
by Baker & Taylor Publisher Services